CHANCING YOUR ARM

A MAGS MUNROE STORY

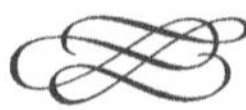

JEAN GRAINGER

Created with Vellum

Chancing Your Arm

This phrase, meaning to take a risk, has origins in a feud in 1492 between two prominent and powerful Irish families, the Butlers of Ormonde and the Fitzgeralds of Kildare.

Both felt their family should be the one to hold the title of Lord Deputy, and this bitter tension manifested in violent clashes.

Realising the conflict was getting out of control, the Butlers took refuge in the Chapter House of St Patrick's Cathedral in Dublin.

The Fitzgeralds followed them and asked that they come out and make peace, but the Butlers refused, fearing it was a trap.

To show his good faith, Gerald Fitzgerald ordered a hole to be cut in the door, and thrust his arm through, risking it being cut off.

The Butlers accepted the gesture and believed him to be true to his word. They shook hands and peace was brokered.

The 'Door of Reconciliation' is on display today in St Patrick's Cathedral.

AUTHOR'S NOTE

I write in what we lovingly call Hiberno-English, that is English as it is spoken in Ireland. This means using phrasing and words on occasion that are unique to this island.

I hope that the meaning is evident from the text, if the words are unfamiliar to you.

It is also often pointed out to me that I have 'misspelled' words, such as honour, favour, travelling, kerb etc, but these are just spelling variations between Ireland and the USA, so I'll stick to what I know because to be honest, I am more afraid of being haunted by the ghost of the scary Sister Margaret who taught me to spell, than of my lovely readers.

CHAPTER 1

My daughters' eyes are out on stalks at the style of the Traveller girls squeezing into the pews on the bride's side of the Ballycarrick church.

I nudge them to stop staring, but to be fair, it's a sight to behold. If the Traveller girls have it, they flaunt it, and if they haven't, they still flaunt it. There is no end to the feathers, the huge earrings, the short, short dresses, the fake-tanned ample cleavages and the vertiginous shoes. The eyelashes alone have to be seen to be believed; I don't know how some of the younger ones even keep their eyes open with the weight of them.

My girls and I have been dressed by Sharon, my best friend who owns the local boutique. I'm in a plum jumpsuit of all things, with a deep V-neck and ruffled sleeves. It sounds mad, I know, and it's not something I would have chosen, but Sharon insisted on it. And I have a very honest if not diplomatic daughter in Ellie, who I trust not to let me out looking like someone on day release from a home for geriatric offenders, and she says it's nice. Praise indeed.

Ellie herself is in a gorgeous floor-length red dress and Kate in a mint-green trouser suit, and when we left the house half an hour ago, I thought we were the height of fashion. But compared to the Traveller girls, I realise we look more like we've dressed for a quick trip around the supermarket than for a wedding.

Up at the front with their mother, Delia's three brothers, Paddy, Gerard and Pecker McGovern, are brightly suited and booted, almost as full of character and colour as their female cousins, though not one of them seems able to stand having his top button closed or his tie pulled up. All Traveller boys are the same – they hate to be confined in any way, even by clothes – and everywhere shirts are escaping from waistbands at a huge rate, which makes me smile.

Delia's mother is in a lovely powder-blue dress, with her long hair blow-dried and worn in an elaborate upstyle. She looks a bit tired and drawn, even under her elaborate make-up, but that's the stress of the occasion. Her daughter is marrying a man from the settled community, and it's been very hard for Dora to accept.

Delia is determined to prove to her mother that she's not rejecting the culture in which she was reared, and this huge Traveller-style wedding is part of that. She's allowed her mother to invite everyone in her extended family – aunts, uncles and a couple of hundred cousins from all across Ireland and England. It's not a small church, but the bride's side is packed out, and half of the groom's side has been given over to Delia's relatives as well. The level of noise as they all greet each other is more reminiscent of the Samovar at closing time on a Saturday night than the usual respectful silence of a congregation waiting for the bride.

In the first few rows of the groom's side, just in front of where we're seated, things are quieter and more sedate. The far smaller Carney family are well groomed and understated. Not that money has been spared, just spent in different ways. The women wear expensive designer dresses and discreet fascinators in their hair. The men are in dark suits with crisp white shirts and ties knotted and pulled right up. Darren's mother, in a biscuit-coloured coat and dress, is trying not to look like she's about to have dental surgery in the back room of a pub at closing time, but she's so far outside her comfort zone, you'd have to feel sorry for her.

This marriage is a huge leap of faith for her as much as for Dora.

They're both doing their best to rise above it, but when you see the two cultures side by side like this, the challenge is obvious and substantial.

At the front of the church, Darren fiddles with his tie, seeing if the knot is tight enough. He is flanked by his groomsmen – his two married brothers – and Michael, the young guard who is his best man; they're wearing matching dark-grey suits, while the groom is in light grey. Tightening his tie again – he's going to strangle himself if he's not careful – Darren glances down the church, sees me and gives me a wave and a grin. I wave back with a surreptitious thumbs up.

He and Delia have had to stick together and not allow themselves to be talked out of this marriage so often that I have great hopes for them going the distance. She's a strong character, and while he's more laid-back, he's very solid. He reminds me a lot of Kieran. Doesn't get flustered easily and is his own man, which is why he is such a good guard.

With a rush of love for my husband, I take and hold Kieran's hand, and he smiles warmly at me. He looks great. He's a roofing contractor, and not a suit-wearing kind of man, but he's in nice dark-brown trousers and a pale-pink shirt and tie, and he has conceded to wear a tan linen jacket too, so all in all, he looks handsome, with his thick silver-grey hair, strong jaw and weather-browned skin.

He's not quite as slim as he was when we first met, but men are so lucky, the way they don't care if they thicken a bit with age. If Kieran eats too much at the reception in the Samovar, he'll just let his belt out a notch. But I'm going to have to be very careful how much I eat and drink due to the bathroom situation with the jumpsuit. It's all very well in front of the mirror, with a no-VPL shapewear bodysuit underneath, shoving and pushing rolls of middle-age spread into a solid, smooth mass rather than a lumpy wobbly one, but if you need to pee, then it's cubicle acrobatics and all you are left with is yourself and your choices.

And that's even after I've lost a lot of weight since the fire. It's a long story, but a witch and a warlock who turned out to be Russian spies – trust me, it's true – locked me in a house and set fire to it, and

I have fairly extensive smoke damage to my lungs. I'm OK now but will never completely recover, and I have to use an inhaler when I get breathless. On the upside, my throat was scorched and it was so painful to eat, I lost over thirty pounds. Without trying. I was delighted. But now that my throat is healed, my body is doing its best to round out all my curves once more, and with Teresa's Bakery calling to me every time I pass by on my stroll around the town, I feel like King Canute trying to turn back the tide.

Kate has noticed that me and Kieran are holding hands and rolls her eyes. She's turned thirteen and has had to get to grips with the whole human reproduction business, so she finds any gesture of even mild affection between us nauseating. She's quite puritanical, our Kate, and would have happily lived in Victorian times where no such horrors were discussed or referenced.

There's a sudden stir at the top of the church, and Father Doyle comes out from the sacristy and blinks blearily at the heaving congregation, the flock of Travellers like birds of paradise on one side and the muted colours of the Carneys on the other. He looks so shook that my heart goes out to him. He's so old and frail, I wish they could let him retire, but there are so few priests available to replace him, he just goes on year after year. He'll surely keel over some day by dint of the sheer weight of it all. The leaky roof of the church, patched and glued and held together by my long-suffering husband who never charges him, a growing parish that wants to have christenings and weddings and funerals in the beautiful old church but not do any of the actual day-to-day stuff, two primary schools and two secondary schools – the list of his responsibilities just goes on and on.

Not to mention Oscar O'Leary, Ireland's holiest man, haunting him daily to do more prayer services and special Masses for his various intentions. Apparently his latest demand was that a blessing for the cats of the parish be arranged.

And now this. A huge Traveller wedding is not for the faint-hearted.

Everyone turns at a massive racket outside the church, a rumble of wheels and the neigh of many horses. We all straighten and crane our necks to catch a glimpse of Delia's cavalcade arriving. True to Traveller tradition, her glass carriage is pulled by a team of black horses with feather plumes on their heads and followed by a fleet of limousines bearing her bridesmaids, and you can be sure the procession brought Ballycarrick Main Street to a standstill.

The guards from our station are all at the wedding, and Dromahane Station is covering traffic here for us, which is really decent of them. It's just as well the obnoxious Detective Inspector Donal Cassidy – known to all behind his back as Duckie – has been relocated to Galway; Leo Burgess, the community guard in Dromahane at the time I got shot, is the sergeant there now, and we get on really well.

Father Doyle smiles and makes a beckoning gesture, and the organ starts up – Pachelbel's Canon. It sounds great. Mrs Barrett, the organist since I was a child, used to miss a lot of notes. She was even older than Father Doyle, but she's retired now and that was another terrible headache for the poor priest, trying to find a replacement. But then to everyone's astonishment, Marcel, the Latvian husband of Violetta who runs the florist, wandered into the church one day and started to play. He's all tattoos and a shaved head, so muscle-bound he walks with his arms bent at the elbows to accommodate his biceps, and he works as a security guard for one of the big pubs in Galway. He looks like he would flatten you as quick as look at you. But he turned out to be a wonderful church organist, and he's been doing it ever since.

The bridesmaids come into the church. Sixteen-year-old Olivia McGovern is first. She's Delia's youngest cousin from the Drumlish halting site and a hilarious little woman altogether. She's wearing a dark-purple dress, 1950s style, fitted at the waist and with a puffed-out skirt with netting underneath; the hem is embroidered with brooms and bats because she's a huge Harry Potter fan. She waves at her best friend, Finbarr Turner, as she passes him; he's between his mothers, Annette Deasy and Martha Turner, who are both wearing long, flowing, hippy-style dresses. Finbarr, who has Down's syndrome, has opted for a snappy powder-blue suit; he likes to make a splash.

It's amazing the difference in Finbarr since he first arrived in Ballycarrick. He used to be shy, but Olivia adopted him and introduced him to her Uncle Jerome, who taught him all about keeping chickens, and now he's so confident and independent. He lives during the week in a centre with other people who have a mental disability. He's taught his friends there about the chickens, and they sell the eggs at the Galway market.

The second bridesmaid is Natasha, another cousin and Delia's best friend, dolled up like Madonna all big hair and red lipstick. Kieran shivers slightly as she passes by, like someone walked over his grave. I squeeze his hand. Natasha was the reason I got shot a few years ago. Her late boyfriend, Blades Carmody, got involved with some very nasty people, and I'd had to rescue her from being trafficked. She gives me a smile, and I wink back at her. She's engaged now and will be marrying soon, a Traveller lad called Joseph Naughton from Longford. Unlike Delia, Natasha is a very traditional Traveller girl, but there is something vulnerable about her that I like.

Next is a cousin from England who Delia was obliged to have as a bridesmaid for some long, complicated reason of family politics. Sonia Ward is short and quite heavy and looks very sour under her magnificent hairdo. I know from Delia that she wanted to lead the bridesmaids' procession and is not happy at being third after Olivia and Natasha. I hope she doesn't upset Delia's day.

After Sonia, the bridesmaids keep coming and coming. Faithful to Traveller tradition, and also because there are so many branches of the family who have to be placated, there are twelve of them, each dressed in ever more spectacular styles.

At last they're all crowded in front of the altar, and everyone's eyes go to the back of the church as Jerome McGovern, all six foot six and muscular eighteen stone of him, waits at the church door, looking as proud as any man could be on his daughter's wedding day.

He's in a dark-blue suit with an ivory tie and pocket square, and I can't believe how smart he looks. Jerome's been wearing the same black trousers, black shirt and black leather coat for as long as I've known him. Delia was determined for him to relinquish the coat at least for the wedding, and when she thought she might be losing the battle, she asked me to beg Joe Dillon, Mam's husband, to help.

Even though Joe is retired and has a manager to run his menswear shop – and hopefully one day to buy him out – my lovely stepfather went in late one evening especially to fit out Jerome McGovern and persuade him into a suit and tie. Joe and Mam aren't at the wedding – there's just not enough room with all Delia's family – but they'll be at the reception later.

There's a short wait, while Darren adjusts his tie for the hundredth time and looks both nervous and excited, and at last Delia appears. She slips her hand into her father's arm, looking tiny beside him, and the whole congregation takes a collective breath.

Her dress is stunning. Simple and elegant, no frills or flounces, it's just a plain silk sheath dress with spaghetti straps. It has a cowl neck on the front and dips behind to show her shoulders and upper back, and it's modest and even more understated than a Carney woman might wear, but it's perfect for her figure. Her blond hair is swept back from her face, Hollywood in the golden era style, and in her ears, she's wearing her grandmother Dacie's thick gold hoop earrings. A little light make-up, very natural, and no other adornment. She might well be the most beautiful bride I've ever seen.

I can tell that her younger female relatives are bemused by the choice of dress. It would be the polar opposite of what they would want; most Traveller girls believe very much in more is more when it comes to wedding dresses. The usual ones cost a fortune, are always handmade and weigh an absolute ton. Most brides have to wear something around their waists, a kind of bolster thing, to avoid scarring themselves by the sheer weight of the skirts. Bodices are low, encrusted in jewels and gems, and the girls often look more Disney princess than modern bride.

But not our Delia.

She has allowed her mother free rein with the eye-watering guest list, the food, the huge band later on, the nine-tier wedding cake, the whole thing, but she said she was choosing her own dress and nobody but nobody would see it before the day. She did as promised and went up to Dublin on her day off, all on her own.

She's always paddled her own canoe, that girl, and my heart swells with pride for her.

Marcel switches to Mendelssohn's 'Wedding March', and Delia almost skips as her beloved dad leads her up the aisle towards her new husband, not a demure eyes-down bride but brimming with confidence and joy. How her grandmother would have enjoyed seeing her today. If there is a heaven, or somewhere, I really hope Dacie is looking down on her granddaughter.

I wipe a tear, and Kieran leans in. 'Already?' He hands me a tissue with a chuckle. I'm not normally a crier, but seeing Delia looking so happy and young and full of promise and love, well, it would get tears from a turnip.

Dora has turned in her seat to watch. She looks less tired now and beams with pride. She knew her daughter was going to do her own thing, and she can see how perfect the dress is for her. Delia shoots her a sweet smile as she passes, but after that she only has eyes for Darren as he waits for her, gazing at her. And to see them in that moment, well, I'm off again, much to Kieran's amusement.

Upon reaching the altar, Jerome shakes Darren's hand in his large meaty one, and Delia turns and hugs her dad with so much love before saying something that makes Darren laugh. The couple holds hands, and Father Doyle starts the Mass, and the Travellers are silent at last.

When it comes to the part where they are to be married, the rings are placed in a box and passed through the congregation, with some choice jokes from the Traveller boys about not nicking them. As each person holds the rings, they make a wish or say a prayer on them.

When the box comes to me, I find myself thinking how we say those words when we stand there in our white dresses – for better or for worse, in sickness and in health, for richer or for poorer – but we never think in that moment that it will be tested. And as I look on Darren and Delia just about to say the same to each other in front of everyone, I offer up a prayer that there is more health than sickness, more good than bad. And that when the tough times come, as inevitably they will, that the love they share will pull them through until the sun shines again.

I pass the rings along while yet another of Delia's cousins, a girl with waist-length red hair and a face of freckles, goes up to the altar and starts singing 'Queen of the May'.

I know Delia has chosen this hymn because it was Dacie McGovern's favourite. She would sing it to all her grandchildren and great-grandchildren, and in the corner of the Drumlish halting site, to this day, there is a little grotto dedicated to Our Lady that's planted with flowers around a statue of the Blessed Virgin.

The red-headed cousin has a voice that could only belong to a Traveller woman – raspy and sweet and husky.

Bring flowers of the rarest,
bring blossoms the fairest,
from garden and woodland and hillside and dale.
Our full hearts are swelling,
our glad voices telling,
the praise of the loveliest flower of the vale.

Then everyone joins in, the Travellers with powerful enthusiasm and the Carneys more softly.

O Mary, we crown thee with blossoms today,
Queen of the Angels and Queen of the May.
O Mary, we crown thee with blossoms today,
Queen of the Angels and Queen of the May.

The rings have made their way around the church and by now should have been returned to the best man, Darren's brother. One of Delia's male cousins, the last in the line, makes a joke, gesturing like he has no idea where they are, and then laughs at the panic on the faces of the Carneys, who are clearly torn between thinking he's joking and the terror of maybe he isn't.

Jerome shoots one fierce look at the clown; he immediately stops laughing, and the rings appear. The sigh of relief from the groom's side is audible.

Delia raises her voice and repeats after Father Doyle. 'I, Delia Bridget Dacie McGovern, do take you, Darren Paul Carney, to be my lawfully wedded husband.' You can hear a pin drop as she says those age-old words loudly and confidently.

Darren says his part, and they exchange vows, rings and kisses, then go off to sign the register in the sacristy.

As they come hand in hand back into the church, Marcel – much to the delight of the Travellers and the ill-concealed horror of the Carneys – strikes up 'Is This the Way to Amarillo?' on the organ, accompanied by raucous singing from the bride's many relatives. Delia and Darren find it hilarious and are the happiest pair you could ever imagine as they rock down the aisle.

Is this the way to Amarillo?
Every night I keep huggin' my pillow,
dreamin' dreams of Amarillo
and sweet Marie, who waits for me.

What that has to do with any kind of wedding at all, I haven't the faintest clue, but it seems to be hitting the spot with Delia's guest list anyway.

The congregation files out, and Delia and Darren stand outside on the gravel, being hugged and kissed by the huge crowd in between having their photos taken.

I look around for any sign of trouble. I'm not going to lie – Traveller weddings bring so many different branches of a huge family together that they can be like tinderboxes. Old feuds are liable to break out just by one person looking at another the wrong way, which is why Delia had to be so political in her choice of bridesmaids.

Out of the corner of my eye, I catch Jerome practically frog-marching a bunch of suited young lads with buzz cuts and diamond earrings around the back of the church. I leave Kieran chatting to Michael and follow Jerome, just in case anything is wrong. I can have the Dromahane lads lift anyone who's likely to cause a problem. Nothing must spoil Delia's day.

The sight I find as I round the corner and duck behind a pillar is the six hardy bucks, not so smart now, lined up against the wall of the church, looking like chastened schoolboys, and Jerome pointing his finger at each in turn.

'I'm gonna say this once right and once only. No fightin'. I don't care who says what to ya, I don't care who does what to ya, there's to be absolutely no fightin'. Right?' He's up close to the nearest lad, right in his face. The boy – the joker who pretended not to have the rings – nods respectfully. Then to each one he goes up, and with a finger in the middle of the chest, he repeats the mantra. 'No fightin'.'

He stands back then, addressing them all. I see two of them are Carmodys – Patrick, who is notorious for scrapping, and Kenneth, who is all talk; his gob is what gets him into the most trouble. The Carmodys and the McGoverns are both Traveller families and related in such a myriad of ways, the entire team of *Who Do You Think You Are?* couldn't get it straight, but they are as different as chalk and cheese.

The other four I don't know, but I assume they are more cousins.

'I swear to God, if I find out that any one of ye drew a clatter on anyone, for any reason, you'll be havin' your meals for the next two months with a straw.' Jerome looks so ferocious, I'm almost scared myself. 'Am I clear?'

They all nod and mumble that it's perfectly clear.

'Right, have a great day,' he concludes, with a big bright smile.

I slip back to Kieran and the girls before Jerome sees me. I need not have worried – nothing will ruin this day. Even the sour-faced Sonia Ward seems to have cheered up, and she's chatting happily to a young man I don't recognise – in fact I'm not sure even whether he's with the bride or the groom, though there's something familiar…

A moment later he notices me noticing him, pats Sonia on the arm and saunters over to say hello. To my amazement it's Lenny Carmody, a cousin of Blades. I haven't seen him in two years; his father, Martin, the patriarch of the Carmodys, sent him to England after he came out of jail the second time, to straighten up in the care of some very strict relatives.

The last time I laid eyes on Lenny, he was terrifying looking, with a shaved head, a livid scar down one side of his face and steely blue eyes, but now I can't recognise the young man in front of me. The skinhead is gone. He has a respectable crew cut, and the scar is a lot less noticeable; even his eyes seem softer. Normally he would be dressed in the most expensive runners on the market and a tracksuit, complete with gold bracelets and that sort of thing. Very showy, gangster style. But today he's wearing a settled-looking suit; his shirt is tucked in, his top button is done up, and the knot of his tie is pulled tight. No jewellery in sight.

'Hi, Sergeant Munroe,' he says.

'Hi, Lenny, welcome back.' I try to sound like I mean it. 'How are you getting on in England?'

'Good, yeah. Staying out of trouble anyway.' He gives me a wry smile. We both know how trouble-prone Lenny Carmody is.

'Well done. What do you get up to over there?'

'Workin' mostly as a stable hand, a few miles outside of London. I'm not makin' a fortune or nothin', but it's grand. And I got married. We have a baby boy and one on the way. She's too far along to travel, which is why I didn't bring her home with me. Sonia there is her younger sister.'

'Really? Congratulations.' I'm delighted for him. I rarely say people are beyond redemption, but Lenny Carmody was a nasty piece of work. Still, this person in front of me seems all right. 'Have you a photo of them?'

He looks at me askance for a moment to see if I'm serious, then realises I am and proudly takes a picture out of his wallet. A really pretty girl of no more than seventeen, looking nothing like Sonia but more like Natasha, with a huge beehive of blond hair, long fake eyelashes and a big grin, holding a chubby baby in a Celtic Football Club jersey, beams out at me.

'Beautiful. What are their names?' I ask, handing him the photo back.

'My wife is Mary, and the small lad is Cristiano, after Ronaldo.'

I don't flinch, but it's very unusual for a traveller to name a chid anything non-traditional and Cristiano Carmody is a mouthful.

'So England was a good move for you then?'

He nods. 'You and I both know where I was headed if I didn't. Mary and Sonia's father, Alphonsus Ward, did you ever hear tell of him?'

I shake my head, though I have a vague idea from something Delia said about Sonia that Alphonsus Ward is a third-generation Irish Traveller, known to be a hard man but also known to steer clear of the law.

'Well, it's him I was sent to work for, and he's tough – he straightened me out a lot. I was still a bit wild, though, so when I put my eye on Mary, he said I could marry her but he wasn't havin' no son-in-law of his banged up. So we made a deal – I could have Mary if I kept out of trouble. So I have.' He shrugs. I know to anyone outside this would sound very transactional, a father giving his daughter as if she had no say, but she probably would have done, and it was the Traveller way. She looks delighted with herself in the photo anyway. Lenny's a good-looking lad now that he's changed his image.

Jerome comes over then and gives Lenny a very suspicious look, as if he is no better than the lads he just lambasted behind the church.

'Hi, Jerome,' says Lenny with a cheeky grin, and after Jerome growls something wordless in return, he saunters off, taking out a packet of cigarettes and offering one to Kenneth, who I think is his brother.

'Don't let him go foolin' you, Mags,' mutters Jerome, glaring after him.

I'm curious at his reaction. 'Lenny seems to have got his act together, to be fair. So what's the matter?' It was Jerome who told Martin Carmody that Lenny had to be sent away, and it looks like Alphonsus Ward has put him on the right path, so that's some achievement.

He shrugs, the massive suit that Joe Dillon picked out for him creasing across his mighty shoulders, and says nothing. This is often his way when he's not sure I'll believe him, or when he thinks something is Traveller business and therefore no business of mine – or more to the point, no business of the guards.

I don't press him; I'm not on duty here, and I'm not out to spoil anyone's day. Besides, I suspect there's nothing to know. Probably Lenny is dressed a bit too like a settled person for Jerome's taste. But that's hardly a crime – and maybe that's the best way for a Traveller to keep out of trouble in England.

'She looks well, doesn't she?' Jerome says, bursting with pride as he looks at Delia, who is posing for the photographer with her many bridesmaids.

'She's beautiful, Jerome, just beautiful,' I agree.

'And she's still a Traveller girl, y'know.' His voice is husky with emotion.

It warms my heart to hear him say it. He and Dora were so worried their beloved daughter might turn away from her heritage – particularly after she and Darren moved into a house instead of a caravan – so it's good to know he feels this way.

'I'm glad you can see that, Jerome,' I say. 'Now I should gather up my own daughters and head over to the Samovar.'

CHAPTER 2

The reception was never intended to be in the Samovar. The original plan was to have it in the Carrick Arms Hotel, a large sprawling place on the Dublin road, but there was a disastrous fire in the kitchen two weeks ago, and they've had to close while the whole place is refurnished and repainted.

There followed twenty-four hours of pure panic. The thing is, it's a rare hotel or pub that agrees to host a Traveller function at the best of times, weddings or funerals, even if there was two years' notice to give, let alone two weeks. Establishments just don't want them, and to be fair, with good reason sometimes.

The last Traveller funeral in Dromahane, six years ago, for the victim of a car accident, was attended by somewhere around three thousand people. Travellers came from all over Ireland, England, some even from the States, and they landed in Dromahane in the space of a few hours. And Travellers do funerals that are every bit as over the top as their weddings, maybe even more so. I wasn't at that one, but Leo Burke told me there were huge floral arrangements representing the life of the deceased. One of Liverpool Football Club, twelve feet long by three feet wide – it was in the shape of the crest of the club but fitted with actual speakers that blasted the anthem 'You'll Never Walk Alone.' And there was another floral tribute in the shape of an American dollar symbol, something to do with a rapper the deceased liked. And another of an actual revolver, for reasons unknown – and perhaps best not inquired into.

Then after the funeral, the younger crowd hit the pubs and the drinking started – in the pubs, out on the street – cars were revved, motorbikes, horses, quad bikes... It was bedlam apparently. The supermarket was cleaned out of slabs of beer and cider, and terrible damage was done; the place was left with bottles and cans everywhere.

Duckie was in Dromahane back then, and in my opinion, he made a pig's ear of policing that day. Donal Cassidy is that unfortunate mixture of someone who absolutely despises Travellers so won't communicate with the older members of the families about the best way to handle things, while at the same time is afraid to confront them when things get out of hand.

As a result, when young Blades Carmody was buried in Ballycarrick, all the businesses in the town, fearing for their stock and their windows, shut up shop, and those with metal shutters pulled them down. Even Tatiana in the Samovar, who can sort out any amount of trouble, shut her doors, the same as the other pubs. There was no fighting at that funeral and there was never going to be, not with myself and Jerome watching over it, but they all get tarred with the one brush, which made for a sad, lonely affair as Blades's last journey wound through the silent town.

This time around, though, when Tatiana found out that Delia and Darren had been left without a venue, she very kindly offered the Samovar to host the wedding.

With Dora's massive guest list – not thousands but maybe two hundred and fifty, plus fifty from the groom's side – the pub and restaurant weren't big enough to host the reception on their own, but Tatiana erected a large marquee outside in the garden, butting up against the open French windows of the restaurant so it's like an extension, and luckily the day is warm and sunny, so more people can sit outside at tables behind the marquee.

The Munroe table is in the marquee space, and I am between Mam and my daughters. Kieran and Joe are opposite, together with my best friend, Sharon, and her boyfriend, Trevor.

As the waitresses take away our soup bowls, fill our glasses and offer everyone beef or salmon, I observe Tatiana as she moves between the marquee and restaurant, directing operations, making sure everyone has what they want, whether a Carney or a McGovern. She is perfectly groomed as always. Her black hair is in a high ponytail, and a sharp blunt fringe stops at her straight black eyebrows. She has green eyes and a wide Slavic face. As Kieran says, she's beautiful but in a scary way. The Samovar is a shining example of a perfectly managed licenced premises; nobody ever misbehaves because Tatiana will deal with it, severely and decisively. I realise with gratitude that there is no better person to run a function like this; any lad inclined to get too rowdy after drinking will be silenced by a single glance from those terrifying eyes.

'Did you see the face on Darren's mam when she thought the rings had been stolen?' Ellie says to Kate with a giggle as she tucks into her salmon. My sixteen-year-old daughter claims to be vegetarian these days because the on-off love of her life – an alarmingly skinny boy called Carrot – has told her that 'meat is murder', but somehow she seems not to think fish are made of meat, and far be it for me to disabuse her, otherwise she'd just eat cheesy pizza and cake.

'Like anyone would do that at a wedding!' agrees Kate, who has just turned thirteen and loves it when Ellie treats her as an equal.

'You have no idea what *anyone* in this life will do, even at a wedding,' says Mam, overhearing, and proceeds to entertain the three of us with a mad story about her friend Ethel who goes salsa dancing with her.

'Ethel was at her niece's wedding up in Mayo, and her brother, the bride's father, had a lot of cash in his pocket to buy drinks and whatnot on the wedding day – he showed it to Ethel when they were getting ready, a wad of fifties in a rubber band – but when he went to pay for a huge round at the bar, he put his hand in his jacket pocket and the cash was gone.'

'What did he do?' The girls are hanging on her every word. Mam can tell a good story when she gets going.

'Well, Ethel could see something was wrong when her brother went white and got out his credit card, but he told her to say nothing, not wanting to ruin his daughter's day. Then the videographer sent over the wedding video while the couple were still on honeymoon – Ethel was still staying with her brother and his wife – and they decided to have a sneaky peek, and they invited the groom's parents over as well. So there they all are, watching the wedding video, and don't they see, clear as day, the groom pickpocketing the money out of his father-in-law's jacket!'

'Did they call the guards?' gasps Kate, shocked, while Ellie's eyes pop with fascinated horror.

Mam shakes her head. 'Oh no, but the money was returned, and the marriage was dissolved as quick as it was done. The girl was lovely, an air hostess for British Airways, I think Ethel said, so she's relocated to Singapore. But wasn't that just terrible?'

'Dreadful,' they chorus, and it is. The poor bride. What an awful thing to find out about the man you love.

There's a gap before dessert for the speeches, and champagne is handed around for the toasts. Kate is thrilled when I let her and Ellie have half a glass. Ellie is annoyed, though; she thinks she is old enough for a full glass now because she's 'not a kid like Kate'. Poor Kate looks crestfallen, the equality of earlier forgotten. But I'm holding out until Ellie is eighteen. I've seen too many casualties to drink among the young people of this town. Caelan Cronin was one for a while, always being frogmarched out of the Samovar by Tatiana. He never got over his mother being mowed down in front of his eyes by a drunk driver. You'd think he'd have sworn off the drink himself as a result, but it seemed to have the opposite effect for a while. Then Jerome had a word with him at my request, the sort of word I couldn't have had myself because it involved the Carmodys, and now Caelan is doing an apprenticeship with Phillip O'Flaherty in the garage. He's still a bit of a tearaway but nothing as bad as he was, so I have hopes.

At the top table, which is at the back of the marquee, Jerome and then Darren's father both make nice, short, polite speeches welcoming each other's children into their respective families, and both Dora – who doesn't seem to be eating; she must be very nervous – and Darren's mother manage to smile and nod. Michael, as best man, gives a speech about how Darren fell in love with Delia the first time he saw her. The couple blush, and I'm using my napkin as a handkerchief while Kieran grins at me, and then the speeches are over and it's time for Baileys cheesecake or rhubarb crumble.

'Poor old Father Doyle was looking a bit shook today,' Sharon remarks, reaching across the table with her spoon to grab a scoop of my delicious cheesecake; she gave hers to Ellie, saying she was full, but now she's regretting it and Ellie has already demolished both portions. 'Did you hear that Oscar is after setting up a special novena to St Gertrude and has asked the poor priest to bless all the cats of the parish?'

'Oh, for God's sake. That poor man.' I'd overheard Teresa talking about it to one of her customers, who was there to buy an apple tart for their tea, but I thought it was just a story having had legs added, as is so often the case in Ballycarrick.

St Gertrude is the patron saint of cats, because in medieval Belgium, she was famous for chasing away rats and mice, so she was thought to be a cat in human form.

'Oh, it's true,' says Mam her mouth in a grim line. She's on the church flower-arranging committee and knows everything about Father Doyle's many trials and tribulations. 'Everyone for fifty miles has been collared by Oscar to present their cats for blessing. I mean, he's even convinced Lelia Kiely, you know, that woman who lives out the Headford road? In the old Carlisle place? She must have twenty cats if she has one – she's a bit daft, if you ask me – but he's told her to bring them all. There'll be hundreds of cats in the church next Sunday after Mass if he's allowed to go ahead with it.'

'But isn't St Gertrude's Day on the same day as St Patrick's Day?'

Ellie asks as she licks her finger and mops the last crumb of cheese-cake from her plate.

'It is, Ellie, but Oscar made an executive decision to move it so Gertrude isn't overshadowed. Give me strength,' says Mam, shaking her head. 'I've a good mind to get the flower-arranging committee to write to the bishop and demand he send some help. Between the roof of the church and all the weddings, funerals and christenings, poor Father Doyle can't be expected to spend Sunday blessing cats all by himself. He just isn't able.'

'It sounds like a nightmare,' I agree, though I hope Mam doesn't get too worked up on Father Doyle's behalf. Oscar is a law unto himself. Trying to stop him when he gets a notion about a prayer service is like trying to stop that bullet train in Japan, so she'd only be frustrating herself. Mam had a heart attack last year and while she made a good recovery and took the sensible decision to retire and allow Sharon to buy the boutique, I wouldn't want Oscar and his cats sending her stress levels sky-high again.

'I think it sounds lovely.' Kate is clearly picturing a congregation of beautiful purring golden-eyed creatures all sitting patiently in the pews, rather than the yowling, spitting, scratching mayhem I'm envisioning. Kate adores animals and is in heaven now that we have two dogs – I know, I can hardly believe it myself; I'll explain later – as well as a huge frilled lizard called Knickers, who is as big as a small dog himself, and a long-haired guinea pig called Meatloaf, courtesy of Ellie's other suitor, the much-scorned Goosey.

'Don't be daft, Kate.' Ellie is dismissive in the way only older sisters can be. 'Mam's right, it will be a nightmare.'

And poor Kate looks crestfallen again. I throw her a sympathetic wink while Mam starts telling another story about her neighbour's cat twice getting stuck up a tree, wailing its head off, and both times waiting till the fire brigade got there to just jump down by itself and stroll off with its nose in the air.

'Seven hundred euro it cost poor Eileen, both times, for an unnecessary call out,' she says, shaking her head. 'I can't believe she fell for it the second time as well.'

Our dessert plates are removed, and soon the tables will be pushed aside for the dancing – there's a huge wedding band setting up behind us in the restaurant. I slip off to the loo, unable any longer to put off the mad contortions necessary to extract myself from the secret armour of elastic hidden under my velvet jumpsuit. Twenty minutes later I emerge only slightly dishevelled from the battle and make my way back through the bar, which is a mixture of industrial chic – brick walls and iron girders – and 1920s American speakeasy – scarlet velvet chairs and tasselled lamps. At the corner of the bar is Tatiana, taking a quick break with a glass of lemonade. She signals me to join her.

I've been meaning to say how impressed I am that she stepped up to host this wedding, and as I take a seat on the stool beside her, I tell her.

She shrugs by way of reply. 'Is easy decision. Two guards getting married, both I like very much.'

'Still, there were a lot of unknowns…' When it comes to the Travellers, I mean.

'Not as unknown to me as you might think.'

I throw her an inquiring look. Tatiana speaks her mind and says what she sees, but when it comes to her background, she's always played her cards very close to her chest. I don't know anything at all about her life before she came here, so I can't help being curious, like I was curious about Jerome's attitude to Lenny Carmody. Maybe curiosity is what makes a good guard.

'Mags, you are very nosy woman, but you keep mouth shut like clam,' Tatiana says, and I realise with a throb of interest that she's about to tell me something. Not wanting her to change her mind, I don't react at all; I just listen.

She twists her glass. 'I don't tell anyone here this, except Jerome and now you.' She shoots me a look, and I nod, keeping my expression neutral.

She drops her eyes again. 'My family were Ruska Roma, what you call gypsies, but in 1956 Khrushchev make it illegal to live nomadic life, so we were forced to live in apartment. Before I was born, of course, but my family remember. Jerome ask me if I know about that life, life of gypsy. I don't know how he knows this about me, but he does. We have many talks. I tell him about my grandfather and his sister who care for me – my parents was both sent to camps. Die there. I don't know what is happened to them, cold, hunger, too much work probably. Jerome is like my grandfather. Big, strong, proud.' She stops and shudders.

I can tell what a big deal it is for her to confide in me like this. 'Have you brothers or sisters?' I ask gently.

She nods once. 'Two brothers, both was in army. I don't know if they dead or not.'

'Is there not a way to find out?'

She sighs. 'Why? I can't see them now anyway. Putin, Ukraine, all of it. No. They don't know where I am. After my grandfather die, I find Russian brides website on computer in library and leave Russia forever. My grandfather's sister was alive when I leave Vladivostok, but now? I don't know.'

'Can't you write? Or ring?'

She shakes her head. 'No mail services, all suspended from Ireland to Russia, and she don't have phone. We are poor, Mags, not like here. We have nothing. Not clothes, not enough food most of the time. I get out. She don't want to hear I come back. Enough for her that I get out. Finding husband in Free World was her dream for me.'

'I'm sorry to hear that, Tatiana.'

She shrugs. 'It is how it is. Now I must check on my guests.' And she's gone. Back to business once more.

I watch her go and slip down off the stool.

Before I re-enter the marquee, I take a stroll around the pub garden, where lots of the guests are sitting out at the wooden tables with their drinks, enjoying the warm evening. Finbarr Turner and his mothers, helped by Olivia McGovern, have done a wonderful job making the place beautiful; there are yellow and purple irises in huge pots, and now with the light fading, the net of solar-powered fairy lights strung along the back wall of the yard begins to glitter. There is a stream that flows along the foot of the wall, the rippling water reflecting the lights, and everything is amazing.

It strikes me how lucky we are to be born where we are, in the time we're in. I know the world can look screwed up, with wars and people living in despair; there's no getting away from it. But when I hear stories like Tatiana's, it makes me so grateful for my life. A nice house, enough food, plenty of clothes, my kids safe, money enough to do as we want – we should all count our blessings maybe and do less whining.

I can't imagine that my dream for either of my girls would be a marriage arranged on a website to some sleazy man on the other side of the world, but that's exactly what it was for Tatiana's grandaunt – she'd been delighted for Tatiana to have the chance. To be fair, Tatiana wasn't a soft touch; she'd dispatched Leery Benny, as he was known, former proprietor of this bar, with all haste as soon as he showed his true colours, and she's made a great life for herself here. She is single again now, Victor the chef, her last boyfriend, getting the high road, as they all do in the end.

Back in the marquee, Mam is waltzing in fine style with Joe. He's a great dancer since he took lessons from Enrico, who is married to Kieran's brother Gearoid. Joe was never interested in ballroom before, said he had two left feet, but he realised it was the only way to woo Mam away from Teo Valdez, the salsa-dancing, Bentley-owning oncology consultant with a full head of silvery-black hair. He still can't believe Mam chose him instead, and he's been on air, as he often says, ever since.

Delia is swaying with Darren, her head on his shoulder. Finbarr is dipping Olivia, both in tears laughing, and Annette and Martha dancing nearby, their long flowing dresses fluttering.

Sharon is draped over Trevor as they move to the music. They're still going strong, I'm happy to say. Trevor Lynch is the drummer of Tequila Mockingbird, a local rock band. He toured the world and then came home to mind his mother. We all had a crush on him when we were in school and he was four years ahead of us; he was very Jon Bon

Jovi back in the day. But now he's different, a meditative kind of man, gentle and deep. I would never have put him with Sharon, but it seems to work. I hope it lasts. It took her far too long to get over the horrific Danny Boylan, who broke her heart when he ran off with Chloe from the chipper – as the now Chloe Boylan will always be known by everyone. Sharon was so badly burnt by Danny's betrayal, she swore she'd never marry again, and I don't think she ever will. She and Trevor live together, and he's wonderful with her son, Sean, who is nine, but I fear that's as far as she's willing to go.

Kate is being hauled around the floor by Kieran. He really does have two left feet and hates dancing, but she's pestered him into it, probably because Ellie is slow dancing with Carrot.

Carrot's real name is Shane; the Carrot moniker comes because he's vegan. He is the sort of dark, skinny, brooding boy teenage girls are suckers for, and Ellie is clearly not immune...

Hang on, how is Carrot here? Surely he's not invited? His parents live in a very posh house and wouldn't stoop to go to a Traveller wedding, not even a half-settled one like this. Ellie must have called him, and he probably came in over the back wall. Yes, he's leaving wet footprints on the dance floor, so he must have waded across the stream. Tatiana has spotted the gate crasher and is headed his way...

Time to go home.

The Carneys have already left, off to their swanky hotels in Galway, and the younger Travellers have dispersed as well, looking for a discreet place to go and drink a few cans and maybe roll some joints, probably up the castle grounds. If they don't make a noise or a mess, I think I'll turn a blind eye. Let Jerome do the policing tonight – like Tatiana, he's shown himself more than capable.

Before I gather up the girls and Kieran, I scan the room for Jerome to say goodnight and see him sitting with Dora in a corner of the restaurant. Her hair has come down slightly, and she's leaning against him, in the circle of his arm, seemingly half asleep. If I didn't know a drop of alcohol never passed her lips, I would assume she's had a glass too many of champagne – it's been flowing very liberally, with Jerome insisting on paying for it all. But Dora never drinks.

I decide just to wave in his direction rather than disturb them; in return he lifts his big hand and smiles, then drops a kiss on his wife's head. He's not a sentimental man, so I'm surprised by the public gesture. Although of course no one is looking at them apart from me, and as Jerome knows – and as Tatiana said earlier – I might be 'very nosy woman', but I 'keep mouth shut like clam'.

CHAPTER 3

Kieran has gone to see his parents. His father, Kevin, has an ingrown toenail and needs him to mow the lawn, which according to his mother, Nora, is 'completely out of control'. In her book that means the grass is over two inches tall. The girls are upstairs, hopefully playing chess or reading but in real life much more likely to be on their phones. Kate has one as well now, a new development; we held out as long as we could.

I'm settled on the couch in the conservatory with my book, *Anxious People* by Fredrik Backman, really good, and I'm reading it while eating the remains of the cream cake we had for dessert. I shouldn't do this – in fact I should stop buying cream cakes from Teresa's altogether – but it's Sunday and you have to have something nice on Sunday, it's a rule, and there was just this small bit left that I didn't want to let go to waste…

I finish the last mouthful and turn the page. The book is about two policemen in Sweden, a father and son, and I'm absorbed by it, and I'm also enjoying the peace and quiet of being all by myself.

It's been a hectic week with both Delia and Darren away on their honeymoon so the rest of us are up to our eyes with work. And it's not like we weren't already snowed under. The new houses built in the town have added considerably to the workload, but there's no sign of any new staff or more resources for our station. The public desk used to be open for four hours a day, two hours in the morning, one in the afternoon and one in the evening to facilitate people with kids or working shifts and all of that. But these days the demand for just basic things – passport applications, bail sign-ons, applications for asylum, general queries – means my officers are run off their feet and things are being allowed to slide. I hate it, but what can we do? We have to prioritise. For example we used to run a great outreach programme with the local secondary schools. The teenagers knew us and knew that we were on their side, and so it meant that if there ever was an issue, we could handle it much better. But that's had to go. We just don't have the staff right now.

My phone rings. I cast a wary eye at the screen – what now? – but then sit up with a smile. It's Mam. I haven't seen her for a few days, and I decide if she wants me to pop over, I will.

'Hi, Mam, will I come round for a cuppa?'

'No, you're grand, Mags. Myself and Joe are going out in a bit to an afternoon tea dance. It was going to be in the Carrick Arms Hotel, but the fire gutted the function room – it was right next to the kitchen – so now it's in Shaw's on the Galway Road and we're meeting Ethel. But wait till I tell you!'

It turns out she's calling because she's bursting to tell me about the stand-off that happened that morning after Mass between the flower-arranging committee and over seventy cat owners, led by Oscar O'Leary, Ireland's most devout Catholic.

'Oscar had promised each cat owner an individual blessing to each cat – can you imagine it? All those poor moggies scratching and yowling in their carriers and baskets and lots of them on leads like dogs, and one lady had hers in a pushchair, can you believe it...'

I can't.

'But I gathered the flower-arranging committee together, and we decided enough was enough for poor Father Doyle. So we hid him in the sacristy, and Maureen went down and closed the main door and the two side doors and slid the bolts. They were all screeching in protest outside and ready to scratch anyone's eyes out, and that was just the owners. Can you imagine the scene, Mags?'

'I'm trying to…' I'm starting to laugh now.

'Eventually we came to a compromise. We said for everyone to control their cats in the car park – there were hundreds of cats, honest to God, hundreds. That lady from Headford had even more than I thought, and there were others as bad. So we said Father Doyle would bless them from the window upstairs, you know the one beside the organ in the gallery?'

'I do, I do…' I'm going to need my inhaler. I'm laughing so much my smoke-damaged lungs are hurting, but I don't want her to stop. This is hilarious.

'So like the pope on Easter Sunday, up went Father Doyle with his holy water and what have you and issued a general blessing on all the cats at once, and there were a few grumbles, mainly from Oscar. But then we brought Father Doyle back to the sacristy again, so in the finish, they had no option but to take the cats away.'

'What will Oscar O'Leary come up with next…' Between gasps, I'm hunting around for my inhaler. Not in my pocket…

'Ah, Oscar would want to wind his neck in now, so he would. I mean, we all go to Mass, we all do our bit, but he's ridiculous at this stage… Yes, Joe, I'm coming! Mags, I'll see you during the week. Lots of love!' And she's gone, leaving me weak and breathless.

Where is my inhaler? Someone has helpfully put it away…

I go through the cupboards in the kitchen, and when I open the one that contains the medicine box, I come eye to eye with Kate's huge frilled lizard, Knickers, who is hiding in there. I'm constantly stuffing the damn thing back into the enclosure Goosey built him in the utility room, which takes up all the space I could more usefully use for drying clothes, but Knickers is the Harry Houdini of the reptile world and always turns up in unexpected places.

He seems almost more alarmed to be discovered than I am to discover him and bursts past me out of the cupboard, leaps to the floor where he scuttles along on his hind legs with the frill standing out around his neck – he's like a mini dinosaur (not mini enough for my liking) – and dives under another cabinet.

He's not usually this nervous, so I suppose he's trying to avoid Princess, who is in heat at the moment and is – how should I put it? – desperate to cultivate a relationship with anything with four legs, whether it's Rollo who's had the snip – or we hope he has as the vet only found one testicle; TMI, I know – or poor Knickers, who is absolutely disgusted by her advances. Obviously. Because he's a lizard and she's a dog.

Oh yes, I did say I'd explain what we're doing with two dogs now as well as all the rest, so here goes.

Rollo, as you know, is the bedraggled Jack Russell that Kieran found in a builder's yard and who has gone from being terrified witless of me to abject devotion; I don't know which is worse. And Princess is the very expensive and formerly highly pampered pooch who used to be owned by Róisín Duggan.

How did the Munroe family end up with my husband's crazy ex-girlfriend's pedigreed Pekingese? You may well ask.

Róisín and her American husband, Joel, came home from New York last year, but it didn't work out. She was hitting the bottle hard and got it into her head that she and Kieran should be together. It was all very stressful, culminating in her arriving to our house plastered out of her mind one night and assaulting me and Kate. She's off the booze now and very sorry and all the rest, but I must say I was relieved when she decided she wouldn't be coming back to Ballycarrick. She set up a new law practice in Dublin instead, where nobody knows her. Joel went back to America, they're getting a divorce, and the house was put on the market.

Which meant somebody had to look after the dog while Róisín found herself a suitable place to live.

For some mad, inexplicable reason, I agreed to do it, on a temporary basis. But of course it's impossible to find a suitable place to rent in Dublin. The only apartment Róisín would consider was a strictly no-pets affair, and so Princess has still not been collected and I'm worried we're all getting used to her, especially Kate, who adores her.

Princess is a bit the worse for wear compared to when she arrived. Róisín had her at the groomer each week and spent a fortune on conditioning fur treatments and getting her nails done and God knows what else, so needless to mention, in our house that's all off the menu. She gets fed and watered, walked and played with, but the cosmetic attention to detail has, I admit, slipped. The one concession I've made to her old pampered way of life is to not get her spayed, because she still – nominally at any rate – belongs to the hapless Róisín, and there's a plan in some unforeseeable future for her to have glamorous pampered and highly expensive puppies by another equally posh Pekingese with his pedigreed papers stamped in triplicate.

Not that Princess cares about posh. I keep her inside when she's in heat, but I've caught her at the window setting her cap at the most disreputable passing canines. She's a dreadful hussy, as poor harassed Knickers can vouch for.

Still looking for my inhaler, I open the door into the living room and catch Rollo having a half-hearted and ineffective go at a desperate Princess on the hearth rug. Seeing me, he bounds over and demands to be picked up, then licks my face, assuring me it is only me he loves. The abandoned Pekingese stalks past me into the kitchen, and the next minute, Knickers comes rushing the other way and swarms up the heavy curtains, where he sways dangerously on the pelmet with an excited Princess yipping at him from below.

I'm tempted to ring Róisín and demand she come and pick up her bloody dog today, now, at once, no-pet rule or not.

'Can't you just tell her she either takes it back or sells it?' Mam asked me last week as I was complaining about Princess. She gets my position on animals – she's much the same as me and thinks they're a lot more trouble than they're worth – but what she doesn't get is why I'm so forgiving of Róisín, especially after she bashed me over the head with an empty wine bottle.

I had to explain that if I did that, Róisín would only dump the problem on her mother, and I didn't want poor Frances Duggan burdened with a yappy sex-crazed dog. It's bad enough her husband,

Martin, has dementia. He's gone into St Clare's as she isn't able to look after him any more, but she visits for hours every day.

Mam had sighed at that; she fears dementia more than anything, even though she's still as sharp as a tack. 'God spare us from that, Mags. That man was so bright and clever. Dementia is such a cruel disease. I'm telling you now, if my mind goes, a pillow over my face and be done with it. I couldn't bear it, to lose yourself a bit more day by day. It's a terrible way to go.'

'I think there are laws against murdering your own mother, Mam,' I'd said with a laugh I didn't really feel. 'I'd have to check exactly – it might have changed – but I don't think it has...'

'Well, I'll find a way to do it myself if that's the case, but I'll tell you here and now, I won't go that way,' she'd answered determinedly.

I find the inhaler on the mantlepiece over the fire in the sitting room and take a big puff, then leave the animals to it and head back into the conservatory to settle down again and read my book.

Except now, instead of feeling relaxed, I'm wracked with guilt about spending all this valuable time alone, away from my loved ones. I am struck by how time is flying by so fast. My mother is still enjoying life, but she's getting older. It's easy to pretend she'll be here forever, but right now, remembering that conversation about the Duggans, I'm acutely aware of how little time might be left.

And it's not only Mam getting older; my little girls are also little no longer. And I'm overwhelmed by a desire to slow it all down. I should be spending my weekends with the people I love, while the girls still want to and my mam is able to.

Mam's off at the tea dance, so maybe I'll suggest bringing the girls to Luigi's for an ice cream sundae. OK, I've had two slices of cake, but this is in the interests of family time, and I'll have a Diet Coke instead of a full-sugar one, even if Carrot has convinced Ellie that diet drinks give you cancer – liquid death, he calls it.

Just as I'm about to get off the couch, a furious fight breaks out upstairs.

I can hear Kate shouting. 'It's not fair! You sent me to get it, and now I need it. Mine's going to die without it, and you've had it for the last hour!'

'It's not yours, you little squib, and get out of my room!' Ellie roars in response.

A thump. A slam of a door. A wordless yell. Wait for it...

'Maaaam...'

I sigh. Oh well, so much for family time. Teenage girls truly are sent to test us. As Kate comes stomping down the stairs, her face dark as thunder, I get ready to channel my inner Kofi Annan.

A second later Kate storms into the conservatory, a look of high dudgeon on her face. Ellie can be moody and sarky, but nobody does indignation like my Kate. To listen to her, you would think she was St Therese of Lisieux going around doing nothing but good works while her sister is the devil incarnate, but I know there are two sides to every story, and they are as bad as each other.

Last Sunday, for example, we went for a walk out on the beach, Kieran and I, with Rollo and Princess. I'd asked the girls to come with us, but Ellie wanted to hang out with Carrot. Kate did come along, in the absence of any better ideas, but to see her pace, you would think we'd asked her to do Lough Derg. Do you know what that is? If not, it's an island in Donegal where people do a three-day pilgrimage, walk around in their bare feet, stay up all night and just eat oatcakes and drink hot water. Las Vegas it ain't, put it that way. She was absolutely allergic to myself and her dad and pounded up the beach with the dogs, looking mutinous.

'Maaaam, Ellie won't give me the charger even though my phone is going to die, and she threw me out of her room and hit me with the door, she slammed it so hard!'

Ah. The charger wars. Every phone that comes through our front door comes with a charger, but for a reason unfathomable, they are constantly disappearing.

'MAAAAM, MY PHONE IS GOING TO DIE!'

Right. This isn't too hard to fix.

'Why don't you use the charger in the kitchen?' Kieran has his plugged in beside the microwave with a big DO NOT REMOVE sign taped to the wall above it. He's told the girls that it is to remain where it is under pain of death, after his last three chargers disappeared into the black hole that lurks somewhere between the girls' bedrooms.

'Because that's the one Ellie made me bring to her upstairs,' wails Kate.

For God's sake. 'Kate, you know that charger is Dad's and you shouldn't have taken it –'

'Ellie made me!'

'Even if Ellie told you to, he'll have a conniption if he comes home and finds it gone from the kitchen. I'm going to tell her it's got to go back, and then you can use it.'

I start to get off the couch, thinking this is an easy one to solve, but it's not finished.

'Maaaam, nooooo, she'll only be horrible to me if you do that. She says she needs it in her bedroom because making videos uses so much battery and her phone is so old, the battery is always dying, and she's up there making a stupid TikTok for pulling up, and it's really, really mean and stupid of her to be doing it...'

This is all delivered in one long breathy tone of deeply wounded hurt.

Right, so the charger is only a small part of what's going on here. I sink back onto the couch – clearly I'm not going to get out of this lightly – and pat the cushion beside me. She sits down, radiating misery.

'Kit Kat, I understand about the charger, but why is it mean for Ellie to be making a TikTok?'

'Mam, you don't get it. Sienna Black is such a legend, and she, like, wants to make the world a better, fairer place. She got where she is by people pulling her up, and she wants us all to do the same for each other. That's why we post TikToks of us doing her songs, and we encourage each other to do them and give and get as many likes as we can. It's all about pulling up...'

'Sorry, what? What are you saying "pulling up" all the time for? I'm confused, Kate. Explain.'

She explains as if I'm ninety-three and in a nursing home and have decided I want to learn to play the stock market online.

'Sienna Black. You remember who that is, don't you? We did tell you?'

Like I have dementia.

Only last month there was huge excitement in our house about Sienna Black coming to Dublin – she's an American singer-songwriter hardly older than Ellie. My girls had entered a lottery to get a ticket code and were so excited when they got a winning number. I was psyching myself up to take them to Dublin to squeeze in with eighty thousand screaming teenagers in Croke Park, because you can be sure that by extraordinary bad luck, the concert would clash with an uilleann piping event that my husband absolutely could not miss.

Until it turned out the lottery win was only *the chance* to sit on my computer for hours, starting at the crack of dawn, for the privilege of *buying* three tickets.

'Please, please, please, please, please, Mam...' they'd chorused.

'Ah, Mags, let them go,' said Kieran, who was reading the *Irish Times* on his phone while eating his breakfast cereal.

Screeches of delight. 'Thanks, Dad, you're the best!'

'Kieran,' I said quietly, 'do you know how much the tickets are?'

'Didn't they just win them?' he asked, his eyes glued to his phone.

'No, Kieran, they won the faint chance of me being able to buy them in the middle of the night, and in the unlikely event I succeed, they cost three hundred and fifty euro. *Each.* So that's over a thousand euro before counting travel or staying over in a hotel...'

The phone went down on the table, and he'd shaken his head in bemused horror. 'Well, that's not going to happen.'

Cue screams of devastation and raging at our parental selfishness, spending money on ourselves while ruining our poor deprived daughters' lives. The selfish bit is that Kieran dared to buy me a night away with him in Castle Dysert, the luxurious five-star resort in Clare, about an hour from here. I can't leave the station while both Delia and Darren are away on honeymoon, but we're going at the end of March.

So yes, I do know who Sienna Black is.

'Right. Well, she is from Washington, DC. That's in America –'

'I'm aware of where Washington, DC, is, Kate. Go on.'

'And she grew up kind of poor and with no connections in the music business or anything.' Kate says this like Sienna Black is some sort of messiah born in a stable. 'Her mam died, and her dad wasn't able to take care of her because he was busy working as a garbage collector' – binman is what they're known as in Ireland, to my generation anyway, but all the kids are American now – 'and her grandmother minded her, but then her grandmother died when she was twelve and she went back to live with her dad. He's now her manager and agent and all of that. She was really talented, but at first no agents or record companies wanted to know about her – she was so young and poor and all of that – so she started putting clips up on TikTok, ones she just made at home herself, and she broke the internet.'

'Really? Is that possible?' I have a brief mental picture of the internet not working any more, no social media, no Google, no 'X', and it feels really pleasant...

Kate rolls her eyes. 'Well, not *literally*, Mam, like that's not how the internet works. It's a load of...um...'

'I know how the internet works, Kate,' I interrupt, although I don't. But then, I suspect, neither does she.

'Anyway, Mam...' She carries on, and I think she's quite glad to be let off the hook about that. 'She's amazing. She won't bow to the patriarchy, she has no filler or Botox –'

'She's seventeen! Of course she hasn't had filler or Botox.

'I know! And she doesn't wear skimpy clothes. She has a kind of vibe, you know? Like empowering girls and women to be themselves, not to change because the media or men or peer pressure tells us to, see? I'm only on three percent, but...'

She scrolls on her phone and shows me a photo of a young woman, pale-skinned to the point of almost albino, dressed in a huge white T-shirt emblazoned with the phrase 'Pulling Up' and even huger white jeans. The only splash of colour is an enormous mop of coppery-red curly hair that grows in every direction off her head but is cut in a very short fringe in front, which has the effect of making her appear a little odd. The colour might be natural; it's hard to tell. But she doesn't resemble any pop star I've ever seen. She is slim, but you'd never know what body shape she has under the enormous clothes, and she wears not a scrape of make-up. It makes a change, I suppose.

'She looks interesting,' I say diplomatically, handing Kate back her phone.

'So she is an advocate for kindness and helping others – she does loads for charities and everything – but her main thing is pulling up, like giving someone a helping hand to get up to your level.'

'So this is what pulling up is about?'

'Yes. She says so many people gave her a hand to get up to where she is, she wants to do the same and empower every young girl with her music.' Kate's face fills with joy at such a prospect, and my heart swells. In a world seemingly so broken and damaged, that young people can still have faith like this is wonderful. 'And that's why everyone is making TikToks of her songs!'

'And Ellie is making one, is that it?'

Kate snorts, plunged into gloom again. 'Yeah, she thinks she's going to get loads of likes, which she definitely won't, but try telling her that. She can't even sing. She's up there warbling like an old crow. She couldn't carry a tune in a bucket.'

'Ah now, Kate…' I'm quite shocked by her vehemence, and also it's not true. Ellie's voice did take a while to settle. She has a natural vibrato that makes it hard for her to sing in tune – she's had to mature into it – while Kate has always had the sort of pure soprano you could listen to all day. 'That's not nice, and Ellie is a great singer now. Sure wasn't she picked to play Mary Poppins in the school musical?'

'That's just because she can fit in the harness, so she can fly. Lydia Doyle is way better at singing, and her mam is English, so she can do the right accent for the part, but she's way too fat to fit in the harness even though the teachers didn't say that was the reason.'

'Kate!' My daughter is not normally mean like this; it's so out of character. 'That's not fair or kind. And what about your hero Sienna? I doubt based on what I've heard that she'd like to hear people calling other people fat now, would she?'

'I suppose not,' Kate sulks.

'Anyway, instead of complaining about Ellie making one, why don't you make one as well, a TikTok, I mean? It might be fun.'

Kate shakes her head, and the tears start to flow. 'I just...'

'What is it, Kit Kat?' I ask gently, putting my arm around her.

'Me and Ellie were going to do one together, and we had it all ready and everything – we practised for ages. But then she said it was crap, and it was, but it was her idea. I had a much better idea that would have really worked, but she wouldn't listen. She said she wanted to do one on her own instead.' Kate's voice is muffled now as she burrows into my shoulder. So this is it.

The truth of the matter is that Kate is feeling a bit abandoned. Throughout their early years, Ellie and Kate, all the fights notwithstanding, were always best friends. They would laugh and giggle for hours, find the same bewildering things hilarious. It was almost at times like they were speaking in code, and neither Kieran nor I had a clue what was going on. But that has changed now. Ellie has turned sixteen and is interested in boys and wants to spend her free time with her mates, and Kate is only thirteen, so too young for that stuff yet.

It's tough being a kid, isn't it? Learning to cope with life's disappointments.

'Ah, I'm sorry, Kit Kat. I can see that hurt you.'

'She never wants to do anything with me any more. She just wants to be with Carrot all the time. And if she's not with him, she's out with her friends or she's at youth theatre doing her drama stuff. It's like she wants to be with everyone but me.'

I kiss the top of her head and let her cry. It's hard but it's life.

When the tears subside, I wipe her face with my thumbs. 'Will we go to Luigi's?' I offer. 'Just for an ice cream?'

She nods.

'We won't tell Ellie,' I whisper, and I'm rewarded with a big grin.

In the car down to Luigi's, which does real Italian ice cream even though Luigi's actual name is Leonard and he comes from County Offaly, not Milan, I flick on the radio; the news is on.

'The investigation into the missing showjumper Chance Your Arm will continue until the valuable animal is recovered safe and well.' It's the distinctive nasal voice of Des Finan, Minister for Sport. 'Chance Your Arm was stolen from the yard of internationally renowned trainer Roger Mulligan in County Galway several days ago, but as yet even the offer of a large cash reward has not yielded any clues as to the animal's whereabouts. I'm joined now by Detective Inspector Donal Cassidy for the latest...'

I groan, and Kate throws me a sympathetic glance. She knows how I feel about Duckie Cassidy because I once blurted it out to Kieran without realising Kate was in the room. He's a misogynistic, rude, ignorant buffoon, and the bane of my life. And now the whole country is going to be treated to his thoughts on the missing Chance Your Arm.

'Thank you for joining us, Detective Inspector Cassidy. Can I begin by asking you if there have been any further developments in the search for Chance Your Arm?'

'Well, Jason,' Duckie's smug, oily tones come over the airwaves; he's loving being the centre of attention. 'The investigation is ongoing, as you know, and all ports, sea and air, were alerted immediately when it came to light. We are confident the animal has not left the jurisdiction.'

'We just heard from the Minister for Sport, and clearly this is a huge blow to the reputation of the country as a centre of excellence for bloodstock. There's to be a government inquiry. Our bloodstock industry is worth two and a half billion to the Exchequer each year, so we don't want people to think that in Ireland a valuable animal like Chance Your Arm can just vanish into thin air.'

'And he hasn't.' Duckie sounds a bit more defensive now. 'As far as I am concerned, Chance Your Arm is still on the island.'

'I believe the owner, Sheikh Al Kharmein, has intimated at a press conference in London that he wants to see quicker results.'

'Naturally he does. The animal is worth millions...'

'And I would imagine in a case such as this, time is of the essence?'

'No one could move faster than I am.' Duckie is bristling now, I can tell. He hates being questioned, however mildly. 'The sheikh, and the minister and everyone else, can rest assured that the horse will soon be found.'

'So you have a definite line of inquiry?'

I smile. Jason Lee is known as being a terrier of an interviewer, and he isn't letting Duckie off the hook. I am enjoying this, however unprofessional that sounds.

'Several leads are being investigated' – which means there is no definite line of inquiry – 'and as always the incident room remains in operation should any member of the public have any information. I need not remind listeners that there is a substantial reward still available for anyone with information that leads to the recovery of the horse.'

'And that number is 1800 565 050. I sincerely hope the helpline number is not indicative of the odds you currently run of finding the horse.'

I laugh then. Good on you, Jason. He's going through Duckie like a hot knife through butter.

'Of course it isn't,' Duckie answers in a huff.

'Well, again, thank you for joining us, Detective Inspector Cassidy.'

He knows he's got nothing out of Duckie except a ton of waffle and little achieved so far.

Kate casts a baleful glance at me. 'Is the poor horse dead, do you think?' she asks. She has a terrible soft spot for all animals, so the thought of Chance Your Arm being dead would really upset her, and she's emotional enough today.

'Oh, definitely not, love. He's worth much more alive,' I assure her. 'There is no possibility that the thieves would let anything happen to him – it would be completely pointless. No, he'll be looked after like a king.'

'But he's probably missing his home now.' She sighs, gazing out the window as the rivulets of rain are accelerated down the glass by the steady speed of the car, and a voice on the radio reads out the number of the incident room once more.

* * *

One of Luigi's special knickerbocker glories cheers Kate right up, and while we're out, I buy two more chargers in the shop at the petrol station, one for Kate and one for Ellie, though I know in both cases it's throwing good money after bad.

While I'm in the garage shop, I get a surly glare from the owner's wife, Gemma, who is behind the counter. She is one of Danny Boylan's many conquests, and I'm sure Danny's bad-mouthed me to her, because I'm Sharon's best friend and he knows I have the measure of him.

Poor Chloe from the chipper. She's in the same position as Sharon now. Everyone knows her husband is sleeping with Gemma – except Phillip, who owns the garage, I assume. I'm glad I'm not responsible for the morals of this town, only for ensuring people keep on the right side of the law – or at least not too far on the wrong side; sensible policing always requires turning a bit of a blind eye.

Back at home I give Ellie her charger and instruct her to never ever again remove her father's charger from beside the microwave, and then while she's feeling grateful to me for saying I won't mention it to Kieran, I talk to her about Kate.

'She has an idea for a TikTok of one of Sienna Black's songs, but it's for two voices, she says, one in English, one in Irish, so she needs you.'

She huffs and pouts. 'Why can't she do it with one of her little friends from school? It's embarrassing to be doing stuff with my little sister all the time…'

'But you said you would make one with her, Ellie, and isn't it all about pulling up?'

'She's not a deprived child –'

'But she feels deprived, Ellie.'

'Of what?' demands the girl whose life was RUINED by my

refusing to get up at four in the morning to queue on my computer to buy a ticket for the Sienna Black concert. Though she's a bit more relaxed about that now, because absolutely nobody in her school got one despite their various mothers being awake for hours. The tickets all sold out in thirty seconds, long before the queue reached any of their lottery numbers.

'She feels deprived of you, sweetheart. She loves you, and you mean everything in the world to her, and she's hurting that she thinks you prefer everyone else to her.'

'Oh, for God's sake...' She throws herself back on her bed, her arm dramatically flung across her eyes.

'Ask yourself, Ellie, what would Sienna Black do?' And with these profound words, I leave the room. Fingers crossed.

CHAPTER 4

The following Sunday – after another week of being up to my eyes at work because Delia and Darren are still on honeymoon; I don't begrudge them the break, but I'm counting the days – is our monthly Sunday lunch at Kieran's parents' house.

Kieran's mother, Nora, greets us at the door, and straight out of the traps, she's off. 'Mags, hello, how are you? Is that your work jacket? It must be very warm. It adds a lot of bulk, of course, but I suppose that's a good thing when enforcing the law, to make you look even bigger than you are.' She tinkles with laughter, and I feel Kieran tense beside me. His mother thinks she's all devious and can get away with saying things as jokes, but she's as mysterious as a bucket and Kieran can spot a nasty dig when he hears one.

I shoot him a sidelong glance. *Let it go.* If I was to take her up on every insult, we'd fight every week, and who has the energy for that?

'No, Nora, this is my own,' I say as I take it off and hang it up before following Kieran into the sitting room. His nice if useless dad, Kevin, is sitting with his feet up in slippers.

'Hi, Kevin, how's the foot?'

'He's like a bag of cats, Mags, is how he is. You'd swear they amputated it rather than a little ingrown toenail to hear him.' Nora rolls her eyes as she follows us in.

Kevin is not a drama queen – he's a man of so few words that for the first few years of our relationship, I wondered if he could speak at all – but anything that takes the spotlight off Nora is not to be tolerated in the Munroe household.

Orla and her husband, Fergus – Nora always describes him as 'Fergus, who is very high up in the bank' – are here already, and their daughter, Evie, jumps up to hug Kate. She and Kate are the same age and were inseparable in nursery and primary school, but then Orla and Fergus decided to send Evie to the same fancy private school as their tech genius son, Tom. It's about twenty miles away, and the girls don't see each other so much. It's sad for both of them, so they love these monthly get-togethers.

Aoife and her husband, Leonard – 'very high up in education' – are here as well, and the third sister, Catriona, turns up while we're still saying our hellos. As usual she is by herself because her husband, Seamus – 'very high up in the health service' – is a cardiologist at Galway University Hospital and always on call, and like Aoife's boys, her children are a bit older and are off doing their own thing.

'That's all of us today,' announces Nora breezily, 'so you might as well come on through. Catriona, you can help me serve.'

I'm sorry that Gearoid – 'very high up in the arts' – and his husband, Enrico, aren't here. I love their company, and they're great at managing Nora, largely by flat-out ignoring her. But I know they're spending the afternoon taking a young boy called Fionn McGuinness out for a Chinese meal and then to a play, *The Crucible*.

Fionn is only thirteen and adores Chinese food – well, the Irish version of Chinese food, which involves more potatoes than I would imagine are popular in Szechuan. He also loves the theatre, and in the last year, he's taken to hanging around the one where Gearoid is artistic director, doing odd jobs. I haven't met him yet, but Ellie knows him a bit from the youth theatre, and apparently he's been in care since he was five. It sounds like his parents were addicts and just weren't able for him. The poor boy never got adopted – he was too old, and everyone wants babies – so he's desperate to have a proper family of his own, and he's sort of attached himself to Gearoid.

They are thinking about fostering him, which if it works out would be wonderful. It was Enrico's idea; he has an enormous family in Spain and misses them.

Gearoid is coming round to the idea, as he's very fond of Fionn, so today is about the three of them talking it through. I hope it goes well. If it does, maybe they'll bring him to the next family gathering. I'm sure the cousins will make him welcome. Ellie says he's lovely if a bit shy, and he's the same age as Kate and Evie.

Oilibhéar MacElroy, Nora and Kevin's long-lost son, and his wife, Muireann, are also absent, but I knew they would be. Oilibhéar is 'very high up' in RTÉ, and it's a long way to travel from Dublin, so he only comes every other month, though we all get along very well when he's here. He's the head cut off Kieran, which is weird because Gearoid looks so different from his brothers.

Those of us who are here move to the dining room, and Catriona helps Nora serve up the Sunday lunch. As usual it is amazing.

My mother-in-law is an absolute penance – she peers down her nose at me because I'm not 'high up' in anything, and she thinks I've held her precious Kieran back because, as he always jokes, the only way he's 'high up' is on other people's rooftops – but she's a fabulous cook. Today it's roast pork with mouthwatering crackling and home-made apple sauce, and two sorts of potatoes, delicious buttery mash and crisp roasties with fluffy centres. I'm ready to burst when I've finished the last mouthful, but she's made an apple cinnamon cake for dessert and resistance is futile.

I reassure myself that the diet will start tomorrow, and it has to. I was doing so well with my smoke-damaged throat – I didn't get really skinny, but at least I was in proportion – but now the ever-expanding waistline situation is taking on a life of its own again.

I might have to go back to Skinny Elaine, who for years has run a slimming club in the damp-smelling basement of the Carrick Arms Hotel on a Tuesday night; she's holding it at Shaw's on the Galway road now while the hotel gets fixed. She stands at the top of the room in her red trouser suit, with her shiny blond bob and scarlet fingernails, and explains to us eejits how we are eating too much and not moving enough. Then we all go and climb on the scales for ritual humiliation. Everyone is supposed to bring their favourite healthy food they've eaten that week and put it on a table, and the person who loses the most weight gets to take home the lot.

Needless to mention I've never won it, and anyway, I know for a fact that Julie Magee, for example, the primary school secretary, eats way more custard slices from Teresa's than bags of kale, but in she troops each week with enough kale to turn the river green in Chicago for St Patrick's Day.

I only go to Elaine in times of dire emergency. Like before Ellie's confirmation when I bought a dress with a 30-inch waist – those were the days – and did not make allowances for the fact that Sharon and I went to Barcelona for her birthday two weeks before and I ate all the patatas bravas and chorizo in the city. Jeggings, leggings, tracksuit pants are not our friends. They tell us lies. Lies like everything is fine. And then you try to wear something with no Lycra and it's a rude awakening.

I dread it, Elaine's condescension, her foghorn voice, and me trying not to notice her huge buck teeth – she looks like she could eat a head of cabbage through a letterbox – but it has to be done and that's all there is to it.

This month's emergency is that Kieran and I are off to Castle Dysert, and I'd love to use the swimming pool in the spa, but I'm worried with the current state of affairs, I won't be able to cram myself into the nice new swimsuit I bought two months ago, let alone risk wearing a bikini – those days are long behind me.

The men all have second portions of the apple cinnamon cake, but I decide to resist and be more like Orla and Catriona and Aoife, even though I haven't a hope of ever being as slender as they are. They're immaculate as usual. They are so well groomed and never put on a pound, and I'm so envious of their figures.

Ellie and Kate and Orla's Evie and Tom are also holding out their bowls, and is it my imagination or does Nora hesitate a moment before giving Ellie less than half the portion she just doled out to the other three teenagers? I really hope I'm mistaken, and thankfully Ellie doesn't seem to notice.

Kate, Evie and Tom are all of the same Munroe greyhound breed. They couldn't put on a pick of weight if they tried, and I just know they'll probably be always like that. But Ellie is like me, a Kelleher.

She's so lovely, my almost-grown-up daughter. She's very like the Munroe side in her colouring. She has Kieran's easily tanned skin and shining curly mahogany hair and dark-blue eyes, and she's very pretty. But her figure is the way mine was at her age, curvy, and she despises exercise to boot, so I hate that she has a struggle with her weight to look forward to when she's older, but she does.

I don't ever talk about diets or weight at home. I think girls get quite enough of that toxic perfection everywhere; they don't need it from their mothers too. Mam was always great when we were growing up, building us up, never undermining us, and she's always told me that I'm grand as I am. She ran her boutique for years and years and made a fine art of making women look more toned, skinnier, flatter, whatever you want to call it. If she had a euro for every mother of the bride who was in tears the week before the wedding because the dress wouldn't fit, she'd be a millionaire. Mam would make them a cup of tea and get out her sewing machine. Panels added, elastics sewn in, seams let out – whatever it took she would do it – and that woman would walk out of my mother's shop with a dress that fit her.

All I hope is that like me, the battle of the bulge won't start for Ellie until she's happily married or settled and not out being judged.

After the cousins finish eating, they take the dessert plates out to the dishwasher in the kitchen and then ask if they can go down the road to the playground, because even though they are doing their best to be grown up, the zip wire is still a major attraction. Meanwhile we adults retire to the sitting room with coffee and tea and sprawl out on the sofas digesting our food. I'm half asleep when I hear my name spoken by Nora – in a tone of approval. I snap awake. This I must hear.

'Oh yes, who would have thought it. Apparently Mags knows Detective Inspector Cassidy very, very well. They've worked together a lot in the past. He's very high up in the guards. There was a rumour he solved a big important case to do with Russians last year, and now he's going to solve the missing horse case. Such an impressive man. Tell us about him, Mags?'

So her approval is for me knowing the obnoxious Duckie, who only got his promotion because I decided I didn't want it and who is so useless, he wouldn't have even been considered for it if it wasn't for his family connections.

'I'm sure Detective Inspector Cassidy is competent to find a missing horse,' I say as politely as I can. Even with Duckie there is a policy in the guards of not trashing your own – at least not to anyone except your nearest and dearest. Just as well Kate is out of the room; she might not be as diplomatic as Kieran, who is managing to keep his expression neutral. It's particularly galling about the Russians, because I'm sworn to secrecy about how I caught those spies, even though I received an accolade from the Garda Commissioner himself. Duckie played no part at all; I don't know how Nora got hold of that rumour.

'I'm sure he's more than *competent*, Mags,' titters Nora. 'I heard him on the radio this morning saying how he had a really important lead. I was hoping you'd know more about it, but maybe you don't work with him any more now he's so high up in Galway. Tell me, Fergus, Leonard or Kieran' – she always addresses her important questions to the men, who are clearly far more knowledgeable than women about anything, even something that's way out of their area of expertise – 'why would anyone steal a showjumping horse? Surely there'd be no point, because if you put them in for a competition, they'd be recognised?'

'I don't really know,' says Fergus, looking puzzled as he thinks about it, and Leonard seems equally flummoxed. But then Kieran speaks up.

'I asked Mags, and she explained that it's to do with breeding. Isn't that right, Mags?'

Everyone turns to me, even Nora, so I have to answer. 'Yes, that's true, Nora. Stud fees for an animal like him would be huge, and unlike racehorses, showjumpers do not need to be reproduced by witnessed live breeding. Mares can be impregnated by artificial insemination. Properly stored and transported, horse semen is quite possibly the world's most expensive liquid, and it's possible that Chance Your Arm's semen is worth, oh, in the millions of euros per litre of it, so that's what the thieves are after.'

I'm expecting my mother-in-law to start fanning herself like a Victorian lady at the mention of the word semen, a bit like Kate does if she catches me and Kieran so much as holding hands. But though Catriona, who is the most like her mother, is a bit po-faced, Nora is nodding with enthusiasm.

'Yes, Mags – you're so right...'

I nearly gasp aloud. It's the first time I've ever heard those words come out of her mouth.

'It's all about having good genes, isn't it? I was explaining this to Gearoid on the phone this morning. I do think, don't you' – she looks around the room at all of us with a bright smile – 'that we should dissuade him from taking on that McGuinness boy. I mean, apparently the parents were drug addicts, so that's the stock the boy has come from. I haven't put my foot down yet, but someone is going to have to say something...'

Aoife and Leonard murmur in low voices about nurture being as important as nature.

'No, no, no.' Nora brushes such nonsense aside. 'All the children you two teach come from decent people, proper homes. They wouldn't be there otherwise.'

I cringe, and Aoife and Leonard shift uncomfortably. They work in very posh private schools teaching the little princes and princesses of the rich. Money is the reason those children are there there, and they know it.

'So I was saying to Gearoid,' Nora continues, 'he should go the surrogacy route like Elton John. He and David Furnish have two lovely boys now, and they're bound to have used Elton's...um, ah...

because they'll want the musical talent, and of course between Gearoid and Enrico, Gearoid would obviously be the best one to…to well, to be the father, because I mean he's so clever and artistic and good-looking, and less of a flibbertigibbet than Enrico. I explained all this to him…'

Kieran is as horrified as I feel, and even Catriona, radiates discomfort. Kieran's father has decided to focus on his bad foot, twitching it back and forth in its slipper.

'I said to him, that's why Oilibhéar turned out so well, you see, because he has my genes…'

'And Dad's genes,' points out Orla, who is fond of her father.

'And wonderful adoptive parents.' Kieran adds much to Nora's displeasure. Instead of being grateful to the people who raised her son, she hated any mention of them.

The one time Kevin stood up to Nora was when he found out he had a biological son she'd never told him about. She had him when she was a teenager, and Kevin went off to college not knowing she was pregnant. Ollie was adopted, and Nora never said a word to anyone all those years. When it came out, she and Kevin had a major problem; he even left her for a while. She was terrified that people would talk about her behind her back, as she would if it was someone else, but it didn't happen. People were kind, and now she takes full credit for Oilibhéar being 'high up in the television'.

'Yes, yes, and your father's genes as well of course. But just think, if Kevin and I had been like that boy's parents, well…' She leaves a short but meaningful silence in which poor Fionn is sentenced to a lifetime of drug addiction. 'So surrogacy is definitely the route to go. Catriona, Seamus is very high up in the hospital – I'm sure he'd be happy to explain about the gene thing to Gearoid. He didn't seem to know what I was going on about when I said about it.' She smiles and nods at her favourite daughter. She's sure Catriona will agree with her.

Catriona mutters something and seems not to know where to look. Then I remember – Nora's completely forgotten that Seamus has an adopted sister. It's not something that gets mentioned much when she comes up in conversation. She's five years older than

Seamus, who was a late miracle baby, and she's a consultant gynaecologist working in Liverpool.

After an awkward silence, Kieran makes a massive effort to rescue the situation. 'Well, Mam, if Gearoid and Enrico do apply to be foster parents, which isn't by any means certain, I think we have to agree not to go interfering. What they do is their business, and I'm sure we'll be informed of their decision in due course. But until then I suggest we all stay out of it.' He runs his hand through his hair as he speaks, the lines of exhaustion – put there by always having to deal with his mother's nonsense – showing on his face.

Aoife and Catriona nod very slightly, and Orla says, 'I agree with that,' which pleases me. Orla is nice but kind of surface, you know? Like she'd never tell you anything real. Her house is always immaculate, the kids are perfect, her husband is wonderful – you know the type. But nice for all of that and would always help you out if she could. I'm glad she's on Gearoid's side – and Fionn's side – in this.

Nora tuts and goes into reasonable mode. 'Of course I'm not going to stay out of it. As a mother it's my job to give my children advice, and of course I'd rather have a grandchild who is biologically related to me. It's so much nicer, and, you know, you get to pick the mother. Like I saw a programme about a gay couple in America using a surrogate from Poland, and how they should do that instead of going to China so the child would blend in better.'

I'm cringing. 'Blend in better' means being white of course.

'And those Polish women are so beautiful. You can meet the mother and find out all about her, what she's like and does she have a degree, so you don't get a child who's going to grow up stupid or ugly…or even fat. If the mother is fat, the daughter will be too.' Her eyes flicker towards me as she says this, and she puts her fingers to her mouth and does her tinkly laugh, like that last awful word slipped out entirely by accident.

Oh. My. God.

I am speechless. My face is burning.

So I didn't imagine it. She really did hesitate about giving Ellie a second portion of the apple cinnamon cake – Kieran noticed it too; I saw his face – because she thinks Ellie has inherited my 'fat genes'.

Orla, Aoife and Catriona shoot each other startled glances and then at Kieran, who has also been shocked into silence.

If this was just the usual dig at me, I would let it pass. But this is too much, her fat-shaming Ellie.

'Nora,' I say, and my voice is shaking. 'Please don't use that word.'

'What word, Mags?' she inquires in pretend amazement.

'The word "fat". It's hurtful and unhelpful.'

'I speak as I find, Mags, you know that about me.' She decrees this as if it is a great virtue, sadly lacking in those around her.

My throat tightens. 'Well, please don't use words around our daughter that could hurt her.'

She titters again. 'Don't be silly, Mags! I wasn't talking about Ellie at all.' I notice she doesn't mention the whippet-thin Kate.

'You were, Nora. I saw that thing with the dessert, acting like Ellie shouldn't really have any more when it was no problem for Kate or Evie or Tom.'

She sees she can't gaslight me so goes for the direct attack. She really doesn't like me, and the feeling is entirely mutual. She's still cranky over her buying dresses for Kate and Ellie last year for Gearoid's wedding that made them look like a pair of Laura Ashley sofas. I returned the dresses, and she's had a face on her since.

'Well, so what if I do think you're storing up trouble for Ellie, the way you let her eat?' she says with a saccharin smile. 'Someone has to show concern, and I'm her grandmother, so I have the right to an opinion on my own grandchild. No wonder you had to return those dresses. Kate's fit perfectly well, she said so, but obviously Ellie's was too small. And I'm not saying she's fa…overweight, if you must. She isn't, not yet, but she sat here today adding butter to her potatoes and not touching her meat. It's all about good parenting. When I was a girl, you wouldn't get your dessert unless you ate everything on your plate.'

'Ellie is a vegetarian,' I say in a hoarse voice, my hands clenched by my sides. My lungs are beginning to hurt with the effort of breathing.

I can't see how Kieran looks. All I can see is Nora, like my vision has narrowed to a tunnel. It's just her and me and this awfulness. I want to point out that when she was a girl, her parents disowned her and put her in a Magdalene Laundry to have her baby – so much for their good parenting. But I won't say it; it would be too cruel.

'You have to use portion control, Mags, unless you want her to turn out like you. And I'll be honest with you. I think it's you, Mags, who doesn't like hearing the fat word said to you, nothing to do with Ellie at all.'

Oh God, this is such a stab to my heart. I can't speak, my throat hurts, my lungs are tightening, I need my inhaler. I start rummaging around in my junk-filled bag, and then it's in my hand because Kieran has noticed and helped find it for me. 'Thank you,' I wheeze, but he is gone. He is on his feet, white-faced, pointing his finger at his mother.

'Listen to me now.' His tone is cold and furious. 'I'm sick to death of the way you speak to Mags. She does nothing but good –'

'It's fine, Kieran, leave it,' I gasp, after using the Ventolin. He's about to blow a gasket, I can tell, and that won't end well. The last big bust-up took months to fix. I'm always trying to smooth things over between him and his mother, however badly Nora treats me, and God knows the fallout from this one will be catastrophic.

'No, Mags, I won't leave it. Enough is enough. You've always worked to keep the peace between me and her, but it's not fair on you and I won't have it any more. Mam, listen to me. My wife is a beautiful woman and a wonderful mother. She does so much good in our family, in our community. She helped you when you were in trouble. And you keep going on with this crap about how I could have done better, but you are so wrong. There is nobody better than Mags. She's always trying to make people's lives easier, including yours. She was nothing but kind to you when you needed her help, and yet every time she comes into this house, she has to face dog's abuse.'

He's on a roll now. His three sisters just watch and listen, while the men keep their heads down. Everyone is shaken and amazed. Kieran gets angry so very rarely, it's quite a sight to see, and it feels nice to have him defend me.

'If it's not insults about her job, it's her friends. If it's not her friends, it's her mother, who, by the way, is a saint and the best mother-in-law a man could want. You criticise her clothes, her body, her hair, how she raises the girls, the food she feeds them, what she lets them wear. It's never-ending with you, the constant carping and whinging and snobbishness about my family, and I'm sick to death of it.' There's no stopping him now.

'Ah now, Kieran, your mother just…' His dad, the henpecked shadow of a man, interjects, then gets painfully to his feet.

'Just wants to have a go at Mags again, like she always does. I'm proud of my sisters, and I'm delighted they all have fellas who appreciate them, but I can tell you now, nobody, not one person in this town or this country or this whole bloody planet, has a wife as wonderful as mine. So Mam, if you ever, and I mean ever again for the rest of your natural life, say one word against her, I swear to God it will be the last conversation you and I will ever have. Am I clear?'

'Kieran, I have never…' Nora's hand is to her chest as if he is giving her a heart attack by speaking like this. 'How could you…' It ends in a theatrical dry sob.

'Don't bother with the waterworks, Mam, they don't work on me. You're trying to manipulate me like you've always done, and I'm not falling for it. Going on all the time about Róisín Duggan, how I'd have been better off sticking with her, and look how she turned out, a drunk with a criminal conviction. Only that Mags intervened she could have been facing a custodial sentence for assaulting my wife and my daughter and driving her car so plastered, it's a pure solid miracle she didn't kill anyone. And you still think she's a better person than Mags. For God's sake, open your eyes, woman, and stop being so pathetic.'

'Kevin, I'm afraid of him, make him leave…' Nora tries to throw herself into her husband's arms, but he doesn't embrace her, and her three daughters and two sons-in-law just sit there like they're watching a play, not coming to her rescue at all. Nobody soothes her or encourages these histrionics.

I also get to my feet. I hate this but it is also necessary. 'Nora, stop this now,' I say. 'You're not afraid of Kieran, because he's not given you cause to be. He had something he needed to say to you, and he's said it. Now, if you'll only listen…'

'Don't you dare talk down to me, Mags Kelleher.' Her eyes glitter. 'Thinking you're so high and mighty, but all you're doing is going around the town checking for bald tyres and expecting my poor Kieran to pay for everything nice you have. Thinking you can come up here to this house and speak to me like this…'

'That's it. Come on, Mags, we're leaving.' Kieran hands me my bag, then crosses two paces to where his mother is pretending to cower behind his father. 'I warned you, but you wouldn't listen, so from now on, you're dead to me. As far as I'm concerned, I don't have a mother. You won't be seeing me or my family again.'

'Ah now, Kieran…' Kevin begins.

'And you'd want to toughen up, Dad. She has a fool made of you. You know she's a horrible person, but you put up with it. The best thing you ever did was leave her that time, and the most foolish thing was to come back. Aoife, Orla, Catriona, I'm sorry but she's all yours now, and all I ask is that you stop her from interfering in Gearoid and Enrico's plans and saying awful things about Fionn to them. It is very, very important she stay out of it entirely, because if she doesn't, I'm pretty certain she won't lose just one son, but two.'

Then, without saying any more, he half pulls me out of the house. I take the car keys from his trembling hands – he's in no fit state to drive – and he takes the passenger seat.

We pick the girls up from the park and send Evie and Tom back to the house, then I drive the girls to my mother and Joe's new house that they bought last year. Mam wants us all to come in, but I explain Kieran and I need a couple of hours of space to process a terrible row he just had with his mother, and she instantly sweeps the girls inside, saying Joe will drop them back later.

They'll be fine, watching TV with my mam. They get involved in all sorts of mad projects with her. Usually from Pinterest, or a programme on the telly. Last year it was making fashion from rubbish, and over Christmas they had great craic making QR codes, but there's been pottery, finding fossils – you'd never know what their latest fad was.

They love *Strictly Come Dancing*, so they watch that religiously every year, experts in paso dobles and charlestons. Now they're stuck in some desperate drivel altogether called *Dance Moms*, an American programme about overly ambitious mothers and their dancing kids. My mam really gets into whatever the girls love and is as enthusiastic as they are, analysing and dissecting each episode after it over tea and home-made buns. She's such a wonderful granny; she adores them and delights in every little achievement.

She and Nora are like night and day.

At home my husband reassures me over and over again – with loving hugs to prove it – how beautiful he thinks I am, and in return I promise him he hasn't inherited any of his mother's personality despite having half her exemplary genes. But we're still so shaken, it's hard to feel good in ourselves. I keep having to use my inhaler.

Kieran repeats what he said to Nora, about her never seeing him or his family again. He says he's let so much go with his mother over the years, but her saying such mean things about me today, he can't get past that.

'Well, however it works out, we'll get a break of a few weeks anyway,' I say, because despite everything, I'm assuming this rift will resolve with time; it's always done before. And it will sort of have to, for everyone's sake; the girls are very close with their Munroe cousins.

He shakes his head. 'No, this time it really is for good. You'll never have to listen to her rubbish again. I'll explain to the girls. I won't tell them what she said exactly, of course, but I'll just say she was very rude to you and I've had enough, and I'll reassure them it won't impact their relationship with their cousins.'

I don't know if he's right about that – he's too wound up and upset to think straight right now – but it's hard to see how it won't have an impact.

I can't imagine Orla holding any family get-togethers without Nora being present. All Kieran's sisters are under their mother's thumb and so will be forced to take her side, and Gearoid tends to avoid family dramas – it's why he didn't tell his parents he was gay until he was forty.

Even if Gearoid finds out what was said and does get involved to back his brother, that's going to heat up everything even more, battle lines being drawn. I love Kieran for feeling the way he does, but I don't want an endless family feud.

I have two sisters, but Kate and Ellie hardly ever see the cousins from my side. Jenny, who is married and lives in the Middle East, has three boys, but they rarely visit, and Delores, who is now called Lori, lives up a tree in America with some hairy hippie called – most unusually – Norman. She had a guy called Hopi on the go for years, but he got the high road for some reason. Norman – we've only seen a photo – looks like a carbon copy of Hopi. All dreadlocks and hairy eyebrows, and could use a good power-hosing. According to Delores, people come from far and wide to have sessions with him in the tree, something involving smoke and hallucinogenic mushrooms. Don't ask me. So on my side of the family, the girls really just have me and Mam.

We're on our second cup of tea in the kitchen when Kieran's phone rings, and he shows me the screen, making an inquiring face. It's Gearoid.

'Yes, answer it,' I say. 'But maybe don't say anything about Nora and what she said about Fionn, even if he has heard from her about the argument. You never know – the girls might have said enough to make her back off.'

'God, I hope so.' He slides his thumb across the screen to answer. 'Gearoid, hi. All OK?'

He waits. Whatever Gearoid says makes him smile. He winks at me and gives me a thumbs-up, so at least it's not about Nora. Gearoid has obviously let his mother's 'advice' about genes run off him like water off a duck; he's so great at ignoring her. And it looks like she hasn't called him since we left.

'Right, I'm glad it went well, and I'll get Mags to call you tomorrow. I'm sure she won't mind doing that for you. Yes, bye, bye, bye.'

Kieran ends the call, beaming. 'He sends his love. They're rushing to get to the theatre – they're going to see *The Crucible*. Anyway, it seems the decision has been made, all three of them are happy, and Gearoid wants to know if you'd mind being interviewed by a social worker. I said you'd call him about it tomorrow.'

'Why me?' I'm confused.

'When you apply to be foster parents, you need character references, he says – he's already checked it out. So they're choosing you and the local priest, who they both get on with really well, and some friend of Enrico's who runs the Mayo youth orchestra.'

I'm flattered. I would have thought they'd go for the 'high ups' like Seamus or Fergus or Leonard, or even Oilibhéar MacElroy, though maybe it is more sensible to ask a guard.

'Of course I will, and they will be fabulous foster parents,' I say, and mean it. All their nieces and nephews love them, especially Enrico. He's a professional flamenco and ballroom dancer, and he's always making up dances together with all the kids. Which reminds me, Kate and Ellie should ask him to help them with their TikTok.

CHAPTER 5

Duckie's car is in the newly tarmacked car park behind the Garda station. He has a huge Range Rover that he always parks across two lines as if he is the most important person on earth.

My heart sinks at the sight of it. I'm not able for him at the best of times, so I go in the back way, past the new women's toilets. Well, I think of them as new, though they're a few years old now. They were a sort of consolation prize to me for getting shot in the line of duty. Then, after I nearly got burnt to death last year, the car park, which used to be full of potholes, suddenly got resurfaced. I wonder what will have to happen to me before I can persuade the powers that be to give me another member of staff.

I pause in the hall, between my office and the public desk, and peep through the glass panel. My nemesis has his back to me, leaning against the public desk, talking to Nicola and Zoë.

Nicola is standing well back with her arms tightly crossed; she finds him repulsive and lecherous, which is a fair assessment. But Zoë has decided that Detective Inspector Duckie – she doesn't seem to have noticed that it's a rude nickname that nobody else ever calls him to his face – is her personal rescue project, which to be fair, is hilarious to listen to.

He's banging on about a golf holiday to Portugal he took last month with the 'top brass' and how they were sunning themselves all day, eating plates of salami and smoked ham, out drinking every night and chatting up women, some stupid story about a Cuban cigar, the implication being – and he's as subtle as a bag of hammers in this regard – that he bedded all these women and did something possibly illegal with the cigar. In his dreams, of course, but we all have to listen to the *nudge, nudge, wink, wink* chat. It would drive you to drink yourself.

'Alcohol, cigarettes, sun radiation and processed meats are the top four carcinogens, Inspector Duckie,' Zoë explains, as if he's a slow four-year-old. 'And it sounds like you had an excess of all four on your trip. You should think about a detox.'

He looks at her like he always does, like she is a delicious morsel but totally confusing. I think he'd love her to never speak, but he does stare at her as if he wants to gobble her up. She's like an advertisement for healthy living.

'Maybe a vampire facial would be good too?'

'A what?' He seems almost frightened, and Nicola finds the contents of the bottom drawer of the filing cabinet fascinating as she stifles a giggle. We all manufacture reasons to be in the office when Zoë and Duckie meet. It's comedy gold, though neither of them is aware of it.

'Vampire facial. It's a microneedling treatment where they inject plasma into your skin. The tiny pricks' – I think Nicola is going to choke at this point – 'created by the needle stimulate collagen production, and the plasma they inject is rich in platelets, so it can have impressive results. It would help with all the thread veins, eye bags, dark circles, rosacea, the dry skin patches and the signs of premature aging you have.' She delivers this devastating diagnosis with huge concern.

'But you probably need a full-body detox too, after that abuse, at your age especially. Geriatric self-care is big now. I read about the devastating impact on old people of not being touched, and it really hurts mental and physical health. Do you find that?' she asks, eyes wide and innocent, and I can't tell if she's aware and taking the mick out of him or is genuine. I suspect the latter. 'I saw one advertised in the Himalayas. You go for a week, and using Ayurvedic cleansing methods, they flush the toxins out of your system. There are things you drink, medicinal mushrooms, yogic cleansing, yoga asanas and most importantly, breathwork. It's great to release physical as well as psychic blockages. You really should consider it, y'know, before…'

'Before what?' Duckie is aghast.

'Well, before you can't travel any more, or before you die.'

'Are you taking drugs?' he asks her, deciding to fight fire with fire, and she turns to him, eyes wide.

'Never. Though I do think there will be a place for microdosing and careful use of psychedelics…'

I decide this has gone far enough.

'But since all of that is illegal and unlegislated at the moment, we wouldn't have any dealings with it on a personal level,' I say, breezing in. 'Hello, Detective Inspector Cassidy, what can I do for you today?'

Duckie stares at me as if I am a plate of cold boiled cabbage, but he follows me into my office, slamming the door behind him.

While he collects himself and recovers his ruffled dignity, I sit at my desk and open up my screen, checking for any messages that came in while I was out or any important updates on the PULSE, the internal Garda network. After a while I hear a self-satisfied grunt and turn to find Duckie has recovered his ego; he's lolling in the chair opposite my desk with his legs spread apart – a revolting habit, particularly from a man in too-tight trousers – showing a length of hairy white leg above his black socks.

He has recently shaved his head after years of dyeing his combover weird plum colours, but the thing that makes me wince to look at him, and nearly shield my eyes as if against bright sunlight, is that he's obviously been to Turkey to get new teeth. His were awful admittedly, but he's after getting a big set of dazzling teeth that are far too white for a man his age and are also too big for his mouth – maybe that's what put Zoë in mind of the 'vampire' facial.

'So how are things in Ballygobackwards, Mags?' he sneers. Ballygobackwards is what he calls Ballycarrick, now that he's been elevated out of neighbouring Dromahane to the teeming metropolis of Galway, population eighty thousand. 'Caught any dogs peeing without a licence recently? Issued any good parking tickets?'

He's always pretending I never do anything important. He can't stand the fact that I got the credit for catching the Russian spies last year. Duckie mocked me for suspecting Neil Jacobson and Minnie Melodie, a very eccentric couple who turned up in Ballycarrick pretending to be a warlock and a white witch, of being the spies we were looking for. In truth, nobody believed me, not even Ronan Brady, but Duckie was downright insulting, in front of other people too.

'Good, Donal. How are things in Galway?' I answer, not playing his game.

'Well, as I expect you know, very, very busy. The Chance Your Arm case is really high profile, top priority, you know yourself. Hush, hush, need-to-know basis...'

Like he can ever keep his mouth shut about anything, and he's clearly here to tell me all about it now. He's so smug. He loves having one up on me. It drives him mental that Ronan Brady, who is the Assistant Garda Commissioner now, is a friend of mine, so he's only dying to lord it over me with his missing horse case.

I'm no lover of animals – I would never harm one or anything like that, but between Rollo, Princess, Meatloaf and Knickers, I have more than enough livestock in my life – so Duckie's welcome to Chance Your Arm, but he thinks I'm mad jealous, the poor deluded fool.

'So you've made good progress?' I ask as I reply to an email from Derry McLoughlin, chairman of the town council, on the subject of illegal dumping of rubbish which is happening all over the town on the country roads where nobody can be seen. It's very frustrating.

'Oh yes, the case is clipping along nicely. In fact I've had a big breakthrough. I'm pretty sure I'll have it wrapped up by the end of the day – keep an eye on the evening news.' He sits there waiting for me to be impressed and beg him for details, so he can make a big song and dance about not wanting to risk the news leaking out, like it's me who can't keep my mouth shut.

I carry on answering emails. The Tidy Towns war between Ballycarrick and Dromahane has escalated, and Lavinia Moran is asking about getting a court order to make Phillip O'Flaherty paint his garage. She says now that he has an apprentice paid for by the government – this is only partly true; small businesses do qualify for a grant, but not nearly enough to cover a wage – why can't he ask Caelan Cronin to do it as a way of giving something back to the taxpayer? Honestly, that woman needs a job. Maybe she should apply for an apprenticeship herself. She could be a painter and decorator – that would kill two birds with one stone.

Duckie has given up waiting for me to show any interest, so he sighs and says like I've been begging him, 'OK, OK, but don't tell a soul please, Mags. Don't be gossiping. I know what you ladies are like. A call came through to me personally, followed by a very clear picture on WhatsApp, so I'm on my way to follow it up. It's not the best news. The horse has turned up dead in an old shed on the outskirts of Dromahane –'

'Dead?' He has my startled attention now, mainly because of the effect I know this is going to have on tenderhearted Kate. 'Are you sure?'

'Oh, don't look so worried.' He grins. 'I know you females get sentimental about animals, but the sheikh's a big boy, he won't mind. It's just money to him, and he will be able to claim on his insurance now and buy another one.'

I doubt that very much. I strongly suspect the insurance money won't come anywhere near pacifying the sheikh. And I'm puzzled as well. It would be crazy to kill an animal like that; it makes no sense. And it does seem strange it's turned up on Duckie's own doorstep, because though he works in Galway now, he still lives in Dromahane.

I decide to just let him get on with it, though. 'Right, well, best of luck with it, Donal. I hope it works out for you. Now I've to get on. I'm meeting the committee who're arranging the Ballycarrick festival. So you get to swank around with the rich and glamorous of the bloodstock industry and I get to discuss parking and public safety around the greasy pole event. Some people get all the luck.' I smile as if I'd much rather be him, which on every level imaginable, I would not, and stand up from my desk.

'Ah, Mags, I'm sure your day will come...' He lays his hand on my sleeve as I usher him out the door. I glance down and he removes it. He thinks he can patronise me because I'm a lowly sergeant, and a woman to boot, but he is kind of nervous of me too, which is great.

* * *

NICOLA AND ZOË are still on the desk and fall quiet until Duckie is out the door, then go back to what they were talking about, which is Lavinia's visit to the station to make sure we got her email about Phillip O'Flaherty's garage. I missed her while I was incarcerated with Duckie, so thank heaven for small mercies.

'Well, I wouldn't mind watching Matteus, his junior mechanic, up a ladder painting away with his shirt off on a hot day.' Nicola sighs.

'Here we go again, objectifying bodies. Honestly, did I teach you nothing?' Zoë complains, half in jest. She knows her political correctness is a source of fun for us in the station. Our Zoë is very Gen Z.

'Ah, shut up, Zoë. He's the dead spit of Johnny Depp, you know he is.' Nicola is having none of it.

'I just think if women want to stop men judging us only on our looks, we should afford them the same courtesy.'

'I'm not objectifying him. It's not like I'd be whistling at him and making rude gestures. If I walked out of somewhere and the men said I was a snack, then I'd be chuffed, not offended. He's a snack, that's all.'

'He's going out with the woman who owns the nail bar in Shannon,' I say, and they both turn, realising I'm there.

Nicola, who is only twenty-five and currently single, is depressed. Her last fella turned out to be a gambling addict. 'I'm doomed. All the good ones are taken, and all that's left is not worth getting out of bed for. I went on a date last weekend with a fella I swiped right on, and you should have seen the state of him. Nothing like his photo, bald, pot-bellied, with breath that smelled of tuna. Maybe I should just get a cat now and be done with it.'

'Oscar can probably get you started,' I joke.

'Maybe you should do some transcendental meditation. It teaches us that consciousness is all there is, that once we transcend and let go, the source of all happiness and peace is there in our inner consciousness,' Zoë suggests. 'But we live our lives on the surface and never explore our own psychological depths.'

'I'd settle for a date with a good-looking lad who isn't a narcissistic, alcoholic, gambling mammy's boy.' Nicola has terrible taste in men by her own admission and has had her heart broken more than once. 'But yeah, failing that I'll explore my own psychological depths and resort to cats.'

Zoë's brow furrows but then her face lights up. 'My cousin Tadhg is coming back from Australia next month. He's been out there for years, but he's missing home and his friend set up a construction firm, so he's coming back to work for him. He's single?'

'Picture,' Nicola demands, holding her hand out for Zoë's phone.

Instead of criticising Nicola for being obsessed with people's looks, Zoë obligingly scrolls, finds a picture and hands the phone to her.

Nicola's eyebrows go up. 'Hmm...potential. Is he drinky?'

Zoë ponders. 'No, I don't think so.'

'A mammy's boy?'

'Well, he's lived away from home for twelve years.'

'Into gambling?'

'I never heard him say anything about it...'

'Crude, rude or mental?'

Zoë considers the questions, then shakes her head. 'No, no and no.'

'Solvent?'

I'm fascinated. This is a very thorough cross-examination.

'Yeah, he owns a few apartments in Dublin. He made loads of money on the oil rigs out there so invested in property here while he was away. He has them rented out.'

'Issues?' Nicola leaves no stone unturned.

Zoë wrinkles her brow again. 'Well, he's not that receptive to personal development. Like, I suggested he go to a wind workshop on the cliffs last time he was home. It's a thing where you stand on the clifftop – you can be naked if you want to, but you don't have to – and howl into the wind all your stresses and traumas. For an extra fee, you can be cuddled by a shaman. He would be naked obviously. But Tadgh said that sounded bonkers and he wouldn't dream of it.'

'Give him my number,' Nicola says decisively. 'He's perfect on paper, so we shall see.'

I leave them to it and return to my office to fetch my notebook. Before heading off to the community centre where the festival meeting is being held, I check myself in the mirror in the women's toilets. There's no getting away from it; the person who stares back at me is a round-faced woman in her fifties.

Unlike the jacket I wore to Sunday lunch, my Garda jacket genuinely is bulky. The Garda uniform…well, to say it wasn't designed with sex appeal in mind is to understate the case, so that doesn't help.

I'm not ugly, but I don't wear make-up at work, or at all really, and I usually keep my long dyed-brown hair in a ponytail. It is badly in need of Gerry the hairdresser's magic touch, but I haven't the time, and it's easier to get an audience with the pope than get an appointment with Gerry these days, so I've grey roots showing, which is aging.

I'm not normally this down on myself, but the horrible phrase 'fat and old' pops into my mind and won't go away. I know I should shake off Nora's remarks about my weight, but they keep echoing round and round in my head. And the conversation between Nicola and Zoë earlier has depressed me, even though it made me laugh at the time.

They're both so beautiful, so to hear Nicola complaining she's too old to get a decent man at twenty-five and might as well resign herself to being a cat lady, it's heartbreaking. And here I am, more than twice her age. Kieran is lovely about saying how attractive he finds me, but is he just being kind?

CHAPTER 6

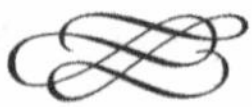

I scan the small gathering in the upstairs room of the community centre, and it lifts my heart. The Ballycarrick Community Association is really a wonderful asset to the town. Small-town policing really can sound like it's all about checking dog licences and bald tyres, but I love helping out these community-minded people, many of whom I've known all my life.

Derry McLoughlin, who taught me in national school, is the chair. He's so willing, and everyone respects him. Annette Deasy, Finbarr Turner's stepmother, is secretary. She's only been here a few years, but she's sensible and a great woman altogether to organise anything. Tatiana is the treasurer; she's meticulous. Julie Dullea, the local pharmacist – she was in my class at school – is in charge of first aid, and Luigi is organising the food side together with Bertie the butcher, another long-standing resident of Ballycarrick. Poor Bertie avoids my gaze as usual. I had the unfortunate job of cautioning him for arranging a dogging event in the local woods a few years ago, and he can't look me in the eye since, but he still turns out for things like this, so fair play to him. In a small town, it takes all sorts, and you have to be able to live things down. Like Dr Harrison's receptionist, Joanna Burke, is the publicity officer for the festival; she is a notorious gossip, has been since primary school, but on the upside, she is also a fabulous networker.

Klara Shevchenko, who runs a cleaning business, isn't able to make today's meeting, but she's dropped in a Spartak cake, and it's sitting there in the middle of the table, calling to me...

Thankfully I don't have to stay to the end of the meeting, when the committee members will all tuck in. I just need to agree to a road closure and barriers for the festival and offer a couple of guards to back up their own stewards.

This summer they are planning a Mardi Gras themed party, with floats from the local businesses and tractors decorated with streamers. The schoolkids are going to dress up as characters from *The Wizard of Oz*, and there will be a small brass band organised by Marcel, who also plays the trumpet – who knew? Klara has promised that all the Ukrainian women will turn out in their national dress.

'So if that's all you need me for, I'll head off,' I say, dragging my eyes away from the cake while getting to my feet and pulling on my frumpy jacket.

'Wait, wait, Mags, you can't go before you have some of this,' insists Julie, and she whips out some paper napkins and insists on serving everyone a piece. I know I shouldn't, but I can't resist, and it is out of this world, chocolate with sour cream layers.

'Melt in the mouth.' Derry sighs as he wets his finger to pick up the final crumbs. 'Don't tell Lillian, Mags. I'm supposed to be off all sweet things. I'm two stone overweight according to Skinny Elaine – Lillian insisted on dragging me along there with her last week – and now my wife is convinced I'm going to die of a heart attack and consign her to a lonely old age.'

Derry saying he's overweight is as depressing to me as Nicola claiming to be old. He's in his late sixties, seventy maybe, and to my eyes, he is a lean, fit man.

If Derry is overweight, what does that make me?

* * *

I WALK BACK down the lane to the station to fetch my car; I didn't drive to the community centre because the doctors say walking is good for my lungs. And in my overly self-critical mood, I decide I should at least try to do something about my hair.

I pop into the station to check everything is OK before going home, and Zoë is on the phone, patiently explaining to somebody that a missing cat is not really the remit of the gardaí but that she'll ask her fellow officers to keep an eye out for Fred as they go about their business.

She really is becoming a wonderful community officer. She has some wacky ideas – she's a bit into healing and energies and has put crystals all over the station – but I'm more and more impressed with her all the time.

'Well, I know that must seem a bit unfair, Mrs Flood... Yes, of course, I understand Fred is every bit as important to you as Chance Your Arm is to his owner, and I know it seems wrong that a domestic cat isn't allocated the same amount of Garda time as an expensive showjumper, but it's a matter of resources...'

She pauses. On the other end of the phone, clearly Mrs Flood is on a roll.

'Do you know, I've just had an idea? Why don't you ring Oscar O'Leary? He's got great devotion to St Gertrude, and she's the patron saint of cats... I think it doesn't matter if the cat was blessed individually by Father Doyle or not, Mrs Flood. I'm sure St Gertrude wouldn't mind...'

I catch her eye, and she gives me a thumbs-up, holding the receiver between her head and shoulder. She scribbles something on a notepad and hands it to me.

Ring Ellie – she couldn't get you on your mobile.

I turned my non-work phone off in the meeting and haven't turned it on again, so I hope it's not an emergency and that's why she's ringing the station. After I've fired it up and entered my passcode, a text pops in from an hour earlier.

Mam can you bring lemongrass and star anise please - making mocktails.

And Kate wants a bottle of kombucha raspberry not ginger and lemon tanx x.

I laugh. It's far from lemongrass and kombucha I was reared. Sometimes I wonder if my kids were transported back even a hundred years, would anyone have the faintest idea what they were on about?

Will do, your highness, I reply.

You are the GOAT – slay queen! is the reply. See? A totally different language.

Bertie the butcher has a whole section of exotic spices now, so I get some star anise and lemongrass there, but I have to stop at the chemist to get the kombucha. Julie Dullea sells all sorts of healthy drinks that are probably as full of sugar as Coca-Cola, but never mind.

While I'm there Julie tells me she needs her security system certified and her safe for management of controlled substances checked, so I say I might as well do it while I'm there. The girls won't die if they don't get their exotic requests for another half hour.

There has not been a robbery yet, but Julie's getting nervous, and I don't blame her. Chemists around the country are being targeted by crime gangs for prescription drugs to sell on the streets. Amphetamines, opioids, barbiturates, benzodiazepines, sleeping tablets, the list goes on. In Dublin last month, a gang robbed a pharmacy with an industrial digger and dug out the safe that was concreted into the wall. The lengths they'll go to nowadays are terrifying.

I inspect the safe and sign and stamp the forms she needs for the Irish pharmaceutical board and her insurance company, and in return she shows me her sparkly new engagement ring. She lost her first fiancé in a motorbike accident over twenty years ago and was sad for so long, but she started dating again last year and met a lovely fella by all accounts. I'm delighted for her finding a new love at her age. Which is also my age, though she looks about five years younger than me. I put it down to having access to all those fancy face creams and no kids.

After I come out, I pop into Gerry's to see what date in the far distant future he can squeeze me in, hopefully this side of Christmas, which is only nine months away.

Ginny, daughter of Teresa who runs the bakery, is on the desk. She's alarmingly big haired, curly with a weird blunt fringe. As I knew she would, she shakes her head as she runs her long black nail over the appointment book, half talking to me and half talking to herself. 'Nothing this week or next week, nothing the following week, nothing, nothing, nothing... Oh!' Her eyes light up. 'I could fit you in on Wednesday the twenty-fourth of July, at four thirty, I have a cancellation. I should really go to the waiting list, but as it's you...?'

She beams at me like an appointment in nearly four months' time is just wonderful and I should be on my knees in gratitude for the opportunity.

I do want to take it, but I shake my head. It sounds trivial, but jumping the queue at Gerry's could destroy my reputation for fair dealing. 'That's really kind of you, but we guards have to be like Caesar's wife, above suspicion.'

Ginny peals with laughter. 'Oh, don't worry, I'm not letting you jump the queue because of you being the sergeant. It's 'cos Mam loves you – she says you're her best customer!'

'Oh well, go on then.' I sigh. Might as well get something out of my relationship with Teresa's cream cakes.

Hearing Ginny laughing, Gerry looks over, sees me and waves.

'Sergeant, in the name of God come into me, the state of your roots.' Gerry doesn't put a tooth in it; he says what he thinks and people love him. He's theatrical but not camp, and getting a hairdo from Gerry is an experience.

'That's what I'm trying to do, Gerry, but you've no appointments for four months almost.'

He says something to a woman whose head is covered in tinfoil and comes over to the reception area, picks up a strand of my dyed-brown ponytail and winces.

'Go to the emergency list, Ginny,' he says, and Ginny gives a professional nod, produces another appointment book and opens it to a page; he leans over and prods an empty square.

'Tomorrow, six thirty,' he says triumphantly.

'After work?' I'm amazed how easy this is.

'No, morning, Mags, in the morning…'

'Since when are you up doing hair at the crack of dawn?' I ask, astonished.

'Since the whole world wants perms,' he says with a chuckle. 'I got two stylists I used to work with back in the eighties out of retirement, because nobody can perm hair like an eighties girl.'

'You're doing perms?' I wonder if he's losing the plot. Perms, the awful frizz we inflicted on our hair in the eighties? I went one further and added a mullet haircut to mine, so shaved sides and a wild mop of curls on top; when the girls see the pictures, they can hardly breathe with laughing. Myself and Sharon thought we were the bee's knees and the sparrow's ankles with our huge hair, and wearing the old suit jackets of our fathers, Doc Martens boots and blue eyeshadow. There's one photo of me with my perm growing out, so I have five inches of straight-as-an-arrow hair from root to ears, which descends into frizz from ears to shoulders. Even Kieran, who hasn't a clue about fashion or hair, finds that one side-splitting. Are women seriously doing that to themselves again, knowing what we know?

'Have you been under a stone, Mags? Sienna Black has the whole world gone curly mad, and if God didn't provide the curls, then Gerry can.' He winks.

I scan the room and sure enough, the junior stylists all seem to be sporting the same huge oddly curly hair as Ginny, with the same blunt fringe.

'I can't tempt you?' He laughs. A touch manically, it must be said.

'No. Definitely not. Mam says when it comes to fashion, if you remember it the first time, best avoid it the second time round, and I think the same might be true of hair.'

'Wise woman, your mother, but we need to make hay while the sun shines, Mags. See you in the morning.'

He's gone back to tinfoil lady and I'm left bemused.

Gerry is a nice man and excellent at hair, but he also is mad for money, everyone knows that. He's married to Louise, who as far as anyone can tell plays golf all day, every day. And when she's not doing that, she's sunning herself in their place in Antibes. Their kids are the same age as ours but go to boarding school in Dublin, which is unheard of for Ballycarrick. I'd say being a mother was far too hard for Louise to squeeze into her busy lifestyle, so she sent them packing, and it must cost a fortune.

On top of that, Gerry loves cars and has a selection of vintage luxury vehicles, Jaguars, Mercs, that sort of thing. He never drives them but has built a glass showroom onto their already gigantic house to show them off.

No wonder he has to do hair at six thirty in the morning.

* * *

KIERAN'S VAN is outside when I get home. I let myself in and dump my jacket on the banister. The living room door is ajar, and Kieran's sitting on the sofa watching the news. Seeing what's just come up, I pause in the doorway of the sitting room without announcing myself.

Duckie's big thick head is on the screen, and his name is scrolling along the chyron as he stands at some kind of podium. It looks like the Garda press room in Galway.

'...was made this morning after a painstaking investigation,' he's saying importantly. This is his big moment. 'The body of Chance Your Arm was found in a shed outside Dromahane, with his carotid artery slashed.'

The reporters are out of shot, but bulbs flash and several microphones are to be seen.

A voice calls out, 'Dermot Quilligan UTV. Are you certain the horse is Chance Your Arm?'

Duckie puffs himself up with a slight frown. 'It's Chance Your Arm undoubtedly. I was informed of his location by a reliable source, and this was followed up with a visual inspection by myself. I'm a senior police officer with excellent knowledge of the equine world. Next question.'

Another voice calls out, 'Alvin Perry, RTÉ. Can you tell us the name of your source?'

'No. This is an ongoing investigation, and therefore we have to be circumspect on the details, but please rest assured that we are leaving no stone unturned and the perpetrators of this heinous crime will be brought before the courts.'

'Paul O'Dowd, BBC. Now that Chance Your Arm has been found, does this mean you're taking all extra security off the air and seaports?'

Duckie looks smug as he answers that one. 'Correct. Finding the horse so early in the investigation has saved the taxpayers a great deal of public money. Now, how about you?' He points at another invisible reporter, favouring this one with his new Turkish smile, the TV lights striking off enormous dazzling white teeth.

'Valerie Dangan, *Irish Times...*'

Ah, that explains the hideous smile. It's a female voice, and no doubt she's young and pretty.

'I'm keen to know your opinion –'

'Ask away, my dear.' His smile is blinding, in a bad way. Like stab-in-the-eye blinding.

'I'm wondering why you think the horse was killed when it would be so much more valuable alive?'

'Well, maybe the thieves realised that no one can jump a horse that's so well known,' Duckie explains in a patronising tone, giving away his complete lack of knowledge of the equine world. 'So they decided to get rid of him. The poor animal,' he adds quickly, to spare her sentimental female feelings.

'Mm.' She sounds very unconvinced, for obvious reasons. Of course they weren't going to jump him; they were going to use him as a stud. 'Did the Garda veterinary surgeon confirm it was Chance Your Arm?'

Duckie runs a finger along the inside of his collar as his face goes pink, ticked off to have his opinion questioned by a woman. 'He certainly did,' he barks.

'Still, given the unusual circumstances, would it not have been better that a DNA sample was taken to check the horse's identity before you removed security from the ports?'

'Now listen here love…'

I'm starting to enjoy this, because Valerie Dangan is spot on and Duckie is getting very uncomfortable, but at that moment, Kieran notices me and flicks off the television. 'Hello, you! I only just realised you were there. How was work? And how are the lungs?'

So that's what alerted him to my presence; my breathing is still a bit raspy since the fire, though sometimes I don't even notice it myself, I'm so used to it. 'Not too bad, but I can't wait until Delia and Darren are back next Monday. It's impossible to keep the patrols going while manning the station as well.'

'And as soon as those lovebirds are back, Castle Dysert for us lovebirds!'

He's absolutely delighted with his present to me, and so am I. I've been looking forward to it for the past month. And in the last week, he's been hinting he has a wonderful surprise for me. I secretly hope this means he's booked the special Castle Dysert lobster dinner for both of us; it's eye-wateringly expensive but by all accounts, out of this world, caught by local fishermen in the bay below the castle. Probably he hasn't – it really would break the bank at two hundred and fifty euro a pop – but a girl can dream, and anyway, all the food there is sublime.

'God yes, I can't wait.' I come in to sit beside him, and he puts his arm around me and pulls me close. Rollo, who is dozing on the rug with Princess, wakes up with a start and leaps to launch himself on me as well. 'Rollo, for God's sake.' I lean against my husband while trying to fend off the dog. 'So how was your day?'

'Mine, or the dog's?'

'You go first, then I'll ask Rollo.'

'Make sure you do. He hates if I get more attention from you than he does.'

'Yeah, yeah, funny. So go on, how was work?'

'Grand, apart from a depressing detour to the church again. That roof really is a danger, and Father Doyle is ancient and exhausted, and even if he had the energy for the job, there is no money to fix it.' Poor Kieran. The church roof keeps him awake nights.

'It's really good of you to keep helping him for free,' I say, and I'm proud of him. He is not just a good worker and businessman, he loves his community.

'Well, I've patched it up as best I can, but I can't keep doing it forever, especially now that…' He stops himself saying something more.

'Especially now that what?' It's not like Kieran to go quiet on me.

He shrugs. 'Especially as I'm not going to be around forever to keep doing it for free.'

I turn my head, suddenly scared there might be something wrong. 'Is everything OK with you, Kieran?'

He laughs, and it sounds genuine. 'I'm grand out, Mags. I'm just worried about Father Doyle. The church needs a whole new roof, simple as that, but that will cost at least a hundred thousand.'

I wince. There is an existing church fund for the roof, but it's only reached ten thousand in the last ten years. Rightly or wrongly the church isn't the centre of the community the way that it was, so asking the congregation to stump up that amount of cash is always going to be hard work.

'And can't the diocese pay?' I have limited patience with the ostentatious wealth of the Catholic Church. We went to Rome a few years ago, and to see the churches dripping with gold and priceless works of art, while the faithful all over the world live in poverty, is hard to justify. They don't even try to justify it either.

'Whether they can or not I've no idea, but I'm going to get onto them about it myself. Things can't go on like this. They either want a church in Ballycarrick or they don't.'

'Well, good luck with that. So, any other news?'

'Mm. Catriona rang, and Aoife. I'm just waiting on Orla now for the complete set,' he adds wryly.

I sigh. I'm not surprised he left this news until last. 'Both of them wanting you to forgive your mother?'

'Variations on that theme, but yeah. I told them both the same thing. I've had enough, my mind is made up. Oh, and Gearoid rang. He spoke to Mam earlier.'

'And what's his take on it all?' I suppose Nora's told him her side of the story, whatever that is, and he's rung to tell Kieran he supports him, though of course he'll stay out of it; Gearoid hates conflict.

'He hadn't heard about the row. It was him that rang her, just to let her know the fostering is going ahead and that he's asked you to be his character witness. And he was kind of laughing, because Mam got up on her high horse that he'd asked you and not her and said she wanted to be interviewed as well.'

'Oh my God, she's ridiculous. I hope he said no?' It would be a total disaster if she went telling the social workers her theories on genetics. He and Enrico would surely get turned down on that alone.

'He did. He was very firm. He told her they have a very considered plan and they're sticking to it, that they badly want this to happen, so it is very, very important she allow them to do the application their own way.'

I heave a wheezy sigh of relief. Gearoid is his own person, and though his strategy is usually more ignore than challenge, he has never been as much a victim of Nora's manipulation as the girls.

'He said she backed down on the interview thing quite quickly, so maybe she heard what I said about losing not one son but two.'

Rollo is flopped across my knee. Princess lifts her head and glances blearily around to see where he is, spots him and settles down again. Clearly she's no longer in heat, which is good. We'll be able to let her out in the garden again without every mongrel in the village hurling themselves over the fence, and Knickers will be able to emerge from wherever he's hiding today without being propositioned.

'Are you hungry?' asks my husband, stroking my hair, which is still in its ponytail.

'Not really. I just had some amazing cake.'

'Well, you'll have to make a bit of room, I'm afraid. Your mam made a Moroccan vegetable tagine. Apparently she and Joe brought a special oven or something back from their trip there, so she's been dying to try it out, and we're invited for dinner. The girls are there already, went from school.'

'Oh God, that sounds delicious.' I groan in despair.

* * *

WE HAVE a lovely evening at Mam and Joe's, and the tagine is a huge success. Mam has really gotten into ethnic cooking since Joe finally convinced her to travel. Sharon, Trevor and Sean are there too, because Sharon rang earlier to ask Mam for advice about the shop, something to do with when is the best time to hold a sale. I don't know if Sharon needs Mam's advice, but it's kind of her to ask for it. Mam is sort of a surrogate mother to Sharon anyway; her own mam had problems when we were growing up, so she was practically reared in our house.

Sharon's nine-year-old son, Sean, is obsessed with football, so Kieran, Trevor and Kate have a kick around with him in the garden after dinner. I love to see the brighter evenings beginning after the dark winter.

Ellie, me, Sharon and Mam sit in the kitchen having a cup of tea, and Mam produces a home-made apple sponge cake with whipped cream, and though I know I should refuse, I can't resist accepting a tiny, tiny sliver.

'Oh, go on, have a proper slice,' urges Mam.

'I shouldn't, Mam. I'll have to go back to Skinny Elaine's, and she's a tyrant.'

'Will you go away with that, Mags, you're gorgeous. You got far too scrawny after the fire. In fact I'm glad to see you looking more like yourself again.'

Typical Mam. She can never see anything wrong with me.

'I wish Nana Nora was more like you, Granny.' Ellie sighs. 'Dad is so upset about her right now. He says he never wants to see her again.'

In response to Mam's look of surprise, we explain a bit about the latest bust-up, though I only say what Kieran told the girls, that she was being rude to me.

Kate and Ellie weren't that surprised when Kieran told them about it yesterday evening. In fact he was impressed how aware they were of how nasty Nora can be to me. Kids see and hear much more than we think they do. He told me they hugged him and said they understood but that Nana Nora was just a bit mental and that he shouldn't take it to heart.

'Well, you can't say she didn't have it coming,' Sharon says. She was never a fan of Nora. 'I know Kieran's stood up for you before, but she really needs to get it in her head that she can't carry on being rude to you.' Best friends since junior infants, she still has my back. To think she and I fell out last year, when Róisín Duggan tried to drive a wedge between us. Never again.

'She's a troubled soul, that's for sure,' Mam adds, a bit more diplomatically. Over the years Nora has done and said some things in my mother's earshot, but Mam, ever the lady, never reacts. She keeps her own counsel when it comes to things like that. It's one of the main things I love about her. 'But I'm sure she'll apologise eventually.'

'I don't know, Granny. I know they've always gone back to talking before, but I think he really means it this time,' Ellie is worried. 'He said this time something just snapped in him and he's determined to cut her out of his life for good.' Even though Ellie loves and supports her dad, it's clear this business is upsetting her.

Mam leans over and pats Ellie's hand. 'And he probably did mean it and still does, but he'll cool down and realise he only has one mother and life is too short. But your nana will have to behave a bit better if she wants your dad back in her life, so maybe it's for the best for now.'

'Give her a bit of time to think, you mean?' Ellie asks.

'Sort of.' Mam nods and my daughter's face relaxes.

My phone pings. I glance at it and see Orla's name. Perhaps she hopes she'll have more luck asking me to persuade Kieran to forgive their mother than she will if she asks him directly. She's probably right. I kind of hate feuding. Don't get me wrong, avoiding that pothole Nora for the next few weeks will be an absolute joy, but as Mam said to Ellie, Kieran only has one mother.

I read Orla's message and can't believe my eyes.

Hi, Mags. I'm so sorry you and Kieran were so upset by Mum this week. And just to let you know, I don't blame Kieran at all for what he said. She's been saying mean things to you and about you for too long, and I can't believe what she said about Kate and Ellie, and it's high time someone stood up to her. Well done xx Fergus and I were hoping you four would come for a BBQ the Sunday after next. The weather is supposed to be nice, and if you can, we're going to ask Gearoid and Enrico to bring Fionn so he can get to know everyone.

I'm shocked. I was sure Orla would be Team Nora. It's a huge leap for her to break ranks like this and really, I'm touched. I read out the text. Mam is delighted, Sharon says, 'I didn't think she had it in her,' and Ellie is so relieved that she can still see at least two of her cousins, and Fionn as well, she can't stop smiling. She rushes off into the garden to tell Kate.

Smiling myself, I text back. *Hi, Orla, thanks for that. It's been a bit 'totes emosh', as my girls say. I'll talk to K. re Sunday week to see if we are free and let you know, but so far I think we are and we'd all love to come. xx*

That's one for the diary. It will be lovely to meet Fionn as well.

CHAPTER 7

It's three in the afternoon when Kieran and I pull up to Castle Dysert, and a valet appears to park our car. Thank God I made Kieran clean out all the sandwich and ice cream wrappers and water bottles. The boot is full of football boots and coats and the detritus of my children's lives that seems to live in my car, but at least the main body is tidy-ish.

I'm also relieved Gerry did my hair, even if I did have to get up at the crack of dawn for it, and I'm wearing a good pair of jeans from Sharon's, the sort that hoick you up and pull you in at the same time, with a white blouse and my favourite earrings. And Mam did my make-up when I dropped off the girls to her, so I'm feeling a bit more confident about my appearance, especially as Kieran wolf-whistled when he saw me and said I was a snack, which made me laugh and tell him I feel more like a three-course meal. To which he said, 'Yes, a delicious one, like Christmas dinner.'

I've brought the plum jumpsuit for later, the one with the deep V-neck and ruffled sleeves that Sharon insisted on me wearing for Delia and Darren's wedding, and the necessary armour to wear underneath it.

We take a moment to stand and admire the panoramic view of the

Atlantic Ocean before climbing the stone steps, worn down by hundreds of years of feet, to the medieval pointed door with the black cast-iron fixings.

The main reception is as I remember it. Octagonal with large cantilever stairs climbing up inside the walls. Sconces that once held torches now are home to electric lights but tasteful and appropriate. Although the hotel exudes luxury, there is nothing fussy or overdone about it.

The floor of the reception is covered in antique Persian rugs, and tapestries hang from the stone walls, blackened with age in some places. To the right is a corridor, modern, made of glass, that leads to the spa and pool complex, and to the left the library, a gorgeous room of perfectly mismatched sofas and easy chairs, tables and lamps, and the walls lined with books. An enormous fireplace that in winter has whole trees burning in it is now filled with an elaborate flower arrangement.

To the back of reception on the far left are the double doors leading to the ballroom, where Gearoid and Enrico's wedding was held earlier this year. And opposite to the ballroom is the entrance to the bar, a warm cosy space, all nooks and crannies, with all sorts of oddities and knick-knacks in glass cases.

I know from before that the story of the castle, from the time it was built in the 1500s to the present day, is presented all around the walls of the bar, and it makes for fascinating reading. By any standards it is an historic place, and lots of interesting things have happened here, murders and tragedies as well as pageants and romantic intrigue. But in its modern incarnation as a hotel, it's a hive of quiet activity. Staff going about their business, the gardeners working on the perfect grounds, housekeepers climbing up and down stairs, and people milling about in the bar, going in and out of the library and walking to and from the spa.

Ana O'Shea, Conor's wife, comes to greet us as we enter. She's so tiny, with an elfin face, blond hair and green eyes. 'Mags, and Kieran, welcome.' She beams, and it's lovely she remembers us. It makes me feel like we're old friends, though I'm sure she treats everyone this way. 'Come on in. Make sure you get your complimentary champagne in the bar after you've checked in.' Her Ukrainian accent is still there despite her years in Ireland. Conor told us the last time we stayed here that they'd met when she was a waitress in a hotel in County Kerry and Conor drove a tour bus. She is a good few years younger than he is, but they are mad about each other; you can tell when you see them together.

'Ooh, champagne sounds lovely,' I say, and smile at Kieran. He must have told them this visit is my birthday treat.

'It's an excellent vintage, our sommelier tells us. Now I'll leave you with Katherine. You're in excellent hands. She and Conor have worked together for many years.' She gestures towards an austere-looking woman of indeterminate age, who stands stiffly behind the reception desk. Her hair is pulled back in a severe bun, and she is wearing a black suit with a white blouse, buttoned to the neck. No make-up or jewellery, apart from a rather large diamond engagement ring and a wide gold wedding band. 'Katherine, the Munroes have been here a few times before. Kieran's brother had his wedding here last year.'

'I'm aware,' she says, without a hint of a smile. She is most disconcerting.

'Now, I need to find Conor,' says Ana. 'My father has decided today he will paint the summer house – so many wet days made it not possible before. He's there since dawn, is crazy, but he can't be made to stop. Conor has gone to help him, but his mobile phone is broken because our daughter, Lily, was watching this cartoon, *Bluey*, on it and then she drop and get it wet, so to dry it, she put it in the microwave. We are lucky our house does not burn down.' She rolls her eyes with a chuckle and disappears into the back of the hotel.

The severe woman eyeballs us as if she thinks we might pocket the silver. 'Good afternoon, Mr and Mrs Munroe. Welcome back to Castle Dysert.'

'Thank you. We couldn't wait to come back after the wonderful day we had with the wedding,' says Kieran as he signs the form she hands him.

'Everything was so perfect,' I add, trying to raise a smile from this forbidding woman.

She merely arches her eyebrows. 'Naturally. We pride ourselves on perfection. Now André will bring your bags to your room, and if you go into the bar, Francois, our sommelier, will serve you your champagne.'

In the bar Francois comes to meet us and settles us in a comfortable nook before bringing us two flutes of champagne. He explains in heavily accented but perfect English the vintage and what we can expect, how it was the result of a manual harvest, using a specific wine press, and how it fermented the second time in the bottle. A far cry from the €12.99 bottle of Rioja from Aldi I treat us to occasionally.

As Francois retreats, I clink glasses with Kieran. 'Thanks for organising the bubbly, my love. It's a lovely surprise.'

'I'd like to take the credit,' he says, almost apologetically, 'but I know nothing about this.'

'Mags, Kieran, how nice to see you again.'

I look up with a smile at the sound of that deep voice, and sure enough it's Conor O'Shea, the handsome owner of the hotel. At the wedding he was in a suit and tie, but today he's wearing jeans with a splash of pale-blue paint on the knee, brown boots and a collared long-sleeved sweatshirt. He's got a day's worth of stubble on his jaw as well that might be scruffy on another man but not on him. It's hard to put an age on him, maybe late fifties, but if anything, he is improving with age.

My husband is good-looking in that rugged Irish way, but Conor O'Shea is not that. He's like an Irish George Clooney – well, I suppose Clooney is kind of Irish, as his ancestors were from Windgap, County Kilkenny. Anyway, Conor is like that, silver-haired, muscular but not too bulky, piercing blue eyes, a warm smile. He's the kind of man who makes you forget what you were saying. When Sharon saw him at Gearoid's wedding, she nicknamed him Mr O'MyGodYes, but the most charming thing about him is he seems to have no vanity. God knows there are plenty of fellas with much less to show and who are full of themselves, but not this one.

'Hi, Conor. The place is amazing as always.' I say as he stands over us.

'A Herculean task, Mags, I won't deny it.' He laughs. 'I've just come back from helping Artur with the summer house – it's the first chance we've had. The weather has been so wet, it had to be done on the first dry day. But listen, I'm sorry for disturbing you, but when I heard you were coming...I thought now's my chance. Could I ask you something?'

Chance for what, I wonder. 'Fire away,' I say.

'Well, the thing is, your brother-in-law Oilibhéar, as you know we're good friends. He's full of praise for you. He says you have some impressive cases behind you, and so I'd like to ask you for a bit of advice.' He throws an apologetic glance towards my husband. 'And Kieran, I was hoping a glass of vintage Dom Pérignon might make up for this intrusion on your time, and for borrowing your wife's ear for just a moment.'

Kieran laughs. 'Oh, any time! For a glass of vintage champagne, she's all yours, as long as you like.'

'Thanks, Kieran, nice to know my price.' I roll my eyes with a grin. 'So what is it you want to know, Conor? I'm afraid Oilibhéar is overestimating my powers of deduction, to be honest, but if I can help you, I will, though I can't guarantee anything.'

'Thanks, Mags.' He pulls up a stool from a nearby table and sits down by my armchair. Then seems not to know where to start. Kieran, who can be very good at reading the room, gets up and strolls away to the huge arched window to admire the view of the bay, glass in hand, giving us some space.

I really hope this is nothing too serious. Ana didn't seem to be upset about anything. 'How are your kids? Well, I hope?'

He smiles and relaxes a bit. 'Grand altogether. The twins are doing great, though Artie passed his driving test first time and Joe has had four goes at it so far and still no luck, so that's a bone of contention. The thing is, if Artie has an exam, he'll work hard for it, leave nothing to chance, where his brother takes after his old man, I'm afraid, winging it. It works sometimes but not always. That's why Artie's at college and Joe works for me.' He laughs. He's clearly bursting with pride for them both. 'And Lily is five and has us all wrapped around her little finger. She's just starting her first year of big school. And yours? Two girls you and Kieran have, isn't it?'

'Yes, Ellie and Kate. Ellie is sixteen and Kate is thirteen, so you can imagine the hormone levels in our house, but they're fine. Ellie is very theatrical, and Kate is mad for sports.'

'It's gas, isn't it?' he muses. 'How they have the same genetics, same upbringing, same everything and are totally different people? Joe and Artie are identical but nothing alike in their personalities. Joe is a natural in the hotel, charming, friendly, but Artie is mad for the books – he'll be one of those fellas in college for twenty years.'

'It really is gas. I suppose we're just how our kids get here. They have their own paths in life to follow.'

He nods. 'Those are the truest words you've ever said. My friend Eddie, he's a priest, always quotes the fella Kahlil Gibran – he was a Turkish mystic or something – but he said, "Your children are not your children, they are the sons and daughters of life's longing for itself."'

I finish the quotation. '"You may house their bodies but not their souls, for their souls live in the world of tomorrow which you cannot visit, not even in your dreams."' I love that book.

He laughs; he's more relaxed now. 'Look at us here quoting philosophy at each other. So I better get on with what I want to ask you – I don't want to keep you from your husband too long.'

'How can I help?'

'I need your advice on a very delicate matter. Well, someone I know needs the advice, and some help if at all possible, but discretion is vital, so I thought of you and thought I'd ask.'

I'm intrigued. 'Go on. Though I do have to warn you that if it relates to any crime, past, present or future, then I can't guarantee my silence.'

'No, no, it's nothing like that.' He folds his forearms on his knees, and leans forwards. 'This person I know, she has…well, she has reason to believe she might have a relative in this part of the country, but she has no contact details for them. She had this idea she might just bump into her somehow, but it's hard for her to go around by herself in public...'

I assume we're talking about some sort of celebrity here. But I'm still a bit surprised that she feels she can't leave the hotel.

Ireland is famously a great place for celebrities to come if they don't want to be hassled. It's kind of a matter of pride for Irish people to treat them like they're completely unimportant, which means people like Beyoncé can cycle around Phoenix Park in Dublin with everyone ignoring her, and Pierce Brosnan can get married by a local priest in Mayo, and Kim Kardashian can go to the cinema in Portlaoise with Kanye West without the girl at the counter batting an eye. Even Matt Damon was able to hang out in Dalkey for the whole of lockdown without anyone peering in his windows, and when a *New York Times* reporter came looking for him, the locals were like, Matt Damon who?

So I wonder who this celebrity is who feels she can't leave her room.

'I was hoping if you could meet with her,' continues Conor, 'and hear her story, maybe you could offer advice about how she could go about finding the relative? Not now, if you don't wish to, but if you were able to spare even twenty minutes today or tomorrow, I'd be very grateful.'

It's hard to understand what he wants from me. 'It's not really my remit,' I explain. 'A missing person, yeah, but an estranged relative... If a person wants to leave for whatever reason, and there is no reason to believe they are hurt or in danger, as a guard I wouldn't really get involved. It's a person's own business if they don't want to be found.'

'I understand, but I think this is a bit different, and maybe more to it than meets the eye. Look, it's not my story to tell, and I don't know all of it truthfully, but this...young woman...she's desperate for some help and it's hard for her to find people she can trust to keep a secret, you know? You might meet her, on a sort of personal level – it won't take long – and just see what you think?'

He holds my gaze with his, and I realise this is a man people find it hard to say no to, and anyway, I'm happy to do a favour for him and talk to this person, whoever she is.

'All right, sure. I doubt I can do much, but I'll certainly speak to her. Let me just ask Kieran if he minds sparing me for half an hour.'

'This is really kind of you. I owe you.'

'I'm not promising anything, mind you, but I'll see.'

Kieran agrees to meet me in the library in half an hour for a coffee and says he'll go and check out our room in the meantime.

Then Conor leads me through the bar and unlocks a heavy oak door with black cast-iron fittings, which opens into a carpeted corridor. Halfway along the corridor, there's a lift, the doors of which open immediately. When we step in, there are only two buttons, Reception and Suite; no other floors are listed. Conor presses the one for Suite, which he explains is the entire fourth floor, a self-contained single unit.

'This person has rented out the whole floor?' I ask, intrigued, wondering how much that must be costing.

'The people that rent it seem to think it's worth it to get five minutes peace,' he says, as if he's read my mind.

'And what happens if they want to use the spa, like the other normal guests?'

'There's a hidden spa on the roof, a pool, hot tub, sauna and loungers placed up in the battlements of the castle. The floor had to be reinforced with steel to take the weight, but it is accessible only from the suite and it's not advertised on the website, so even the press don't know about it. It's all word of mouth,' he explains, then adds proudly, 'It was Ana's idea of course.'

When we reach the suite, we pass down another silk-carpeted corridor, where Conor unlocks the door to a small room and asks me to take a seat, then closes the door behind me.

The room reminds me of a waiting room in a fancy doctor's office. Three coral suede slipper chairs sit on the cream deep-pile carpet. There's a glass-topped oval table with a crystal water decanter and three glasses resting on what looks like a copper tree, and a large elegant standard lamp. On the blank wall is a canvas – it must be ten feet by six – with an abstract painting, what might be feathers, in corals, coppers, creams and burgundies. It is the kind of room you see on that programme about hoarders, when they go into people's houses and take out six hundred china teapots or eighty boxes of old car racing magazines and replace it with something classy and zen.

I go to peer down from the window. The rose garden is far below, and I can see the freshly painted pale-blue summer house in the distance. I wonder what on earth all the secrecy is about and who I'm about to meet.

Five minutes later I hear muffled voices from outside and the door opens. Conor walks in, and behind him…well, I can't believe it.

'Sergeant Mags Munroe, let me introduce Sienna Black. Sienna, Mags is the person I told you about. She might be able to help you.'

CHAPTER 8

If Kate or Ellie could see this, I doubt they'd be able to speak. Sienna Black, as I'm reliably informed by my daughters, is the winner of five Grammys and an Oscar for best supporting actress in some musical film, and she has outsold Beyoncé, Taylor Swift, Pink and Billie Eilish, becoming a billionaire last year. All over the world, her concerts sell out in a matter of minutes. And here she is standing in front of me.

She's tiny is the first thing. No taller than five feet if she was barefoot, and she can't weigh more than fifty kilos, if that. The wild copper corkscrew curls are untamed and the fringe looks like it was cut by a blind child with rusty clippers, but what do I know about hair fashion?

'Hello, Sergeant,' she says, and her American accent comes out in a low gentle growl, totally incongruous with her image. She extends her hand and I take it; it's tiny and bony like herself.

She's dressed as she seems to always be, in clothes far too big for her. An enormous off-white hoodie with a black dripping heart on the front and a logo saying 'Zadig & Voltaire', and jeans with rips and buckles and straps that look like six of her would fit in them. On her feet she wears big chunky platform sneakers that add at least three inches to her height. I recognise them as Buffalo London because Ellie was trying to convince me to shell out two hundred and sixty euro for a pair last weekend. Needless to mention, I did no such thing.

'Hello, it's nice to meet you,' I say awkwardly.

'Thank you for making the time for me, especially when you're here as a guest, but Conor says you can be trusted. It's a problem for me, as you can imagine.' She shrugs, her thin shoulders raising the large sweater. 'It's very hard to find people who aren't willing to spill the beans, for money, y'know, and tell all sorts of stories about me.'

'Yes, I can imagine. So umm, umm…' Why am I tongue-tied? She's just a kid of seventeen, but I'm really on the back foot. 'So what can I do for you, Sienna?'

'Well, I…um…well, I think…' She casts a glance at Conor, and she looks as self-conscious as I feel. She really is very young.

'It's OK,' he says gently. 'Why don't we all take a seat first?' He gestures towards the three coral suede armless chairs, and we all sit. I find it's necessary to kind of recline in mine, which feels odd but sitting upright would be bonkers, and then he pours her a glass of water from the decanter and hands it to her. She takes it and sips, gathering her thoughts.

'Well, umm… Gee, it's hard to know where to start.'

'Just tell your story in your own words,' I say, trying to remember she's only a year older than Ellie. 'There's no rush.'

She takes a deep breath. 'See, my mom died when I was six, breast cancer.' She stops again.

'I'm sorry, that's very hard,' I say.

She nods. 'And it was just me and my dad, y'know? I was the only kid they had. My mom got cancer soon after I was born, and it was on and off, so she was on medication and couldn't risk having another child, though I always wanted a little brother or sister…'

I nod but don't speak.

She swallows. 'My father was so deep in grief, he couldn't do much, so my grandmother took care of me for a while – well, that's what we say to people, though…'

She sips her water again, and I notice she's trembling.

'Whatever you tell me won't go any further, I give you my word, Sienna,' I say.

She looks at me then with her green eyes – they're surely fake lenses; nobody's eyes are that green – weighing up if I can be trusted or not. There's a long pause.

She inhales and exhales loudly. 'OK, it wasn't really my grandmother. My father was drinking and, well...not really coping, so I went from group home to foster home and back to group homes. I was bullied and all of that. It was bad. Girls in the system are targets for creeps and predators, and I was no different. Nobody cares about those kids, so they're the ones people pick on.'

I hate that she's right. There's no self-pity in her tone, just a factual retelling. I think of Fionn McGuinness, and I hope the social workers allow Gearoid and Enrico to foster him.

'So I started making music then, just on my phone. There was a piano in one of the schools I went to, and I had kind of taught myself by then, and I uploaded some songs to TikTok, and stuff slowly started happening. I was eleven.'

I know some of this rags-to-riches story from the girls, the sanitised version with the grandmother anyway, but I don't say anything.

'All the time, though, since the day I went into foster care, I didn't know it, but my father was fighting the system to get me back. His name's Tony. I never got to see him. They said he didn't care and wasn't in touch, but then I found out – well, he told me – he was kept away from me because they thought he'd be bad for me, but he never gave up. He went to rehab, got sober. It took a few attempts, but he did it to get me back, and eventually, supervised at first, he was allowed to be my dad again, even though the authorities never liked him because he was poor and lived in a trailer, but we had a flower bed and everything, and it was warm. It was OK.'

She glances from me to Conor, defensive and so proud of her father for fighting for her. 'He's been sober now for six years, three months, one week and four days – we tick the calendar together every morning – and he's my manager, my protector. He does everything for me. He's like my guardian angel. He's great, isn't he, Conor?'

'He's very protective,' Conor says quietly, and I get a slight vibe off him that he doesn't think Tony Black is quite the angel his daughter believes him to be. Sienna doesn't notice, as Conor hides it well; it's only that I've done a million police interviews and I've learnt to pick these things up.

'I know, he is,' she agrees. 'I had to pretend I was going to the ladies' room to come here – he worries so much about me. After I won my first Grammy, the press hounded me all the time, up in my grill. One time it got so bad, he rented us a cottage up in the Rockies in Montana. And the lies they printed about Dad neglecting me and only being interested when I got famous... That's why he told everyone it was my grandmother who looked after me while he worked as a garbage man. It sounds better than me being in foster care while he got sober.'

She blushes, her cheeks blazing, clashing with her hair. 'But he was just doing it to protect me, and it worked. It put them off the scent, 'cause my grandmother backed up his story. I didn't really know her, but she must have been a nice woman to go along with it and help to pull me up. She's dead now.'

'It must have been very hard to have everyone trying to find out everything about your upbringing and interested in everything about you,' I say gently, then add, because it seems strange not to, 'My daughters are huge fans of yours.'

She smiles then, a warm, more open smile. 'They are? Way cool. What are their names? How old are they?'

'Kate and Ellie. Kate's thirteen, Ellie's sixteen.'

'Tell them I said hello,' she says, and there's a note of sincerity there that I find endearing.

'So what happened then, Sienna?' I don't want to leave Kieran alone too long, even if he is perfectly happy looking after himself. I want to enjoy this lovely place with him.

'Well, my dad, he got a girlfriend, Charlotte Whelan, and she was my dancing instructor. I was really happy they were seeing each other. They kept it quiet, though, because of the press intrusion, but she was nice, really kind to me. They had a baby, a little girl called Phoebe. I really loved her, but Charlotte went kind of strange as Phoebe got older…'

She swallows again, and I wonder where this is going.

'Charlotte kept saying to me, like… Well, it was mad, what she said. She said we should leave my dad and everything, and of course I said no, that was crazy. I love my dad and I wouldn't go, and I didn't want her to go either – I loved her and my baby sister. Then one day she just disappeared. Phoebe was only two. I was heartbroken and Dad was as well, but he explained the problem to me. See, Charlotte had told him Phoebe wasn't his after all, that her father was some other man she was seeing, and so when she and Phoebe disappeared, Dad said to just leave it. But I'm worried about Phoebe, you know? And I miss her. I want her to have good things and pull her up, and I don't know what's happening to her. She must be three years old by now. I loved being her older sister and –'

'Sienna, are you sure Charlotte is back in Ireland?'

She blushes again. 'I'm not, I'm sorry. It's just she was Irish, y'know, and sometimes she said about how she missed a place called Lisdoonvarna. That's near here, isn't it?'

I nod. Lisdoonvarna is only a few miles away from here.

'Well, I remembered the name, and when I realised Castle Dysert was so nearby, I sort of got talking to Conor about it.'

She throws Conor a shy smile, and he smiles back at her. I'm not surprised she confided in him; he's the sort of man you do confide in.

'I don't really want Dad to know I'm looking, you see. Charlotte broke his heart, and I don't want to upset him all over again. I love him so much, and I owe him for pulling me up. I just want to do what's best for Phoebe, even secretly, y'know? Make sure she's all right and not poor like I was, and I want to pull her up too, even if she isn't my biological sister, you know, because I love her like a sister anyway.'

I like her even more for that. 'Do you have a picture of Phoebe?'

'I wish I did, but Charlotte and Dad never wanted Phoebe put on social media anywhere, and they were right, because of how everyone was hounding us because of me, and so I only had a picture of her on my phone. And then after Charlotte disappeared, my phone went missing, I don't know how. Dad was so worried it had been stolen, and I had to change my number, though nothing turned up on social media, so I guess I just lost it. It's lucky no one found it. I'm so stupid. So no, I don't have a picture, or Charlotte's old number even. I wish I did…' Tears pool on her lower lids. 'Please can you help me, Sergeant Mags? I don't have any money to pay you right now. I don't have my own bank account. I'm too young, Dad says.'

This poor girl. My heart goes out to her. 'Don't worry about money, Sienna. I would love to help put your mind at rest about your little sister. And I know your motives for finding her are good, but if her mother doesn't want to be found, that's her prerogative. You do understand that, don't you?'

'I do, and I won't go near her if she doesn't want me to. I just want to know everything is OK, and I was hoping… I mean, Ireland is such a small place…'

'It is, Sienna, compared to America, but there are still five million people here, and…well, I'd hate to give you false hope.'

'I have a photograph of Charlotte. It's not very good but…' She is pleading now, holding out one of those tiny photos that are taken on the modern equivalent of Instamatic cameras, the sort people buy and throw away. I reach for it. It's an unhelpfully small shot of a woman in profile, sitting on a couch, in her thirties with cropped bleached-blond hair. Her bare arms are toned, and she has several piercings in the ear and one in her nose. *Love ya, Sienna, Charlotte xxxx* is written in small letters on the back of the photo.

I turn to Conor. 'And has Google Images thrown up anything for this photo?'

'Nothing. It's not great quality. So we're stumped, and we thought you might have some other ideas.' Conor holds up his hands. 'And I'm not asking you to use Garda resources or anything. I just hoped you might have an idea.'

'I can check if she's on the Garda system, that's legitimate, but unless she's committed a crime, she won't be on there.'

'She won't be,' says Sienna. 'She's a really good person. I mean, she was until…' She blushes again. 'I mean, until she upset my dad and all…'

I rack my brain. 'There is Finders International, but that's just for probate genealogy.'

'What's that?' Sienna asks.

'It's an agency that will find beneficiaries of wills, people who are out of contact or distant relatives, that sort of thing.'

'But not for living people?' she asks.

'No.' I'm trying to think of another way. 'What line of work was she in? You could try LinkedIn?'

'Just, y'know, my dance instructor before I even got famous, and then she stopped when she had Phoebe. So I've tried LinkedIn, yeah, but I couldn't find anything.'

'What's going on in here?' The door opens, and a broad, tall man stands beaming in the doorway. He's in track pants and a polo shirt, and his forearms are tattooed and so are his hands, badly, telling of a life not always lived in the lap of luxury like now. His head is shaved; he was balding and decided to go the whole hog. He's not exactly handsome but he's pleasant looking.

Sienna springs to her feet with a wide, welcoming smile. 'Dad!'

'What happened to you, darling?' He has large, warm, brown eyes. 'When you didn't come back, I thought maybe you were sick or something. I've been searching everywhere.'

'No, no, sorry, Dad, I'm fine. I just met Conor. He was showing this police officer around. She's one of the undercover security for the week – you'll see her around the hotel – and he was showing her the elevator. I met her in the hall, and she has two daughters who are fans of mine, and we got talking…'

I'm impressed how smoothly she lies to him, and doing it the best possible way, which is by almost telling the truth. I guess if you've spent a lot of time being bullied in care, you might get good at lying, though it doesn't chime very well with how much she keeps saying she loves him.

Tony nods, switching his warm smile to me. 'Awesome. How old are your girls?'

'Sixteen and thirteen, and they love your daughter.' I stand up, and so does Conor.

'Anyone Conor feels is suitable to bring onto his security team is OK by me. He is doing a great job, covering all the angles, so thanks for being a part of it, Officer…er…'

'Munroe,' I say. I understand now why I picked up that slight vibe off Conor earlier, that he doesn't quite trust or like this guy. It's impossible to put a finger on – on the surface he seems nothing but normal – but there's something there, enough for me not to want him to call me Mags. 'It's been a pleasure to meet your daughter.'

'I think I'll try out the hot tub now, Dad!' Sienna sounds childishly hopeful.

He laughs and shakes his head. 'No, you don't want to do that, and anyway, you have to meet the voice coach, and then a PT session, so we've got to go. Nice to meet you, Officer Munroe, and thanks for your help with our security. I'll see you later, Conor.' And he ushers Sienna out, closing the door behind them.

Conor and I remain in the room alone, standing by the glass table.

'Well? What do you reckon?' he asks, pouring out another two glasses of water and offering one to me.

I shrug as I take it. 'She's not like I expected. There's something very vulnerable about her.' It's strange – she rather reminds me of Delia's cousin Natasha, the girl I had to save from being trafficked.

Conor nods and drinks some water. 'Yes, to see her up on stage, owning the whole thing, and being so outspoken in the media and all the rest, you'd imagine her to be much more confident or mature or something, when she's just a kid really.'

'I know, only a year older than Ellie. It's amazing.'

'And a year younger than my boys. I'd like to help her. I don't know why really, but the people who came on my tours, now the people that stay here, there always seems to be something I can help them with. But I'm stumped with this one.'

'About finding Charlotte Whelan, or stumped in general?' I ask.

He smiles, realising that I've also picked up a subtle sign of something being off. He's very good at reading people; it must be from years of working with a wide variety of customers and staff. 'Her father, you mean?'

'If you like.'

He nods, but answers diplomatically. 'He's very charming, softly spoken like his daughter…nice, friendly and professional. He's very protective of Sienna, but I can kind of get that. We might be the same if we had a daughter as famous as her. You should see the security bill. You won't have noticed because they're very discreet, but we have to have 24/7 patrols of the perimeter, and we've seen off four paparazzi already this week. So I suppose the way he watches her every move, maybe it's understandable.'

'What a life. I don't envy her. Though my daughters regularly moan about how boring and ordinary we are.'

He nods. 'There's a lot to be said for being ordinary, Mags. I see a lot of wealth and privilege in this place, and I can tell you one thing for nothing – it doesn't make them happy.' We are on the move now, leaving the room and heading for the lift, which is standing open.

'So any thoughts on how to help her?' he asks as we step into it. He presses the button marked Reception.

'Leave it with me. I'll have a think and see what I can do. I didn't have a chance to ask before her father turned up, but a date of birth would be very useful.'

'Thanks, Mags, you're a star. Now what's your and Kieran's very favourite meal?'

'Oh goodness, I'm sure everything here is my favourite. I can't wait to see the menu.'

'Lobster?' he asks as the doors slide open onto the discreet corridor behind the bar.

I almost laugh; he really is a mind-reader. 'Well, I loved it the few times I've tried it but…'

'Done. Lobster dinner for you both this evening, on me, and a full bottle of Dom Pérignon this time, and your room for the night is on us as well.'

'Oh, Conor, that's so not necessary…'

But he brushes away my protests, walks me through the bar and leaves me at the door of the library where Kieran is waiting, reading the paper and enjoying the peace and quiet with a cappuccino in his hand.

There are a few groups also having coffee, and some drinking cocktails, and a man in a bow tie and tails is playing 1940s jazz on the grand piano. The aroma of old leather, beeswax polish and lilies from the huge arrangement on a table in the window is lovely.

'Look at you, lord of the manor,' I say, sliding into the armchair beside my lovely husband.

'I could get used to this.' He grins. 'Imagine living here in the old days as members of the aristocracy, never having to lift a finger from dawn to dusk, not light your own fires or take out your own rubbish or mow your own lawn...'

'No more housework or cooking or washing up. Ringing a little bell every time I feel like a cuppa or a foot rub.' I join in the fantasy.

'You do know that if we travelled back in time, though, we wouldn't be the ones ringing the bells. We'd be the ones making the tea and chopping the firewood.' He laughs, pricking the bubble.

'That's probably true, but we can dream,' I say, picking up a small leather-bound menu. 'Now, what will I have? Maybe a cinnamon latte...'

As if he's heard me from across the room, a young man wearing a name tag saying Artie materialises. 'What would you like?' he asks. 'My dad says you are to have whatever you want.'

'Oh, are you Conor's son?' I ask. We met his other boy, Joe, once before, and now that I look at him, of course he is; the boys are identical twins, though Artie's curly blond hair is longer and tied back in an elastic.

'Yes, I'm Artie. Joe works here full time – that's my brother – but I'm on study leave, which somehow in my father's head means me waiting tables.' He rolls his eyes.

'Conor told me you're at college, but not what you are studying?'

'Joe always says I'm studying the hardest sums you can imagine, but I'm doing applied physics. I love it.' I realise he's less like Conor and more like his mother.

'And what would you do with that afterwards, like what line of work would you go into?' Kieran asks. It's one of the many things I love about him – he's interested in people and what they do. He spent about three hours discussing the working of leather with Jerome one day, saddles, bridles, tanning, all of that; I left them at it. But he's genuinely fascinated with other people's lives while being totally content with his own.

'I'm hoping to do a post grad in artificial intelligence and machine learning.'

'That's interesting, though I have to admit I'm kind of terrified of AI,' I say.

'I suppose it's how you look at it. People were worried about electricity at the start, but now we can't live without it, same with smartphones. And of course there are some downsides, but on balance we'd all rather keep our phones, so I think AI will be the same, a tool we use. But for sure we need to regulate it and ensure it doesn't end up regulating us.' He smiles, and I know if my daughters were here right now, they would swoon. 'I'm interested in being a part of that.'

'Well, I'm glad we are educating our young people to be able to do it, because I can barely work the TV remote,' Kieran says with a chuckle.

Artie laughs. 'My dad is the same. He has a computer for work and a phone obviously, but once he comes home, he turns off the phone. He has no social media and refuses to even consider it. He reads the actual paper, like the paper version.' He says this like Conor comes to work by chariot rather than by car.

'Ah, we're not alone so,' Kieran replies. 'Our daughters think we're in the dark ages too because we have a conservatory that we've made sure has no screens or Wi-Fi.'

'Yeah, same. Dad and my mam have a room in our house like that, and they'd live in it if they could, but my little sister, Lily, loves TV and she's the boss of our house. Thank God for her, because Joe and I are scared we'll go home some day and they'll have got rid of all the technology completely. All that would be left would be an old radio from the 1950s with big dials and all the cities of the world marked on it that my granda bought my dad, which he loves.'

'Oh, I had one of those when I was a kid. My father let me take it apart to see how it worked,' Kieran reminisces.

'It probably wasn't complicated. There were no processors or microchips or anything, but I suppose it was good technology for the time,' Artie says kindly, not to hurt the feelings of the elderly. 'Now, what can I get you…'

I had been going to have coffee, but the jazz is putting me in the mood. 'A pina colada. I haven't had one of those for at least twenty years. Do you fancy a cocktail, Kieran?'

Kieran beams at Artie. 'A Black Russian?'

'Sure thing…'

As Artie goes off to get our drinks, I look at my husband, thinking about all the young people around us. We are pushing on, no doubt about it. It's weird how you get old in your body but not in your mind. I wonder about that. Is the me of now different to the me of, say, twenty or thirty? I don't think so, but I don't know. Kieran was talking about a retirement plan recently. We went to see our accountant, and he was suggesting we invest a bit more now as retirement is approaching. I was kind of shocked. Though of course it is approaching. I'm fifty-two, and if I do the full term, I'll be retiring in eight years, though I can't imagine life without my job.

Don't get me wrong. I'm not so devoted to law enforcement that I have no life, quite the opposite, but being a guard is kind of part of who I am, and so the idea of not being one feels strange.

'Penny for them?' Kieran says, interrupting my reverie.

I don't like to mention I was thinking about us getting older, let alone retiring, so I shrug and say, 'Just thinking about the crazy half hour I just had.'

'I know you probably can't tell me, but was it interesting?'

'Very, *very* interesting, and I can tell you as it's not Garda business, but not here, and you have to promise not to breathe a word to anyone else ever.'

He's delighted. He hates when I have to keep secrets from him because it's police business. 'It must be something big, given we're getting cocktails on the house as well as champagne. And I wasn't going to tell you, but I'm sure the room is a serious upgrade on the one I booked.'

'And there's a free lobster dinner for two, and the room is paid for.'

He laughs in disbelief, then sees I'm serious. 'Hang on, what did you do this time, Mags? Find some guest's diamond necklace worth billions or something like that?'

'No, but keep guessing.' I wink, knowing he never will.

'Chance Your Arm is alive and living in the stables here at the castle?'

'No, though that would be almost as astonishing as the truth.' The cocktails have arrived, and I'm happy to see there's no paper umbrellas to contend with – this place is far too sophisticated – only long silver straws.

'What could be more amazing than that?' He's astonished, then looks scared. 'This isn't something dangerous, is it? Because I don't think I can cope with nearly losing you again...'

'Nothing like that,' I reassure him, patting his hand as I sip my delicious pina colada. 'Relax and enjoy, Kieran, and I promise I'll tell you when we're safely alone.'

* * *

He's right, our bedroom is incredible. It has a huge four-poster bed with heavy brocade curtains tied back and a high window with shutters, and there are flowers everywhere and a really big comfortable blue velvet sofa that you can sink into and still see out over the bay. There are oil paintings on the walls that look like originals, and the Persian carpet lays over polished dark floorboards that are two feet wide and uneven with age.

We sit there leaning against each other while I tell Kieran about Sienna Black, and he's fascinated, and also relieved it's not some mad dangerous James Bond–style mission, though as I get up to go for a shower, he calls after me that he still thinks it would be even more interesting to find Chance Your Arm in the stables, 'because it would put that bozo's big nose out of joint forever'. Kieran is very protective of me around Duckie.

'You're definitely showing your age, not getting how much more massive Sienna Black is than even a really famous horse.' I tease him through the bathroom door as I wriggle out of my jeans, and he takes that as a challenge and insists on joining me in the shower, which is lovely.

Half a very pleasant hour later, it's coming up to dinner time and I need to get dressed. I shoo him off downstairs before the whole secret process of heaving and tugging at elasticated underwear, then with triumphant ease, I slip on the purple jumpsuit with the V-neck and ruffles.

I got one of those hot-air blow-dry brushes from the girls for Christmas, and it really works great. So after much pulling and pushing of shapewear, spraying and teasing of hair, applying of make-up, I slip my feet into gold high heels and look in the mirror. Not bad.

I see his admiring glance as I enter the dining room and a waiter shows me to our table.

'Hey, you better get out of here soon. My wife will be here any minute, and she'll be savage if she finds me ogling you...' he murmurs as I sit down.

I laugh. A bottle of Dom Pérignon is already open, and he pours us both a glass. 'Don't get used to it. As of tomorrow it's back to hoodies and jeans.'

'I'd love you if you wore a bin bag,' he says simply. 'But you are stunning tonight.'

'You clean up well yourself,' I say, toasting him. He's in an open-necked white Ralph Lauren shirt and navy chinos, and he's gorgeous.

'Thanks. It's because I'm not allowed any unsupervised purchases, so I always wear clothes my wife likes.' He grins. 'Anyway, don't mind the clothes. I've a surprise for you.'

In the excitement of the afternoon, I'd completely forgotten he'd promised me a surprise. At first I'd assumed it was the champagne, and we're having the lobster dinner anyway, so it's obviously not that, so what is it?

The waiter arrives with a basket of delicious breads and home-made butter, and we decide on six oysters each for starters, caught today from the bay outside. They come quickly, served very simply with a lemony white-wine vinaigrette with finely chopped red onions, and they are incredibly sweet and tender.

'So what's my surprise?' I ask as I dip my fingers in the glass finger bowl provided.

'Early retirement!' he says, with an enormous smile.

I sit looking at him, wiping my clean fingers on my linen napkin. 'I'm sorry?'

He's fizzing with excitement at telling me. 'It only just happened last week, and I wanted to surprise you here, in the lap of luxury, to give you a taste of what's to come. You know Wojtec?'

'Of course I know Wojtec.' He's one of Kieran's employees, a Polish man, very kind and hard-working. I'm still confused, though.

'Well, he came to me to tell me the inheritance he's been waiting for is going to come through a lot earlier than he was expecting, and added to what he's saved so far, he wants to offer me a million euros for the business, sometime next year. The equipment is worth a lot, and the rest is for the customer base.'

'Oh, Kieran, wow, that's amazing!' I'm so pleased for him, though also taken aback. As far as I was aware, he loves his job as a roofer. 'That's fabulous, but I thought you were content with your life and wanted to keep going for a few more years yet?'

'No, I've been thinking about it since our trip to the accountant, and I've decided I don't want to wait. It's a young man's game climbing up on roofs all day in all weathers, and I'm not young any more, Mags, my knees are getting stiff. I even said to Foxy Clancy, I might ask him to find a buyer for me –'

'You did?' I'm startled. Foxy Clancy is the local estate agent and is an oily, untrustworthy man. I'd hate for us to be involved with him in any way.

He nods. 'But it all worked out much better, because Wojtec

offered and that's who I want to have it, so I told Foxy not to bother even though he said he could get me a better deal because of climate change, which being Foxy he managed to make sound like a great thing. God, he's a dose.'

I wince. I can imagine Foxy celebrating climate change. Probably he's hoping everyone will have to start moving to higher ground so there'll be lots of house sales in it for him. I know what Foxy means about roofers, though. There was a terrible storm last winter – we are getting them more often and more intensely now – and it has meant more jobs than Kieran's firm can ever take on. And I suppose I have noticed he's working harder than he ever did.

'So…' I say cautiously, and I know I should be more enthusiastic – he deserves this – but at the same time, I'm stunned. Somehow I can't imagine him as anything other than a fit, strong outdoors man going up and down ladders in rain and shine. I have a weird thought – what is poor Father Doyle going to do? But instead I say, 'What are you going to do with your time?'

He stares at me as if I've got two heads. 'Music, of course!'

'Music…'

'Yes, Mags.' He's slightly offended now. 'You might not have noticed, but I'm quite good at the uilleann pipes now and I've been at it just over a year. But I want to get better still. I want to get *good*, Mags, and that means putting in a lot more hours.' He pauses, and I see the disappointment on his face; this is not the reaction he was expecting. 'What is it? I thought you'd be happy.'

'I'm not… I mean, I am… I just, well, I just didn't realise you were considering retiring so soon.'

I'm not going to lie. My heart is sinking at the thought of yet more piping in the house. It's hard to believe it's only been a year, it feels more like a lifetime. I suppose I have sort of noticed he's getting better – well, you know, it's not like tomcats on a wall anyway, so it's an improvement, but even so…

And at least if he's retired, he can do it during the day while I'm out at work, so there's that. I pull myself together and say what I should be saying. 'I think it's a wonderful idea. You've worked very hard and it's a fantastic offer, so of course you should pursue your dreams.'

'And of course it won't be just music. We'll be able to go travelling half the time, living the life of Riley – just like your mam and Joe!'

'We?' I stare at him, wondering if I've heard him right.

He's so happy, he is on a roll. He's usually better at picking up cues than this, but he's too excited. 'Well, as I say, the business is worth a million, and selling it will set us up for the rest of our lives. It will put the girls through college, and together with the pension I've been paying into, and with the pension you'd get from the guards, which I googled – and you can retire as early as you like after the damage the smoke did to your lungs, on the full benefit – financially we'd be grand.'

I continue to stare at him without saying anything. But inside I'm really hurt.

Does he really think my job is that unimportant to me that I would give it up without a second thought for the joy of sitting at home listening to him playing the pipes in between cruising the Mediterranean with other retirees? And yes, I know Mam and Joe have been having a wonderful time, but they're *retired*, for goodness' sake, by which I mean *old*, though even now it's hard for me to think of Mam as old.

But I'm not old. I'm not incapacitated either. Yes, I know I wheeze a lot if I've had a long day, but I'm not on the scrap heap yet – am I? *Am I?*

His face slowly falls as I sit there in silence; he realises this isn't going down well. 'I get scared when you go quiet,' he says, trying to make a feeble joke of it.

I don't want to ruin this evening, and maybe I'm overreacting because I've been feeling bad about myself getting older, which is not his fault, but I do want to say one thing before we go any further. 'I don't want to retire, Kieran.'

'You're thick with me now,' he says as a waiter takes away the plates of empty oyster shells and the finger bowl.

'No, I'm not. You just felt this was so right for you, you thought I'd feel the same way, but I don't, at least not right now. So let's please just celebrate your incredible news, and I promise we'll have great holidays, though maybe not a cruise just yet – not until Kate's off in college anyway.'

He relaxes and smiles again, then starts telling me at length about the expensive set of pipes he's planning to buy, and I try to be as interested as I can be. Another waiter arrives with our lobster and refills our glasses.

'Well, isn't this something...' my husband declares as we get to work with silver claw crackers and the delicate picks that come with the opened lobsters and dip the delicious meat in the melted garlic butter. He's right – it's out of this world.

* * *

WE'RE EITHER LATER or earlier than the other guests for breakfast, I don't know which, but we're almost alone in the pleasant little breakfast room, its French windows already open because it's a lovely warm day with the softest of Atlantic breezes.

The coffee is gorgeous, and we have fresh-squeezed orange juice, and we decide on the scrambled egg and smoked salmon, with a side of sourdough toast with home-made butter.

'God above, that's some mess, and your man leading the investigation. I mean, in all fairness what kind of a clown goes on TV to say he's found the horse without checking? No disrespect to the guards, but seriously...' The two young waiters standing in the corner with nothing to do are chatting quietly to each other.

Kieran shoots me a glance, but I'm already on my phone. It's all over the morning news – the DNA results have come in on the dead horse. It's not Chance Your Arm, it's some poor twenty-five-year-old cob that was already dead before it was 'murdered'.

GALWAY INSPECTOR FALLS AT FIRST FENCE

A man passing himself off as a horse expert unseated the Garda investigation into the disappearance of Chance Your Arm last week, saddling Detective Inspector Donal Cassidy with a nagging headache.

DI Cassidy bridled with rage yesterday, accusing a journalist of being a naysayer...

Oh my God, the tabloid press are having such fun with this. Even I can't believe that Duckie was thick enough to go in front of the cameras without any evidence at all; he must have lied about the police veterinary surgeon examining the poor beast. What an utter plonker.

Kieran, who is also scrolling on his phone, laughs, then grins across the table at me. 'Good treat, Mags?'

'The best,' I reply.

CHAPTER 9

Delia and Darren, who are back from their honeymoon, and Nicola, Michael and Zoë are all in the station, having great craic about Duckie making such an eejit of himself.

I should probably row in behind my senior colleague. We support each other well usually within the force, and normally younger members would be reprimanded for being disrespectful to their superior officers. But he's the last word, so while I won't join in with the teasing, I can't help smiling at a few of the texts and memes they keep showing me. He is not well liked, our Duckie.

'Now come on, everyone, back to work,' I say.

Michael and Delia are covering the desk today, and Darren and Zoë are off on patrol. There's a Tidy Towns meeting that I would normally cover, but I ask Nicola to take it. This gives me a spare five minutes that I use to retire to my office and log into the PULSE system.

I put in the name 'Charlotte Whelan' and her age when she left America, which Conor got from Sienna and texted to me, though Sienna couldn't remember her exact birthday.

Nothing comes up.

I add in 'Lisdoonvarna'.

Nothing.

I google Charlotte Whelan and refine the search with the two possible years of her birth, the tiny photo I've taken a copy of on my phone and Lisdoonvarna. As Conor had already discovered, lots of hits but still, nothing.

Then I have an idea. Lots of people use the Irish version of their name on social media for a bit of anonymity.

I try Searlait Ní Fhaoileán, and there are still a few hits, not on PULSE but on Google, but when I refine the search with the photo, I stumble on someone. It might be her.

She's shared a link to a podcast. I recognise the host; she's a columnist on one of the broadsheets here and has a women's podcast I listen to sometimes. She is one of the main journalists who highlights the ongoing failure of the Catholic Church to pay reparations to the women they incarcerated in the so-called mother-and-baby homes. I really like her.

I open Facebook on my work computer, search for the person who shared the link and find the woman I think might be who we are looking for. Her hair is longer now, and golden brown rather than blond, but it could be her.

I toy with the idea of just sending Conor the link to the page, let Sienna take it from here if she wants to, but something stops me. One of the few profile photos is of her with one of those frames, you know the way people can have them saying 'I stand with Ukraine' or for a charity or something? Well, this profile photo is of her, with a banner beneath of Sonas. The only Sonas I know of is a charity that supports women and children through domestic violence and abuse.

It might be just that she thinks Sonas is a good cause – who wouldn't? But a tiny alarm goes off in my mind. The sort of alarm that rang very, very faintly when I was in the room with Tony Black.

Searlait ní Faoileann is not a serial poster; she shares an odd article. She seems interested in the environment, so a piece about the disappearance of the corncrake and another article about windfarms. A photo of a dog but none of a child. That doesn't mean she doesn't have a child obviously; she might just be keeping her off social media, which is probably wise.

There's no address, but I see she's shared a competition to win a picnic hamper from a Centra shop in Ennis. Another town that is near to Castle Dysert.

I pick up the phone to text Hazel O'Flynn, a detective I know from another case and who I heard was moved to Ennis. *Hi, Hazel, Mags Munroe, Ballycarrick, here. Would you have come across either a Charlotte Whelan or a Searlait ní Faoileann, late thirties, around Ennis?*

I send it and it's seen and delivered. She responds right away. *I know her. Charlotte runs a charity shop here in the town. For Sonas. All OK?*

Absolutely, no problem whatsoever. Thanks – hope you're loving life in the wild west!

Delighted to be out of Dublin. Getting too old!

I google 'Sonas charity shop Ennis' and find the address. It's in a little precinct off the main street. Before I can read any more, there's a knock on my half-open door. I glance up and it's Delia.

'Sarge?'

'Delia, come in.'

She comes in and sits down opposite me, her face expressionless, not the smiling, joking, just-back-off-her-honeymoon, Duckie-mocking Delia she was five minutes ago.

'How can I help you, Delia?'

She says in a flat voice, 'I know I'm only just back, and I know I've taken all my holidays this year and I don't want to let you down, but can I take tomorrow off as unpaid leave?'

I'm startled. In the four years since she joined, I don't think she's ever asked for a day off in this way; something very bad must have happened.

'Delia, what –'

'Darren will do the district court for me,' she says. 'It's just the arraignment of the Murphy case. And Nicola says she'll cover my shift on the public desk in the afternoon.'

I look at her. She is hard to read, never showing emotions on her face; she'd be great at poker. 'Of course you can have the day off, but can I ask why? Not as the boss, but just out of concern?'

Delia is tough as old boots and never cries, not even when the Carrick Arms Hotel burnt down and she thought her wedding plans were ruined, but now to my astonishment, her eyes fill with tears.

'Mammy isn't doing good, Sarge. She can't stop coughing, and none of the remedies her sister Kathleen gave her helped, so Kathleen told Daddy to take her to Dr Harrison. Dr Harrison sent her to A&E, and now they want to keep her in. She's had an X-ray, and tomorrow she's scheduled for another different scan, a CT scan, because they're worried about a shadow on her lung. I want to be with Daddy in the hospital – he needs me there.'

'Oh, Delia, I'm sorry.' I'd noticed that Dora seemed a bit drawn and tired at the wedding three weeks ago, but this sounds really serious. I scramble for something to say that's not falsely reassuring. There isn't anything really.

I remember when my dad was dying, people were trying to be helpful by saying 'I'm sure he'll improve' or 'if anyone can beat this, it's your father', but it didn't help, and in reality it made me want to scream. Of course there's no reason to think Dora has cancer like my father, a shadow could be anything, but still, saying 'I'm sure she will be all right' doesn't cut it, because how would I know.

So I just say, 'Of course. Take as much time as you need, Delia. Don't worry about it, we'll manage. And it doesn't have to be unpaid. If necessary, I'll put in an application for personal leave for you – we can get a cert from Dr Harrison. But your family need you at the moment.'

'Ah, Sarge, thanks, but this might go on for a while...'

'Well, let's just take each day as it comes, OK? And for now stay out anyway. We have enough cover.'

'Are you sure?' She is unconvinced.

'Absolutely sure. Just look after your parents, Delia, and call if we can help with anything.'

'Thanks, Sarge.' She wipes her eyes on her sleeve and gets up to go.

'Delia?'

She turns.

'Are you on for the rest of today?'

She nods.

'OK, finish up what you're doing and head away. We're all here, we can handle it. Your dad needs you more than we do now.'

As a guard, Delia will do better than her parents in the hospital, dealing with the staff and talking to the doctors.

Her mother, Dora, is very wary of settled people and modern medicine, and in return, settled people are very wary of Jerome, who looks terrifying, a solid eighteen stone of muscle and six foot six, with a big pelt of black hair oiled back and tattooed hands and gold jewellery. He's a lovely gentle giant, but you'd have to know him to realise it. There is still prejudice against Travellers, and I hope Delia's presence will go some way to ameliorating that. She has a foot in both camps as it were.

'Thanks, Sarge, thanks very much,' she says.

As I gaze after her with a worried frown, my personal phone rings; it's Ronan Brady. Even though we're friends, I'm surprised to see his name. Being second in command in the Irish police force is a demanding job, and he's so busy, I hardly ever hear from him these days.

'Mags, hi, how are things in Ballycarrick?' he asks as I answer on the second ring.

'Grand, thanks, Ronan. How are you?' I'm sure he hasn't just called for a chat.

'Up the walls, you know yourself. How are the lungs? I hope you're taking things easy?' Not another one. I feel a rush of intense anger against men who think I'm over the hill and should retire.

I inhale, exhale. I read in one of those self-help articles about how between the trigger and the response is power. 'I'm grand. Now what can I do for you?'

'Find that flipping horse?' he says with a chuckle.

I relax. 'Still no sign?'

'Not a dickie bird. But the Horse Board are doing their nut, and the minister is on our necks about it. Between the huge influx of international protection applicants, the feud in Drimnagh and a big operation on dissident republicans with the Police Service of Northern Ireland, I'm pulled in fifty directions.'

'I can imagine. Wasn't there a big roundup of the gang in Drimnagh, though? CAB got them in the end, didn't they?'

CAB, the Criminal Assets Bureau, was set up in 1994 after the murders of a Garda detective and a female journalist who was outspoken about a particular gangland boss, and it was specifically tasked with going after the proceeds of organised crime. They've been fantastically successful in doing it too.

'They did, great job, but Europol are in on it too. The Meeghans have links everywhere, Holland, Colombia, Australia. For a bunch of thickos, they seem to have spread their net wide. I have a feeling we only got the foot soldiers this time, though. The generals are still on the loose, but we're getting there.'

'I'm sure you will,' I say, wondering where he's going with this, because the Meeghan crime family are definitely nothing to do with me. Or at least they better not be.

'Now, Mags, I was only half joking about the horse...'

Ah, here we go.

'Normally this isn't even my remit, but it landed on my desk because Duckie is stomping all over this like a bull in a china shop, getting nowhere and upsetting everyone, so somehow this has become my thing.'

'Oh dear,' I say. Nothing but nothing will force me ever to work with Duckie Cassidy again.

'He's an absolute liability. Imagine announcing you found the animal without checking bloods? And taking security off the ports? We put it back as soon as we found out, but God knows if the flipping animal is even in the country still...'

'It's a tough one.'

'Have you any ideas, Mags, like even a wild guess?'

'Not a clue, Ronan, sorry.'

He gives up waiting for me to volunteer myself, then cuts to the chase. 'I don't suppose you'd help Duckie with the search, would you?'

I laugh. 'Er…you suppose right, Assistant Commissioner Brady.'

'But what am I going to do with him, Mags?' He doesn't push it, but I hear the frustration in his voice.

'Get rid of him, put someone else in charge.'

'I would if I could, Mags. If it was up to me, I'd give him a golden handshake and be shot of him for once and for all, but his uncle is Minister for Agriculture and his father was regional commissioner, and besides, the optics of doing that at this juncture would make a bad situation a hundred times worse.' I hear the exhaustion in his voice. He's right, the gardai are looking like bungling idiots where the horse is concerned now thanks to Duckie, and so if we remove the lead investigator the press will have a field day. 'If I take him off this case now, it's going to become as big a story as the missing horse and make us look even more like we don't know what we're doing. I did try appointing a good officer to work under him, but she lasted less than a day, said he was sexually harassing her, and then I found a young male detective from Galway who agreed to do it, but when he questioned something Duckie was doing, Duckie lost the head, threatened him, the usual rubbish, and so that guy reported him to HR and that's now ongoing, but he's off the case. I need someone competent, sensible, who isn't wound up by DI Cassidy, but I doubt someone like that even exists…'

I have a thought. 'Ronan, leave this with me.'

A note of hope comes into his voice. 'You'll do it?'

'No, I definitely won't. But like I said, leave this with me.'

'Mags, if you can think of someone, I swear I'll do anything…'

'Hmm, I'll have a think. I'll give you a shout later on.'

I hang up. I know someone who is entirely oblivious to Duckie's ham-fisted flirting, and who he can't offend. If it's made clear to him that he cannot dismiss her and has to work with her on pain of being publicly removed from this high-profile case, it might just work.

'Zoë,' I call. 'Can you come in here a second?'

* * *

ZOË BLINKS, and I wonder if she has grasped what I asked. She's prone to a long pause. We're used to that; she really thinks before she speaks now as per my suggestion. She was a divil for oversharing when she first came, and the day she told a mortified Foxy Clancy about a new device that had been invented for making pap smears more comfortable, complete with actions, I knew I had to say something. So now she pauses deliberately before answering, and there's no choice but wait.

Long seconds pass.

'Do I have to do this or is it a choice?' she asks eventually.

'Absolutely a choice, but it will be noted by management what an asset you are, and if it works out and you'd like to move up, having that experience under your belt would help your application.'

'And I'd be working with DI Cassidy?' she asks, and I hold her gaze for a second. It's hard to tell if she's much smarter than she lets on or if she really is very innocent.

'Well, you'd be reporting to him, but you've done very well here, and you're learning how things are done, so I think you could bring fresh eyes to the investigation into the disappearance of Chance Your Arm, and that can only be a good thing.'

'He's a bit…' she says, and halts.

Duckie is a prize eejit, no doubt about it, but the chain of command is important in our organisation. I try to stay professional even if he doesn't. I wait for her to say lecherous, creepy, misogynistic, thick, smelly – the list is endless – but she surprises me.

'Hurt?'

'Er…how do you mean?' I ask.

'Well, he's clearly a sex addict, and in the case of addiction, there's no point in asking why drink or why drugs or why sex – the only question is why the hurt? I suspect childhood trauma, but it could be something else, I suppose…'

'Hmm…' I take a long pause myself before I reply. 'I suppose the thing here, Zoë, is to get to the bottom of what happened to the horse, and DI Cassidy's personal life isn't relevant really?'

'Oh, but it is, Sarge, because we aren't robots. If we are living in a state of fight or flight, our sympathetic nervous systems are on high alert all the time, never allowing our parasympathetic systems to put the brakes on, to calm us, and he lives very much in that mode. And I'm sure his failure to find the horse and his humiliation in front of the whole country won't be helping his already battered self-esteem one bit. Often a healing session with a cuddle yogi can really have benefits, help him return to his baby state. Some people even wear baby clothes or a nappy and get cuddled, and it's almost a way to revisit babyhood and rewrite that memory…'

'Maybe so.' I'm not sure where to go with this. Duckie in a Babygro is an image I would rather erase from my mind immediately. She's a kooky one, no doubt about it. But the fact that she is impervious to Duckie as a lecherous old creep is a huge advantage. She just pities him and wants to psychoanalyse him. It drives him to distraction.

'Do you think I could help him, Sarge, really?'

'I think you might be one of the only members of the force that could, Zoë,' I say truthfully.

'Then I'll do it of course.'

'Wonderful. But you do understand your job is to help find the horse, first and foremost?'

'Of course. DI Duckie needs a boost of endorphin, success in this case, and peer admiration will do that.'

I debate explaining further but decide against it. Who cares why she tries to find the animal; it's just important that she does. 'I'll speak to someone and find out the next move,' I say.

She leaves and I pick up the phone to ring Ronan. I get straight to the point. 'Do you know Zoë O'Donoghue?'

'I do. I met her when that pair of Russians tried to burn you to death. She told me that she thought I had sad eyes but that I should have my teeth whitened. I'm not sure if white teeth would make me less sad, but we never got to dig deeper.'

'Yup, that would be her all right. Well, the thing is, she's the only person I've ever met in my entire life that isn't wound up by Duckie. He tries flirting with her, but she either can't or won't hear it. She's convinced he's full of childhood trauma or he's got all sorts of issues, addictions and the whole shebang – she's probably not wrong. But anyway, she can manage him in a way I've never seen. He can't flirt with her. He can't bully her because she just tells him he's behaving like that because he's hurt and she understands. It's comical to watch, but she might be the only officer in the country that can bear to be around him.'

'Interesting, but is she a bit of a… Well, she seemed a bit…um… unconventional, when I met her.'

'Oh, she's that all right. She's unique but efficient and sensible too. She's got the makings of a fine officer, but yeah, definitely a bit unusual.'

'And you reckon she can handle Duckie?'

'Well, currently nobody will work with him, he's making a total dog's dinner of the investigation, and there's no sign of the horse, so you know? How much worse can it get?' I laugh and Ronan groans.

'This would be funny if it wasn't so serious, you know that?'

'I do.'

'And you definitely won't do it?'

'I definitely won't,' I say with conviction.

'Fine, tell her to report to Galway tomorrow. I'll be there with Duckie, and I can broach the partnership with him then. He probably won't be thrilled.'

'I don't know, he might be delighted. Now this is on the condition that I get a replacement for Zoë right away.'

'A replacement, that's a push…'

'I need someone. The population of the town is growing by the week, and we're flat to the mat. Things are sliding and I don't like it, but I can't change it without more people.'

He sighs. 'Fine, I'll send someone, but only till she's got this thing sorted.'

'Deal,' I say, delighted. It's better than I thought I would get. I've been plaguing personnel for more staff for months but getting nowhere.

'Right, send Garda O'Donoghue to me and try to explain she needs to be a bit less…'

'Oh, there's no explaining. She is what she is. Anyway, I'll tell her. Bye, Ronan.'

'Bye, Mags, take care.' He hangs up.

I text Kieran. *Ellie has rehearsal and she's got a lift, Kate has camogie practice and she has one too, and Joe's collecting afterwards and bringing them to Mam's, so do you want to go to Luigi's after work? Just us? x*

It will be good for us to have some time together. We had a fabulous stay at Castle Dysert, but since then every time we discuss his retirement, it's like there's an elephant in the room. It's fine, it's not fraught. I've made it clear I don't want to retire, and he hasn't said anything about it since, but judging by the way I nearly slammed the phone down on Ronan just now, I'm clearly still seething about it underneath and need to get over that.

See you there at six. x

He'd normally say something funny or sweet, so maybe he is a bit annoyed with me as well. We definitely need to have a nice, relaxed time together.

* * *

THE AFTERNOON IS BUSY.

Danny Boylan's flash car turns up. He had it stolen a few days ago. He came in to report it when I was at the festival meeting, and Nicola told me he'd been strangely reluctant to admit where it was parked. She got the location out of him eventually, explaining we needed it to know which CCTV to check. And it's obvious why he didn't want to say. He knows as soon as I see the report that I'll guess what he's been up to. Seeing Gemma O'Flaherty. He always took Chloe to the same hotel, a little place up a side street in Galway, when he was cheating on my best friend, Sharon.

Anyway, the brand-new BMW has been found at the Carmody halting site, wrecked, and Darren and Nicola go to bring the culprit, Kenneth Carmody, into the cells. He is out on bail pending around fifty charges, so he's going back inside either way, and he reckoned one more charge was nothing and he was bored according to himself. At least he doesn't waste Garda time by trying to say he didn't do it.

Michael and Zoë are called to the local secondary school because some kids were messing and rang in a bomb scare. We all know there is nothing in it, but procedure has to be followed and the school has to be evacuated. The two boys responsible are in a lot of trouble, and I'll be meeting with them and their parents to give them a stern talking to about wasting Garda time. I just hope getting out of the biology exam was worth bringing all this down on their heads.

I've cleared half an hour at the end of the afternoon because a social worker is coming to interview me. I don't know why she wants to come here to the station rather than the house, but maybe it's to make sure I am who I say I am and not some mad actress friend of Gearoid's dressing up pretending to be a policewoman.

Anyway, it's fine, no hard questions. She just checks that I've never had any problems with Gearoid, and I tell her what a wonderful uncle he's been to my daughters and what a family man he is, and mention the barbecue at Orla's that is coming up this weekend, and where I hope I'm going to meet Fionn, who is the same age as my youngest daughter and who already knows my older daughter from the youth theatre. And she says it sounds like a readymade family with lots of support. I feel slightly guilty about not mentioning there's a nasty grandmother in the mix, but at the same time, I'm not going to let Nora scupper this chance for Gearoid. And it's not like he's fallen out with her himself; he's very capable of handling his mother by ignoring her.

After the social worker is gone, I check the work calendar and decide I can pop down to Ennis this coming Friday to see if the woman in the charity shop really is Charlotte Whelan. I will do it discreetly, without saying anything to Sienna. I'm even in two minds about whether to tell Conor.

Darren is at the front desk. He's just come off his phone and looks worried.

'Any word of Dora?' I ask him.

'No change. Delia just texted. She's on oxygen to help the breathing, so she's resting better.'

'Well, tell Delia to take as much time as she needs. And keep me updated please, Darren. I don't want to be bothering her, but if there's anything I can do...'

'Will do, Sarge.'

I'm so glad Delia has Darren. She will need him now like she never has before, and I know he's up to the job. Delia and her mother have not always had the most harmonious of relationships. Dora could never understand her daughter's need to live a different life and took her rejection of early marriage to a Traveller boy and a tribe of kids as a personal insult. But still and all, they are family, and they love each other. Like Mam says, you only get one mother.

As I stroll towards Luigi's, I promise myself that Dora will be all right, that it's probably a touch of pneumonia, that it can happen to anyone. Or maybe it's COPD. Dora never smoked but Jerome does, and I suppose the damp and the turf fires of her childhood and all the rest didn't help. COPD wouldn't be great – it's a progressive lung disease – but if you're careful, you can still live a long life.

I really hope it's nothing worse.

For all Jerome being the big man, I can't imagine what it would be like for him if anything happens to Dora. Like Delia, he's so stoic; he never lets on how worried he is or anything. The only time I ever saw him emotional was the day his daughter got married. He was so proud, and I could see him choking up over it all, but apart from that...

An image comes into my head. When I was looking around to say goodbye to Jerome at the wedding, I saw him with his arm around his wife, and he did something I'd never seen him do before, which was drop a kiss onto her head in public.

I dig for a tissue in my pocket, because I'm tearing up myself.

CHAPTER 10

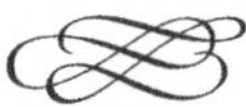

When I open the door of Luigi's, I see Kieran already there. I go over and give him a kiss before sitting opposite him. Thinking of Jerome and Dora makes me realise how important it is to value every moment I have with the man I love.

Luigi's has a real trattoria feel – checked tablecloths, cheap and cheerful food, chianti bottles as candlesticks, encrusted in melted candle wax. It should be tacky and a bit old-fashioned, and it is, but there's something lovely about it. It smells of garlic and basil, and there's always something like Dean Martin or Édith Piaf on the stereo.

'Hello, you. How was your day?' Kieran asks, pouring me a glass of wine from the bottle he's ordered.

'A few different things…' I pause to take a sip of the Rioja, my favourite, then tell him about Dora, which makes him sigh and squeeze my hand.

'It's so important to spend as much time together as we can, isn't it? Life is so short.'

I get the same rush of irrational anger that I felt towards Ronan earlier. It's unreasonable of me, I know that, especially given that I've just been thinking the same thing myself about valuing our time together. But I can't help myself. It feels like my husband is hinting at me to retire.

I swallow my irritation and continue. 'Then the social worker came to interview me, and I told her about the barbecue at Orla's this weekend, and that went down well. She was impressed with our extended family life. Obviously I didn't mention the bust-up.'

He winces slightly. 'If you think I'm going to make it up with my mother, think again.'

Ah. I've just poked Kieran's sore spot, the way he just poked mine. I haven't said anything directly to him about making up with Nora, but he knows I hate family feuds, so I suppose he feels a sort of unspoken pressure from me.

'I didn't mean to say –'

'I'm sure you didn't, but –'

Before we get any further, Cat O'Leary, Ellie's friend, comes to take our order.

'Hi, Mags, hi, Kieran, what can I get ye?' she asks cheerfully, and we both turn on our best smiles.

'Nice to have you waiting on us for a change,' Kieran teases. The O'Leary twins, Cat and Trish, are always at our house. 'I'll have the tagliatelle with the chicken please.'

'Great, and what for you, Mags?' She turns to me.

'I'll have the spinach and ricotta tortellini please, love. What did I hear yourself, Trish and Ellie plotting on the phone last night?'

'Party next Saturday. Well, not this weekend, the next. Ellie's getting ready at our place,' Cat says cheerfully.

'Ah, fantastic, so it's your carpets will get the fake tan and your bathrooms fumigated with hairspray then,' Kieran says, mock relieved.

'My dad went mental after the last time, so all tanning to be done on the tiles…new rule.' Cat rolls her eyes as if Humphrey O'Leary is a tyrant, which he is most certainly not.

'Whose party is it?' I ask.

'The last Sienna Black concert is being livestreamed. She's so good.

She wants everyone that didn't get a ticket for any of the shows to be a part of it, so it's a free livestream and we're all watching it in the community hall.'

'The whole country is gone mad over this young one, whatever it is about her,' says Kieran. He doesn't mention that I met her at Castle Dysert; he knows not to. I felt a bit guilty at first asking him not to tell the girls – he hates keeping secrets – but he doesn't seem to find it hard to keep this one because Sienna's music means nothing to him; he doesn't get what all the fuss is about. But if she was playing the uilleann pipes now, he'd be following her around himself.

'She's amazing, seriously, and her dad manages her. He's great. He really pulled her up. So if Ellie gets famous, which she's determined to do, by the way, maybe you can give up roofing and become her manager,' Cat suggests with a grin.

'When I give up roofing, it won't be to do that, I can assure you.' He nods. 'I could never manage that child. If I could get her to pick her shoes up off the sitting room floor, it would be a start,' my poor long-suffering husband says, with a deep sigh.

I know what he means. Our daughters seem to leave their shoes everywhere in our house. Upstairs. Downstairs. On the actual stairs. It's hard to know how they have so many of them when they're always complaining they have no money.

When Cat has gone off with our order, I tell Kieran about my trip to Ennis on Friday to find Charlotte Whelan.

'Conor going with you?' he asks.

'No. I did think about mentioning it to him, but it's not necessary.'

'Well, I think you should ask him to come,' he says, and I raise my eyebrows at him in surprise. He shrugs. 'It's an unknown situation, Mags, and I'd rather someone was with you.'

'Kieran, I'm going to see a woman who works in a charity shop.' I suppose it's sweet of him to worry about my safety, but he's really pushing my buttons now.

'Mags, it's like she's hiding, and when people are hiding and you find them, well then, the people they're hiding from might come down on you as well. So I think you should ask Conor, as he's the one who got you into this.'

'No, Kieran, and he didn't get me into anything. This is probably the easiest thing I've ever done for anyone. You wouldn't believe how simple it was to find her – if it is her, of course.' I'm shaking my head.

'Well, if you won't ask him, then I'll come myself. Like you said, it's not police business, so I can.'

'No, you cannot!' I'm between laughter and annoyance now. 'Anyway, you haven't the time.' The weather is fine at the moment, and he's got to get a roof on a milking parlour for a big dairy farm, so he can't afford to go haring off to Ennis with me for a whole day while the sun is shining; it's ridiculous.

'Your safety is more important to me than work.' He's being mulish.

'Oh, for goodness' sake, Kieran.' I never worry about danger. It's unfortunate if you find yourself in a tight spot, but it's very unusual. We Irish guards are not armed, but to be fair, neither are most of the criminals, so it's safer to be a police officer here than most places. But I don't want to fall out with my husband; this is supposed to be a nice evening. 'OK, I'll say it to him. I'll do it now. But I'm not asking him if he wants to come – he can say himself if he does.' I take out my phone and text Conor.

Between us and the wall, I think our friend is in Ennis. Going down in the morning, I'll be there 11 a.m. Don't tell your guest. Our friend might not want to be found.

The ticks go blue, and he replies straight away. *Let's meet outside the Old Ground Hotel, 11 a.m. The manager is a friend, so we can leave the cars there.*

I send back a thumbs-up and turn the phone towards Kieran. He nods.

I decide to give him further proof that I'm not always running off on wild goose chases with the intent of getting into danger and leaving him widowed in his old age. 'Ronan Brady offered me a big case today,' I say.

He lowers his fork. 'What is it this time? Sex traffickers, gangland feuds, Russian spies? Which?'

'A horse.'

'Chance Your Arm? Ronan wants you to chase down the gang who stole him?' He's very alarmed, but at the same time, his lack of incredulity is flattering. He clearly doesn't think it's weird that I'd be selected by the second-highest-ranking police officer in Ireland to crack this notorious case.

'Well, he's having a nightmare managing Duckie, who's making such a pig's ear of the whole thing, so he asked if I'd step in. But...' I leave a beat, then say triumphantly, 'But I said no.'

'You said no? To Ronan Brady?' Instead of being relieved, he raises an eyebrow.

'What's that supposed to mean?' I ask, prickly again.

'Just that you don't usually say no to him,' he answers.

'Well, he is my boss, so I doubt people often refuse their employers when they ask them to do something?' I'm so disappointed. I hoped he would be happy or grateful or something that I turned down a big investigation like that, considering he says he's so worried about me all the time.

'Signoria Mags, Signor Kieran...'

'Oh, hi, Luigi.' I smile as the restaurant owner himself delivers our food.

'I heard Dora is in hospital,' he leans down to say quietly as he places our plates in front of us. News travels fast in Ballycarrick.

I nod. 'Hopefully it's nothing too serious.'

'I'll just say a prayer that it all goes well with her.'

'It's all we can do.'

'It is, Mags, and she'll be in a lot of prayers tonight.'

'So,' I say to my husband as Luigi retreats, 'I relinquished my big chance of being famous on television to Zoë.'

For some reason he laughs. 'Oh yeah, I forgot to tell you,' he says. 'I saw Zoë a couple of days ago. She told me I was looking a bit slimmer, which I was delighted about, but then she went on to tell me that I was probably burning fat at a higher metabolic rate than anyone else because of spending so much time at higher altitudes.'

My indignation with him subsides, and I laugh as well. This sounds like classic Zoë.

'I said I think that only matters over two thousand feet and not at twenty or thirty feet, but she wasn't having it. She claims that the best thing for health is to stay up high.'

'She's got some crackpot notions, that girl, no doubt about it, but hopefully somehow it will work with this investigation. She certainly thinks outside the box.'

We move on to talking about the kids and the various things we have to do, like ordering a Black Forest log from Teresa's to take to Orla's on Saturday, but we eat in silence mostly. Despite our best efforts, something is not right with us. He's upset by the fight with his mother, I know, and I'm upset by feeling old and what I feel is his attempt to consign me to the scrap heap. My meal is nice, but I don't taste it. I only drink half a glass of wine, and for the first time ever, I want to just go home.

'Are you cross with me?' he asks eventually.

'No,' I answer, and I'm not. I know it's because he loves me that he hates the idea of me being in danger, and when I got shot, and admittedly it was the hand of God I didn't die that time, he took it very hard. And then there was the fire...

'So what's up?'

I think about it. What is up? I need to get it straight in my head and explain, rather than just going around a bit depressed and expecting him to understand why.

'OK, I suppose I'm a bit annoyed that I turn down a big chance, and I thought you'd be happy that I wasn't putting myself in danger or whatever by taking on the Chance Your Arm case, but you didn't seem to care except to say I never say no to Ronan Brady.'

He sighs. 'OK, fair enough. He's your boss, I get it. But I... Look, Mags, I'm not the jealous type, you know that, but I just know he feels something about you over and above work. And I know you've never done anything or said anything to encourage that, but I still don't like it, so I'm a bit ratty when his name is mentioned, OK?'

He's not wrong. I am not exactly the *femme fatale* type, but Ronan is a deep person. He's got a lot of pain – he never really got over his wife's death from breast cancer – and he finds me easy to talk to, I know.

'Fair enough,' I say, and he seems surprised. 'No, I mean it. I know you weren't interested in Róisín Duggan either, but it was still annoying to feel everyone was talking about her and you last year. But Kieran, the relationship I have with Ronan, it's just work, I swear to you.'

He reaches over and holds my hand again. 'I know, love. It's him that winds me up, and then I feel bad because he's never done or said anything to bug me, but he just does.'

I squeeze his hand back. 'I get it.'

We go back to eating, and I should feel better because we've talked things through, but I still feel down.

'Is there something else bothering you?' he asks after a while.

'No, I think I'm just tired.'

'Is it because of your lungs?'

And once more I feel like he's pushing me to retire, and it really annoys me. 'Look, I know you hate me being a guard...'

He's hurt. 'That's not fair, Mags. I don't hate it. I hate that you're in danger, and come on, let's face it, you get yourself into more dangerous situations than your average cop. You must admit that much at least?'

'I've been a bit unlucky once or twice, yeah, but I'm grand, can't you see that?'

'If you call a gunshot wound that missed your heart by inches and scarring to your lungs that will never fully repair grand, then yeah, I suppose you are,' he says. 'And for God's sake, Mags, don't try and pretend you said no to Ronan for my sake. You know and I know it's just because you couldn't stand the idea of working with Duckie.'

I push my plate aside without saying anything. I want to say he's being really unfair, that I was doing it for him, but if I'm honest, he's kind of right, and that makes it all the more annoying.

'Finished?' he says, looking at my half-empty plate.

'Like I said, I'm tired.'

He calls Luigi and we pay the bill, though he hasn't finished his meal either and half of the wine is still in the bottle.

Luigi puts a cork in it and gives it to us, concern on his face.

'Thanks, Luigi,' Kieran says, walking out in front of me, leaving me to follow him.

CHAPTER 11

I say I will collect the girls from Mam's new house, and Kieran says he'll head home. He's left his van there, and it's only a twenty-minute walk.

I set off for Mam's, collecting my car at the station.

Before they got married, Mam and Joe lived over their respective shops, but rather than move into one or the other, they decided to buy a new house together. It is in the new development out the Limerick road, and it is really nice, bright and sunny and with plenty of room. I'm delighted Mam has such a lovely home now. The old one was always cluttered and a bit higgledy-piggledy because it was so small, so this clear, calm place is wonderful.

Mam immediately sees there's something wrong when I arrive alone, and she sends Joe to play forty-fives with the girls. They're a pair of card sharps now; he's taught them all his tricks.

'What's up?' she asks, putting the kettle on. She's dressed in smart cream linen trousers and an emerald-green jumper, and her short silver-and-blond hair is in perfect shape and condition. I don't know how she does it, but Mam always looks so well put together. Sometimes I wonder how I'm her daughter at all.

'I don't know. Things are a bit off with Kieran is all.'

'Why so? Did you have a row or something?' She puts two cups with saucers on the kitchen table and offers me a slice of coffee cake from her famous tin that has always had home baking in it as long as I can remember.

I shake my head. 'Just the tea, Mam. I'm not hungry.'

She looks worried as she closes the tin. Being not hungry is not usually a good enough reason for me to refuse her cake.

'Well?' she prompts again as she fills the teapot from the kettle and brings it over.

'No, not a row exactly. He's just... I don't know...' I try to think what I'm really annoyed with him about. It's not Ronan; we cleared the air on that. 'He's been talking about retirement.'

'For him or for you?'

'For both. Wojtec is going to be in a position to buy the roofing business next year for an amount of money that will set us up for life, and he says it means we can both retire early.'

'And you don't want to?'

'Of course I don't want to. I've years to go yet.'

'But he's insisting even though you don't want to?'

'Well, no. I said no, so he dropped it, but I can feel he still wants me to.'

'And you won't even consider it?'

'No!' I'm incredulous my mother would even ask me such a thing.

'So he was just saying you could go now if you liked and then left it?' Her question is mild, but I know where it's going. Did I overreact to a perfectly plausible and rational suggestion? My mother knows me well, better than anyone in fact, and I am inclined to dig my heels in if I think I'm being pushed.

'He keeps going on about my lungs...'

'Which we know were damaged by being exposed to toxic smoke in the line of duty, despite you always saying your work is nothing but dog licences and bald tyres, and laughing at us for worrying about you. Even after you got shot by a bullet that missed your heart by inches.'

'Oh, that's how it is, is it? You're on his side too?' I'm hurt and upset now.

She pours me a cup of tea and one for herself. 'No, there are no sides in this, Mags love, only that you'd make it so. But sometimes we can't see what's good for us and we need to rely on people we love and trust to tell us. I should know.'

I know she's referring to the fact that I was years trying to get her to give up the shop, and it took a heart attack and marriage to Joe Dillon, her old friend, to make it happen.

'You were in your seventies to be fair, not fifty-two.'

'Yes, but I was not well and neither are you, pet. I can hear your laboured breathing and how you rely on the inhaler, and I know you had a good recovery, but there is damage done, long-lasting damage.'

So even my mother thinks I'm old. 'I was back at the consultant last month, and he said he was impressed at my healing...'

'He didn't say you were healed, though. You know yourself you're still not able to climb the stairs without puffing, and before you say it's because you're not fit or something, we both know it's since the fire.'

I'm getting really annoyed with Mam now. 'Fine, you're right, I rely on an inhaler most days, but so do lots of people of all ages, and it's not a reason to give up my job and sit in a rocking chair waiting to die.'

'But that's the point, love. Kieran doesn't want you to die. He wants you to be around forever because he loves you so much.'

'And if he loves me, surely he wants me to be happy, and being a guard makes me happy.' I know I sound sulky. I sip my tea.

'He knows that too,' she says. 'So do I.'

'But you agree with him.' A statement not a question.

'I think you should give it some serious thought.' She sips her own tea, and a silence hangs between us.

'I don't feel retirement age, Mam, nothing close to it. In my head I'm –'

'Twenty-five?' She chuckles. 'That's the thing about getting old, love. Your body does it, but your brain stays the same. I'm about thirty, but the mirror and the doctor and the tablets I have to take every morning would suggest otherwise.'

'Mam, you only retired last year. And you were ready to do it.'

'I know that, love, but your circumstances are different. You'll have your full pension, and the money from Kieran's business. It's not as if he thinks you should pack it all in this week – he's just asking you if you want to do the full term.'

'I think he'd love nothing better than for me to pack it all in this week,' I say with a sigh. 'He's like a bag of cats anyway since the bust-up with Nora. He's as prickly about that as I am about this. I daren't say a word about it.'

'Then don't. Don't give it any thought, love. Don't engage at all would be my advice. An unfed fire can't burn, so if you want it all to die down, just don't fuel it.'

My mother would give the Dalai Lama a run for his money on wisdom.

'I know. He was just defending me, and I'm grateful. And I know plenty of people like Nora – they see everything as a fight for supremacy. Any olive branch would be seen as weakness. He gives in, she wins with a cackle. But the alternative is to live in this stupid feud state that's upsetting everyone, and I can't bear it, the family being torn apart all over something to do with me.'

My mother reaches over to squeeze my hand, and I'm ten again, and I know I need her advice even if I don't want it.

'It's not just to do with you, my love. It's all sorts of things that have gone on since long before you ever came on the scene. Nora Munroe was always and ever a cantankerous old snob. She has her own demons, God love her, and is, I think, deeply unhappy for reasons we'll never fully understand. I don't even know if she understands, but it all comes from childhood, I'm convinced.'

She opens the cake tin again and gives us both a slice of the coffee cake, and this time I don't refuse.

'When it comes to life, I've noticed this. On account of me being officially ancient, you understand.' She winks and I smile. 'You can get over a broken heart, a terrible friend, a sibling rivalry, even an abusive father, but there is one relationship that if it's broken, it's very hard to recover from, maybe even impossible, and that is if your mother rejects you. It doesn't matter the reason. The person who gave you life is supposed to love you unconditionally – it's the rule of the animal kingdom, of everything. So if that's not the case, then a person goes through the world with a profound sense that they are somehow unlovable, if even their own mother can't love them.'

'And you think Nora feels that?'

She shrugs. 'I don't know, but to rear her children to believe her parents were dead when they weren't, to have had her mother throw her out when she got pregnant, it doesn't suggest a warm relationship, does it?'

'I suppose not.'

'It doesn't excuse her behaviour, but it might help to explain it. Happy people don't go through this life hurting others. They have no reason to. And it's a testament to her and Kevin that their children all turned out so well.'

'Don't we all know it,' I say wryly. The shrine of photos, medals, trophies and certificates on every spare inch of wall in the Munroe house is evidence of the exceptionalism of Nora's offspring.

Mam sighs and nods. 'She's broken, Mags, and I doubt there's much hope of repair at this stage. If finding Ollie and him being fine and her family embracing him didn't fix her, then nothing will. She's got her own path to walk, and all the troubles she has, like us all, are her own to manage. Misery loves company, so my advice is to stay out of it, because I honestly believe, love, this fight is about more than just the way she speaks to you. It's between Kieran and his mother, and it's been a long time coming. He's had too many years of her nonsense. You can't fix this for him, love.'

Loud protests come from the next room. Joe has won all the money back from the girls, which makes us smile. He doesn't deliberately let them win ever – bad training, he says – so they know if they do win money from him, they've truly done it themselves.

'I suppose you're right about Nora, Mam. But…'

'But?' she asks gently as she tops up my cup.

'The retirement thing… It just all feels a bit like…it's all going too fast, you know? Ellie is sixteen. Two more years and she'll be going off to university or whatever she decides, then Kate behind her. And it makes me feel so… I'm feeling like I'm on a ride that's speeding up and I want to get off.'

She nods, setting the teapot back down. 'I remember that feeling when I was your age. I think it's menopause too. Your fertile years are behind you, your kids are growing up and moving on, and there's a sense of loss there definitely. It's a bit like puberty in reverse, I think. Everything is blossoming in puberty while –'

'It's all dying and falling down at my age,' I interject mournfully.

'Well, something is, and that's normal to feel its loss. But Mags, another whole phase is about to open up, something exciting. Yes, it's sad the girls won't live at home forever, but imagine not having to worry about who was being dropped and collected here and there? Or deciding you're not hungry so you won't bother making a dinner? And all of this freedom against the background of knowing you raised two beautiful young women who are out there making their own way in the world?'

I try to imagine the house without them and can't.

'And you and I are every bit as close as when you lived at home. Relationships, good ones, don't disappear, but they do change and we have to let them. And as for work, I know you love it and you're so good at it, but you've been a guard since you were twenty-one. There must be other things you'd like to do? Maybe let the next while be your time to dream it up?'

I give a small laugh. 'You sound like Zoë now.'

'She might be daft as the crows, that girl, but not all of it is nonsense, you know,' Mam says sagely. 'Look at me. You can't keep me at home these days. Sure aren't Joe and myself going on a painting trip to Florence soon? And before I retired, I'd hardly go to Galway for the day. But I love to travel, and I would never have known that if I hadn't retired.'

'I can't see myself and Kieran painting in Florence, Mam.' I sigh. 'He's threatening to spend all his time playing the pipes.'

'Grand, the pipes for him then, but for you it might be something else – golf, cooking, bridge…'

The look on my face says it all, clearly.

She laughs. 'Well, maybe not them either, but Mags, there is more to life than being a guard, even a very good one. It's what you do, not who you are. And there's more to life than loading the dishwasher and making school lunches too. But in order to find that other thing, you have to allow the space for it to happen.'

'I suppose you're right,' I concede. 'I'm just scared, I think, like Kieran and I have a great life and a great marriage, but we don't see each other all day and we have our own lives.'

'And you will continue to have your own lives. I see too much of that, men usually, retiring and deciding their wife is now to be their sole playmate, when she's had her own things going on for years while he was at work.'

More protests from the card game waft through from the sitting room as Mam closes the cake tin and clears away the plates and cups. 'Did I tell you about Liz McSweeney?'

'No, what about her?' I can feel a story coming on. Liz is a friend of Mam's; they are both expert seamstresses.

'Well, you know she's been making curtains since God was a child, brilliant at it she is. She's just done that abbey out towards Castlebar, the new five-star hotel. They brought the damask in from Syria, would you believe, it cost a fortune. And anyway, she made them all, stunning.'

I nod. Liz McSweeney's curtains are legendary. She has a waiting list of years.

'Well, she built that business up from scratch, making curtains in her dining room before she built on the workshop, and the money reared her family, it put all five of hers through college, the whole shebang. And so then two months ago, her husband, Johnny, you know him? Bit of a know-it-all, if truth be told. Anyway, he retires from the Office of Public Works and decides he's going to help her in her business, the one she's run without his so-called help for thirty years.' Mam's voice rises in indignation at this outrage. 'So last

Tuesday she's fitting Lavinia Moran's new curtains, and on comes my man Johnny with her, and he standing there, hands in his pockets as she's hanging the curtains, and he's saying, "I don't know, Liz, maybe they're a bit high? Maybe bring them down a few inches." The barefaced cheek of it!'

I laugh at Mam's righteous resentment in her friend's defence. She's big on women entrepreneurs and told Sharon not to let Trevor, nice and all as he is, next nor near the boutique.

'She nearly blew a gasket. She called into me afterwards, and she said, "Marie, don't mind the kettle. Pour me a glass of wine before I put these talented, hard-working hands around Johnny McSweeney's neck and squeeze till he's blue."'

'That would drive you to drink right enough,' I agree.

'Ah, the neck of him, thinking he had a clue about curtains, and he spending his entire career showing tourists around the old fort. What would he know about curtains? Nothing, that's what.'

We chat easily for another few minutes, she's getting a bunion from her new dancing shoes so she's going to Limerick to a special podiatrist that all the dancers go to, and I tell her about a lime and ginger dessert I had in Castle Dysert, and then I round up the girls. As we leave, I hug her tightly. 'Nobody can talk me off a ledge like you can,' I whisper in her ear.

'That's what mammies are for, love.' She hugs me back.

CHAPTER 12

I switch my engine off in the car park of the Galway Garda Station and steel myself. It's nine thirty in the morning, and I have a meeting.

Zoë and Duckie will be there, as well as an equine forensics expert brought in from the United Arab Emirates, a representative of the Minister for Tourism, Culture, Arts, Gaeltacht, Sport and the Islands – who decided that big mouthful was a portfolio? – and two people from the Irish Horse Board.

After the short meeting yesterday, where he briefed Zoë and Duckie together, Ronan is staying out of this as much as he can. That's the only reason I'm here – not to be involved, just to observe and report back to him. Duckie will hate it, but Ronan asked me to go to this one, and it wasn't in a 'Mags, could you do me a big favour?' kind of way, more a request being the polite wrapping on an order. So here I am.

Ronan says the minister is having a hairy canary over the loss of Chance Your Arm, and the owner is threatening all sorts if the animal isn't found. It looks terrible for the Irish Horse Board, who actively promote Ireland as a top-notch training location for the best of the best when it comes to bloodstock, so they're driven demented as well.

Apparently Duckie tried to object to the Garda Commissioner, Ronan's boss, when he was told Zoë was coming on board, but the Garda Commissioner merely pointed out in no uncertain terms that if he'd found the horse in the first place, it wouldn't be necessary, and that Garda O'Donoghue is, according to her superior officer, very astute and also has a proficiency in social media surveillance that DI Cassidy lacks.

I walk in and catch the eye of Tim O'Halloran, a detective who knows Duckie of old.

'Good luck.' He winks at me, and I know he's thanking his lucky stars this missing horse has nothing to do with him.

In the meeting room, everyone is assembled but not yet seated. Duckie has moved a big office chair into the room for him to sit on at the head of the table, presumably so he's on a throne and the rest of us are just on ordinary chairs.

Zoë gives me a little wave and makes an excited face, which looks unprofessional, but at this stage, I suppose that hardly matters. Everyone gathered is tense and stressed except for Zoë.

Duckie ignores me completely – he knows well who Zoë's superior officer is – and calls the meeting to order.

The woman from the UAE, the forensic scientist Farah Sadiq, is wary as her dark eyes dart from person to person. She is dressed in a hijab, and I remember Ronan telling me that she is the daughter of someone 'very high up in the government', as Nora might say, as well as a cousin of Aziz Al Mabrouk, a wealthy horse trainer from Abu Dhabi.

The man and woman from the Horse Board, Pauline Cross and Donnchadh de Bruin, both in their forties, I would guess, are expressionless but clearly not happy. He wears a Rolex, and she has that ultra-polished sheen – very expensive charcoal suit with a baby-blue silk top, diamonds at her throat and ears.

The Minister for Sport, Des Finane, isn't here, but he has sent a representative, Barry Dowling. He is in his sixties, overweight, with a puffy face; he's sweating and looks unwell.

Duckie does a quick introduction, and when he comes to Farah

Sadiq, he winces as he introduces her, as if having to try to pronounce her name is a source of pain to him. It comes out as 'Sarah Saddy', which everyone notices. I cringe. I can't believe he's still on this investigation, whatever the optics Ronan was talking about.

He tries to get the screen in the room to work to show something but fails. Abandoning it with a guffaw and a 'We don't need technology, we just need good policework', he rambles on, aggrandising himself and his role in the investigation so far, glossing over his misidentification of the dead horse. To hear him you would think he just did it to throw the thieves off the scent, that anything else the newspapers are saying is fake news and in reality we are seconds away from finding the animal, which of course we are not. He's totally lost the room. De Bruin from the IHB checks his Rolex, and Farah Sadiq is scrolling on her iPhone.

As Duckie drones on about having so many useful leads – which means he has nothing useful, just a bunch of tips from the sort of people who think the earth is flat – Zoë stands up and cuts across him. I suppress a smile. This is so against everything we believe about the chain of command, but I admire her, and nobody else can stop this old windbag.

'Sorry, DI Cassidy, but if I could just show everyone what I think might work?'

All eyes go to her. She's dressed in civvies, jeans and a white jumper, and her caramel-coloured hair is in two French plaits, making her look about seventeen when she is, in fact, twenty-four. She wears no make-up, but Zoë is more into skincare than make-up. Women painting their faces to please men, another sign of the patriarchy, is her take on a bit of mascara.

Duckie is incensed to be interrupted, but Farah Sadiq cuts in, 'Please do.' The inference clearly being that anything is better than listening to Duckie.

'Well, everyone in the whole country was very interested in Chance Your Arm at first, but that kind of died off after DI Duckie thought he'd found him. It's not Duckie's fault – he needs the attention because he didn't get enough skin-to-skin with his mother when he was a baby…'

I glance at Duckie, who's gone a violent shade of purple. Everyone else is not sure what they just heard.

'Anyway, after it was just an ordinary dead horse, people got sort of Chance Your Arm–weary, like they get weary of stuff they think isn't going to work out, like you know, wars that go on too long. So I thought if I made a TikTok video, showing what Chance Your Arm looks like, a funny one so it will go viral, then everyone will get interested again, and this time they'll know what to watch out for as opposed to just the gardaí knowing, so it will make life very tricky for whoever has him.'

It seems a sensible idea to me, and I'm intrigued by what she's going to come up with.

She opens her laptop and picks up a small remote control. Instantly a video file on pause appears on the screen that Duckie was unable to work.

'Now for context I have to explain something that happened a few years ago to anyone not from Ireland. There's a TV show here called *Father Ted*, and it's a hilarious sitcom about three priests who live on an island called Craggy Island. It's one of the funniest shows I've ever seen. In one episode Father Ted and Father Dougal entered the Eurovision Song Contest with a song called 'My Lovely Horse'. They made a video and everything. Eurovision is traditionally very sparkly and over the top, and the song was a mad jingly thing about fetlocks blowing in the wind that just poked fun at the whole song contest. Anyway, the song, 'My Lovely Horse', was a huge comedy hit and everyone was singing it. She points to the screen,

'The still image here is of Father Ted, a middle-aged priest in a black shirt, clerical collar and a sequinned baby-blue jacket, and Father Dougal, a gormless thirty-year-old who looks like a choir boy and doesn't quite grasp most things, also in priestly attire and a sequinned jacket. In between the two priests is not the horse of the 'My Lovely Horse' video but an image of Chance Your Arm.'

She presses play. The intro is the opening bars of the familiar to everyone song and the two priests, and then it cuts to Zoë standing in the yard of the old stables at Ballycarrick Castle.

'Ladies and gentlemen, boys and girls, all genders and none, as you'll know from the news, the showjumper Chance Your Arm has disappeared. Despite extensive investigation, the gardaí are drawing a blank when it comes to locating this lovely horse. Can you help us?'

The image fades to several photos of Chance Your Arm, a chestnut stallion with a white star on his forehead. Zoë's voice continues.

'The marvellous thing about Chance Your Arm is he has the most amazing blue eyes. Blue is a rare colour in a horse's eyes, but we are fortunate in that Chance Your Arm has this distinctive feature. And while the white star can be dyed brown, his eyes will remain blue. We don't believe at this stage he's been taken from the island, so we need you, the people of Ireland, to help us find him.'

The video cuts back to Zoë in the stable yard again.

'We need to return Chance Your Arm to his owners. We need to show the world that Ireland is a wonderful, safe place for horses. So please keep your eyes peeled for a blue-eyed horse. If you find him, or even think you know where he might be, then call me, Zoë, at Ballycarrick Garda Station, County Galway.'

The station's phone number appears across the bottom of the screen, and the outro fades into another few bars of 'My Lovely Horse', only this time the voices are singing 'my blue-eyed horse' instead. I think it's Darren and Michael, though they're making a great job of imitating Father Ted and Father Dougal. And we get a sight of Chance Your Arm jumping a clear round at the World Equestrian Festival in Aachen in June.

As it ends, everyone is silent. And I can't tell if it's in awe or horror. I don't even know myself. She is suggesting the members of the public call her, Zoë, and she's drawn this whole thing down on my station. We don't do things like this. I mean, we appeal to the public for help all the time, but in a sober way that indicates we are taking the crime seriously. Duckie looks like he's going to combust.

De Bruin passes verdict. 'That's genius.'

'Can you make this TikTok go viral?' Farah Sadiq asks.

'Well, that would need to be discussed at management level, and frankly I don't think –' Duckie splutters.

Zoë cuts in. 'Well, I put it up last night and it's had' – she pulls up her phone and checks something – 'four hundred thousand views already, so I think it will.'

My heart sinks. She really made a solo run here, something that's out of the question within the force.

'This is exactly what we need.' Barry Dowling appears relieved for the first time.

'If everyone in Ireland is on the lookout for Chance Your Arm, it will make it harder for whoever has anything to do with him,' agrees Farah Sadiq.

'Except kill him,' Duckie interjects, hating being upstaged.

'Well, Detective Inspector Cassidy,' Pauline Cross replies acidly – she has no time for Duckie, you can tell – 'I think you should be grateful to Garda O'Donoghue for saving the day after you managed to make people lose interest in the whole business. We need public cooperation in cases like this, and Garda O'Donoghue's idea makes a lot of sense. It's funny and it will – it already has – captured the public's attention, so I think it's a stroke of genius.'

'Did we always know the horse had blue eyes, DI Cassidy?' asks de Bruin.

Duckie mutters something into his chest, but Zoë says brightly, 'We did. I read all the notes, and it was in the first briefing.'

'A pity for whatever reason it didn't filter through as something useful.' I hear the frustration in Barry Dowling's voice. 'There's a lot of money at stake here.' He means this by way of support, but Zoë turns to him most seriously.

'And the well-being of a sentient creature, Mr Dowling, that's the most important thing. I'm a vegan –'

'Of course you are,' Duckie mutters, more audibly this time.

'– and I abhor so-called sports that exploit animals. I'm trying to find Chance Your Arm because he was taken against his will away from his environment, and I am very fearful for what this will do to his attachment. Human attachment theory would suggest secure attachment means the child is confident in the care of their caregiver and secure in the knowledge that they will not be abandoned. Lack of secure attachment leads to self-destructive behaviour.' She throws a pitying glance at Duckie. 'So if it is the same for horses...' She turns to Farah. 'Is it the same, Madam Sadiq?' She pronounces Sadiq perfectly.

Farah Sadiq appraises her coolly, considering the question, and I wonder if she thinks Zoë is a genius or a bit unhinged. It's a question everyone who knows her asks themselves from time to time. Well, all the time actually.

She decides to take the question seriously. 'It depends. Some are, some are not particularly attached. Some horses will bond easily with others, in a matter of a day or two, but in the case of Chance Your Arm, he is a highly strung, emotionally needy animal. I can imagine that this situation is extremely stressful for him, and it will certainly affect his behaviour.'

'So that's why we must return him to his familiar surroundings and those he loves and trusts.'

I'm not sure that's the motivation of the gathering, but nobody objects. They don't care why Zoë wants to find him; they just care that she does. She got no Garda approval for this, and she should be reprimanded by rights, but if this works, then nobody will say a cross word to her.

CHAPTER 13

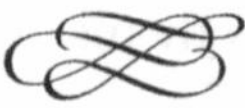

I ring Ronan from the Galway Garda Station car park to report on the meeting, and I'm laughing so hard, I have to use my inhaler. He's bewildered at first, especially by the skin-to-skin thing, but he gets up the viral video on his desk computer and loves it.

He chuckles. 'They'll want Garda O'Donoghue on TV next.'

'On your own head be it. She's a great person and a fine officer, but she's a bit of a loose cannon in terms of saying what she thinks…'

'Yeah, I remember, but for some reason she doesn't offend. She's entirely guileless.'

'I'm not sure it's innocence, it's hard to tell, but either way she feels very strongly about things and is not shy about making her point, so an interview about the horse could easily turn into a TED Talk on the patriarchy, veganism, animal testing of cosmetics, over-fishing, naked shamans… She's got a lot of thoughts about a lot of things that may not exactly reflect the Garda viewpoint,' I warn.

'Hmm, well, it's going to be out of our hands. It is already. It's at' – there's a pause as he checks – '750,000 views already. They're bound to want to interview her on the morning shows.'

'Well, everyone except Duckie was delighted with it, so let's hope it yields some results.'

'Indeed. Thanks, Mags. You and your officers never cease to amaze me. Right then…'

'Ronan?' I say, before he has the chance to ring off.

'Yes, Mags?'

'If Zoë finds Chance Your Arm, will we get an extra officer, do you think?'

He laughs. He knows what I'm talking about. 'We'll see, we'll see.' But he goes off the line without promising anything.

* * *

Before driving back to Ballycarrick, I drop into the hospital to see Dora.

Darren has updated me that the CT scan found a shadow in her lung, but the hospital says it could easily be an abscess and only a biopsy will tell if it's malignant, so we are all praying for a good result. Jerome isn't leaving her side apparently, only if someone else he trusts is there. Delia stayed all last night but has gone home to sleep, so maybe if I pop in now, he'll take the chance to go out for a cigarette and a walk in the garden or get something to eat.

I find out from reception which ward she is in, and once there, I ask the nurse sitting at the desk for Dora's room number.

'Is it the husband ye're after?' she asks knowingly, registering my Garda uniform. 'He'd put the heart crossways in ya all right.' And I realise she assumes I've come to arrest Jerome for some crime and that she's more relieved than horrified by this.

'No, though he's a friend of mine, and so is Dora McGovern, which is why I've brought her these flowers,' I say, staring her down, daring her to make another derogatory comment. I give her the small bunch of roses in my hand. 'And I'd appreciate it if you could pop them in a vase with some water and bring them down to her.'

She looks abashed, but not much, and takes the roses and puts them aside, like she will when she's ready but is not going to be told to jump up for the sake of some Traveller woman by anybody. 'Room 4,' she snaps. 'She's in a private one so her visitors don't disturb anyone –

her sons are a bit loud. But it's only the husband at the moment, he won't leave ever, so if you don't mind him, you can go in.'

I walk back down the corridor and knock gently on the closed door. Jerome opens it.

He's wearing the usual black trousers and black shirt, but the leather jacket is on the back of a chair and the shirt is a new one, I can see; the creases from the packaging are still in it. Delia must have bought it for him. He's always clean-shaven, but now there's a day or two of stubble on his face and his eyes are tired.

'Mags, how are ya?' he asks.

'I'm grand. I thought I'd pop in to see Dora.' I smile, and he gestures towards the bed. I walk over.

It's a shock. She's different from the last time I saw her, at the wedding, hardly a month ago. She was never a big woman, and she always seemed even smaller next to her bear of a husband, but she looks so much tinier now. Even in the single bed, she's like a child, and her pink pyjamas are much too loose on her. Her hair is long, as all Traveller women's hair is – no Traveller woman would cut their crowning glory – but it is limp and grey and tied up in a ponytail, and her skin is almost translucent on her temples.

Seeing me, she removes the oxygen mask from her face. 'Hello… Sergeant…Munroe,' she whispers.

'Hi, Dora, and will you ever call me Mags, in the name of God,' I tease her. Dora refuses to ever use my first name, though everyone else does.

She shakes her head with a little smile.

'How are you doing?' I ask, sitting down on the plastic chair beside her.

'All right… But…I want…to go…home.' Talking is hard for her; even uttering one word seems to make her breathless.

'You will soon, Dora,' I say, and I hope I'm right. 'But you need the medical care right now.'

She just shakes her head again, then places the mask over her face and breathes.

Jerome shows no sign of taking the opportunity of my presence to pop out for a cigarette or anything, and I wonder if I should go. I'm close to Jerome and Delia, but Dora is very much a Traveller woman and has an inherent mistrust of people like me, which is no doubt why he doesn't want to leave me alone with her.

As I'm thinking this, she takes the mask down again and turns her head to look at her husband. 'Go…eat.'

He's nonplussed and objects. 'I'm grand. I had a bar.'

Again she shakes her head. 'Not…chocolate. Food. Sandwich. Café.'

'I'll go down to the café when Delia comes in, I promise.'

'Now. While…Mags…is here.' She's finally done it; she's finally called me Mags instead of Sergeant Munroe. Maybe it's just to save her breath, but it means a lot to me.

'Yes, go on Jerome,' I say. 'Dora's right, you'd eat nothing but biscuits and chocolate bars off the trolley if you were left, so take this chance to go and get something proper into you.'

'But…'

'Jerome…go…' breathes Dora.

So he does, reluctantly, taking his leather coat and saying he won't be more than ten minutes, and I stay sitting by the bed, not sure what to do, wondering if I should make conversation or just let Dora rest.

'Mind Jerome…and Delia…for me.'

I look at her, startled. 'Dora, you'll be home to mind them yourself soon enough.'

But she shakes her head once more, very slowly, left to right, the effort to do so visibly sapping her energy.

'Don't…Mags,' she says. She's used my first name again. Maybe this is the way it will be from now on. 'Don't…say…that. Because…I… know. Kathleen…knows.'

Dora's sister Kathleen has the sight, or so the Travellers believe. I wonder if she's told Dora she's dying, or if Dora has just seen it on her face. Either way my first instinct is to insist that whatever Kathleen has seen in the tea leaves or cards or whatever, that everything is OK, that there's no need to assume the worst, the doctors say it's probably just an abscess…

Then I remember again how it made me want to scream when people denied to my face that my father was dying when I knew differently.

'I don't know what you know, Dora, but if anything...well, anything bad happens, I will look after them, Dora, I promise. I'll look after them both, and the boys.'

'Boys...grand...'

I nod. I know what she means. The McGovern boys, Gerard, Paddy and Pecker, are younger than Delia and run with a tribe of cousins and second cousins. And with Jerome overseeing them to make sure the antics don't get too out of hand, they'll be fine. They'll marry Traveller girls in due course and be subsumed into their wives' families.

'You're right, they will be,' I say.

'Delia...'

'Delia will be fine as well. Darren is a good man, and he loves her so much. But I'll keep a close eye all the same.'

She closes her eyes to rest after the effort of speaking. 'Jerome... he...he doesn't...know...'

'I won't say anything about this conversation to him, Dora.'

She smiles with her eyes still closed, and she stays like that for so long, I think she's sleeping, but then she opens them again. 'Take care of...Jerome...'

'Jerome will be fine, Dora. If he loses you, he will be very sad for a long time – he'll be lost without you is the truth. We all know who rules the roost in your house.' I'm rewarded with a hint of a smile. 'But he has Delia and the lads and all the family, and more than that, he is very well liked and respected in Ballycarrick, so everyone will want to help him. And I will too.'

She nods, a slight gesture, and she reaches over with her thin small hand and places it on mine. It's the first time I think Dora and I have ever touched. 'Thanks...Mags.'

She replaces the mask before shutting her eyes once more and falling asleep. I adjust the mask to a better position on her face and bend and kiss her forehead.

'God bless, Dora,' I whisper.

A few minutes later, Jerome is back, and I put my finger to my lips and creep out.

* * *

ON THE DRIVE HOME, I pray that Dora is wrong and the hospital will find nothing more than an abscess, which is serious of course – it's obviously making her very ill – but surely they can treat it. I'm glad I had that conversation with her, though; it seemed to ease her mind.

I know both times I thought I was dying – the first time after being shot and then again as the toxic smoke rose around me in the Lodge – the only thing I could think of was Kieran and the girls and hope they would be OK without me.

I love my family so much, just as Dora loves hers.

As I'm on the road already, I go home to make a sandwich for my lunch and find Kieran has done the same thing. He's constructed a doorstopper, ham, coleslaw, cheese, onion, stuffing and relish and when I come into the kitchen, he glances at me, wordlessly makes another, leaving out the stuffing and onion as he knows I don't like them, and pushes it over to me on a plate, while I boil the kettle and make a big mug of tea.

'You want another cup?' I ask, breaking the silence.

He shakes his head; he's got most of his pint mug left. He goes to sit at the table by himself.

I remain standing at the counter, feeling very flat. Life is too short to have this distance between us. I don't like it. Maybe I am overreacting about the retirement thing. To be fair, like Mam said, he didn't demand I give up work; he just said it was an option to think about. And it's hard for him about Nora, and Mam's right about that as well. It's not just about me.

I need to have a proper talk with my husband. I need to explain how I feel instead of just telling him I'm tired.

He was working late on a job last night, and I was asleep when he got in. And he was gone early this morning too. He is meeting someone from the diocese later today about the church roof, and he's going to a traditional music thing tonight, so though this isn't the ideal time, with both of us on the way out again any minute, it will have to do.

'Kieran, can we talk?' I say, and he glances up from his sandwich, which he's finishing off while scrolling on his phone.

'We are talking?' he says warily, after chewing and swallowing. He often says 'we need to talk' is the most terrifying thing a woman can say to a man.

'I know, but just about the thing the other night, in Luigi's,' I say tentatively.

'OK…' he says, putting his phone on the table and taking the last bite of his sandwich. Both dogs are sitting watching him avidly, hoping for a bit of crust. I make a mental note that we should really stop feeding Princess scraps; she's getting very rotund, though Rollo is as lean as ever.

I bring my own half-eaten sandwich and tea over to the table. 'Well, I just think I might have overreacted, and I'm sorry for that. But I want you to understand why I got so upset.'

'And why did you?' he asks.

'Well, I was annoyed at you for saying that thing about me never saying no to Ronan Brady.'

'I thought I explained –'

'I know, but it's not that, Kieran. The thing is…' I try to gather my thoughts and be honest with myself as well as with him. 'Look, I know not wanting to work with Duckie was part of it, but that wasn't the whole story. I've turned down lots of chances and offers of promotion so as not to be too busy for you and the girls. And yes, I know that's my choice, but I've made it with you and them in mind. It's part of the reason your mother is so awful to me, because I'm not "high up" enough that she can be bragging about me.'

He holds his hands up as if warding off an attack. 'Mags, I don't care about you not being high up –'

'Kieran, wait, I'm not accusing you of that.'

He drops his hands but still he's tense.

I have another think. 'I know I'm always saying how unimportant and lowly my job is, and I'm always telling people I make a living checking for bald tyres, but sometimes it is important.'

He looks agonised. 'I know it is, but I can't help worrying when you get into danger.'

I shake my head. He's missing the point again, but that's not his fault. I think I've missed the point myself for a long time, downplaying the way I feel about my job, the one I've stuck with year after year, refusing all those promotions. That's one reason Nora thinks my work is so worthless – I've played into that narrative – and maybe that's why Kieran didn't realise how important my job is to me. And to be honest, how important I am to the job, though I don't like to say it normally.

'I know that, and I promise I'm not angry with you for worrying about me. But it's not the dangerous stuff I'm talking about. It's the day-to-day stuff, the way I've stopped young kids like Caelan Cronin going off the rails, the way I've protected the Drumlish halting site, how I've saved women from domestic violence. I haven't gone mad enforcing the law. I've listened to people, and made allowances, and I've rescued a lot of people from doing things they'd regret for the rest of their lives. I really want you to see that, and not talk about me retiring like all I've been doing is a couple of hours a week ironing for someone for pocket money and it's not a real career.'

He's bewildered. 'I honestly didn't mean it like that. It's just I love you, Mags, and I wanted us to be off having fun together.'

'I know. I get it, I really do. I just needed to explain what's been in my mind. And now the last thing.'

He steels himself. 'Go on…'

'Your mother.'

'No, Mags.' He shakes his head. 'No way. I meant what I said that day, and I'm fine with my decision. And don't tell me you miss being dragged up there to be insulted. I've had enough of her and her crap. I've listened to it for decades, and no more.'

Now it's my turn to raise my hands in defence. 'Calm down…'

He laughs. It's a running joke of ours, that nobody in the history of human interaction ever calmed down on demand. 'OK, but I'm not apologising to her.'

'I'm not asking you to,' I say, and I channel Mam. 'It's between you and your mother, and I suppose it's a long time coming. And it's about more than just the way she speaks to me – it's lots of things. So it's up to you what you're prepared to put up with. I just want to see how you are doing on the whole thing. You hate fighting with people, so I just want to check and make sure you're OK.'

He stands and draws me up beside him, puts his arms around me and kisses me in a way we don't do if the girls are around because they claim it's so gross to see. I kiss him back, and it doesn't feel one bit gross. It's lovely, and who needs to rush back to work? He's his own boss, and the station is fully staffed apart from Delia.

His eyebrows raise in question. I nod – suddenly I'm not tired any more – and he leads me upstairs.

Everything is fine with us again, and we're both relieved. We don't like it when we're at odds.

The only fly – or should I say lizard – in the ointment is that when we roll apart, Knickers is eyeballing us from the top of the wardrobe.

CHAPTER 14

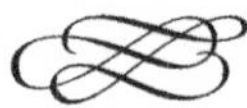

On Friday morning I meet Conor outside the Old Ground Hotel in Ennis, and as we begin the walk to the charity shop, he tells me of how the paparazzi are becoming insistent. They hired a helicopter yesterday to fly over the castle. There's a retractable awning over the rooftop spa, and it was closed against the rain.

I can sympathise, to a small extent.

As Ronan predicted, Zoë's TikTok appeal has gained so much traction that all of the news outlets are covering it.

Kate and Ellie say they're like celebrities in school because everyone is singing 'My Blue-Eyed Horse' and is impressed my girls are on first-name terms with Zoë. Kate has to keep repeating the story about how Zoë saved her from 'my dad's mad girlfriend' when Róisín nearly broke Kate's nose. Not the sort of story I'd prefer her to be telling around the town, but it seems her friends think it's great.

The most annoying thing is, a handful of reporters seem to be under the impression that the hunt for Chance Your Arm is somehow to do with Ballycarrick Garda Station and have camped outside, and they yell questions about the case at us as we go in and out.

Of course the hassle we're getting from the press is a small fry compared to being buzzed by a helicopter jammed with hacks.

'I'm glad she has you and Castle Dysert to protect her from that.'

'Honestly those photographers will stop at nothing. We found one climbing a drainpipe – he could have killed himself. I don't get the obsession with celebrity and never will.'

'You're no stranger to the camera yourself, though, are you?'

There was a TV show a while ago called *Grandma Says We're Irish* about people finding their Irish roots, and Conor featured heavily in it, as did Castle Dysert. It did really well and was aired in Ireland as well as in the States.

'None of that was my choice.' He bristles, a bit embarrassed. 'We had a terrible flood – the sea rose and broke the tide wall – and the damage was so extensive, I was struggling to come up with a way to pay for the repairs. They came along with this idea, and I had to take it – the money was too good to turn down. But it was a nightmare.'

I can see why they wanted him to present the programme, though. Something about Conor, the candid way he speaks, is endearing. He looks polished, as someone in his position would, but beneath the expensive clothes and the expertly cut hair, there is a lovely ordinariness to him. He is just a normal person, albeit a drop-dead-gorgeous one.

'Well, you came across very well. And how you handled some of those people, you have the patience of a saint is all I'll say.'

He laughs. 'You get used to that after a while. Between the hotel and the tours, I've had my fair share of difficult people.'

'I'd say you get a few oddballs all right.' I'm thinking his job and mine are not that far apart. It's all about troubleshooting. The difficult cases constitute maybe two percent of the population – most people are great – but those few can cause a lot of havoc.

'I could write a book.' He says, 'we had a wedding here a while back, and the mother of the groom, I think it was, she was a complete nightmare, kept ringing us to "tweak", as she called it, things that the couple had arranged. She monopolised the photographer all day, ensuring she was in every shot. She was rude to the staff, and her poor husband was so embarrassed, though he never said a word. And to cap it all, she even wore white…' He pales then and blushes.

'It was my mother-in-law, wasn't it?' I say, chuckling.

'Ah no…it was…' Conor is horrified at his gaffe.

'It's OK. I call her my monster-in-law. She's a nightmare. Gearoid nearly choked her before the day was out.'

'Is there a point to insisting it was a different nightmare mother-in-law?' he asks with a wince as we pass a small church.

I smile. 'None. She's a one-off.'

'Please, Mags, don't repeat what I said to Kieran. I can't believe I was so… It's not like me. And I know Ollie well, so it was just a –'

'Conor, if I had a euro for every time I put my foot in it, I would not be earning a living checking for bald tyres,' I reassure him, slipping into the usual way I talk about my job. 'Relax, it's grand. She'd test the patience of a saint. I can well imagine she's the worst.'

'Thanks.' He's still discomfited.

'Do you miss doing the tours?' I ask, to distract him from his mistake.

He cheers up a bit. 'Funnily enough I don't, but I loved the job when I was doing it. I couldn't have imagined doing anything else, but then I met Ana and we got married and had the kids, and being away all the time was awful, more for her than for me but for me too… Eddie!'

With a smile of pleasure, Conor stops to shake hands with a small round priest who has just come out of the parish house beside the church.

'Eddie, this is a friend of mine, Sergeant Mags Munroe from Ballycarrick. Mags, this is Father Eddie, scratch golfer and local parish priest.' Conor winks at me.

'In that order?' Eddie is mock hurt. 'Don't mind him, Mags, and it's nice to meet you. Is it Ned Doyle who is still in Ballycarrick?'

'It is,' I say. 'Poor man should have been retired years ago. He'll be eighty-four next month, and he's gone very frail.'

Eddie sighs. 'I must call up to see him.' He doesn't seem surprised at all that his colleague is still working so late in life; it is the same everywhere. 'The last time I met him, he was telling me about the roof of the church being in a diabolical condition. Only for some local man going up there every second week to patch it up, the whole thing would be down on their heads. Ned was full of praise for him.'

'That local man is my husband,' I say with a smile, and again I wonder what will happen to poor Father Doyle when Kieran retires. 'And he met with someone from the diocese the other day to see what can be done, because it so badly needs to be replaced.'

'Any luck?'

'Not really. They told him if Father Doyle raised fifty thousand of the hundred needed, they'd match it, but in the last ten years, there's only ten thousand gone into the Ballycarrick church roof fund. It's going to take another ninety years at that rate.'

Kieran had been extremely annoyed. He said it was just a way of the diocese sounding generous while being sure they didn't have to put their hand in their pocket, but I don't say that because...well, Eddie is a priest.

'Well, let's hope it happens. I'll say a prayer for him and the roof. What's his name?' Eddie asks.

'Kieran, Kieran Munroe.' I'm not sure what good a small chubby priest can do about Kieran and the church roof, which is threatening to haunt his retirement, but it seems churlish not to be grateful. 'Thanks.'

'Come here to me, Conor – your Joe shot an eighty-two last week?' Eddie is impressed. 'He made a four with me and Robert and Dan O'Herlihy.'

'He did. Sure what is it, only ground hurling?' Conor laughs, but I can see the pride there.

'And a fine hurler he is too. Will he be called up, do you think?'

To play for your county in the sport of hurling or Gaelic football in the All-Ireland Championship is the greatest honour in Ireland and one bestowed on few. To be a county hurler or footballer, especially for counties that excel like Clare does at hurling, is a passport to legend status and a shoo-in to any walk of life in this country.

Conor shrugs. 'Hard to say. He was minor last year, but he's still a bit young. He might be, but we'll have to wait and see.'

'They'd be foolish to leave him out, and we facing Cork in the first round.'

'Well, that's going to be a tricky one for me then, Eddie.' Conor smiles. 'I'm a Rebel first and foremost.' There's a trace of Cork in his accent, the rebel county as its known, and people take their county loyalty very seriously when it comes to such matters.

'Ara, not at all. There's enough of those Rebels below in Cork to shout louder than we can. Up the Banner!' He raises his fists in victory for Clare, the Banner County.

'I'll give you a shout later in the week, but we better get on now,' Conor says, clapping Eddie on the shoulder as we walk on.

We find the charity shop, and the window display is of a beach scene, with piles of sand, buckets and spades and a striped deckchair. On the mannequins are summer dresses and shorts. It looks cheerful and welcoming, but I see Conor take note that it's run in support of a women's aid shelter and wonder if he's thinking what I've been thinking since I found out someone called Charlotte Whelan, aka Searlait ní Faoileann, is raising money in aid of Sonas.

He pushes the door open and holds it for me.

The shop is bright but has that smell that all charity shops have. Whoever runs it has decided to coordinate it by colour, so there are racks of red clothing, racks of purple and so on. Preloved shoes are on every shelf and stand, and a big basket with a variety of handbags stands in the centre. There are bookshelves in the back corner filled with paperbacks and some CDs, long gone beyond use. I remember when people bought records, and then CDs were the modern thing, and now they're gone too.

On the opposite corner is a children's section with books and toys and children's clothes. An Indian woman dressed in a flame orange sari with two boisterous little boys smiles at us as she tries to get one of them to fit on a coat.

A few other people are browsing, and the woman at the till, head lowered over a list of some kind, is our person, I'm sure of it. She's tall, and her bare arms are toned. Her hair is longer than in the photo Sienna showed us, but she has a lot of piercings. Ears several times, nose. She's wearing a vest top that skims her navel, which is also pierced, and camouflage-pattern cargo trousers. On her feet are those heavy army-style boots.

'Charlotte?' I say, and she looks up from her work with a smile.

'Yes?'

I'm not wearing my uniform, just jeans and a plain sweatshirt, my hair tied back in a ponytail, but I introduce myself as Sergeant Mags Munroe from Ballycarrick because people hate if they reveal things to you and later find out you're a guard.

Her smile fades. 'What... How can I help?' She is trying not to panic.

'Don't worry, nothing is wrong,' I hasten to reassure her. 'I'm here with Conor O'Shea...' I turn to him, and he steps forwards.

'Hi, Charlotte,' he says, and it's lovely to see the way she relaxes when he speaks to her. He really is good at this, and I'm glad Kieran made me text him that night in Luigi's.

'So what can I do for you?'

'I wonder if we could have a chat about something, nothing bad, but if we could talk in private? It's to do with someone staying at my hotel, Castle Dysert?'

A shadow crosses her face when he mentions the hotel. She must have seen in the papers and on social media who is staying there.

'I don't want to see anybody,' she says. 'I don't want –'

'Nobody except us knows you're here, Charlotte, and we're not intending to tell anyone either,' I say. 'But if we can have a moment of your time, I'd like to explain, and then you can make up your own mind what to do.'

She looks at me and then at Conor for several long seconds, and finally decides to trust us a little, just for now. With her gaze still on us, she calls through a door into the back, 'Mariola, can you leave the steamer and come out here and keep an eye for a while? I need to go upstairs.'

'Of course, Charlotte.' A dark-haired woman with an Eastern European accent emerges, giving Conor an admiring glance as she takes up her position behind the till.

Charlotte beckons us in behind, past the black bin bags of donations, through the room where Mariola has been working with a steamer on some donated clothes, and then through another door to a staircase.

'I live upstairs. We can talk up there.'

She goes up first, and Conor and I follow her.

Upstairs, the little flat is home to her and a young child, you can see at a glance by the coats hanging up and the box of Duplo bricks on the table along with some coloured crayons and pencils.

There's a little kitchenette in the corner and a table with two dining chairs, and the rest of the room is a sitting space, with a TV against the left-hand wall, opposite a small squashy orange couch. There are two doors, one presumably to the bathroom and the other to a single bedroom, which mother and daughter must share. It's a long way from the lifestyle she must have had with Tony Black and his billionaire daughter, Sienna. I think about Sienna talking about wanting to pull her little sister up.

'Have a seat?' she offers, and Conor and I sit on the couch while she pulls over a dining chair.

'So what do you want with me?' she asks, with a hint of belligerence. 'I don't have long. I have to collect my daughter from nursery.'

'First, I don't want to waste your time, so I'd like to make certain you are who I think you are and not a different Charlotte Whelan,' I say.

'Why do you want to know who I am?' She's definitely belligerent now.

'Not for any bad reason,' Conor says then, in his deep, soothing voice, 'a guest in my hotel knew someone that went by your name in the United States, and if that's you, they'd like to make contact, that's all.'

'Who is your friend?' she asks, not turning her suspicious gaze on Conor but keeping it on me.

'I'd rather not say,' I reply, 'until we can establish if you are the person our friend knows. It's tricky, because they're trying to keep a low profile as well. Did you live in the US for a time? And do you have a daughter called Phoebe?'

'Is it Tony Black?' she asks then. She's gone pale and looks…well, it's hard to say, but she's not overjoyed, put it that way.

Conor and I exchange a glance. We have the right woman for sure. 'His daughter.' I say.

'Oh.' Her face softens. 'Sienna… Is she well?'

'She certainly seems to be.'

'Did you tell her you'd found me?' She's alarmed again.

'No, as I said, we've told nobody, only Conor and I know. He introduced me to Sienna because she wanted professional help finding you without letting her father know she was looking for you.'

'Ah, that's good.' She lets out a ragged breath. 'Does that mean she understands now why I had to leave?'

I glance at Conor again. 'Mm…I don't think she does, not from what she said to us. What she wants is to know if Phoebe is OK. She says she wants to help her sister, financially, I suppose, even if you don't want to see her? But she really does love Phoebe and she says she loves you too, though she doesn't understand why you left?'

'Oh, poor Sienna.' She puts her elbows on her knees and her head in her hands. 'I did try to get her to see it, how he controls her every move, her money, everything. He tried to do the same to me, controlling my social media, cutting me off from my friends, all in the name of protecting Phoebe. But he didn't care about Phoebe. He hated if I gave her any attention. He wanted me to leave her alone when she cried, said she needed discipline if she wanted to be like Sienna. He was starting to control her as well, trying to break the bond I had with her as her mother, encouraging her only to listen to him – she was only a toddler! I had to go. It took time – I had to hide money from him to make my escape. I asked Sienna to come with me, but she just couldn't imagine life without her father. He's like a god to her. He's taught her to think he rescued her from foster care, when it was his fault she was there in the first place. It was only when she started to get noticed…' Her anxiety and anger are palpable; she is shaking.

She's clearly been the victim of coercive control, which is a crime in Ireland.

I say gently, 'We won't tell her we found you if you don't want us to?'

'Oh God. I don't know.' Her gaze darts about, as if she feels trapped. 'If there was some sort of way we could communicate without Tony knowing? But I don't know if that's possible? I daren't let him get his hands on Phoebe, and I suppose as her father, he has legal rights. I don't know how I'd fight him with all that money behind him.'

'And he is Phoebe's father?' I ask carefully, remembering what Sienna said.

She stares at me. 'I'm sorry?'

For a moment I'm not sure whether to tell her this, but Sienna believes it and if they're going to communicate, I need to warn her. 'He told Sienna that you left because Phoebe… That she wasn't… Well, he said you told him she wasn't his child.'

'Oh.' She looks wounded. 'How could he say… How could he even think that? I had no friends. I was never out of his sight. Sienna needs to know that's not true. That's so cruel, for her to think Phoebe isn't her real sister…'

'Sienna has never stopped thinking of Phoebe as her real sister,' I assure her. 'But of course it's better if she knows the full truth, so if you want to get a message to her…' I shoot Conor a glance, wondering if he'd be prepared to act as some sort of go-between while Sienna is still in Ireland, which is for another week at least – her three concerts are on Thursday, Friday and Saturday of next week, the last one being the one my girls will be watching livestreamed in the community hall.

He sits forwards. 'Charlotte, your business is your own, and as Mags said, we won't say anything if you don't want us to. But – and I'm not saying you should, it's up to you – but if you want to write Sienna a letter or card or something, I will give it to her without anyone else knowing, and then if you both want, I can bring a letter back to you from Sienna as well?'

Her face lights up with relief; the defensive belligerence is gone. 'Oh, would you... Please, that's wonderful... Oh...do I have a pen? I can use one of Phoebe's pencils...'

Conor passes her a black and gold ball point pen from his inside jacket pocket – it has 'Castle Dysert' written up the side – and she takes a sheet of Phoebe's drawing paper and uses a book of fairy tales to rest it on while she writes a paragraph or so, then she folds the paper and gives it with a grateful half-smile to Conor. 'I need to go to pick her up now,' she says as we all stand. 'I'd like to write more – will you explain I didn't have the time? And I know you know this, but Tony will suspect something if... Well, he's just very tuned in to the slightest thing. He's a bad person, you can't believe it. I know it's hard to imagine when he can be so charming, but... I've wanted to explain to Sienna since I left, but she refuses to believe anything bad about Tony. He's careful to behave himself around her, but she's seen and heard some things, and now that she's older, she might believe it. I haven't said where I am, so even if she does tell him, he won't know where to find me...'

With the same pen Conor scribbles something on the back of an embossed white business card. 'That's my private mobile number and email on the back,' he says, giving it to her. 'Anything else you want to say, you can send a document to my email, which I'll print out and give to her without reading it. I promise you he won't hear a word about this from me. And neither Mags nor I will reveal where you are, I assure you of that. Just text me when it's sent so I know it's there.'

'Thank you, Conor.' She is tearful. 'And thank you so much, Sergeant. When I escaped from him, I was terrified and broken, but I'm not that person now. Sonas helped me, and Sienna needs at least the chance to get away from him. If she doesn't take it, then that's her choice, but I have to offer it to her.'

* * *

CONOR and I are back in the meeting room at Castle Dysert with Sienna Black, sitting in those strange chairs that force you to lean backwards. Her copper curls still spring from her head, and she's had her fringe cut again since I saw her last. Today she's wearing black denim dungarees, five sizes too big, with a silver thing underneath that looks for all the world like chain mail.

And she's crying quietly as she reads Charlotte's letter.

'Why would Dad say that about Phoebe if it wasn't true? That's so cruel… Do you think it's not true?' She appeals to us, as if we're people she can trust, and I feel I have to tell her the truth, though she may not like it. I believe what Charlotte has told us, but victims of coercive control often mistake the constant monitoring of their movements and relationships for love, when in fact it's nothing to do with love.

'Charlotte said your father controlled everything she was doing, her finances as well – she had to hide money to be able to run away – and that he was starting to do the same thing to Phoebe as well, taking her over, stopping Charlotte from comforting Phoebe when she cried, trying to break the bond between them.'

'Yeah, well, but…' Sienna's face shows she knows what I'm talking about; but it makes her uncomfortable. 'He said it was for Phoebe's own good, that Charlotte was spoiling her, that it was only because he loved her so much…' I can tell by her expression that in her heart she knows differently; it's just so hard for her to admit it to herself.

'He didn't love Phoebe enough not to make up lies about who her father was,' says Conor, a little forcefully. It's clear that he doesn't like Tony Black, and Sienna casts him a scared glance and then looks towards the door. And I don't think it's Conor she's afraid of – it's her father.

'He's been so good to me, though, my dad,' she says. She's torn. 'Managing everything I couldn't do for myself, all my social media and tour dates and finances…' Again her voice wavers and trails off. It's like she knows the truth but doesn't want to face it. 'The accountant, his name was Michael Defoe, I really liked him. He was so nice. And he said something about when I reach eighteen, he could help me set up my own bank account, but Dad said…' She stops for a long moment, and it clearly costs her a huge psychological effort to say the next bit. 'He said I wasn't to talk to Michael any more, and he sacked him, and then Dad told me I shouldn't trust anyone, that nobody is trustworthy around that amount of money, not unless they really, really love you like he does me.'

We sit in silence for a while, and I think it's a good idea to leave space for Sienna to hear what she's just said.

After more than a minute, Conor says, 'If you would like to write back to Charlotte without using your phone, I can get you some hotel notepaper and a pen for that. And also for anyone else you wish to write to.'

Again, that scared glance. 'Anyone else? I don't know anyone else.'

'Well,' he says gently, 'how about Michael Defoe? You said he was nice. And you can use my email if you prefer.' He shows his phone. 'I have it here, and you can write and send a message without…well…'

'Without my father knowing,' she says, again with that nervous glance towards the door.

'Maybe you do need to hear what Michael has to say about having your own bank account,' I suggest.

She sits for a while longer, thinking. Then she says, 'I would like to write back to Charlotte, Conor, and if I can use your phone to email Michael, that would be very kind. I don't know his email address, but he works for a big firm back home called Defoe, Shropshire and Leibowitz. I think they're based in New York.'

'I'll find it for you,' says Conor. 'And I'll deliver your letter to Charlotte.'

She says in a rush, 'But you know, Dad's been so good to me. He's given up so much for me, and he worked so hard to get me back so he could help me with my music…'

Again her voice tails off, and we three sit a while in silence. And I remember what Charlotte said, that Tony Black only developed an interest in his daughter after she showed signs of becoming famous.

With a shake of her head, she stands. I get to my feet as well, and she puts out her hand to shake mine.

'Sergeant Munroe, you did what I asked you to do, and I'm sorry I don't have a way to pay you. So I was wondering, would you like to take your daughters to Saturday's show in Dublin? It's the last one of the three, the one that's going to be livestreamed?'

'Oh, wow, my two would absolutely love that,' I say immediately. 'Thank you.' It's not my idea of a good time, but I put my best face on being consigned for a whole evening to the company of eighty thousand screaming teenaged girls in Croke Park, Ireland's biggest stadium. Not every present can be a free lobster dinner and a night away in Castle Dysert, I suppose. 'I really appreciate it, Sienna.'

Normally I couldn't accept something like this – it would be a conflict of interest – but I did this investigation as a favour to Conor, not in my role as a guard, and besides, it would be an experience of a lifetime for my girls.

'No problem. If you give Conor your email, I'll send you three QR codes later today. Just show them as you go in, and once you get to the main stadium, someone will direct you to one of the corporate boxes. I'll arrange for some merch for them too.'

'Thank you so much, that's so kind.' I'm relieved by the idea of a box; maybe the concert will be more bearable this way.

She waves her hand as if it's nothing.

We all leave the room together, and as we do, Tony Black comes down the corridor. A dark shadow crosses his face when he sees it's me again.

'Sienna, sweetheart, your masseuse is looking for you...' He puts his arm around her as he stares at me, and though he is smiling, there is no warmth in his brown eyes.

'Oh, shoot, yeah, I forgot. Thanks, Sergeant Munroe, that move is really useful. She was just showing me some self-defence moves, Dad, just in case any crazy fan or pap comes for me. And thanks for showing me the spa, Conor.' She hands him Charlotte's letter, folded, which she still has in her hand, and smiles up at her father. 'I was a bit worried about going up to the roof, Dad, after the helicopter, but Conor reminded me the awning over the spa is one-way glass and no one can see down through it – did you know that?'

'I don't want you using it whatever anyone tells you. It's too risky,' he says, and there's an edge to his voice. 'Now come on, you know you were complaining about tightness around your shoulder. You have to be in perfect condition for these concerts.'

'Yes, Dad.' She trips up the corridor with him to be massaged, and I feel so sorry for her, but at the same time, what a life. I'm impressed at Charlotte Whelan for walking away from such wealth, and I wonder if Sienna will ever have the courage to challenge her father.

Conor offers me lunch, but I tell him I can't stay; I've to collect Ellie, and we're going to watch Kate play camogie. Ballycarrick Under 14s qualified for the county final and the boys didn't, much to the delight of my daughters, who are fed up of women's sports being usurped by men's, and it's this afternoon straight after school, so I need to be back in time.

'Well, after this is all over, I'd like to invite you and your husband for a long weekend here.' He smiles. 'Spa and everything.'

'Conor, no, you've already done enough...'

He raises a hand, palm forwards, to stop my protests. 'I'll be emailing you the voucher, Mags, and don't pretend you won't need a good relaxing rest after taking the girls to a Sienna Black concert.'

I groan. 'Oh God, did it show on my face?'

'Not at all, but it wouldn't be my idea of a good time either. Thank God Lily is too young for things like that.' He laughs as he walks me out to my car and waves me off.

CHAPTER 15

I'm listening to Sienna Black in the car as I draw up outside Ellie's school; I'm mentally preparing myself.

You ain't got the balls for that,
you ain't got the call for that.
My life is my own,
my crib, my car, my phone.
I ain't askin' you for nothing, bruh,
'cause I can fend all on my own...

I'll give her this, Longfellow she isn't, but there is something catchy about her music, a combination of rapping and hip-hop, and the message is clear. Girls don't need boys, women don't need men, she can earn her own money and make her own decisions. Fair enough.

As I'm waiting for Ellie to appear, my phone buzzes. It's a text from Kieran. *G&E approved for fostering. They're over the moon.*

I text back. *Brilliant. See you later after the match. Have news as well.*

'Oh, I love this one. I tried to make a TikTok of it, but I couldn't really get it...' says Ellie as she climbs into the car.

I can't wait to tell her that she's going to the concert, but I want to do it with her and Kate together, so I ask, 'Are you making that

TikTok with Kate we talked about?' I think she is, because Kate is so much happier these days and they keep disappearing into Ellie's bedroom together and they've lost another of Kieran's chargers already and were very defensive of each other about it.

'Yeah, we're working on it. It's Kate's idea, a version of her "Scared but Standing Tall" track. Kate has some killer dance moves, like a mixture of Irish and hip-hop. She's so athletic, unlike me. But she taught me to follow her, and I think it's coming together. We're going to sing it in a mixture of English and Irish. Kate's really sure we'll get loads of likes, so I hope for her sake we do.'

'You'd like that too, wouldn't you?'

'Yeah…' She gazes wistfully out the window. 'We're having a Sienna Black karaoke at the community hall party, before the Sienna Black livestream, so we might try it out there first.'

'Sounds fun.' I'm wondering why she's so listless; she's usually more engaged than this.

'Yeah, I suppose…'

'You're not tiring of Sienna Black, are you?' I hope not; that would be a disaster.

She looks shocked. 'No way! No. And I know next Saturday will be the best fun, and the concert tickets were way too dear, but, well, I was so jealous today. Clodagh Dunlea just got her birthday present from her grandmother in Dublin today, and she's going on the Saturday night. She wouldn't stop going on about it today in school, and she was all like' – Ellie puts on her poshest Galway voice – 'I'm sure the livestream party will be lovely, but it's just not the same as being there in *person*, I mean, the *atmosphere…*'

'Ah, don't mind her, she's just trying to wind you up. Don't give in to her.'

I can just imagine Clodagh lording it over everyone like that. Her mother, Pamela was in my class at school, and a bigger show-off you couldn't meet. I remember her bragging about going to Romania on holidays when the rest of us were lucky to get a day to the seaside. Of course as an adult, I realised they went there during the reign of Nicolae Ceausescu, so what on earth the McLoughlins were doing in

Romania while a despotic dictator was in charge, I'll never know. But it sounded very flashy in 1982 to us who had never been anywhere.

'I know...but she's such a pain, Mam, she really is.' It's very unlike Ellie to get upset by something like that, but I hear a quiver in her voice and think there's something deeper going on here.

'Is everything OK apart from that, Ellie?' I ask. She was bullied once before by her so-called best friend Jess, who was only using Ellie to do her homework.

'Ah yeah, she's just bugging me, and...well, she said she was kissing Carrot at Sally McGann's birthday two weeks ago, and she knows I like him...'

Ah, so that's the problem. 'And was he kissing her back?' The perfidy of men and boys.

'Yes, and she just keeps rubbing my nose in it, and I just...I can't stand her...'

I need to tread very carefully here. Ellie tells me very little about the love life situation, so I don't want to blow it. 'And did you and Carrot have...' I just stop myself saying 'an understanding'. Wake up, Mags, it's not the 1950s.

'We're not exclusive. Like, well...I sort of am...but he's...' A fat tear rolls down her cheek.

'He's not,' I finish for her.

'No, and Clodagh wasn't just kissing him. She said they were talking about setting up a hip-hop band, and he knows I love hip-hop but he never said anything about it to me...'

Poor Ellie. The feckless Carrot is clearly breaking her heart. And I know I'm being the protective mama bear here, but honestly he's not worth her tears, if you saw the state of this kid. Ellie's so gorgeous, bright and bubbly, and he's like a long drink of water, not a pick on him, long hair hanging over his face. He might seem all dark and brooding, and I know that's catnip to teenage girls, but it's all a pose.

'Well, ask yourself, what would Sienna Black tell you to do about him?' I say with a smile.

Ellie laughs. 'Throw him in the trash, like last night's pizza, nice in the moment, but you don't need him to complete ya...' she raps, quoting a Sienna lyric.

'Exactly. So my advice is, channel Sienna.'

'I suppose.' She sighs, and she doesn't sound completely convinced.

* * *

KATE IS IN GOAL, and the winning shot gets past her, so she's gutted. One of the trainers, a father of one of the girls, lets out a roar of frustration at her, which is understandable but harsh, and she takes it personally, so both my girls are very subdued on the drive home. It's part of life, but it's hard to see them battered by the waves of fortune.

I still don't mention the concert. I'd like them to be in a better frame of mind before I do the big reveal.

Kieran is piping in the kitchen when we get in, and though usually they claim to love the sound of him playing, they just glower at him as they slope in, so he puts the pipes aside.

'Well, this is a lovely sight to behold, I must say,' he says, observing their two morose faces. 'What's up?'

'I hate men,' Ellie says.

Kate nods vigorously. 'I don't hate *all* men, but Christy Coughlan was so mean to me. I let a goal in, and it's not like I did it on purpose, and I saved around four attempts, but he was roaring at me anyway.'

Kieran casts a glance at me to see if this is something serious or not. I give a small shake of the head.

I turn the heat on under the veggie curry I made last night and get out two microwave pouches of rice. I know it's cheaper and better and all the rest to boil rice from scratch, but those little pouches are a godsend.

Over dinner Kieran gently gets it out of them. He tells Kate that Christy's reaction was involuntary, men can't help it, and reminds her how he roars at the TV when the hurling or the rugby is on. And he offers to drop something heavy from a height on Carrot if Ellie wants him to.

'I don't want you to kill him,' she says sadly, 'just all the other girls.

It's not just Clodagh. He met Justine Livingstone on the bus coming back from the ploughing, and Cat said he was with Eabha Healy after the county final.'

He stands up, goes around the table and pulls her into a big bear hug. 'You're worth fifty Carrots, a hundred Carrots, and don't you bother your head with some eejit who can't see that. You deserve a lad who can't see any other girl in the whole world, only you...'

'If you say like you and Mam, I'm putting myself up for adoption,' Kate warns him, finishing her curry.

'Well, I won't say it, but...'

'La-la-la-la-la-la!' They both put their hands up to their ears and sing tunelessly, and we are soon all laughing. Rollo bounds around yapping, and Princess regards us disdainfully from her cushion by the door. No wonder she's getting fat; she's become very lazy.

'I hope you'll be in better voice next Saturday than you are now, girls,' I say mildly.

'For Orla's barbecue?' Kate asks. 'Why? You're not going to make us sing at that, are you?'

'No, I don't mean tomorrow at Orla's, I mean the following Saturday. I thought we'd take a trip up to Dublin...'

Ellie is scrolling on her phone. 'No, we can't go to Dublin that Saturday, Mam. We have the livestream party of Sienna Black's concert in the community hall.'

'Ah well, if you prefer the livestream to the real thing, then OK.'

'Ha, ha, yeah, course we do,' Ellie says, still scrolling.

'Well, that's a shame, because I met Sienna Black today and she offered us tickets for the Saturday night show.'

'You did, yeah...' She is dismissive.

Kate gazes at me, though, her big blue eyes wide. 'Ellie,' she says slowly, 'I don't think she's messing.'

Ellie looks up then, her face comical. 'Say that again?'

'I met Sienna Black earlier, and she offered me three tickets for Saturday night in Dublin, and special passes so we can watch it from a corporate box.'

'You *met* Sienna Black?' Ellie is not taking it in at all.

'I did.' I'm enjoying this.

'Where?'

'Castle Dysert,' I answer nonchalantly, like it's no big deal.

'Mam, don't be playing with us now... Did you really?' Kate is teetering between hope and terror.

'I did, I swear. I met her, and she's lovely, and I said you were fans, and she asked would you like to come as her guests, and I said you probably would, and...'

The screaming can be heard four fields away.

The dogs go demented, Kieran and I have our hands over our ears, and Knickers flees into the laundry room and crouches on top of Meatloaf's cage, while the huge smelly guinea pig glumly munches his cabbage stalks and pays no attention to anything as usual.

* * *

THE BARBECUE at Orla's is a really happy affair, completely different from the fraught Sunday lunches we have to endure at Kieran's parents.

The girls are still on a mad high about Sienna Black, and Evie is so sweet; she's delighted for them. Gearoid and Enrico appear with their future foster son, and Fionn is gorgeous, with jet-black hair and bright blue eyes and a shy but endearing smile.

He's a bit overwhelmed by the three girls, who are excited enough as it is and descend on him with screeches and hugs, but luckily the geeky Tom is there to save him. The two boys slink off with plates piled high with chicken wings, smoky ribs and potato salad to play computer games in the shed, a purpose-built room with screens and a pool table and exercise equipment, which Orla and Fergus have had built at the bottom of their huge, beautifully tended garden. It looks nothing like a shed.

Fergus and Kieran have a long chat about how to invest his money from when he sells his business, and I secretly admit that sometimes it is quite useful to have someone 'high up in the bank' in the family, despite Nora being so snobby about it.

Enrico helps Kate and Ellie polish up their Sienna Black TikTok dance, while Evie is an enthusiastic audience. From where I'm sitting, it's really good. Kate sings and raps in English, while Ellie follows on in Irish, which suits her natural vibrato, and their dance is a clever mixture of Irish dancing and hip-hop.

On the deckchairs next to mine, Gearoid gets advice from Orla about having a teenage son, while I sit relaxing with my head tilted back, my face to the sun, listening to them all chatting and laughing. I am so enjoying this gathering.

Nobody has mentioned Nora at all, but both Orla and Fergus are much more relaxed than usual. Orla has never *not* been nice to me – we've always had a friendly and polite relationship – but she seems warmer towards me today, like she's decided to take off a mask she's been wearing for years. She's always pretended not to notice how horrible Nora is to me, and I'm not expecting her to stop seeing her mother, but maybe it's a relief for her not to have to pretend any more that there isn't a problem.

My phone buzzes, and I pull it out of my pocket. It's a text from Delia.

OK to talk?

In ordinary times I might text back to say I'm busy with family and will call her later. But these aren't ordinary times. Dora is in hospital. I get up and walk away into a quiet corner of the enormous garden, the phone to my ear.

'Hello, Delia?'

There are a few gasps at the far end, and when she manages to speak, her voice is choked. 'The biopsy came back yesterday, and it was a tumour. They were going to operate today, but this morning they did a bone scan, and now they say the cancer is so widespread there's nothing to be done, just keeping her comfortable is all they can do. They say she has two months at the most.'

Oh no, that was far too quick, God love them. A profound feeling of sadness washes over me. 'I'm so sorry, Delia…'

'And Sarge, I don't know what to do.' She sounds so young and scared. She's such a capable guard, I forget sometimes she's still only twenty-two. 'Mam keeps saying she wants to come home, but she needs oxygen all the time now and palliative care, and the nurses here say that can't be done in the caravan. It's not safe – I don't know why. So they say she has to stay in hospital, but she hates it here so much. She says she feels trapped, like she's in a concrete box, and she thinks they don't like her. They act scared of Jerome and the boys and keep talking about her having too many visitors, but our family is so big…'

Poor Delia. I was hoping her presence would stop that sort of thing happening, but of course in the hospital she's not wearing her Garda uniform, and despite her career and her experience, she can still exude that mixture of resentment and fear of authority, like all Travellers, which doesn't help.

'What about the new hospice, Delia? I've heard it's lovely there, lovely and bright and airy and lots of greenery around, nothing like a hospital?' I've never had reason to visit it, but I've heard Catriona's husband, Seamus, the cardiologist in Galway hospital, saying how good it is.

'I don't know. No one said anything about that,' she replies despairingly.

'Mm…' I don't want to make assumptions, but you have to work with reality, and I can just imagine the likes of the nurse I met on Dora's ward thinking the quiet, peaceful, beautifully appointed hospice is no place to send a Traveller woman, with her noisy, dangerous family. 'Leave it with me, Delia,' I say. 'I'll try and find out for you.'

'Thanks, Sarge…' She sounds choked again as she goes off the phone.

As soon as she's gone, I scroll through my mobile and dial a number I very rarely use. It is answered on the second ring.

'Hello, Seamus Linehan speaking.'

'Seamus, hi, it's Mags. I hope I'm not bothering you at work?' Seamus is married to Kieran's sister Catriona, and we've never seen much of him, even when we were having Sunday lunches with Nora. He's the leading cardiologist in the west of Ireland and always incredibly busy.

'I'm at the hospital, but it's fine. What can I do for you?'

I like Seamus, he's a decent man. But he does not do small talk. At all.

'I want to ask a favour of you if I can,' I say.

'Fire away.'

'There's a patient in the hospital, Dora McGovern. She's a Traveller woman, and a friend of mine, and she is dying of cancer. They say she has two months at the most.'

'Sorry to hear that, Mags.'

'The thing is, she's very unhappy in the hospital – she feels very confined. But they don't want to provide palliative care on a Traveller site, and no one has mentioned the hospice to her. So I wonder if you could look into it and just make sure that she...well, that she and her family are getting all the support they need, the same as anyone else might?'

He doesn't ask me what I mean by that. He just says, 'Her name's Dora McGovern?'

'That's right.'

I hear scratching of pen on paper.

'I'll do that.'

'Thanks, Seamus, I appreciate it.'

'No problem, Mags. Bye.'

The exchange has taken less than a minute, but I'll put my house on the fact that he will do as he says. And if I know him, he will make it clear the McGoverns are to be treated like anyone else. I can't do much for them, but I'm glad I can do this.

I go back to my deckchair in the sun, and I'm relieved everyone else is still deep in conversation or practising dance steps, because I need a few quiet minutes to absorb what I've just been told.

Poor Dora. And poor Jerome. What will he do without her? Death is a natural part of life, it's one of the few guarantees, but it feels so wrong when it comes for someone we love. A person is there one day, a huge part of your life, and just gone the next, never to be seen again on this earth. It's so deeply unsettling and so very sad.

My phone rings, startling me out of my reverie, and though only five minutes have passed, it's Seamus.

'Mags, hi. I checked in on your friend, and then I spoke to Professor Grainne Kinsella, the palliative care consultant, and Dora is being transferred to Hollymount Hospice this evening.'

'I appreciate it, Seamus, that's so kind of you –'

'I didn't do much, but call me if you need anything else.'

'I will, thanks.'

'Bye, Mags.' The phone goes down again. Ten-second phone call, max. Another gold star for the high-ups in Kieran's family.

CHAPTER 16

On Tuesday evening Kieran and I take the dogs for a long walk on the beach. Both Princess and I need the exercise, especially after the dinner we've just had, battered cod and chips and mushy peas from the chipper, where Chloe Boylan is still working despite being pregnant again. Poor Chloe, she looks so miserable; I suppose she knows all about Gemma O'Flaherty.

Princess has developed a gargantuan appetite for such a small dog. I did try to stop the girls feeding her surreptitiously under the table – she especially loves the batter off the fish – as she really needs to lose a few pounds. If Róisín Duggan could see her now, she'd have a fit.

Oh well. I suppose one advantage of having so many greedy animals is you don't have much food waste to get rid of. Even the carrot peelings and cabbage stalks don't go to waste, thanks to Meatloaf. And Knickers loves green salad along with the supply of worms and woodlice that Goosey drops off every week in a bucket in return for a brief few minutes of Ellie's attention.

Poor Goosey. He's a sweet boy, but Ellie is still lovelorn over Carrot. She keeps playing Sienna Black's music at full blast in her room. It's driving us mad, though we don't stop her because she says she needs it to get over her broken heart, that it's so empowering.

She's back at the house now with Kate, practising their TikTok routine. They won't be showing it off at the community hall livestream party now, because they're going to the real concert instead, but they're still planning to upload it.

After the walk Princess collapses exhausted onto her cushion, while Kieran takes his revenge on the Sienna Black music throbbing down the stairs by playing his pipes in the conservatory.

In desperate search of peace, I retreat into the sitting room. I've a book I want to finish, but I find myself sitting there, thinking about Dora. After a while I take out my phone. I pause with my finger over the call button, then decide to press it, and after four or five rings, Jerome answers.

'Mags, how are ya?'

'I'm all right, Jerome, how are you all doing?'

A pause. Silence. Have I intruded? Then I hear the muffled sound. He's crying.

'Where are you, Jerome? At Hollymount?'

'Yeah, I'm sorry… I… Mags, could you come?'

'I'm on my way, Jerome, just wait there.'

I end the call, tell Kieran where I'm going and leave by the kitchen door.

I drive the fifteen minutes to the hospice and pull into the car park. It's beautifully landscaped, and the building itself is only a few years old. It was designed by a famous Irish architect and won loads of prizes, but none of that can take from what it is. I steel myself as I sit in the car. People coming and going, in and out of cars in the car park, all with the same reason to be here – someone they love is dying. A man walks out of the double glass doors holding a little girl's hand; she can't be more than six or seven. His is face grey and drawn. Another older lady is in the disabled spot and slowly extracts herself from her adapted vehicle with the help of a younger woman, her daughter I would guess. All human life is here. It's the great leveller. And it's coming to us all.

I get out and walk towards the reception. Inside is a huge fountain and a bright sunny atrium. There's art on the walls and gentle classical music being piped through an expensive-sounding system.

I pass a café that is bright and sunny. One wall made of glass overlooks a courtyard, where flowers tumble from stone urns and a fountain tinkles in the middle. Groups of comfortable-looking sofas and armchairs dot the large space, among huge yuccas and cheese plants. Some patients well enough to come down sit in wheelchairs, having lunch with their families at the tables. There are three young people playing gentle music – a harpist, a fiddle player and an accordionist – and a more tranquil, peaceful place it would be hard to imagine. They've done everything possible to make this a welcoming space.

There's a bald man on the desk, and I go up and give Dora's name. He checks the computer and smiles.

'Dora is in Room 7 on the Orchid Corridor, third floor. The lifts are behind us here.'

'Thanks,' I say, and head to the lift. I've never been in here before, though I've driven past thousands of times. I've been lucky that this hasn't touched my life so far. My dad died, but he died at home, and it was a long time ago now. Hard at the time, but he'd been sick for so long, it was sadness tinged with relief, for him and for us.

I'm here, I text Jerome.

And he immediately replies, *I'll meet you at the lift.*

As the lift door opens, there he is, and though Jerome is a huge man by every standard, he's diminished somehow. His black hair, normally oiled back, falls over his forehead, and his black leather coat seems to be hanging off him.

There's a rugged toughness to Jerome. He doesn't feel cold or heat. He was reared in a roll-top wagon, slept under a tarp thrown across the shafts, winter and summer. He's hardy in a way no settled person is, but this is breaking him.

I hug him, then he leads me over to an alcove where brightly upholstered sofas face each other across a large glass coffee table.

'Will I get you tea?' he asks, and I shake my head.

Wearily he sinks into the sofa. 'She's going to leave me, Mags. She doesn't want to, but she's going, and there's nothing we can do about it.'

'I know, Jerome, and I'm so sorry,' I say, the words so inadequate.

He nods. 'They're after giving her a beautiful room, very airy, and we can have the long windows wide open. There's bird feeders on the balcony, and they even put nyjer seeds to draw the goldfinches. Today we watched them for hours.' His voice gets stronger as we talk. 'She got her hair done, and they came and painted her nails – she never had that done in her life – and even gave her a massage. She's not in any pain, so she says anyway – I don't think she is – they're being very good to us.'

His eyes are bright with unshed tears. 'Imagine, she has her own bathroom off the bedroom. I swear to you, Mags, 'tis the most luxury either of us have ever seen, and they brought in a bed for me so I'm not in a chair.'

'It's a hard, lonely, heartbreaking time in anyone's life, but at least the place is nice and they've tried to make it not feel like a hospital,' I say.

'Oh, it's totally different. When we were in the hospital, we were stuck in a room like a box and you could feel visitors weren't welcome, especially the boys, but here everyone is allowed in, no question. Lovely grub. And yesterday a woman with a fiddle came in and asked if we'd like her to play for us. Dora loves Big Tom, but I didn't think someone like her would know any of his songs. But a nurse that was in earlier – and we were talking about the music Dora liked – asked the woman if she knew any Big Tom, and sure enough didn't she come back with a fella with a guitar, and they played "Four Roads to Glenamaddy".'

'I'm so glad.' I swallow. Jerome McGovern would not be used to being prioritised. Like all Travellers, discrimination and suspicion are so endemic to how they are treated that they have come to expect nothing else.

'And we've plenty of freedom to come and go. The staff say how me and Delia and the boys are to treat this place like our home for as long as Dora is here. Tatiana came to visit this morning. 'Twas nice to see her. And Finbarr made Dora a bracelet – he gave it to Olivia for her. And Dora knows how nice it is here, Mags, and we're grateful, but...'

His face crumples then. He tries to stop it, pursing his lips, shutting his eyes tightly, but it is as if the floodgates have opened. I move to sit beside him, put my arms around this huge man and hold him as he sobs in my arms, his heart breaking.

'She's still asking me to take her home to die, Mags, even though the public health nurse says it's not possible, not in a caravan. She won't get the palliative care she needs, and she'll be in pain. But she doesn't want to die in here, nice as they are...'

Poor, poor Dora. And poor Jerome. He can't have his wife die in pain, at home in the caravan. He's not able for that. No one would be able for that.

'Delia offered her house to her,' he sobs, 'and she said to Delia that she has no bad feeling towards her, and thinks Darren is a grand lad and the house is lovely, and she knows how Delia hasn't turned her back on her culture, but she still doesn't want to die in a house herself. She wants to die how she's always lived, in a caravan, unrestricted by four concrete walls.'

* * *

I CALL Seamus on the hands-free phone on my way back to Ballycarrick, to explain.

'I'm sorry to bother you again, Seamus...'

'Mags, when I said to call me if you need anything else, I meant it.' He's a straightforward man, no beating about the bush.

'OK, well...the hospice is wonderful, and Dora's family are so grateful, but she's still begging to be allowed home. There's something about Travellers – they don't like being closed in, no matter how luxurious the surroundings or how kind the staff. Seamus, do you know why the palliative team can't manage to care for her in the caravan? There have been a lot of changes to the halting site since the Maguire thing – it's got a bathroom block now and hot running water and a gas supply. It's really very nice, and the McGoverns keep the place immaculate.'

Two years ago a corrupt county councillor called Andy Maguire paid a criminal to wreck the Drumlish site in an attempt to get the McGoverns pushed off their land and rezone it for the private school next door, St Colm's. Finbarr Turner nearly died of exposure as a result. He was there minding the chickens and ran away and fell in a deep ditch and didn't dare come out, and but for Jerome finding him, who knows what might have happened. So in the interests of hushing everything up, the council paid for the upgrade.

Seamus sighs. 'Even so, Mags, the palliative care in Hollymount is second to none.'

'She's in the best place I know, but she's so determined, and poor Jerome, her husband, is just crushed. He doesn't know what to do.'

'Mm…' He's thinking, and I can hear his pen scratching. 'It's hard on the family if the patient is trying to leave. Look, let me talk to Professor Kinsella again and find out what the issues are.'

Just as before, he calls me back in five minutes. He is a one-man masterclass in efficiency.

'Grainne says she's spoken to the public health nurse about the caravan, and there's no room for a hospital bed or a morphine pump, no private space for nurses, she's anxious about all the coming and going, the kitchen is part of the main space – it's just too crowded. Plus the palliative team can't provide round-the-clock care like the hospice. There would be a strong chance of Dora experiencing long periods of pain.'

'Ah…OK.' So it is hopeless then. I'll have to go back to Jerome and tell him going home is not an option.

'So I explained about the recent upgrades to the halting site and asked her if anything could be done, and she said the interior of the caravan would have to be remodelled to accommodate the hospital bed and other equipment, proper paths would have to be laid across the site so no one is walking in dirt, and there has to be a separate annex for nurses to get washed and changed and safely store their equipment. The palliative team will be able to cover 9 a.m. to 9 p.m.

care, but for the other twelve hours, you'll need to employ a private agency. She gave me the number for one. It's called Harmony Homecare and it's expensive, but if the money can be raised, Grainne is prepared to play ball.'

My heart lifts, though only so far. The expense of remodelling the caravan, paving paths across the site, building an annex, the cost of private nursing – would it even be a runner for the McGoverns? Kieran and I would help of course, but... 'Thanks, Seamus, that's very helpful of you. I'll pass it on. And thank Professor Kinsella for her advice.'

'Mags?'

'Yes?' I'm surprised. I was expecting him to say 'Bye, Mags' and ring off, job done, as he's done the previous two times.

'I know that sounds like it will cost a lot of money, and I'm not familiar with the McGoverns, but I suspect they won't be able to afford it.'

'Mm...' I'm not sure where this is going.

'But I know you've worked hard to build bridges between the Travellers and the settled community in Ballycarrick, so if you put up a GoFundMe page, you might be surprised who responds. I'm sure myself and Catriona would contribute.'

I'm astonished, and grateful for the suggestion. 'Seamus, that's a brilliant idea, thank you. You really are a star.'

'Oh, and by the way...'

This is unheard of; he's getting positively chatty.

'Yes, Seamus?'

'I hear you had fun at Orla's last Saturday. Myself and Catriona would love to join in the next time.'

My head spins. Is this what I think it is? Seamus and Catriona are prepared to do the same as Orla and Gearoid, and take Kieran's side in his fallout with Nora? There's something big happening behind the scenes here. I take a moment, then say as nonchalantly as possible, 'I hope you do. It was lovely, and you'll love your new nephew, Fionn.'

'I'm sure I will. Good genes, like yourself. Bye, Mags.' And he is gone.

CHAPTER 17

I have a long chat with Kieran, who agrees the GoFundMe is a good idea – hopefully it will raise something – and maybe if he pulls in a few favours from the many tradespeople he knows that he's helped out in the past… Sure, anything's worth a try.

First thing in the morning, I text my best friend and most long-standing comrade-in-arms, Sharon.

She set up a GoFundMe page for Trevor's band a few months ago to raise money for a tour after Covid killed live music, and Tequila Mockingbird, Ballycarrick's answer to U2, turned out to have so many old fans willing to contribute that the boys were able to buy a little bus and do several small gigs around Ireland in pubs and clubs.

She texts back that she will see me for elevenses, and she appears in the station at ten to eleven.

'Will we go out for a coffee?'

'Yes, let's.' I'm keen to get away from the station phone, which is still ringing off the hook, newspaper editors wanting updates on 'My Blue-Eyed Horse', as if I'm running the investigation, which I am not.

'Will we go to the hotel? You won't get a second's peace from those reporters in Teresa's or the Samovar.'

'Good idea.'

We sneak out the back and into Sharon's car, and she speeds past the handful of rain-bedraggled hacks who are camped out front, with alarming disregard for life and limb.

'From a mad witch and warlock to a missing horse. It's never-ending with you,' Sharon says, fiddling with her phone – definitely not hands-free – with one hand and fixing her hair with the other while steering with her knees.

'Sharon, God almighty, I'd be giving you about ten penalty points if I stopped you now.'

'Relax, Mags. Gerry did something weird with my layers. He's all about the perms these days and has forgotten how to cut hair,' she says, pulling at a chunk of hair on the side of her head. She seems fine to me, but my opinion on such matters counts for zero.

'I won't relax – hold the steering wheel!' I command.

'All right, all right, don't get your knickers in a twist.' She sighs like I'm the most unreasonable person she's ever had to deal with but does place her hands on the steering wheel as Beyoncé's 'Texas Hold 'Em' fills the car. Sharon is a huge Beyoncé fan.

'So how is Jerome?' she asks, as she indicates onto the main road.

'I saw him yesterday at the hospice. He's not coping well at all. He might look like the bruiser in that family, and God knows a person would do well not to cross him, but Dora is the boss of Jerome and always was, and he's having an awful time trying to persuade her he can't bring her home.'

'I can imagine. Well, hopefully we can sort it out for them. We just need to write a good statement, one that really tugs at the heartstrings and makes people want to help.'

She pulls into the car park of the Carrick Arms Hotel, which has opened its bar again, though renovations are continuing in other parts of the building. As we enter, there's still a slightly acrid smell of smoke in the air, mixed in with the smell of new paint. We take our seats by the window, and Sharon orders coffee and scones. I try to protest that I'll just have coffee, no scone, but Sharon is having none of it.

'Stop worrying about your weight all the time, Mags. You're still not anything like where you were before the fire,' she says, with uncharacteristic kindness. 'Maybe in another year, but it's not going back on that fast.'

'Thanks, Sharon.'

'You could even have some cream with that jam,' she adds, even more kindly.

'Get behind me, Satan!'

'I thought it was your behind that was the problem…'

'Ha, funny. But seriously, Shar, what do you think of Seamus's GoFundMe idea? Would people contribute, do you think?'

'I think people would,' she says as the waitress arrives with our coffee and scones and a sinful amount of jam and cream in white pots. 'People know you get on with them, and you're well liked. And Delia is very well liked too.'

'But what if we do it and then we don't raise enough for it to be useful?'

'Then we can return their money to the donors and we don't have to say anything to the McGoverns about it, but I'd say we'll raise enough no bother. How much do you think we'll need?'

I grimace. 'A lot.' Kieran spent two hours on the phone this morning to different tradespeople, calling in favours from some and getting quotes from others for a fast turnaround, while I checked the Harmony Homecare site to see how much two private nurses were to cover all Dora's nighttime care for at least two months. 'Around forty thousand euro.' I wait for Sharon's face to fall, but it doesn't.

'Right, let's do it.' She takes a sip of coffee and a bite of her scone, then gets her laptop out of her bag, puts it on the table and pulls up the GoFundMe website. 'What we need is a really clear, simple headline followed by a detailed explanation.'

I'm encouraged by her confidence. 'Help Dora come home?' I suggest.

'Perfect.' She types it into the first box, then goes to the second box. 'Now what do we want to say? We can always edit it.'

I drink my coffee and eat my scone while I think for a bit, and then I say, 'OK, how about "Local family the McGoverns are facing something we all must face at some point. The serious illness of a loved one. Jerome and Dora McGovern are central members of our community here in Ballycarrick, and while the care and attention Dora is receiving in Hollymount Hospice is second to none, it is her fervent wish to come home. To achieve that, considerable moves will need to be made to ensure appropriate nursing care and equipment is employed. This is expensive, and so we, the community and friends of the McGovern family, would like to help to make it happen for them. If you are in a position to donate anything, big or small, it would be very much appreciated."'

'Perfect,' says Sharon again, her fingers flying as she types it in. 'Now have we got a picture we can use?'

'I do.' I have a load of photos from Delia's wedding on my phone, and there's a lovely back view of Jerome sitting on one of the outside benches with his arm around Dora. If you didn't know them, you wouldn't know who they were, but you can see the love in the way they're leaning together. I show it to Sharon. 'What do you think?'

She nods approvingly. 'WhatsApp me.'

I do, and she uploads it to the page, and then it's done, there, up on the internet. 'So here's the link,' she says, and my phone pings. 'And you share it with all your family and friends, and I will too. And Trevor and Kieran – get everyone to keep sharing it. You know the way Ballycarrick is – it will reach everyone.'

'And what happens next?' I'm amazed how simple this seems to be.

'I'll monitor the page – I've put up my details in the background – and when there's a reasonable amount of money, GoFundMe will contact me and off we go. Now hang on…it's good to get a big fat donation right at the top, to encourage others… I'll stick in a thousand, hang on. I'll get my online banking app up on screen…'

'A thousand?' I can't believe she's breezily announcing that she's going to donate one thousand euro.

'Yes, there was that much left over from Trevor's tour. I emailed all the fans to say I was going to divide it up and send everyone something back, but they all said to keep it and put it towards a good cause, and this is a good cause. I'll let them know, and they'll be delighted.'

'Oh, Shar.' I'm so touched. 'But shouldn't you check with Trevor first?'

'Already checked, and he's happy out.' She hits a key. 'Now it's done. First donation, in the name of Fans of Tequila Mockingbird. They'll love that.'

'Well, thank Trevor from me. We have to all go out together soon.'

'Sounds good. How are things with Kieran? Is he back talking to his mam yet?'

'No, and I'm leaving it up to him. And so much else has been happening, I've almost forgotten about it.'

'Like what? You haven't said anything to me?' She sounds slightly aggrieved; she hates if I leave her out of the loop. She'll absolutely kill me when she finds out I've met Sienna Black… Though maybe not, as she's all about Beyoncé.

I start with the less complicated news. 'Sorry, Shar. It's been a whirlwind, and we'll need a longer catch-up to cover everything. I guess the most important thing that's happened since I last saw you is Wojtec wants to buy the roofing business and Kieran's agreed.'

She applauds, beaming. 'Woohoo! Well done, Kieran!'

'Yeah…' I raise my cup.

She spots my hesitation and grins broadly. 'Oh, OK, let me guess… He wants you to retire as well and join him on a permanent Caribbean cruise with a boatload of trad musicians?'

I nearly choke on my coffee. 'You've no idea how close you are to hitting the nail on the head.'

'Oh dear… So I take it you said we have to talk?' She rolls her eyes, grinning. 'Poor Kieran.'

Sharon is like Kieran. She hates the words 'we have to talk'; she prefers to ignore the elephant in the room and hope it goes away. It's why she was able to put up with the awful Danny Boylan and his affairs for so long. She doesn't say much on the subject of her present relationship, but I hope she and Trevor talk; I'd love her to trust him enough to show him her true feelings. But she's been so vulnerable since her divorce, I don't know if she'll ever let him get that close.

'We did indeed have the talk.' I smile at her good-natured teasing. 'And after that, everything was fine.'

'Fine, how…?' She raises one eyebrow.

'We just needed to clear the air.'

'Oh, I know that look, Mags Munroe!' she cackles, pointing at me. 'There's life in the old dog yet.'

I slap her hand. 'I should hope so. I'm not in my dotage despite everything. And now that you've made me reveal all, it's your turn – how's things with Trevor?'

'He asked me to marry him.'

'What?' I sit up straight and stare at her, not sure I've heard right.

'Trevor asked me to marry him,' she repeats quietly.

'Oh…wow… When?' I'm trying to gauge her feelings about this, but she's playing her cards close to her chest.

'Last night, as I was standing at the kitchen sink scrubbing a grass stain out of Sean's football shorts.'

'Go on.' I'm praying she didn't give the poor man too short a shrift; he really loves her.

'Well, I had just gone for a walk – I'm listening to that true crime podcast I told you about. It's so good. You should listen to it yourself.'

The idea that I would spend my leisure time listening to a true crime podcast doesn't seem as ridiculous to Sharon as it does to me. 'Get to the point, Shar,' I prompt.

'Well, you should. Anyway, I came home and Sean was playing a match today – they're through to the primary school final against Dromahane. Trevor washed his kit in the machine, but it wouldn't shift the big grass skid mark on the back of his shorts, so I got it out with Vanish and a nail brush. And there I am, sweaty as you like, hair scraped up in a ponytail, no make-up, scrubbing at the sink and splashing water everywhere, and when I turn around, there he is on one knee in the middle of the kitchen floor, which is wet, so I thought he was after slipping. I'm just about to pull him up when he takes a ring out of his pocket. No box, just a ring.'

'Oh my God…' It all seems so mad. 'What did he say?'

'Nothing too embarrassing. Just, "Shar, please will you marry me?" and then he stayed down, the knee of his jeans getting all damp.'

'And what did you…?' I'm on edge with expectation, and worry for Trevor.

'I said yes.'

'You said *yes*?' I can hardly believe my ears. She's always been so adamant she would never trust a man again enough to marry him.

'I did.' She has a slight smile on her face, but otherwise she's calm. There's none of the hysterics she had when Danny proposed to her, squealing how he was the best, most handsome man in the world while the rest of us held our tongues.

'Oh, Shar. Congratulations. And is the ring nice?' I ask, fearful of the answer. I do hope she'll be happy with whatever Trevor could afford; she's such a fashionista. When she and Danny got engaged, people used to joke she'd need a wheelbarrow for the massive rock he got her.

Still with that small smile, she lifts her left hand, and there on her finger – how did I not notice before? I suppose I was too worried she was going to crash the car – is a lovely, simple diamond ring. Old-fashioned, a brilliant-cut solitaire on a yellow gold band with pinched shoulders.

'Oh, Shar, it's lovely.'

'It's an antique. It belonged to his great-grandmother, then his granny, then his mam.' Her voice is soft, and I realise how much this means to her. I'm glad. She never was one for sentimental value, but she's changing, it seems.

'I'm so pleased for you, Shar – and amazed. I thought you'd never marry again.'

She shrugs. 'Neither did I, but Trevor really wants it, and Sean loves him. So…'

'And you, do you love him?' I ask gently. She has never said.

'I do, as it happens.' She's uncharacteristically shy when she says it. My friend Sharon is a lot of things, but shy isn't one. 'We're happy, you know? And he loves me for me, not the hair or the make-up or the clothes. If I wore a bin bag, he wouldn't care. And he's decent, Mags, you know, a good, decent man with morals.'

'He is,' I agree, and I'm so glad she's finally found happiness.

'There was a time I thought we'd never last. I mean, how could I spend my life with a man who wears snow-washed jeans and has a mullet...'

I chuckle. Trevor is good-looking but in a weird late-eighties, Iron Maiden kind of a way, which I know Sharon found hard to get her head around at first, as did I.

'But he loves me, Mags, like really loves me. Apart from you, I've never had that. My mam was a disaster, as you know – not her fault, but she was never there for me – and then there was Danny. And I know a lot of that is me. I don't let people get close. But I've come to trust Trevor. He's never let me down, and I don't think he ever will. And he loves Sean, and we all have such a laugh together. So yeah, I'm going to marry him and glad to do it.'

Sharon and I are not huggers really, but I lean over and give her a huge squeeze. 'I'm delighted for you, truly.'

She hugs me back, then says, 'Great, so you can't refuse my request then.'

'What request?' I ask, instantly wary. You never know what Sharon is going to come out with next.

'Be my maid of honour,' she says, and I hoot with laughter.

'Only if I can wear peach taffeta!'

'Done.' She nods. 'And Gerry is going to give you a permed mullet too – we're having an eighties-themed wedding.'

'Sure, I can't wait...' But I'm not even sure she's joking.

CHAPTER 18

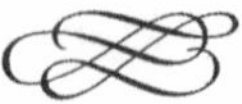

I'm back home for lunch. It's impossible for me to get a sandwich in the town now without being harassed by a reporter from the *Irish Times* or the *Western People* or whatever.

After I've fed myself, I feed the animals. A handful of hay and some aging asparagus and half a red bell pepper I just found in the back of the fridge for Meatloaf. The tops and tails of last night's green beans and a scoop of wriggling woodlice and worms for Knickers – I can't believe I'm doing this, but the girls and Kieran pretend they're too squeamish. A forgotten packet of cooked chicken on its sell-by date for Rollo. And for Princess...

She really should be on fat-free yoghurt and a lettuce leaf, but she's just pinched the chicken off Rollo and is wolfing it down. That dog just never stops eating.

I'm beginning to wonder if Princess's mother had fat genes, despite having a list of pedigreed papers as long as your arm, because her daughter now resembles a hairy white balloon with the face of a Pekingese.

I find an old packet of ham to feed Rollo instead. For some reason he's not objecting to her thieving his chicken. He's sort of smiling at her as she eats it, in a benign doggy way...

A terrible thought strikes me. I've been pretty vigilant about not letting Princess out when she's in heat, but when was the last time she... Could herself and Rollo... No. Impossible. Though now I think about it, there was that issue with the vet and the missing testicle...

Aagh!!!

I text Kieran, who is on a job in Castlebar. *Think Princess might have succeeded in seducing Rollo. She's like a barrel and he looks pleased as punch. PS – WE HAVE TOO MANY ANIMALS ALREADY!!!!!! XXX*

I get a reply almost straight away.

Suspected that, was scared to mention it. Don't worry, I'll make Rollo stand by her. Or Knickers if they come out as lizard-dogs. Pekizards? xxx

I hope and pray we're both wrong, and not just about the Pekizards. The girls will lose their minds if they think puppies are coming, so we'll have to have a strategy from the off that they are not staying. And they are *not* staying.

* * *

BACK IN THE STATION, I drive past the reporters shouting my name, and when I park around the back, Sharon's car is there.

As I come in past the toilets, I can see her inside through the glass panel, talking to Nicola at the front desk; the two of them shush each other as I open the door.

'What's going on?' I stare from one to the other.

'Tell her, Sharon,' says Nicola in a slightly strangled voice. Her cheeks are very pink.

'Something has happened,' Sharon begins, and she's trying her best to look serious, but then her face lights up and she can't contain her excitement. 'You'll never guess what, Mags!'

'Go on.' I smile cautiously.

'There's nearly twenty-five thousand in it already!'

'Twenty-five...in what?' I'm confused.

'Every shop and pub in the town has made a donation, none of them less than five hundred! Look!' She takes out her phone and shows me the fundraiser. 'Even that tight-fisted Danny Boylan' –

Sharon's ex is an accountant and normally wouldn't spend Christmas unless he's trying to impress his latest woman – 'put in a thousand, Mags, probably 'cos he didn't want to be shown up by Trevor in front of Chloe from the chipper, not that he minds cheating on her with Gemma O'Flaherty.'

It's the first time I've heard her refer to Chloe from the chipper with a touch of sympathy rather than a wolverine snarl.

I scroll down the list of donations, stunned into speechlessness. After I went home last night, myself and Kieran put in one thousand from our savings, and now Gerry the hairdresser has given a thousand as well, and so has Luigi. Teresa from the bakery, Violetta of the flower shop and Julie Dullea are down for five hundred each, as is Sharon's Boutique – I beam at my best friend, who shrugs and says, 'Well, the thousand wasn't mine.' And Bertie the Butcher has pushed the limit up to a thousand again, followed by two thousand from Castle Dysert. That's so kind of Conor and Ana.

'And see here.' Nicola leans over my shoulder. 'The board of management of St Colm's made a donation of seventeen hundred, can you imagine that?'

I can. Matthew Hilser, who became principal of the exclusive boy's school a couple of years ago, is a decent man. The chair of the school's management board, Lavinia Moran's husband, Richard, was involved in the plot against the halting site, so Matthew got rid of him off the board, and Matthew and Jerome became good friends. They share a love of horses, and now Jerome looks after the school stables. That's the thing about Jerome – he has friends in all walks of life because he doesn't see people as high or low, the way my mother-in-law does.

Annette and Martha have donated six hundred. That's a huge amount for them, but they love Jerome, who saved Finbarr that time the site was attacked and also taught him about minding chickens, and above all about being true to yourself, no matter what society says about you.

Finbarr himself has put in forty euro. He's very proud to be earning his own money now. Annette told me that as well as selling eggs, he's set up an urban garden support kind of thing. People in Galway who only have a balcony or a tiny bit of space can get a starter kit and advice from Finbarr, who runs it, and they can grow a few new potatoes or tomatoes or peppers or whatever they like.

I keep scrolling, and my heart swells with pride for my community, all these ordinary people, with all their foibles and faults, that have stepped up to do a good thing, with no fanfare or fuss. I'm so grateful to live here, to bring my kids up here.

All of Kieran's siblings have given generously, one thousand from each couple: Catriona and Seamus, Orla and Fergus, Aoife and Leonard, Gearoid and Enrico, Oilibhéar and Muireann. And to my surprise, five hundred from Nora and Kevin – what on earth is going on there? I suppose Nora feels she has to fall in line with the 'high-ups'. Mam and Joe have put in seven hundred and fifty, and every Polish guy who works with Kieran has donated one hundred.

Liam Cronin, Caelan's father, has donated seventy, and even Oscar O'Leary has given twenty euro, bless him, as has Dave Coo-Coo, the owner of Jules Verne, the most famous racing pigeon in Ireland.

Ronan Brady is down for five hundred, also Padraig McCarthy, the leader of the Galway council.

Klara Shevchenko, who has the cleaning business, has put in three hundred, and Deirdre Hickey, the ancient Irish dancing teacher, has put in fifty euro – how is she still alive, let alone on the internet?

The refugees who live in Horsehead have raised two hundred and fifty euro between them. They held a bake sale after Mass last Sunday in the parish hall. They have barely any money and what they have they send home to Ukraine, but their message reads 'We don't forget friends who stand by us in our time of need, and we pray that Jerome can bring Dora home.'

I know what they're referring to. It was Jerome who organised a posse of Travellers to drive away some nasty out-of-town protesters threatening to burn out the Ukrainian women and their children, and who also took a delivery to Ukraine and brought one woman's injured husband back from the front.

There are so many other messages of goodwill, prayers and kind thoughts, it would bring a tear to a stone.

Delia's in-laws in Tipperary, who were initially horrified that their son was marrying a Traveller girl, have written 'So grateful to be related to Jerome and Dora.' The Carney family – Darren's parents, two brothers, uncles and one aunt – have donated nearly four thousand between them.

Tatiana has put in twelve hundred, with the coded message, 'From a fellow Traveller'.

Then there are donations of a few hundred each from Phillip O'Flaherty, who 'appreciates the help with the tow chain', and the Carrick Arms Hotel – they've written one word, 'Respect' – and three of Gearoid's posh arty colleagues in Galway and a couple of consultant friends of Seamus.

The elderly people who live in St Anna's sheltered housing clubbed together and donated six hundred.

Together with a mass of small individual donations, we're looking at 24,977 euro, and the counter is still ticking; it's not slowing yet.

The Travellers wouldn't be big on bank accounts – they don't trust banks and deal only in cash – so I'm not surprised to see none of their names here, but I suspect that they won't like to be found wanting, and hopefully that will help to get us over the hill. If not we'll have to cut our cloth, but I think it's time for us to get the ball rolling.

'This is incredible,' I say. 'But now someone needs to tell Jerome what we're planning. Sharon, you set it up…'

'No way. You, Mags, you,' Sharon says. 'It wouldn't have happened without you.'

I hesitate, but I suppose this is my responsibility. Jerome might be angry and reject this as charity, so maybe I should be the one to go in there and admit what we've done.

'I'll go over there now,' I say, handing Sharon back her phone. 'Nicola, are you OK to hold the fort?'

'Sure thing, Sarge.' She has the GoFundMe page up on her own phone now, ready to make a donation.

'Sharon, at least come along for the ride?'

'Will do. I've already put up a notice saying the boutique is closed for the afternoon. I'm far too excited to be selling a beige cardigan to Mrs Harris.'

'Are you surprised at the response? I am,' she says as we head out to the car, then navigate our way past the reporters – rather more carefully now that it's me driving and not Sharon.

'I am and I'm not,' I say as I pull out onto the main street of this ordinary Irish town. 'Jerome and Delia have done a lot for the people of Ballycarrick. Finbarr's urban garden project is only the latest. They're using Jerome's recipe for a spray for greenfly, totally organic and safe to pets and people. Then Delia haunted the council until they put a pedestrian crossing between St Anna's and the church because she hated how the old people were terrified to cross the road for Mass – all the building of the new estates out that way meant the road was so busy. Dora and the boys are more distant, more like the way Travellers are, but those two are fully involved in the community, and you don't hear a word against them.'

'I think it's great, though. I mean, they wouldn't do it for the Carmodys, but they'll do it for the McGoverns,' Sharon says.

'Exactly, and the Carmodys add very little to this place, except keeping us busy. Though I have to say, Lenny is a changed man. He went over to England and got married and has a baby and all. His father-in-law threatened him that if he got into any trouble, he'd be sorry, so it seems to be working.'

'But it's good, isn't it? That not all Travellers are being tarred with the one brush.'

'It really is.' I turn onto the motorway that will take us to Hollymount, and a few minutes later, I pull into the car park of the hospice and find a space. I sit there for a few moments after I've parked, without getting out. 'I'm sick over this now,' I say. 'What if he hates the idea?'

'It's fine. Just tell him the truth, show him all the donations, then it's up to him,' Sharon says airily.

'So are you coming in?'

'God no, I'll wait here. You don't need me. You'll be fine.'

'Oh right, "you'll be fine,"' I say wryly. 'Do you feel like one of those mad generals in the first world war? "Don't worry, chaps, over the barbed wire with you now. I'll have a brandy here and watch. It will all be fine."'

'Something like that.' She laughs as I get out of the car.

CHAPTER 19

I get in the lift, which is big enough to accommodate a bed, and as the door opens on the third floor, I see Delia straight away. She's pouring herself a drink from the water cooler in the alcove, next to the tea and coffee dock, which is surrounded by those brightly upholstered sofas.

'Hi, Delia,' I say, crossing towards her.

'Hi, Sarge,' she replies, in a flat, dull voice.

I stand beside her as she fills the cup and drinks it down. I want to tell her about the fundraising, but I need to tell Jerome first. 'How's your mam?'

'She keeps trying to get out of the bed, even though she can't stand. All she wants is to go home, but the pain relief and everything she needs is here, but it's all she wants…' She looks wretched.

'Have you eaten? Slept?'

She shakes her head, then sinks onto one of the sofas and just disintegrates.

'She was clear yesterday, talking like.' She sobs into her hands as I crouch down beside her. 'She begged me to take her back to the van, and I said again, what about the house, and she says she loves my house but she can't die inside, not like that, not without wheels beneath her. And she was talking like she still lived in a caravan like the one in which she was born, where at night you could lie under a tarp slung across the shafts and gaze up at the sky, and you were always on the road...'

The lift pings, and Darren appears. He's just arrived, and I beckon him over. 'I need to talk to Jerome. I've something really important to tell him that I think will help, so will you stay with Delia a moment, and then when she feels a bit better, come to the room so I can bring Jerome out here?'

'Give us five minutes.' He sits by her on the sofa, drawing his heartbroken wife into his arms.

* * *

Dora's even smaller than when I last saw her. Her hair is loose now on the pillow. She always wore it tied back, but this way must be more comfortable. Her face is careworn, as if she's wincing, and she's wired up to oxygen and another machine on her right. Jerome sees me noticing it.

'It's a pump for pain relief. They're keeping the worst of the pain away with that. It rears up now and again, but mostly she's resting easy,' he says quietly.

There are big recliner chairs on both sides of the bed. He offers one of them to me, and we sit down, him on an ordinary plastic chair that he pulls up beside me.

'She's awake, you can talk to her,' he says. 'She's just very tired today.'

I lean forwards. 'Hi, Dora, it's Mags. You don't mind calling me Mags still, do you?'

She gives a ghost of a smile without opening her eyes.

'Everything is fine in Ballycarrick, the boys are all OK, and everyone is looking after your family. Darren just arrived – he's having a cup of tea with Delia – and when they come back to the room, I'm going to bring Jerome to get a cup of tea with me.'

Jerome frowns, but I shake my head and put my finger to my mouth, indicating I can't say why in front of his wife.

When Darren and Delia arrive, she's much calmer; it's lovely to see how much strength she draws from her young husband's presence.

Jerome follows me to the alcove with the sofas, and I make us a pot of tea as he rests on one and closes his eyes, his long legs in his black trousers stretched out. I find myself nervous, dreading telling him what we've done.

Sharon texts me. *All OK?*

I send her back a thumbs-up, then bring over the tray with tea and biscuits to the large glass coffee table, pour us a mug each and push his and the biscuits towards him. He picks up his tea but then sits hunched and listless, the mug nearly invisible in his huge hands, his shoulders drooping. He doesn't even ask what I've brought him out here for, he's so crushed by the weight of his grief.

I finally manage to get the words out. 'Jerome, I hope you won't be angry or upset, but we've done something,' I begin.

'Done what?' he asks.

'Well, I spoke to Seamus again…you know, my brother-in-law…'

He nods; he doesn't mind that.

'Well, he spoke to Professor Kinsella, and she says if you can make certain modifications to the caravan and the site, and employ a private company, Harmony Homecare, to provide the overnight nursing, then the hospital palliative team will do the rest.'

He stares at me, my words slowly sinking into his exhausted brain. A faint flicker of hope crosses his face.

'Myself and Kieran costed it out. Lots of Kieran's friends in construction will help, and altogether it will come to about forty thousand, we think, because it will have to be done fast and all at once.'

The flicker of hope dies, and his head droops.

'I haven't…' he begins but I interrupt.

'The community has got together and set up a fundraiser and… well, look.'

I take out my phone and show him the GoFundMe page. It's nearly twenty-eight thousand euro now. He stares at it, and I can see by the worry on his handsome face that he doesn't understand.

'It's a fundraising page, and see, there's enough money to get started already…'

He stares at the amount raised as the figure ticks up to 28,045.

'Did you do this?' he asks. His expression is impossible to read.

'Well, Seamus suggested it, and Sharon set it up, but this is from everyone in Ballycarrick, Jerome. They want to help you to bring Dora home. If you scroll down there, you can see, and people wrote messages too…'

Jerome's meaty calloused finger scrolls down the screen, page after page of donations and messages of goodwill. Jerome is well able to read. Some older Travellers can't, but when he and his family got put on the halting site in Ballycarrick, Derry McLoughlin, then the very young master of the national school, taught the youthful Jerome to read and write. Travellers lived in fear of the 'cruelty man' then, who would take their children away if they didn't go to school, but when they came for Jerome, Derry wouldn't allow it.

I say nothing as he reads each entry, his face immobile. Derry McLoughlin is one of the most recent donors. He and his wife have put in four hundred and fifty, with a message praising Jerome and Dora for raising wonderful children with great curiosity about the world and a strong belief in themselves.

'Did you ask people yourself to give this money?' His voice is husky now. I wish I knew if it was gratitude or fury.

'No, Sharon just put the fundraiser up on the community social media, and it took off by itself. Nobody was harassed or anything, if that's what you're worried about.'

He nods slowly and returns my phone, and then I see them, the fat tears rolling down this big man's face.

'They did that for us?' he asks, and I nod.

'Yes, and it should be enough to remodel the caravan to fit in a hospital bed and the oxygen cylinder and morphine pump. Kieran can call in favours to get paths put across the site, and we can make a start on an annex for the nurses to get changed and rest and store their stuff safely. Everyone is ready to get to work, if you give us the go-ahead.'

'And if you do all this, then I can bring Dora home?'

'You can.'

He is silent for a long time. Finally he says, 'I went to the chapel this mornin', and I prayed to my mother. I begged her to find a way for me to do as Dora wants, though I didn't think there was goin' to be one. Dacie McGovern is on your shoulder, Mags, and she's so grateful to you. And I am too.'

'It was everyone, Jerome, not just me, but thank you.' I stand then and so does he. 'Kieran is just waiting on the call, and so is Selena, the lady from Harmony Homecare, who wants to know when to start, so I'll go and ring them now. They'll get everything set up as soon as possible, and we'll get Dora home.'

Jerome is not comfortable with physical affection, but he takes my hand and shakes it several times, up and down. 'While I'm alive, Mags, you and your family will never want for anything I can give you,' he says, and then he keeps my hand in his for a long moment, pressing it silently.

He seems old and beaten, not just in the weathered way I'm used to him being, but in the way grief can just knock the stuffing out of you. Mam looked that way for a long time after my dad died.

'I was glad to help. We're friends, Jerome,' I say. 'That's what friends do.'

He nods and smiles as if the notion that I, a settled woman and a guard, could ever be a friend of a Travelling man amuses him even in the middle of his grief. But he says, 'We are, I suppose.' Then he's serious again. 'If you're ever in need of anything, ever, Mags, anything at all, as a friend, you need only ask, and I'll make it right for you.'

It's my turn to smile. After Princess being pregnant, which there's not much Jerome can do about, my biggest problem is all those reporters camped outside the station and trailing me everywhere around the town. I wish I could ask Jerome to run them off, like he did those out-of-town lunatics who threatened to burn Horsehead House. But I can't, not really.

'You don't know where that bloody horse is, do you? I think I'm only going to get my life back if Chance Your Arm turns up.'

CHAPTER 20

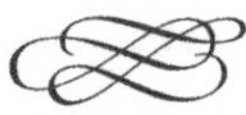

'Can you believe all the money raised?' Ellie asks. 'It's amazing. The transition year class in our school did a car wash today – they washed all the teachers' cars – and the money is going to Mrs McGovern's fund. And you know Snipe?'

'I do.' I wonder how she knows the man nicknamed Sniper's Nightmare on account of his pronounced limp. He moves between the Samovar and the bookie's with his long hair and Grateful Dead T-shirt, winter and summer.

'He won three hundred euro on an accumulator, and he gave it straight to Tatiana to put in for the cause.'

'And you know this how?' I wonder at the types of people my sixteen-year-old seems to be familiar with.

'Goosey told me. He was in the kitchen of the Samovar laying a humane trap. Tatiana thinks she saw a rat around the bins out the back of the bar, and she said she would shoot it if she had a gun, and poor Goosey, you know the way he is, begged her to let him trap it and release it into the wild. She looked at him like he was totally nuts but gave him twenty-four hours. Then she says she's putting down poison and a huge trap. Then Winky Costello, who's working in the bookie's now, said he'd give Goosey odds of fifty to one to catch the rat if he put the money into Mrs McGovern's fund if he wins, and Goosey put in two euro, so hopefully that's another hundred coming.'

'Never a dull moment in Ballycarrick,' I say, shaking my head.

It's Saturday, and Kieran's up at the halting site. There's work been going on up there but here at home, we're getting ready to drive up to Dublin for Sienna Black, and the girls are up to ninety with excitement.

Ellie's bedroom floor is covered with outfits chosen and discarded, and the whole place smells of a toxic combination of sprays, gels, serums and glitter.

'What are you wearing Mam?' Kate demands anxiously.

'Jeans and a hoodie?' I say hopefully. At the moment I'm wearing a bathrobe, having just had a shower.

'Ah, are you high?' asks my thirteen-year-old. It's the phrase of the moment apparently.

'No, Kate, I am not high, nor have I ever *been* high, on account of hallucinogenic drugs being illegal, and as a member of An Garda Síochána, taking such would be a sackable offence, and then we'd be destitute and starving and the only avenue open to you and your sister would be a life of crime, which would culminate fairly rapidly, I suspect, to apprehension and incarceration for the rest of your natural life, where the high point of your day would be a particularly neat line of stitching on a post bag.'

This, my daughters find hilarious.

Kate giggles. 'Mam, you're a nutter!'

'I got you this.' Ellie grins and hands me a bag, and I investigate. It's a Sienna Black T-shirt in a size that would fit a sumo wrestler. It's black and held together with what look like huge safety pins.

'Are you joking?' I ask hopefully.

'Ah, Mam, please, we're wearing the same, so we'll all match.' Kate pleads, and I realise this might be the first and last time in our lives that my daughters want to match clothes with me.

'Right, bring on the safety pins,' I say, resigned, retreating into my bedroom to get dressed.

I pull on a pair of jeans, once more offering a silent prayer of gratitude to whoever invented Lycra. The old unforgiving hard jeans of the past that cut in and slipped down are a dim and distant memory. They were uncomfortable enough when I was young and lithe; they would be inconceivable now.

After I've donned the T-shirt, I throw on my 'good' runners, not the ones I use to walk Rollo and the increasingly rotund Princess. Sharon made me buy them because she said I needed 'going out' runners. These are white and have a label and are, according to my daughters, 'not too embarrassing'. It's my first time wearing them, but they do look better than my old ones.

I bring my hoodie and walk onto the landing.

'Right, you two, let's get going.' I would normally demand they clean up Ellie's bedroom first, but they're on such a high, I let it go, and anyway, I want to get there in plenty of time before the concert. And for once my daughters jump up to leave immediately, and I'm able to get them out of the house without the usual last-minute delaying tactics.

We have Sienna on loud all the way to Dublin, the girls singing along at the tops of their voices.

It's not like it was for us gals in the old days...

They belt out along with their idol, and it might be me, but I think their two voice styles chime well together.

Being tied to the railings and getting kicked by their horses.
Respect to those sisters, honest and brave,
burning their bras and cutting their corsets.
But things are all changed now, it's no longer that way.
We still fight for our rights and demand equal pay,
we won't do what you say, it ain't gonna happen that way.
So listen up, dudes, we got something to say...
We won't dress like you tell us to, of our bodies be ashamed.
We won't squeeze our feet into shoes so that walking is pain.
We will love you and help you but on our own terms.
The patriarchy's dead, let's all watch it burn.

I wonder how Sienna is getting along with her father, and if she made contact with Charlotte or that accountant – Michael Defoe, was it? I hope one day she gets to take her own advice about not letting toxic men like him boss her around and control her life.

Two hours later we arrive and park and make our way with the hordes of Sienna Black fans to the gates of Croke Park, Ireland's biggest stadium. It's mostly girls, and all are wearing mad, huge clothes and many are sporting perms with blunt fringes. Lining the route are hawkers selling T-shirts and hats and even red curly wigs, and I can see the glee on my daughters' faces as they soak up the atmosphere.

The codes Sienna Black gave me work perfectly and we go through several security checkpoints, until one young woman, dressed in black, scans them and smiles. 'You lucky things.' She says something I don't understand into a walkie-talkie, then tells us, 'Follow me.'

She leads us away from the main throng and through a door in the base of the stadium. We are in the tunnel where the dressing rooms are for the teams that play here. It's eerily quiet compared to the excited cacophony outside.

'Sienna and the band are upstairs, but I'll just take you to the corporate suites. Her people will take care of you from there.'

She leads us through a warren of doors and corridors, each one needing a security fob to get through. The concrete floors give way to plush carpets and subdued lighting. We arrive into the suite, and another girl dressed in black greets us – nobody in this world seems to have clothing of any other colour. 'Hi, Mags, Ellie and Kate, right?' She's got an American accent and is sweet and smiling.

'That's us,' I say.

'You're so welcome. I'm Jax, one of Sienna's assistants. Sienna has asked me to settle you in one of the corporate boxes.'

I suppress a smile. I just know on the way home my two will be bemoaning being called Kate and Ellie, incredibly boring names apparently, and will be wishing instead to be called Sienna and Jax. It might work in Hollywood but not in Ballycarrick, but they won't see that.

The young woman leads the way into a small luxurious space with a balcony within fifty feet of the stage overlooking the thronged pitch. We'll have all the atmosphere and none of the pushing and shoving – perfect. There are sandwiches and cakes and a coffee machine and champagne on a table at the back of the box. Myself and the girls are the only ones here.

'Help yourselves, and call me if you need anything else,' Jax says as she leaves us.

I take one of the soft leather seats near the front of the box; my lungs are aching from all that walking, and I need to rest. Kate and Ellie run out onto the balcony, towering over the stands and the pitch, which is almost full already. The huge screens and giant set are something to behold. I've been in Croke Park before to watch Gaelic football when Galway made it to the final against Dublin, and I found this state-of-the-art stadium very impressive then, but from up here, it's truly amazing.

In their huge excitement, my girls burst into another Sienna Black song, her breakout hit 'Scared but Standing Tall', the one they've been practising in Irish and English with their own dance routine.

'You said I had to believe whatever you said,' sings Kate, taking slow and mournful steps. She's holding out her arms to the oblivious crowd below, pretending the balcony is a stage, although of course they can't hear her.

'Bhí orm chreidiúint gach rud a dúirt tú.' Ellie joins in, singing the lines in Irish, also dancing slowly but in a more modern style, as below them the stadium continues to fill, colourful girls pouring in through every gate.

'You said I was too weak and scared to leave your bed…'

'Dúirt tú go raibh mé rómh lag agus eaglach do leaba a fhágáil…'

Then Kate bursts into that very fast exhilarating mixture of hip-hop and Irish dancing that Enrico perfected with them at Orla's. 'But now I'm on my feet, I'm strong, I'm free…'

And Ellie joins in with her. *'Ach anois táim ar mo chosa, táim láidir, táim saor…'* Their very different voices work together, overlapping, as the melancholic first verse becomes a typically rousing Sienna Black anthem.

'I'm scared but standing tall. If I don't fight back, I'll fall. I know I got it in me, you're never gonna kill me.'

'Tá eagla orm ach táim i mo sheasamh ard, más na troideann me, thitfidh me, tá a fhios agam go feidir liom, ní maróidh tú mé riamh.'

It's a splendid hymn to female empowerment and freedom, everything that Sienna aspires to but has not got, and they sing their hearts out until they finish on the famous lines.

'It's you who is broken…'

'Is tusa atá briste…'

'You will never break me…'

'Ní bhrisfidh tú go deo mé.'

They bow triumphantly to the stadium as I applaud, and then a second pair of hands starts clapping. I twist in my chair with a smile, expecting to see another of the ubiquitous black-clad staff.

It's Sienna Black, tiny in another outsized T-shirt – you could fit four of her in that shirt – and huge cargo pants.

'That's really good, girls,' she says, still clapping, as Kate and Ellie slowly turn to stare at their diminutive idol, open-mouthed.

'Ah… Oh…' they breathe, like she's the vision of a saint or something.

'I guess you're Sergeant Munroe's daughters?' she asks, with her sweet smile. 'Your mom has been a great friend to me. I owe her a lot.'

'Yes, this is Ellie and this is Kate,' I answer for them, getting to my feet. They finally manage a couple of feeble hellos, but they're white as sheets.

'Well, I'm Sienna, and it's lovely to meet you!' She beams at them, her wild curls springing in all directions and her intense green eyes shining. 'And I hope you'll all enjoy the show. Now, me and your mom need to have a quiet chat, so if you don't mind… Caleb!' she calls over her shoulder.

A slight young Black man appears, smiling. He's also dressed in black, with a tattooed neck and silver rings on every finger. 'Yo, Sienna?'

'Caleb, this is Ellie and Kate, friends of mine, so can you bring them down to the merch store and let them choose anything they want? Something for each of their friends as well – give them a big bag each to fill.'

'You got it, Sienna,' says Caleb, who is also American. 'I'll have them back in time for the opening act. Come on, girls!'

'Oh…' Kate's eyes open wide at me. 'Can we go, Mam?'

'Go for it, Kit Kat.'

'And don't worry, Mom, I'll take good care of them.' Caleb grins as he ushers them away.

'Coffee, Sergeant Munroe?' asks Sienna, going to the table.

'Yes, let me…'

'No, sit down and I'll make it for you. Latte or Americano?'

'Latte, please.' I sink into my chair, and secretly, even though Sienna is just a teenage girl, I'm a bit overawed by being waited on by someone so famous, which makes me feel like a teenager myself.

She brings me the coffee, then grabs a Coke Zero from the table for herself and takes a seat in another leather chair that she turns to face mine, drawing her feet up under her, popping open the tab of the Coke and taking a swig.

'So how are you?' she asks. 'Has everyone here been looking after you?'

'They have, and the girls are delirious with joy,' I say, taking a sip of my coffee. 'Thanks for being so kind to them. That's something they'll never forget, you clapping and saying they were good.'

'Oh, I meant it. I wouldn't lie.' She is serious. 'I thought it was very professional. Do they take lessons?'

I can't wait to tell the girls this. 'Well, Ellie is in a youth theatre – she wants to be an actor – and Kate does Irish dancing. They do singing in school, and their uncle-in-law is a professional flamenco dancer and helped them with the routine…'

'Lots of people pulling them up then.' She nods. 'It's the only way. Do they get the talent from you or their dad or both?'

I laugh. 'Not me, certainly. But their dad is a keen musician, Irish trad, though. He plays the uilleann pipes.'

'Oh, I love those,' she breathes. 'So atmospheric. Lucky you, having an Irish piper in the house.'

'Ah…mm…' It's another astonishing moment in a generally astonishing day.

'So,' she continues cheerfully, 'I wanted to see you to thank you again for all your help.'

'That's no problem. Have you been in contact with Charlotte again?'

'Yes, Conor got me a different phone, so we've been WhatsApping a lot. She explained more about why she left, and I understand it better now. I even had a FaceTime with Phoebe – she's grown so much.'

She seems really happy as she tells me this. It's sad she has to use a secret phone to hide things from her dad, but I don't comment, I just let her talk.

'And I spoke to Michael as well, you know, the accountant Dad fired, and he told me all the rights I'll have when I'm eighteen, so I'm still thinking about that. It's a big step to do things for myself, even with Michael's help. I'm not used to it. It's a scary thought.' She stops and looks at me as if to see what I think. There's a youthful innocence to her that's very endearing.

'You can be scared and still stand tall.' I smile at her.

She's surprised, then laughs. 'Yeah, I see what you mean… If I don't fight back, I'll fall, won't I? Crazy, isn't it, that I spend all my time singing about empowerment and don't do anything about it.' She pulls a face, disappointed in herself. 'I guess I'm talking the talk without walking the walk.'

'I think you are walking the walk, but at your own pace,' I say gently. 'Finding your sister, making contact with Michael, those are both steps in the right direction.'

The door at the back of the box flies open, and there he is, Tony Black, in a tight black T-shirt, his tattoos on show down his muscular arms and a suspicious glare on his face that he is trying to mask with a big, fake, loving smile. 'There you are, baby. Time to do your warm-up vocals – the opening act is going on soon. And give me that. You know you shouldn't…' He whips the Coke out of her hand.

I expect her to apologise and jump up at once like she usually does for him, but this time, with a glance at me, she says, 'I'll be there in a minute, Dad. I'm just talking to Sergeant Munroe.'

'Ah yes, Officer Munroe. You sure do pop up everywhere, don't you?' He's pretending to joke, but his eyes are icy cold. 'But there's no time to chat, baby. Your voice coach is waiting.'

She half gets up, changes her mind and sits down again. 'No, Dad. Tell Alicia I'll come when I'm ready.'

'Sienna.' This is a man who does not like to be crossed. 'This isn't you. Come on, baby. Now.'

She sits there, not moving but not saying anything either. Her chin is stuck out, but I know that look, when a woman or girl is cowering inside. I've seen it on the faces of domestic abuse victims – and yes, they are almost all women – time and again when I call to their houses.

'Come with me, baby.' There's a menacing note in his voice, and he puts his hand on her, hard fingers digging into that thin little shoulder under the huge shirt.

She quivers and shifts a little in her chair; she's going to get up. She throws me a despairing glance.

'You don't have to do what he says, Sienna,' I say quietly, putting down my cup.

He throws me a withering glance. 'Stay out of this, Officer. This is none of your business.'

I hold his gaze as I get to my feet. 'You're wrong, Mr Black. Coercive control is against the law, so that makes it my business. I advise you to take your hand off your daughter.'

He pretends to be amazed, though he does let her go. 'Coercive… What? Officer Munroe, I'm a loving father taking care of his daughter's best interests. I'm not controlling anyone. Someone's gotta protect my girl in a world full of sharks…' That fake smile again. 'Now, leave us, please.' He jabs his big finger at me and then the door.

'No, I don't want Sergeant Munroe to leave.' Sienna is on her feet now, rubbing her shoulder. He's hurt her, and I wonder suddenly what those huge baggy shirts and cargo pants are intended to hide; maybe they're not about empowerment after all. 'And she's right, Dad, about you being controlling. It's ridiculous. I go out on stage singing songs like "Scared but Standing Tall", all these songs about being brave and free, and here I am, without access to my own money, my passport, anything. It needs to change. If my fans found out you treat me this way, like I'm helpless…'

'Sienna, I treat you this way because without me, you *are* helpless.' He says it almost kindly, but he grabs hold of her again, hustling her towards the door.

I get in between them and the door. 'Mr Black, I'm warning you for the second time to take your hands off your daughter.'

'Who the hell do you think you are? Get out of our way, lady!'

'Sergeant…' Sienna's voice is pleading; she has tears in her eyes.

I need to take him on, but I've no backup, he's a huge man, my lungs are shot, and everyone and everything keeps reminding me I'm getting old. 'I'm going to call security, Sienna,' I say.

I turn to open the door to the suite when an arm goes around my neck and I am yanked backwards. Tony Black has me in a headlock, crushing my windpipe so I can't shout out or breathe.

'Stop interfering,' he snarls in my ear.

'Dad, let her go!' gasps Sienna, sobbing.

'You shouldn't have been talking to this woman behind my back, Sienna. She's just after your money, just like Michael…' The arm tightens around my neck, and his other hand is on the back of my neck; it's a Krav Maga chokehold. He's very strong. My lungs are fighting for air, things are going dark, I'm getting scared for my life…

'Dad, please, I'll do whatever you want, I'll say whatever you want…' Such terror in that young girl's voice.

'Will you, baby? Will you?' His voice softens a little. 'Promise me?'

'I promise, Dad, just let her go…'

'Tell her she has to leave or you'll get security to throw her out.'

'Sergeant Munroe, you have to leave!'

And that's the point at which I decide to be scared but stand tall anyway, even if I am only fit for the scrap heap.

I summon up my Garda training, dip my chin to protect my neck and reach back, grabbing the hand holding my head. I manage to get a grip on two of his fingers and bend them back hard and fast, causing him to yelp with pain and let go of my neck. Then as it comes down, I grab his wrist in a C-grip and hug it to my chest, immobilising his right hand. I pull the arm he had across my throat downwards and rotate out of the hold, so I am face to face with him. I swiftly knee him hard in the groin. He doubles over, and as he does, I interlace my fingers and, using the strength of two hands, land a blow to the back of his neck that sends him forwards onto his stomach. Once he's down, I slam my knees into his back and pin him down, all the while gasping gratefully for air.

'Get off me,' roars Tony Black, puce with rage at being overpowered. 'Sienna, call security!'

At once I hear her open the door and start shrieking for someone called Dave. Heavy feet come running, and I don't know what's going to happen, but I'm damned if I'm letting this man off the floor.

'Get this woman off me and throw her out!' howls Black, his cheek pinned to the cream wool carpet.

'Yes, boss.' Huge hands take hold of my shoulders. Dave is a Pacific islander of some sort, like a cross between Dwayne 'The Rock' Johnson and Jason Momoa, all tattoos and a shaved head – and utterly terrifying. Three other men, bulky but nothing like Dave, run in behind him, all with earpieces and wearing black T-shirts and black cargo pants.

But Sienna shouts, 'Don't touch her!'

'Sienna?' The security guard takes his hands away, though he sounds very confused.

'Do as I say, Dave!' roars Tony Black. 'Get rid of this woman! I'm the boss here! Remember who pays your wages!'

'You're not the boss any more, Dad. You're fired,' says Sienna, and though there's fear in her voice, I can feel she's stepping into her power. 'Dave, I'm your boss now. I am Sienna Black. Everyone in this entourage has their wages paid by me and me alone, and now I'm telling you to remove my father from the premises. He is no longer my manager and no longer welcome here.'

'If you say so, Sienna.' Dave sounds a bit happier now. 'Umm… ma'am…'

'Munroe,' I croak. The pressure to my windpipe has left me even hoarser than usual.

'Mrs Munroe, if you could, umm, just move aside a bit.'

Slowly I release my grip on Tony Black and get to my feet. Black gets up as well, shaking his shoulders, and for a moment just stands there facing Dave, who is far bigger even than Tony Black, bigger than Jerome – a wall of American muscle, arms big as my legs.

'OK, Tony, you heard her…' Despite his size, he's a bit awed by his mission to escort his former boss off the premises, and Tony Black takes advantage of his uncertainty, gesturing at him to stand aside.

'Let me out of here, Dave. Sienna, I'll be waiting upstairs.'

'No, Dad, you're to go now.' But her voice wavers.

'Don't be silly, baby,' he snaps.

'I know what you did to Charlotte, about Phoebe, what you threatened to do to Michael. I know about it all, Dad.'

I get out my phone, dial Ronan's work phone and put him on loudspeaker.

'Assistant Garda Commissioner Ronan Brady,' he says as he picks up.

'Hi, Ronan.' My voice is a bit less croaky now.

'Hi, Mags, good to hear from you. What can I do for you?'

'I need you to send some officers to Croke Park. I've been assaulted and threatened, a struggle ensued…'

'Oh my God, Mags, are you all right?'

'Yes, I'm fine. I easily overpowered my assailant. But security here needs help ejecting him, and I don't want to do it myself. I'm here with my daughters to see the concert.'

'Happy to help. What's his name and where are you?'

'In the corporate suite, and the man's name is Tony Black.'

'Officers on the way.'

'Thanks, Ronan.' I ring off.

Tony Black is choking with rage, Dave is looking more confident but still not sure what to do, and Sienna is white with the effort of standing up to her father; she's ready to collapse.

'Dave, why don't you and your colleagues bring Tony into the neighbouring box and stay with him until the guards arrive,' I suggest. 'And Sienna, you should sit down and take a moment to recover.'

While Dave escorts the speechless and seething Black out of the box, Sienna sinks into one of the leather chairs. As I bring her a bottle of water, my two girls arrive back with Caleb, loaded down with merchandise, happy and joyful and completely unaware of the drama that's just occurred.

'Mam, we got so much stuff... Oh, sorry, Sienna...' They've just realised their idol is still here and go all shy again.

'Thanks so much for all the merch,' says Kate awkwardly, and Ellie doesn't know where to put herself.

The support act has just started on the stage outside, warming the crowd up for the main event. It's some woman I've never heard of, but I know the girls were excited to see her on stage. They glance in the direction of the music, hesitating, not wanting to seem rude.

'Go on, go and watch, that's what you're here for.' Sienna smiles, and their faces light up as they skip out onto the balcony.

Myself and Sienna remain sitting in the chairs side by side. She doesn't seem to want to leave, though I'm sure she should be getting ready.

A short while later, there's a tap on the door, and it's Caleb, who shows in a female liaison police officer. And with the girls still out on the balcony, too absorbed to notice what's going on behind them, the officer, who introduces herself as Garda Madden takes a statement from me and then Sienna, who's still drained and scared but gives a truthful account of what happened and even lets Garda Madden examine her shoulder, which is bruised with the imprint of her father's fingers. There are other bruises as well, I notice, on her upper arms.

'And has he ever hurt you before, Sienna?' asks the female officer, who's clearly noticed as well.

Sienna's green eyes are shadowed before she closes them, a single tear seeping out.

'Were you frightened of him, Sienna?'

She nods.

The officer closes her notebook. 'I'll leave you now, Miss Black, but are you prepared to give evidence against your father if you decide to press charges on your own account?'

Another nod, her eyes still closed.

Down in the arena, the support act finishes and the crowd begins to chant Sienna's name, eagerly awaiting her on stage. Kate and Ellie are still out on the balcony, hanging over it, absorbing the atmosphere.

I sit waiting for Sienna to leave, to get ready, to do something, but she remains here with her eyes closed. Eventually I say softly, 'Sienna?'

She shudders, her eyes still closed. 'What should I do, Sergeant Munroe?'

She's so used to having her father push her this way and that, and maybe it was the same when she was in care. She seems lost without someone to order her around. I don't want to do the same.

'Do whatever you think is right, Sienna.'

The chanting from outside is becoming more insistent. 'Sien-na, Sien-na, Sien-na…'

'I don't know what the right thing is to do. I'm not sure I can face it…'

'You decide.' I won't push her.

Kate and Ellie have turned away from the balcony and are gazing in at us, puzzled. They don't understand why their idol is still just sitting here, her eyes closed, doing nothing.

Sienna says so softly I have to lean close to hear her words, 'I think the right thing is to go out there, not to let people down…'

Kate and Ellie draw closer now, anxious and worried.

'I just don't think I have the strength.' She sighs.

'I think you do have the strength, though, Sienna,' I say, now that I'm sure this is what she wants. 'And you give Kate and Ellie here strength as well. Every song you write is about overcoming the odds, digging deep into yourself…'

She inhales. The chanting is louder than ever now. And then finally she opens her eyes and fixes her gaze on me and then on Kate and Ellie.

'Can you two come with me?' she asks.

'Come… What? Where?' Ellie is bewildered.

'Out on stage. You can help me start with my song "Scared but Standing Tall", right?'

'We… With you…' Kate looks nearly sick.

'I can do it if you guys come with me. I'm going to open with it. You two are my pulling up today. I'm feeling small and weak, and I need you out there with me. Are you able to help me?'

'Oh…oh…' Ellie's voice is faint.

'Are we able to help Sienna, Ellie?' Kate gazes up at her big sister with huge, scared eyes. 'Are we?'

No more than Kate, Ellie is white as a sheet and shaking, but still to her little sister, she is the final arbiter of all things. She pulls Kate up. I hope they stay like this their whole lives long.

Ellie throws a terrified glance at me, and I think of all the people who saved up, the kids whose birthday or Christmas present this concert was, the mothers who sat up all night, and I give her a nod. If this is the only way to get Sienna out there, let it be done. And let my girls prove to themselves that it's possible to be scared, terrified even, and do it anyway.

Ellie steels herself and nods at Kate. 'Let's go,' she says, and Sienna gets to her feet.

'Brave girls.' I stand as well and hug my daughters, and I don't invite Sienna, but she steps forwards and I have the three of them in my arms. 'Scared but standing tall,' I say, trying to breathe confidence into all three. I can feel them trembling, but somehow I know they're going to be OK.

When Sienna opens the door at the back of the box, the team who have clearly been loitering outside waiting for her spring to attention, and when Sienna explains to them what's going to happen, they nod and rush to action.

As my daughters are swept away, Kate slips her hand into her big sister's. Ellie looks down, gives her an encouraging smile and puts her arm around Kate's thin shoulders. This is the sisterhood right in front of me. I know my girls will stick together, no matter what happens.

'Sien-na, Sien-na, Sien-na…' Her fans are getting louder and louder as they wait for her. I go out to the balcony to watch, and my heart races nervously. Will Ellie and Kate really have the courage to go out there, to support Sienna as she sings? And what will Sienna ask them to do? Time ticks by, and I wonder what's happening backstage.

Twenty long noisy minutes later, explosions go off, there's a burst of *It's not like it was for us girls in the old days*, and the crowd goes wild as a hydraulic platform rises through the swirling smoke, to reveal not one but three figures with radio mikes on their heads and with their arms raised – Sienna Black, international superstar, and on either side of her, Kate and Ellie Munroe, Irish schoolgirls from Ballycarrick.

Oh, my brave girls, hold your nerve, I pray for them fervently.

'Good evening, Dublin!' Sienna calls from the platform in her signature raspy voice.

'Good evening, Sienna!' eighty thousand teenage girls shout back.

'How are you all doing?' She beams then, her face appearing on fifty-foot screens each side of the stage, and it's as if she is spreading the glow of her pleasure on the crowd; they almost sigh as they bask in the warmth of her love.

'Ladies and gentlemen, girls and boys, let me introduce my friends, all the way from the county of Galway, Ellie and Kate Munroe!' More whoops and screaming – the crowd is happy to follow wherever Sienna leads.

'We're doing something cool this time, Ireland – are you ready?' she calls, to a cacophonous response.

The slow opening bars of 'Scared but Standing Tall' ring out around the arena, and the platform descends until it's level with the boards. Sienna and Kate take one step forwards onto the stage, and they sing the first line together in English.

'You said I had to believe whatever you said...'

Then Sienna turns and stretches out her other hand, and Ellie comes forwards to sing the Irish words by herself in her husky vibrato, an ordinary Irish teenager, standing beside one of the biggest stars the world has ever seen.

Sienna and Kate sing the second line, the two of them projected together onto the screen to the left of the stage. 'You said I was too weak and scared to leave your bed...'

Ellie follows on in Irish, appearing by herself on the fifty-foot screen to the right of the stage.

And then the music bursts out into the deafening uplifting part of the anthem, and they burst into that mixture of Irish dancing and hip-hop. Sienna is such a pro; in those twenty minutes backstage, she's learnt the girls' routine and is doing it ten times better than either of them. But it's fine. They're perfectly professional beside her, not a step out of place, and they're singing at the same time, English and Irish together. 'I'm scared but standing tall. If I don't fight back, I'll fall. I know I got it in me, you're never gonna kill me...'

At a gesture from Sienna, the audience picks up the next verse, while on stage, Sienna hugs first Ellie and then Kate, then hands them over to two stagehands, who bring them aside into the wings while Sienna moves to the front. She puts her hand on the microphone stand but then just smiles and waits, letting the stadium continue to sing without her. On the huge screen, her eyelashes and eyebrows are delicate amber gold and her green eyes are mesmerizingly bright – glazed over with tears?

It's deafening, thousands of girls singing at the tops of their lungs, and I look at my two, arms around each other in the wings, so happy. I think maybe the gender gap really is closing, and sure, it's thanks to the suffragettes and those women who in every walk of life for the last hundred years refused to be subjugated, but maybe it's down to people like Sienna Black too, who know what's right even when they're being treated wrong.

Finally the last lines are coming, and Sienna raises her hand and stops the crowd. The music, while still played at ear-splitting volume, slows down…

And Sienna, in her husky, enthralling voice, sings all alone at the front of the stage, slowly and softly. 'It's you who is broken.'

The crowd starts to cheer, and she stops and holds up her hand for more silence before she brings her mouth back to the mike and breathes, 'You will never break me.'

As the anthem ends, she remains where she is at the microphone, and slowly a deep hush descends over the crowd. When you could hear a pin drop, she begins to speak. 'The only way one of us can be equal is if we are all equal. Tonight I was pulled up by two friends who helped me when I was weak and small…'

Ninety-two beats per minute. That's how she speaks, like she is Martin Luther King Jr at the Lincoln Memorial. But there is something so compelling about her, so much more powerful on stage than in real life.

'So everywhere you go, I want you to pull someone up. We are the sisterhood, and what raises one, raises all. Ellie and Kate Munroe from Ballycarrick, County Galway, come out here and take a bow.'

A huge cheer goes up as she beckons to my daughters. The camera goes to the three of them, arms around each other for a few sweet seconds, before the opening riff of the next song played at ear-splitting volume sends the already overexcited crowd into paroxysms of ecstasy, and my brave, lovely daughters leave the stage hand in hand.

CHAPTER 21

We have quite a drive home. The girls are having their ten minutes of fame, at least among the teenagers of Ballycarrick. Despite the late hour, their phones beep non-stop all the way, so much so I have to order them to put them on silent – I keep thinking it is something wrong with the car.

Kate says it's even more thrilling than being best friends with Zoë after the 'Blue-Eyed Horse' TikTok came out, and Ellie is on such a feminist high after the concert that when Carrot texts to ask her to be the singer in his hip-hop band instead of Clodagh, she tells him to crawl back under his rock and blocks him.

Kieran is awake when we get there, having been texted by everyone congratulating our girls, and over tea and chocolate biscuits, he is enthralled to hear the whole story, before we all finally hit our beds at three in the morning. He's been working non-stop, some of the crews working through the night, and Kieran has become the foreman, organising the work on the Drumlish site and Dora McGovern's caravan, but apparently it's nearly complete. One more day will do it if everyone works Sunday.

* * *

On Monday I go up with Kieran to Drumlish to admire the completed work.

The paths across the site have been concreted, so no one has to walk through mud, and Violetta the florist has sent up some lovely hanging baskets to dot around the place.

The secure annex for the nurses has been built onto the toilet block, so they have their own bathroom facilities and changing room, as well as a safe to keep the medications.

I admire the annex floor, and Kieran explains that Mairead Cullen of the neighbourhood watch posted that she had a laminate floor going spare. They had been going to use it but decided against it in the end and carpeted the spare bedroom, but the floor was non-refundable and so that was collected and used, and Kieran had Marius and Jack, two of his roofers, fit it. 'A click laminate floor shouldn't confuse two experienced carpenters, I suppose,' he remarks with a grin when I tell him how impressed I am with the job they've done.

The flat roof my husband did himself, and he says if they decide to keep the annex, it will last for years. 'Unlike the bloody patchwork quilt I've had to make of the church roof,' he says. He hates doing a botch job. 'I suppose I'll never be rid of it until it crashes down and kills poor Father Doyle.'

In the caravan the huge double-fitted bed Dora shared with her enormous husband is gone, and the partition wall between that and the boys' room has been removed. The hospital bed has arrived, delivered this morning, and it has plenty of chairs around it for visitors to sit. Delia's old bedroom at the far end is reserved for the night nurses. Harmony Homecare is supplying two nurses for the 9 p.m. to 9 a.m. shift, and one of them will be in attendance at all times; the one not on duty will get a few hours' sleep in Delia's single bed, which has a new mattress.

The caravan's very neat and clean inside despite the flurry of work. Foxy Clancy's brother Bingo, who spends his life trying to explain to people that though he looks like his brother, they are nothing alike, is the best painter in Ballycarrick and has made the place elegant and bright.

One of the nicest changes, and this was Delia's idea, is that the local double-glazing firm has put a window into the ceiling above the hospital bed, so when Dora opens her eyes, she will see the sky, the sun and rain by day, the stars by night, just as she did sleeping under the tarp thrown over the shafts when she was a child.

There's also a portacabin supplied by one of Kieran's builder friends to use as a café for visitors, which is a great idea; there are bound to be loads. Dora is usually desperate to make everyone a cuppa, so she'll be happy to know it's there. Luigi has promised to send up lasagne, Bertie is going to supply sausage rolls, and Lavinia Moran has donated an old – read, four years old – three-piece suite; Lavinia upgrades her perfect house constantly ever since it was featured in the interiors magazine of the *Western People* somewhere between ten and fifteen years ago.

Between people's generosity with both money and time, it's amazing what has been accomplished in such a short period, and how cheaply. It's very reassuring, because it means we should be able to keep the night care nurses on for as long as necessary.

We are over the forty thousand mark on the GoFundMe page, and that's just the settled community.

Delia tells me her enormous extended family, not to be outdone, has been donating a lot of cash, matching the GoFundMe almost penny for penny, and she's been keeping a running account. One donation caused her a lot of astonishment. Lenny Carmody gave ten thousand pounds, appearing at her door in person despite him having a wife and small child back in England and apparently working a low-paid stable-hand job for his father-in-law, Alphonsus Ward, somewhere in Kent.

DORA IS due home on Tuesday.

Delia waits at the site for the arrival of the ambulance, ensuring everything is perfect and the boys are looked after, and I go to the hospice because a number of Travellers are expected; they want to pay their respects as Dora is brought home to die.

I get to Hollymount for ten in the morning, and the car park is full of vans and four-wheel drives. When I get out of my car in my uniform, the Travellers also exit their vehicles, old and young, men and women. Jerome must have told them to wait for me to arrive. There are whispers and nudging among the children, but the adults are quiet.

Martin Carmody comes up to me as I approach the front door.

'We're not here to make any trouble for the hospice, Sergeant. We just wanted to…' He can't find the words. Dora was a Carmody before she married Jerome, and she's maintained her links to her original family all her life.

'Be here for her, I know, Martin. I'm sure they'll appreciate it,' I say, and he nods.

Inside, Jerome is standing with a tall, grey-haired woman, and he beckons me over and introduces me to Professor Kinsella, the palliative care consultant who Seamus recruited to our cause. After greeting me politely, she turns back to Jerome.

'So, Mr McGovern, Dora has been given adequate pain relief for the journey, and she'll get oxygen in the ambulance. It's all set up for her to go. The porters will bring her down now.' She shakes his hand. 'And for what it's worth, though I was against the idea of you taking her home in the beginning – my colleague, Professor Linehan, had to persuade me – I can see now how important this is to your wife and your family.'

'Thanks, Professor Kinsella. We couldn't have done it at all without everyone's help. And everyone here, you've been very good to us, and we'll never forget it,' says Jerome.

She nods and smiles, then her beeper goes off and she heads off down another corridor.

'Are you ready?' I ask him, and he nods. His face is a mask of pain and loss, and he knows as well as everyone else this is Dora's final journey. I'm just so glad he's been able to do it her way, and even if she dies tonight, he will know he's honoured her last wishes.

Together we go up to the room, and there are two porters there ahead of us. Dora's belongings have been sent back to the site already.

'We can take you in a wheelchair or on a trolley. Which would you prefer, Mrs McGovern?' the older of the porters says.

She looks past him, so tiny and birdlike in the bed, her grey hair in a neat plait now. She removes the oxygen mask and puts her hand out to Jerome. 'Will you?' she whispers.

Saying nothing to anyone there, Jerome McGovern, his huge bulk filling the small room, gently pulls back the covers to reveal his tiny wife, reaches down and puts his arms under her.

The porters exchange a worried glance and make like they are going to intervene – this is very irregular – but I hold my hand out to stop them.

'It's all right,' I say, as Jerome stands with Dora in his arms. Her weight is nothing to him. I've seen Jerome McGovern stop a cantering pony with his shoulder; he's powerfully strong.

I place her fur-lined slippers on her feet, a warm dark-green beanie hat on her head and a fleece banket over her, tucking it around her. She gives me a small smile.

He walks out of the room, cradling his wife gently in his arms like he's carrying a baby, and all the way down the corridor, the nurses on duty stop and stand, each saying goodbye to the McGoverns.

They pass the alcove with the sofas and enter the huge lift, and I join them, keeping a respectful distance. Jerome stares straight ahead, and Dora rests against his chest.

As the lift descends, he lowers his head and murmurs something to her. It's in Cant, their language, and I don't know what it is he says, but though she's so very ill, she smiles.

More staff and some visitors stop to watch as Jerome steps out of the lift, his wife in his arms. This is an unusual sight, and Jerome is every inch a Travelling man, so people will be wondering what's happening. They don't seem disapproving, but they are clearly puzzled.

Outside the breeze is fresh with a little heat in it. Dora turns her face to it, and I wonder if she feels like a bird released from a cage.

The Travellers have lined the path from the main door to where the private ambulance is parked, McGoverns and Carmodys standing three deep, some in tears, all solemn. Jerome walks through them, head and shoulders above most, and brings Dora to the ambulance. Two paramedics appear to receive her and settle her in, fixing another oxygen mask to her face. Without asking if he can, Jerome gets in beside her, his bulk dipping the vehicle on its springs.

The paramedics close the door, and the ambulance drives away as the Travellers disperse.

CHAPTER 22

Ten days later, Dora dies peacefully in Jerome's arms, surrounded by her family, gazing up at the stars through the new window in the roof of the caravan, which is open.

Three days after that, to my relief, the funeral goes off without a hitch. There are huge numbers, but everyone, and I mean everyone, behaves with respect. The people of Ballycarrick, though nervous, don't close their doors and shutter their shops and pubs as they did for Blades's funeral, and the Travellers in return do nothing to upset anyone.

As at Delia and Darren's wedding, the Dromahane guards do the honours, and with Leo Burke as the sergeant, they don't make the pig's ear that Duckie made of the last Traveller funeral there. Everything remains calm, no disrespect on either side.

Dora's coffin is drawn up Main Street in a glass hearse pulled by black horses and filled to the brim with white lilies, the coffin buried beneath their weight. Behind the hearse, Jerome walks slowly through the rain with his head bowed, followed by Delia and her brothers. It's been raining all week.

My heart goes out to the boys.

Gerard and Paddy stare blankly ahead of them as they walk, taking nothing in, and the other lad, the youngest, Pecker, leans against Delia; she strokes his head. He's only thirteen, too young to lose his mother.

The church bells toll mournfully as we take our places, and Kieran is torn between his sadness for the McGoverns and his grief for the state of the roof; there's a constant pinging going on, not unlike my daughters' phones that night two weeks ago as we drove back from Dublin, but in this case, it's the pinging of rain dripping into buckets all over the church.

After the funeral Tatiana caters for everyone in the Samovar. Sandwiches and soup are available all day, and the cost of it all is covered. I know Tatiana would have done it for free, but that's what the fund is for. The money that was needed for everything in the end barely put a dent in the final sum collected, and that's without taking into account anything donated by the Travellers. Delia has shown me the tally she's keeping, and the cash sum matches the amount donated by the settled community. So 110,000 altogether. And in the end, the full cost of bringing Dora home was only twenty thousand.

'If all the bills are paid out of the GoFundMe side of things, and we pay back anything left over from there to the donors, Jerome will still wind up with a nice little sum because he'll be able to keep all the cash contributions from the Traveller side,' says Sharon, when we discuss what to do with the remaining money.

I shake my head. 'I don't think he'll want to keep anything that was intended for Dora's homecoming.'

'You think?' Sharon thinks I'm a bit starry-eyed over the Travellers, where she's a bit more cynical. She isn't racist, nothing like it, and she was proud of the GoFundMe page, but some of the younger Carmody girls do shoplift from her boutique, and despite her good heart and not wanting to tar everyone with the same brush, she can't help assuming Travellers aren't strictly honest, even Jerome.

Around eight o'clock, on my fifth sparkling water, I give Kieran the nod that we'll go. He looks as tired as I feel after this long day of celebrating Dora's life. The girls are around somewhere with Fionn and Evie, and I go searching for them in the yard, where the spring evening is still bright. Fionn has blended into the family as if he's always been part of it, and he told Gearoid and Enrico that it was great at school telling everyone that the two girls who sang with Sienna Black were his cousins. He clearly loves his new life, and Gearoid and Enrico love him too. It's wonderful to see.

The marquee has been erected again, and the tables are full, but no sign of my two. I check around the back, but the outside benches are wet because it's been raining all day, in keeping with the mood, so nobody is around except for Jerome, smoking a cigarette by the stream.

I feel I shouldn't be here, interrupting his private grief. I turn to leave, but he says my name and I turn back again.

'How are you?' I ask, going up to him.

He sighs, a deep, sad, ragged exhale. 'Ara, terrible, but sure what can I do, only keep going?'

'That's all you can do. There's plenty of rearing left in your lads – they'll need you.'

'They'll be grand.' He flicks the cigarette into the bubbling stream and shoves his huge hands in the pockets of his black leather coat, watching the little red burning light go out. 'She was peaceful at the end, Mags. We were all there, me and Delia and the lads, and she went easy. God rest her. She was talking to her mother, like she could see her, so please God, they came for her.'

'I'm so sorry for your loss, Jerome. She was a special person.'

He shakes his head. 'She wasn't really, Mags. She was a very ordinary person. She had no airs or graces, but she was a good mother and a good wife, and it won't be the same without her.'

'Well, she was special to you.'

'She was.'

'We're going now, Jerome, but I'll call in the next few days. Take care.' I turn to go – I need to find the girls – but again he stops me leaving, touching my arm.

'I owe you, Mags. None of this, Dora coming home, the funeral, none of it would have been the way I wanted it to be only for you.

Delia's been keeping a record, and the money will be given back to all the GoFundMe donors –'

'Jerome, let's not talk about that today. There's no need.' But I'm glad I was right about him not wanting to keep any money meant for Dora.

'Well, we'll talk about it later, Mags,' he says. 'Are you workin' tomorrow?'

'I am. We missed our team meeting this week with one thing and another, so I've everyone coming in a bit early at seven thirty. Hopefully we'll get there before the reporters.'

'Half seven…' It's like he's making a note of it.

'Except Delia, of course,' I reassure him. 'She can take the rest of the week off.'

'No, I think Delia will be there. I'll say it to her…'

I'm puzzled. 'Do not, Jerome. If you really want her to talk to me about the money, I'll see her next week.'

Instead of answering me, he pats my shoulder, as if he's soothing a skittish mare. 'Well, thanks again, Mags, for everything,' he says, and turns away from me, lighting another cigarette.

I go off in search of the girls again. They've school tomorrow and need to get to bed. Kate and Evie are squished into a corner of the restaurant, still talking about Sienna Black. It's the topic of conversation for the year, nothing else is worthy, and Evie is loving basking in the reflected glory. I beckon them to come with me and park them with Kieran, then go off again to find Ellie.

My older daughter is in a passionate embrace with the fickle Carrot, wrapped around each other in the lane at the side of the pub where Teresa from the bakery once rifled through all the empty packages in the Samovar's bins searching for the mysterious source of Tatiana's unbeatable coffee.

I clear my throat, and Ellie and Carrot spring apart. He saunters off nonchalantly, and my daughter comes sheepishly towards me while I hum a few bars of 'Scared but Standing Tall'.

Seems like you can sing as many female anthems as you like, but teenage hormones will get you every time.

CHAPTER 23

The alarm seems to go off about fifteen minutes after I fall asleep, and I groan, rolling over to find my beeping phone.

Kieran is already gone; he's a great one for leaping out of bed when he has a job on. But I have to drag myself from the bed to the shower and stand under it for a full ten minutes to wake up. I hate early meetings, especially on Mondays.

I rap on the girls' bedroom doors to remind them to get out of bed and have their breakfasts eaten. I'll pop home after the briefing to take them to school.

I drive down. After the activity of Dora's funeral, the town is quiet; there's not a soul about. None of the shops will be open for another two hours at least, and I'm happy to see the reporters haven't arrived yet – that was part of the reason for meeting early.

I pull into the car park at the back of the station…and slam on the brakes.

What on earth?

There, tied to the railings of the wheelchair access ramp is a huge truly beautiful chestnut-coloured horse. He looks up at the sound of my car, stamps his back nearside hoof and gives a whinny. There's a bucket of water on the ground and a small heap of hay, which he goes back to investigating.

At first I think it's a wind-up, like the dead cob in Dromahane, only alive this time. Someone's idea of a joke. There's no white star on his forehead, so it can't be him.

But as I get out and gingerly approach the animal, he turns his big head towards me, and sure enough, he has blue eyes.

'Are you Chance Your Arm?' I whisper as I continue my approach, hardly daring to believe it. 'Did they cover over your star?' I'd like to examine his forehead, but he flattens his ears and I don't go any closer. I don't want to spook him or have him damage himself or me trying to get away.

All showjumpers need expert handling, and according to Farah Sadiq, Chance Your Arm is a particularly highly strung, emotionally needy animal. Livestock is not my area of expertise; I have enough problems in that direction with the animals I've already got.

I ring Zoë, who is on her way in as well.

'I'm two minutes away, Sarge,' she says as she answers the phone.

'Park outside on the road,' I say, 'and contact the others to park outside too.'

'Sure, Sarge. Is something wrong?'

'Nothing's wrong, Zoë. But I think you might deserve a medal.'

I hang up while she's still asking what on earth I'm on about and stand watching the gorgeous horse with my hands in my pockets. After a long suspicious look at me, he seems content to let me stay there while he goes back to eating his hay, crunching and masticating.

Though I didn't ask her to come in today, Delia turns up before Zoë, a folder under her arm. 'Sarge, Zoë said we were to park out on the road…' She sees the horse. 'Oh my God, is that… No… What…?'

Zoë walks into the car park right behind her and comes to a stunned halt, also incredulous. 'It's not, is it?'

'I think it might be,' I say quietly. 'He has blue eyes.'

'There's no star, though?' Delia hands me the folder and goes right up to him and examines his forehead, pushing her fingers through his coat. Chance Your Arm, if it is indeed him, has no problem with her touching him; he even gives a contented snicker. She's clearly a horse whisperer, like most Travellers, especially her daddy. 'Yeah, this is dyed. Let me run into the station and get some cleaning wipes.'

'No, no, wait.' Zoë roots in her huge fake-leather vegan bag and takes out a packet of hypo-allergenic, no-chemical, not-tested-on-animals wipes and hands them to Delia, who gently rubs the horse's forehead. Lo and behold a white star appears.

'It's him,' Delia says with confidence, and Zoë's face illuminates with sheer joy.

'Oh, Sarge, he'll be so glad to get back to the people he knows and loves, rebuild his attachments until he is confident and secure in the knowledge that he will never be abandoned again –'

'Meanwhile, Zoë,' I cut in, 'why don't I and Delia stay here and make sure he doesn't get unattached again, while you go and ring Assistant Garda Commissioner Brady to tell him the news that you've recovered Chance Your Arm.'

'But I didn't, and anyway…it's too early to call someone that important, isn't it?' She's alarmed, like a rabbit in the headlights.

'Well, you did, because you made that video and asked that anyone with any information contact you. You gave out your own name, as well as the number of this station' – I raise an eyebrow as she blushes; she knows now that was a rookie mistake, but nonetheless – 'and so whoever returned Chance Your Arm returned him to you. You asked for him back and you got him. And as for it being too early, the whole country has been waiting on this news. Ronan won't care if you wake him.'

'Shouldn't I ring Inspector Duckie first?'

Probably she should, that's the chain of command, but if she does, he'll take all the credit.

'No, this is your case, Zoë. You solved it, you make the call. You can call Duckie afterwards and tell him to organise a horsebox.' Even Duckie, whose mystery-solving skills are around the same standard as Scooby-Doo's, should be able to source one of those in Dromahane, where he lives. There are lots of posh types out there with girls in the pony club.

'Are you sure you don't want to call the Assistant Commissioner, Sarge?' she asks.

I shake my head. 'It's nothing whatsoever to do with me. Now go.'

Nicola, Michael and Darren turn up next and stand there blinking.

Michael speaks first. 'Am I dreaming or is that…'

'Not dreaming,' I confirm. 'Zoë has just gone to ring it in now.'

And we all laugh as Zoë's blue-eyed horse whinnies contentedly again; Delia is stroking his neck.

The rest of the day is bedlam.

The first to arrive is Duckie, throwing his weight around like this is all him. He's got a battered old trailer and a mutinous farmer with him, but the trailer is clearly too small and has been used for sheep, and Delia tells me it's dangerous, that Chance Your Arm will injure himself in it and probably pick up some awful infection if he cuts himself. So I was wrong – Duckie isn't even capable of finding a suitable horsebox.

Duckie tries to override Delia. The reporters are turning up now, and he's keen to get a photo opportunity of himself leading Chance Your Arm into the sheep trailer in time for the morning news. 'I know you ladies are all about animal welfare,' he says in his most patronising tone, like this is a case of some doting old woman with a cat she treats as her baby, 'but take it from one who knows something about horses…'

Delia doesn't even bother arguing back; she just stares at him in blank contempt, her arms folded, blocking his way.

Zoë is more sympathetic. 'Detective Inspector Duckie,' she says, 'I think Delia knows better than any of us, so maybe we'll let her deal with it. Remember we talked about your control issues? This is a good opportunity to practise your mindfulness techniques?'

Duckie loses it. 'I think you should be locked up, seriously, in a lunatic asylum! You're mad!'

The horse whinnies in alarm. Delia has to soothe him by rubbing his neck and mumbling in Cant.

'Maybe it's best if you go inside, Donal.' I say. The press would love nothing more than a bust-up between us at this stage.

He does it reluctantly.

Meanwhile I get on the phone to Matthew Hilser. The headmaster of St Colm's is a horse fanatic, which is why the school now has its own stables, cared for by Jerome, and he's delighted to help. Fifteen minutes later, a huge gleaming horsebox arrives, big enough for four horses. Duckie appears out on the road and immediately takes ownership of that as well, waving his arms around as he directs it to park outside; it's too big to turn into our car park. He also encourages the reporters to set up their cameras and flashes. 'I'll be bringing the animal out shortly, so you'll get a good shot.'

I go back behind to where Delia and Chance Your Arm are still waiting, followed by Duckie. He will hog this limelight, hell or high water.

'Sarge,' says Delia, 'I really don't think it's a good idea to let Detective Inspector Cassidy do this.'

'Donal, can we discuss this for a minute?' I ask Duckie, trying not to be overheard by the crowding reporters.

'Oh, get out of my way!' he barks. He brushes me aside and then goes barging past Delia, who looks like she'd brain him if he wasn't her superior officer.

'Donal, please…' I beg as Duckie grabs the halter.

I'm praying Chance Your Arm takes a well-deserved chunk out of him before the stupid man can untie him, but unfortunately the halter and rope are secured by a slip knot, which is easily released by tugging on the right end of the rope. Duckie does this the first time – more by luck than on purpose – and jerks the horse's head up out of the hay.

'Come on.'

Chance Your Arm doesn't do anything for a moment, just stares at him in haughty astonishment. Then he rolls his eyes and bares his enormous teeth, which are even bigger and whiter than Duckie's own.

'Whoa, whoa!' roars Duckie, alarmed.

With a furious snort, the huge chestnut rears up on his powerful hind legs, hanging for a moment in the air, while Duckie hangs on to the rope in terror.

'Let go, Duckie, let go!' shouts Delia, in her horror forgetting not to use his nickname.

But the eejit can't let go; he has the rope wrapped around his hand. Chance Your Arm bolts, dragging Duckie out of the car park behind him, puce-faced and still tangled.

'Hold on, Detective Inspector Duckie!' yell the delighted reporters. 'Don't let go!'

'Oh no, oh no!' Zoë is panicking; I am as well. The flashes and clicking of the photographers are enraging the horse still further, and Duckie is flung around everywhere, on his front, on his back. Then Chance Your Arm turns and lashes out with his forelegs, and finally Duckie is thrown onto his back in the middle of the street as the whooping reporters applaud his spectacular acrobatics.

'We're going to lose Chance Your Arm! He's going to go charging out into the main road – he'll get knocked down!' groans Zoë.

'Everyone, in your cars! We'll see if we can head him off!' I shout.

The others scatter towards their cars left out on the road, and I dive into mine. But before I pull away, I hear a cool clear whistle, and then another, and then a sudden silence. No more laughter, no more whooping, no applause. Not even cameras clicking. Only many voices going, 'Shh, shh…'

I turn off the engine again, step out and go to the railing overlooking the road. Delia is walking towards the horse that is now standing outside Mam's boutique, stock-still, his rope hanging down. She approaches him and holds out her hand to the horse, who is quivering and sweating.

When she gets beside him, the horse ducks his head to allow her to scratch him between the ears, and then she takes the halter in one hand, flipping the rope over his head. Instead of walking him back to the box, she, in one agile movement, without use of stirrup or saddle to help her, pops up on his back.

Using only the halter and rope, she rides back in our direction, bent low over his neck, patting and murmuring to him, and it soothes him. He walks calmly, like a different animal. Delia gets as far as the horsebox, then jumps down and walks him up the lowered tailgate, where she secures him safely in one of the four stalls.

A huge round of applause erupts, from reporters and my colleagues alike, and a cry of 'Go, Delia!' from Darren.

After which Zoë – ever compassionate to the underdog – goes to check on Duckie, who is slumped on the footpath, his head in his hands. She sits beside him, her hand on his shoulder. Another great photo op for the papers and the morning news.

After Duckie is escorted away in the ambulance I've called for him – he's fine, but I still want him off the scene – I pop home for five minutes to bring the girls to school.

When I come back, Delia is still in the horsebox, calming Chance Your Arm, which is fine; she wasn't scheduled for anything else because I wasn't expecting her in. The others have gone about their daily tasks, as I told them to before I left – we're skipping the briefing meeting today – but Zoë is in the car park giving an interview to a television reporter from RTÉ who's just turned up.

I pause to listen.

She's given quite a few interviews since her TikTok took off. I warned her before the first about being too...well, too herself, and in all fairness, so far she's kept it fairly professional, and she continues to do so today despite an aside about attachment theory and a brief speculation about Duckie's childhood.

Donnchadh de Bruin from the Irish Horse Board turns up next, along with Farah Sadiq. They both make a statement to the cameras, commending Zoë and Ballycarrick Garda Station, and then they talk to Delia and Matthew Hilser. A very fancy Land Rover turns up with a groom, trainer and vet from Roger Mulligan's yard in County Galway, and finally the famous animal is driven away, with an escort of Garda motorbikes provided by Galway.

The Minister for Sport, Des Finane, arrives; his representative, Barry Dowling, doesn't get a look in this time. Finane does his own piece for the cameras, and I have to say he's good at it; he is surprisingly young and dishy, and very suave despite the nasal voice. He comes into the station to thank Zoë personally, then puts his arm around her for a photo op.

I spend my morning fielding calls and texts, before Ronan finally manages to get onto me, grumbling that he's tried me about a hundred times.

'Well, you did it, Mags,' he says.

'I did nothing whatsoever,' I say, thinking about that brief chat with Jerome at the hospice. But I say nothing about that, because it was, of course, nothing. 'It was all Zoë.'

'Who you recommended, Mags, when no one else would have... er...'

'Chanced their arm?' I suggest with a grin.

'I wasn't going to say it.' He chuckles. 'But yes.'

'I suppose it was a bit of a gamble, but it was the only thing I could think of. Are there any leads on who took him?'

'Not really, and to be honest, I get the impression the Irish Horse Board would rather leave it that way, make out like he probably escaped on his own and that valuable horses in Ireland aren't targeted by criminal gangs that we have no way of catching...'

'I'm sorry... What?' I'm having a problem getting my head around this. 'So they want it to be like, "Oh, he just wandered off and clearly someone found him in their back garden and were too modest to claim the enormous reward"?' I ask incredulously.

'Something like that.'

'O...K...' It's not my case, so I'm not that bothered. Not my circus, not my monkeys, but still. 'Well, I'm glad he's all right and the search is over. I can get Zoë back to normal work before she decides she's the new James Bond.'

I hang up and sit there at my desk, thinking. Remembering Jerome at the hospice, saying, 'If you're ever in need of anything, ever, Mags, anything at all, as a friend, you need only ask, and I'll make it right for you.'

And me answering, 'You don't know where that bloody horse is, do you? I think I'm only going to get my life back if Chance Your Arm turns up.'

Could Jerome really have had anything to do with this?

I run a few possibilities through my head, and one stands out. Lenny Carmody works for a stable in Kent, for his father-in-law, Alphonsus Ward, a hard man who is known to steer clear of the law. Or perhaps is just very good at not getting caught…

I've sent Delia home again now that the horse is gone, but I have in front of me the folder she brought in with her this morning, where she's kept a record of all the cash that came in for Dora. A bell rings in my head. I open the folder and flip through the pages. Hundreds of donations, most of them small. But one jumps out. Ten thousand euro, from Lenny Carmody, who, as Delia already told me, delivered it to her door in person.

Was this what alerted Jerome? Did he go in search of the truth, and convince Lenny to give up the horse? Or am I wandering down the Scooby-Doo school of investigation myself now?

The horse is back. It's not my concern. And as far as I know, Lenny Carmody has returned to his wife and child and new baby in England. And Alphonsus Ward is outside my jurisdiction anyway.

CHAPTER 24

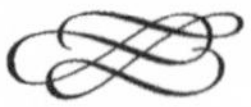

Press and television have an absolute field day with Chance Your Arm, who seems to have suffered no ill effects from the whole episode. Unlike Duckie, whose reputation is now surely beyond repair; every newspaper has a picture of him flying through the air with a terrified expression on his face.

His nickname seems to be common knowledge these days, because several tabloids have come up with the same front-page headline: FLYING DUCKIE! And half the pictures are of him sitting on the footpath, being comforted by Zoë. The duck puns abound, though one tabloid went with 'Beauty and the Beast' in the headline.

A few days later, the Irish Horse Board and the owner of Chance Your Arm contact Ballycarrick station, wanting to give Zoë and a friend a month's luxury resort holiday in the UAE as a gesture of gratitude for the excellent policing she displayed in retrieving their precious horse.

There's a strict policy against taking gifts for doing our work, otherwise Zoë would be owed the enormous reward for finding him, but Ronan Brady manages to swing it for her that she can accept the holiday. He's also hinted to me that my request for an extra team member might not fall on deaf ears.

Well, I'll believe that when I see it.

'I hope you're going to take me as your plus one. We're a team, remember.' Nicola nudges Zoë as we gather in my office for our team meeting.

'Well, it should be Inspector Cassidy by rights,' points out Michael, very seriously.

Zoë's face drops; she can still find it hard to tell if someone's joking or not. 'Oh no, but…'

'Oh, stop it, Michael.' I grin. 'And Zoë, don't panic, he's out on stress leave anyway, playing golf in Portugal – lucky Portugal.'

'Besides, rumour has it that a certain suave young unmarried Minister for Sport has asked Zoë on a date,' murmurs Darren, making Zoë go pink and mutter something about how they get on well because they're both vegan, that's all.

How Des Finane being a vegan sits with the portfolio he has, I've no idea, but I'll be watching the news to see if he finds a good political reason to pop over to the Emirates during the month Zoë is there with whoever she decides to take as her plus one. I think it might be Nicola if I can spare her. I suppose I can. Short-staffed yet again…

* * *

After we wrap up the meeting, with Chance Your Arm safely gone, there's nothing much on, so I stroll up Main Street, thinking about dropping into Teresa's for elevenses, then remember I should be slimming for Sharon's wedding, then decide to ask Sharon if she fancies coming to Teresa's for a cream cake, which I realise is an illogical train of thought, but never mind.

As I reach the boutique, I feel the slight pang I always do, seeing the sign that says 'Sharon's Boutique' instead of 'Marie's Boutique'. I know Mam's happy to be retired – she and Joe are gone to Tuscany, painting for the week – but change is hard, even though Sharon is my bestie.

'How's Operation Peach Taffeta coming along?' Sharon asks from inside the window display, where she's doing the mannequins.

'Oh, I've the perfect one got already,' I say as I give her a hand to climb out of the window space. 'So have you set a date?'

Sharon laughs. 'If Trevor Lynch had his way, we'd be doing it Thursday. He says he's terrified I'll change my mind.'

'You won't, though, will you?' I ask, worried.

'No, I won't. He's the best thing to ever happen to me, Mags. I'll be grabbing him with both hands and holding on.'

'Good woman yourself,' I reply.

'I am doing the right thing, aren't I?' She's suddenly not so sure.

'You are.' Sharon likes it when I'm decisive in my answers. She needs me to be. She was always a ditherer, as my mother says. 'He's kind and decent and handsome in his own way, and he's a good laugh. And he's never let you down.'

She nods, satisfied. 'He wouldn't.'

'So when is this wedding? When do I have to start going to insufferable Elaine in the slimming club again?'

'On the third of August in the registry office in Galway, and afterwards to that new tapas place El Camino Español by the Spanish Arch. It's Sean's favourite, so he picked it. And no, don't go to Elaine, because, Mags Munroe, you are perfect exactly as you are, and Skinny Elaine with her buck teeth and her twig like thighs has nothing to offer you or me.'

'Aw, shucks.' I smile. 'So maybe you fancy a cream cake in Teresa's?'

'Sure thing.' She immediately turns the sign to 'CLOSED FOR LUNCH', though it's nowhere near lunchtime, and we stroll up the town together.

'And the perm?' I ask as we pass Gerry's Hairdressers.

'I don't think any of us need to see you with a mullety perm ever again in this lifetime,' she replies dryly. 'Once was enough. The image from 1987 is still burnt on my eyeballs.'

'Oh, thank God.' I'm relieved, to be honest. I did hope she was joking all along about the eighties-themed wedding, but with Sharon you never know, and she *is* madly in love with a man who still wears snow-washed jeans.

'If you hadn't called, I was going to come up to you at lunchtime,' she says as we settle down with our coffees that are almost but not quite as good as Tatiana's, to Teresa's frustration, and cream cakes. Well, I'm having a custard slice, with the vague idea that the eggs make it protein so more like the keto diet. 'I've got something amazing to tell you.'

'Trevor's decided to move on to the nineties?' I ask.

'Ha, ha, no. Give the poor man time. His fashion years are kind of the opposite of dog years – ten years for us is only one fashion year for him. No, it's about the money.'

'You managed to sort out the GoFundMe stuff?' I'm so grateful to her for taking this on; I hate dealing with numbers.

'Much better than that…'

'What then?'

'Mags, what's Kieran's biggest problem?'

'Huh?' I stare at her, confused.

'Go on, think about it.' She seems thrilled with herself. 'What keeps Kieran awake at night?'

'Sharon, what are you on about?'

'Come on, you must know the answer!'

Is she talking about my refusal to retire? But that's not an issue any more.

Kieran and I had a lovely conversation about my job on the day of the funeral. As the horses drew Dora's coffin up Main Street, followed by the long line of Travellers and the townspeople standing along the pavement with their heads lowered, showing their respect, Kieran nudged me and whispered, 'I've had a thought, Mags, about your job.' Naturally I felt the usual stab of irritation.

'Today's not the time to discuss this, Kieran.'

'Yes, it is,' he said, 'because today has made me realise nobody else could have brought the whole community together like this and made it work. And I get it. I get why you don't want to leave your job. It's more than just money, and this place would be the worse for it if you did retire.'

Now, in Teresa's, I take a contented sip of my coffee. 'Well, it's not about my job. He says he's happy for me to keep on working.'

'Good to hear it, but no, I'm not talking about that.'

'The rift with Nora? He's still set on that, and it's easier on hin now that Orla and Catriona and Aoife as well have rallied around There's another barbecue coming up at Orla's that all the siblings ar planning to attend, even Oilibhéar.

'No, not Nora. Come on, Mags, it's the bane of his life?'

I rack my brains. 'Princess? Knickers?'

'No, the animals are the bane of *your* life, Mags. Think about it.'

'I don't really…'

'The church roof! Surely you realise he's always talking about th bloody church roof and poor Father Doyle and all that?'

'Oh, of course, sorry. Stupid of me. I suppose I have kind o screened it out, it's such a constant in our lives. But what has that go to do with anything?' I've completely lost track of this conversatio and can't remember where it started or figure out how it ended u here.

'OK,' says Sharon. 'So I went to Delia like you asked me to, an we discussed the remaining money. Delia was adamant tha everyone on the GoFundMe page needed to be paid back – Jerom didn't want to keep any money donated for Dora while the settle community were out of pocket. And yes, I know I doubte Jerome…'

I raise an eyebrow and give her a wry 'I told you so' smile.

'Thank you.' She bites into her cake, cream everywhere. 'Well, w worked it out that even after we'd paid everyone back every penny there was still ten grand left over thanks to that Lenny Carmody – who would have thought it? So we were wondering what to do wit it, and then I had a thought and Delia liked it.'

I love the way two of my favourite people are bonding. 'So wha was it?'

'You know the way Travellers are very religious, very Catholic Well, I suggested that maybe Jerome would like to put the last te grand into the church roof fund, and Delia asked him, and Jerome wa all for it.'

I'm delighted. Clearly it wasn't only Kieran at the funeral wh noticed the rain pinging into buckets everywhere. 'That's great. That doubles what's in there in one go.'

'No wait, there's more.' A big grin spreads across her face. 'I updated the GoFundMe page to explain the McGoverns were very, very grateful for all the help and were going to pay everyone back with the money donated from their extended family, and that the ten thousand left over would go to the church roof. And guess what happened then?'

'Go on...' I'm intrigued.

'Well, one by one, they came back and said, no, it's all right, give it to the church roof fund or a local fund or whatever.'

I'm struggling to work it out. Numbers aren't my favourite thing, despite Derry McLoughlin always being so kind to me about my tables when I was in school.

'So how much...?'

'Well, it's roughly sixty plus fifty minus twenty, so ninety thousand. And so with the original ten thousand he collected over the last ten years, Father Doyle is going to have about one hundred thousand in the roof fund, which has surely got to be enough...'

I'm gasping with joy. 'It is. But Kieran made the diocese promise if Father Doyle ever raised half the amount, they would match it! Oh, Sharon, this is amazing. It means Kieran can retire with a clean conscience, no more sleepless nights about leaving poor Father Doyle in the lurch...'

She's delighted. 'Do you think he will have time to do the job before he retires?' she asks. 'Have the satisfaction of finishing it off?'

'Oh, it will have to go to tender and the diocese will get a few quotes and decide, but honestly I don't know. Kieran says he never, ever wants to go up on that roof again, and I'm sure the diocese only promised because they never expected Father Doyle to raise such an enormous amount that quickly, so hopefully they'll drag their feet over it and it'll be Wojtec that has to deal with it.'

'But the diocese will come through, do you think?' Sharon is worried. 'I mean, are we doing the right thing?'

'Yes, you are, and they have to – Kieran had them write it down, so it's a contract,' I say decisively, the way I spoke about Trevor when she had a wobble and needed reassurance.

And the rest can go into the community fund, which means Ballycarrick might beat Dromahane in the Tidy Towns for once, and the community hall badly needs a makeover.

She looks relieved. 'That's great then... So will you tell Father Doyle?'

What is this obsession for getting me to be the one to tell people things? 'No, Sharon, you and Delia should tell him. It's you two who have sorted this out.'

'No, we talked about it. We think it should be you.'

'Why on earth...'

'Look, to be honest, we're kind of worried it will give the poor man a heart attack, so it needs to be someone very, very calm.'

* * *

Later, after I've told Kieran about the fund – and he nearly weeps tears of relief – I tell him what Sharon said about me being the least likely person to give someone a heart attack, and his tears of relief turn to tears of laughter.

CHAPTER 25

Kieran and I are at Castle Dysert again, this time with the girls. We've taken up Conor's invitation to come for the weekend, which he's been reminding us of ever since the Sienna Black concert.

We're sitting at a table on the patio of the sumptuous hotel in the sunshine, sipping the delicious summer punch the waitress has brought us and watching Kate and Ellie, who are trotting along the shoreline on a pair of yellow ponies from the Castle Dysert stables; they are under the care of Conor's eighteen-year-old twin boys, who are both expert riders.

Ellie and Kate's bragging rights are gone off the charts now, between hanging out at Ireland's premier five-star resort and regularly DMing Sienna, who says they are her new 'besties.'

There are a lot of girls wanting to be 'besties' with my daughters now, including Clodagh Dunlea, who has invited Ellie into her coven, but I'm glad to say that Ellie, while being polite to Clodagh and friendly to Sienna, hasn't forgotten that her real besties are the O'Leary twins, the ones who have stuck by her through thick and thin. And Kate I know feels the same way about Evie.

'Mags!' Conor crosses the courtyard to where Kieran and I are sitting. 'How are you?' He shakes Kieran's hand, then hugs me. 'I feel so terrible for getting you involved with your man Black.'

'You didn't know.' I smile as he releases me. 'You were trying to do a good deed.'

'I'm normally a better judge of character than that. I knew he was a bit off, but…'

'He was a classic controlling sociopath, no empathy. They're hard to spot. Don't beat yourself up over it.'

He still looks worried. 'I just didn't realise he'd be mad enough to attack you.'

'Anyone trying to put my wife in a chokehold would have to be mad for sure,' says Kieran cheerfully, adding, 'Not that I would know from personal experience of course…'

I've downplayed the whole thing with Tony Black to Kieran, which is why he's able to joke about it. This time it was only a few bruises, not a bullet wound or scarring to the lungs, so I've managed to persuade him it was a routine police incident. A man easily overpowered, security backup there in seconds.

And I don't think it's going to come up in court, so hopefully my story can stay that way. Sienna decided not to press charges against her father, so I've taken her lead; she's been pushed around enough. So Tony Black was released and has gone back to America, where he's still trying to monetise his daughter by giving nasty interviews about her to the press. She just sent out one tweet. *Love is not hurt. Love is not control. #scaredbutstandingtall*

She never mentioned his name, but people saw him scrambling to get interviews to bad mouth her and put two and two together.

None of her fans seem to care what he has to say.

'And the girls, are they all right?'

'They didn't witness it. Their only fright was finding themselves on stage with Sienna Black in front of eighty thousand people.' I chuckle. 'We're watching for signs of PTSD from that, but they seem to be surviving so far.'

Conor draws up another chair to sit beside us. 'I just spoke to Sienna. She's doing OK. She's mad about your two girls. After her

European tour, she says she's coming back here for a few weeks to spend some time with Charlotte and her sister, Phoebe, and she's hoping the girls can come and hang out with her one of the days.'

'I'm sure they'll be delighted to,' I say with a smile. 'And thanks for having us all for the weekend, Conor. We really feel like we are taking advantage now.'

'Absolutely not. You are more than welcome, and make sure the girls or yourselves do whatever you want. There's archery, and they can take quads over the grounds if they like. And I've told the staff in the spa to expect you – have whatever treatments you like, all of you, please.'

'We could get used to this, Conor.' Kieran grins.

'Well, and I don't know if I should even bring this up...' He looks awkward and stops.

'Go on,' I say, because as Tatiana would say, I am 'very nosy woman'.

'Ok, but this is just a suggestion...' He pauses again. 'if you ever considered retiring early...'

Oh God, here we go. Even though it's Conor, I feel a flash of irritation. When will the men in my life stop treating me like I'm fit for the scrap heap?

Kieran jumps in. 'Mags isn't interested in retirement, Conor.'

Conor looks surprised. 'Oh, obviously not, and I didn't mean retire retire. I just meant leaving the guards. I'm hoping to recruit a full-time head of security. We're having to get more serious with the like of Sienna Black turning up, and I could really do with someone with your skills, Mags. We have a lot of' – he makes a face – 'unusual situations that crop up from time to time. It might not be as exciting as life as a Garda sergeant, but it would be more lucrative, I can promise you that.'

I laugh until I realise he's serious, then just stare at him.

'Look, I know you'd have to think about it at least. I'll go twenty-five percent over your current salary, all the benefits you currently have, pension, health, all of that. You choose your hours, and you'd be answerable only to me.' His smile is so genuine and persuasive, I can't imagine how anyone can refuse him anything. 'There's a tied cottage that goes with it, on the grounds. And of course your family can use the hotel as they wish.'

'I'm very flattered, Conor. Thanks for the offer,' is the best I can manage.

'Right so' – he winks – 'after dropping that bombshell, I'll take my leave and give you some time to unwind. Remember, anything at all food, drinks, treatments, activities, just sign for it. There won't be a bill. I owe you big time.'

'Not at all,' I say, still shaken, 'but thank you.'

* * *

'DON'T,' I warn my husband as soon as Conor is gone.

'I didn't say a word.'

'You don't have to,' I reply dryly. 'And I agree, it's an incredible offer, and it would be ridiculous to say no.'

'Yes it is, a wonderful offer, but I want you to know I still stand by what I said at the funeral.'

I smile and sip my cocktail, remembering that day and the pleasure Kieran's little speech gave me. Of all the people in Ballycarrick, in Ireland, in all the world, it's my husband's opinion that matters to me the most. Not that he's always right, but…

Down on the beach, the girls are learning to canter. What would it be like to live here?

'This arrived this morning.' Kieran pulls out a card in an envelope from his jacket pocket and hands it to me. 'I thought I'd wait till we got here to show it to you, when we had some peace and quiet to think about it.'

The card has a kitten on the front holding a flower with *I'm Sorry* written on it in curly writing.

I open the card with a puzzled glance at my husband.

Dear Mags and Kieran,

I am truly sorry for my behaviour and for anything I said or did to offend either of you. I admit I have been hard on Mags, and that is unforgiv-

able, because contrary to what I might have said in the past, Mags, you are a wonderful wife and mother and Kieran is lucky to have you. He knows that and so do I.

I miss you both and the girls very much, and I would like to find a way for us to get past this. I promise to never say anything derogatory again if we can patch it up.

Nora

I finish reading and turn to Kieran to see what he thinks. I'm glad she wrote the card. I know she's a very proud person, so it would have been hard for her to do it, but as Mam said, this is his call. It's his mother. It's not all about me.

To my surprise, his lips are twitching as if there's something very funny about all this.

'What? What is it?'

'Look on the back,' he says.

I turn it over, and there's a postscript.

PS. I heard that new sports minister, Des Finane, on the TV praising everyone at Ballycarrick Garda Station, and he singled you out, Mags, for finding Chance Your Arm. He's very impressive, and I never knew you were on such friendly terms with someone so high up in the government.

For a moment I can hardly believe my eyes. She's incorrigible.

I have to laugh. With my mother-in-law, it's all you can do.

'She never lost it.' He shakes his head with a smile.

No, she hasn't. And I don't think she ever will.

CHAPTER 26

Oscar is bending Father Doyle's ear in the churchyard as I walk by, and for once the elderly priest doesn't look browbeaten and depressed but quite upright and cheerful, and he waves to me as I pass.

He's so much happier now that the church roof is going to be replaced.

There was a sticky moment when I first told him the news. We were in the sitting room of the parochial house, and he paled and could hardly get a word out. The relief was enormous. Since then it's like ten years has gone off him. He tells me he feels like a young man of seventy-four again. Father Eddie, Conor's friend from Ennis, came up to see him the other day, and he told me he's taking full credit for the miracle because of the prayers he said for Kieran and the roof. He had a twinkle in his eyes when he said it, but... You never can tell what priests believe.

Further up the street, Annette and Martha are delivering vegetables to Bertie the butcher's, and jars of honey as well. Finbarr got interested in bees a while back, so they've put some hives in the rocky upper field behind their cottage and they're all learning about beekeeping together at weekends. They're so supportive of him.

Luigi is out writing the specials on his blackboard, and Tatiana is chatting to Klara, who has a bucket of soapy water in her hand – she's doing the windows of the Samovar. Snipe comes out of the bookie's and gives me a cheery wave.

Can I leave this place and move to Clare? Could I come back to visit my mother and Sharon and all my old friends, and walk down the street knowing someone else was sergeant here now, someone else entrusted with the safety and security of this town? I'll have to sometime in the future, I suppose, so why not now? I don't know. One minute I think I can, that I'd be mad to turn down the offer Conor made me, and in the next minute, leaving seems inconceivable.

As I walk past Teresa's Bakery, I spot Nora inside with Orla, so I push the door open and cross to the booth where they're sitting.

I know Kieran finally had the big talk with my monster-in-law last weekend. He didn't go running the minute we got the card; he didn't want her to think it was that easy. So he left it for a good while and then went up and gave her a lecture that this was her last chance. Time to see if now she knows she's back in, she'll stick to her promise to behave.

'Mags, how lovely to see you,' Nora trills. 'And your hair is beautiful. Did you get it done recently?'

'Not for a while. My roots need to be touched up, but trying to get an appointment with Gerry… Well, you know how it is.'

'I've an appointment for Friday morning – you could go instead if you like?' she offers. Now if you're not from Ballycarrick, this might not seem like a huge offer, but if you are… Well, suffice to say nobody would give up their appointment unless for a truly great cause.

'Ah, not at all, Nora, but thanks. Mind if I join you?'

'No, no…we'd be delighted, wouldn't we, Orla? What can I get you, Mags, anything at all?'

Oh dear. Nora tripping over herself to be nice is almost as irritating as Nora being rude. It's like the Rollo situation all over again, when our Jack Russell stopped shrinking from me like I was a dangerous monster and fell in love with me instead.

I'm still Rollo's number one woman, by the way, despite it being

Princess who has just given birth to six puppies – six more flippin' animals in the house. And it was definitely Rollo who did the damage. They're a bizarre, silky, multi-coloured, snub-nosed and, even to my jaundiced eye, incredibly cute mixture of Pekingese and Jack Russell, which apparently is a *thing*. It's called a Peke-a-Jack. All of the girls' friends at school are begging their parents if they can have one, especially now that Sienna Black has shared the picture Ellie sent her of them all gambolling cutely around a bemused frilly lizard called Knickers. It's like the brainless pups think Knickers is their dad, though thankfully there's no resemblance. They're definitely not Pekizards, though one of them does have a bit of a ruff.

'I'd love a coffee and a scone please, Nora,' I say, and she leaps up and goes rushing to the counter.

'She's been so happy since Kieran forgave her,' Orla murmurs. 'She was like a hen with an egg after sending that card. She kept wanting the rest of us to phone him to see what he was going to do, but we told her she had to leave him alone to make up his own mind. He was dead right to take his time, Mags, and I really think it's helped get through to her.'

'So were you behind her sending that card, or Catriona or Gearoid or what?' I ask, equally sotto voce.

'None of us. It was all her own doing. She was like a briar since the fight, tears, the whole lot. And Evie let slip about the barbecue and that Catriona and Aoife were planning to come to the next one, and Oilibhéar, and that must have really hit home even though she said nothing to me about it.'

'So the puppies are all going to find new homes, I think,' I say as Nora starts back towards us bearing my scone and coffee. 'It really helped Sienna Black sharing that video of them dancing around. I need them like a hole in the head, however cute they are.'

'You're too modest, Mags!' Nora beams. 'They're not just cute, they are amazing. I was saying to Orla, they were better than that Sienna Black, really and truly. Ellie was like a natural superstar, and Kate as well…'

She obviously thinks I'm talking about my daughters rather than the puppies, but I don't correct her. I let her gush on; she's fit to burst with enthusiasm.

'They're both real beauties, and Kate is so like your mother when she was young. God, I remember everyone saying how the lads used to stand up to look at Marie – she was the belle of the ball for miles. But once she laid eyes on Milo Kelleher, God rest his gentle soul, all the others had to make way. He was handsome too, your dad, reminded me of James Dean.'

I think in all the years I'm with Kieran, this is the first time Nora has said anything nice about my family, and I swallow the lump in my throat.

Orla then tells us about Evie being the most popular girl at her posh private school these days because of her cousins, and how she was showing her friends pictures of Kate, Ellie and Sienna together in the green room on her phone and got caught, so Orla was called in. The deputy principal had Evie in her office when Orla arrived. They are very strict on phones apparently – they're not supposed to be brought into school – and Orla expected a right grilling. But the woman only wanted to see if they could get tickets for the London concert at the end of the month. I had no idea of this, but Evie texted Kate, who texted Sienna, and now the deputy principal is going with her daughter and Evie is her pet for the rest of her time in school.

We all three laugh at that, and then Nora tells us everyone at the bridge club is singing 'Scared but Standing Tall' for the over-sixties talent contest and that Dorothy O'Halloran has offered to do the rap parts. Dorothy O'Halloran is ninety if she's a day, so that will be a sight to see, I'm sure.

'Now tell me, how have you been? I heard about that awful thing in Dublin, that man attacking you. Thank God you weren't hurt, Mags.'

'It was all over in a matter of seconds really. It was nothing, Nora.' I'm sticking to my story. I don't want Kieran having wakeful nights again; he's been sleeping like a baby now that the church roof is sorted.

'You would say that. You're always so brave.'

'Ah no, all in a day's work.'

We chat away for another twenty minutes, getting caught up on all the Munroe family news. Orla tells me that Seamus is working with Professor Kinsella to get a review made of the palliative care arrangements for Travelling families after Dora, and that's good to hear. I'm so proud of how Seamus stepped up to help. When Nora made snide remarks about Travellers, he never reacted or contradicted her, but it's clearly not the way he feels himself.

'Poor Mrs McGovern, and wasn't it wonderful of her family to pay so much money towards the new church roof,' Nora says. 'I sent Jerome a card thanking him and telling him what an asset his family is to the community, and how I think when the new roof is done it should be dedicated to Dora.'

'You did?' I ask, failing to hide my incredulity.

'I did. I know I'm old and set in my ways, Mags, but I was wrong about the McGoverns – they're decent people. I've been wrong about a lot of things,' she finishes quietly.

Something about it, the way she's saying these things, is starting to make me believe she is genuine. Maybe I'm being foolish – leopards don't change their spots and all of that – but she sounds sincere.

'We all make mistakes, Nora. That's what being human is all about And it takes a big person to say they're sorry, so you have no fight with me.'

She reaches over and grabs my hand, holding it tight. 'Thank you Mags,' she says humbly.

She tells us then about Kevin's plantar fasciitis – he's having injections into his heels, which sounds grim – and Oilibhéar's meeting with someone 'very high up' in the BBC, and when it's time to go, she asks very shyly and tentatively if I would mind coming to Sunday lunch next weekend.

'Or whichever weekend suits, Mags, you decide. We'll fit it in around you.'

I drain my coffee and stand. 'I'll talk to Kieran, but I'm sure next weekend will be fine with both of us.' She hasn't mentioned Kieran yet in the conversation, but I know he's at the centre of all of this. She absolutely idolises him, more than even Gearoid or the girls.

'Thank you, Mags, thank you very much,' she says, and there are tears in her eyes.

* * *

I HAVE one last person to see before I head home for the day. I drive to Drumlish, but he's not there, at least his van isn't, and I can guess where he might be.

I'm right. I pull in behind his van in the car park of the cemetery and enter through the pedestrian gate.

He sees me – we're the only two people here – and waves. I walk towards him.

It's too soon for a headstone – traditionally you wait a year – and the mound is still bare earth. He's removing the many wreaths that are turning brown now.

'Hi, Jerome, how are you doing?'

I stand beside him, both our eyes on the little wooden cross with the brass plaque that reads *Dora McGovern*.

'Still trying to believe she's gone, Mags, and that's the truth.'

'I know. It takes a while to sink in. Even when you know it's going to happen, it's still a shock, and it was only weeks that you knew.'

He nods.

'How are the lads?'

He shrugs. 'You know young *sublicks*, Mags, they don't say much.' He uses Cant words around me sometimes now, and I'm happy when he does it; it makes me feel accepted.

'It's bound to be hard for them, though, all the same.'

''Tis. Sure they had an eejit made of her.' He gives a half laugh. I know he means that she spoiled them, and it was true. Dora loved her boys; there wasn't anything she wouldn't do for them.

'She loved every bit of it,' I agree.

We gather the last few wreaths while we chat about the funeral, how well it all went, and the church roof. He mentions all the sympathy and thank-you cards he's got from people in the town, including Nora and Kevin, and tells me Dora in heaven will be delighted that her fund is going to help the church. She was very devout, as most Travellers are.

Then we walk back towards the vehicles, dropping the dead flowers in the big bins on the way.

In the car park, I pause by my car without opening the door. 'I know it was you, by the way.'

He regards me, his head slightly to one side. 'Me who done what?' he asks innocently.

'You know very well what. And I know you won't tell me, so I don't even know why I'm asking, but was it Lenny Carmody who stole the horse on behalf of Alphonsus Ward?'

'You're dead right,' he says with a wicked smile. He opens my car door for me, and I sit in. He leans down and winks. 'I won't tell you.'

The End

I SINCERELY HOPE you enjoyed this story. If you did, I would really appreciate a review on Amazon. If you would like to hear more about my other books, or join my readers club where I will give you a free novel as a thank you for joining up, just pop over to www.jean grainger.com. It's 100% free and always will be.

If you'd like to read more about Conor O'Shea, he is the central character of another series of mine, which you can find here:

The Tour - Book 1

IF YOU WOULD LIKE to try something else from me, here is the start of my latest novel Lilac Ink, The Knocknashee Story Book 1

. . .

Chapter 1

KNOCKNASHEE, DINGLE PENINSULA, CO KERRY

April 1938

Grace Fitzgerald studiously applied a modest scrape of butter to her morning toast as her older sister, Agnes, while spreading a lot more butter on her own toast and marmalade as well, grumbled on and on about all the immoral shenanigans in the sleepy town of Knocknashee.

Today's diatribe was mostly to do with Peggy Donnelly, and the new range of pink and mauve cardigans and scandalously short skirts – barely reaching the knee – she'd put in the window of her shop, the wearing of which was bound to lead to dreadful behaviour among the young people of the town.

'So we won't be shopping in Peggy's until they're taken down. I don't know what's come over her. Grace, are you listening to me?' Agnes leaned in and pointed with her knife.

'Yes, Agnes,' Grace replied gazing down at her plate. Secretly, she thought Peggy's new display brightened the place up and doubted very much it would lead to naked dancing and satanic rituals on the strand. But she couldn't say that sort of thing to Agnes, not even as a joke.

Anyway, she didn't want to be cheeky to her sister. She was entirely dependent on Agnes, who had been like a mother to her – as she was often reminded – since their parents died.

It had been horrible, and so sudden; it still upset Grace to think of it. Eddie and Kathleen Fitzgerald had served as the master and mistress of the school attached to this big stone house. They were on their way back from one of the islands dotted off the coast, where they'd set up a school for the island children and visited twice a year to bring more resources for the only teacher, a past pupil of theirs who had married an islander. On the way back to Knocknashee, their little boat was caught in a squall and capsized, and they drowned.

Grace had just turned eleven when it happened. The Fitzgeralds' only son, Father Maurice, had been away on the missions in the Philippines and couldn't come home. So it was Agnes, the second oldest at twenty-six, who had to take over the running of the household and the school. Grace had been a surprise baby, arriving many years after her parents were sure their family was complete.

Together she and Agnes ran the school now, though her sister had no desire to be a teacher. Unlike their parents, who had been much loved, Agnes had no vocation for it. But she did it anyway, she said, to put food on the table for Grace. It was a big sacrifice for her, because it had meant giving up on her plans to marry Cyril Clifford, the son of the local hotelier.

Before Mammy and Daddy drowned, Agnes had been sure of a proposal from Cyril. They'd been doing a strong line together for years, and he was considered a fine catch; it was just a matter of time before he put a ring on her finger. But after the accident, everything changed.

If Agnes married, the law required her to give up teaching, and Cyril could hardly be expected to take over responsibility for Grace as well as a new wife and any future children they might have, so until Grace was old enough to look after herself, the marriage was put on hold.

Grace knew to be very grateful, because Agnes could have solved the problem in a second by putting her into an orphanage, the same way Charlie McKenna's children had been sent away when the postman was left unable to cope after his wife died in childbirth.

To make matters even worse for Agnes, a year after their parents died, Grace contracted polio and was rushed to the hospital in Cork.

Agnes tried desperately to keep it quiet – people were so frightened of the disease – but of course it got out. And Cyril wrote to Agnes, saying his parents were afraid of him catching polio from the furnishings in her house, and then guests would be put off coming to their hotel, and that it would be best all round to discontinue what he referred to as 'their friendship'. Poor Agnes was humiliated and disgraced in front of the whole place when he married a woman from Limerick not a wet week after he'd finished it with her.

For the next four years, Grace was in hospital. Agnes was unable to visit because the school board forbade it on account of the risk to the schoolchildren in her charge. Agnes had to manage everything all alone, with a broken heart. No wonder she'd become so unhappy and saw badness everywhere.

Grace had been lucky by comparison. She'd had to have a lot of painful operations and therapies, but at least she'd been well looked-after in Cork. The consultant, Dr Warrington, had such a bright, kind face; just the memory of him cheered her up. He went so far and beyond for his patients. His wife was a wonderful woman too; she'd put Grace through her school exams, as she did all the children. The couple had no family of their own, and all their loving energy seemed to go into nurturing the suffering youngsters in their care whose lives had been devastated by the terrible disease.

One of Grace's happiest memories was when Mrs Warrington told her she was so clever that she should train as a teacher at one of the new colleges instead of learning on the job as lots of rural teachers did. Though it turned out the doctor's wife had overestimated Grace's abilities.

The summer of Grace's leaving cert, when she was sixteen, she'd finally been allowed home from the hospital. Dr Warrington had driven her to Knocknashee from Cork himself so she didn't have to take the train and bus alone, and like his wife, he'd told her he was sure she'd do very well in her exams. But when the results arrived, she'd failed so badly that Agnes was too kind to even show them to her; she'd put the letter into the fire instead.

It was probably for the best, as Agnes said. Even if her marks had been good enough, Grace would never have been able to go to teacher training college in Limerick or Dublin; she'd never manage alone, not with a twisted leg in a calliper. And though that door was closed, a window opened. Agnes persuaded Canon Rafferty, the chairman of the school board, to appoint Grace as her teaching assistant. For a small wage from the Department of Education, she could take the four- to eight-year-olds off Agnes's hands.

Grace knew this was good of Agnes, and it was also kind of her sister not to take a penny of her wages for her bed and board. The polio meant she could never be married, not now that she was a cripple, so Agnes insisted that every penny Grace earned went into a savings account in the post office so she could pay someone to look after her when she was left alone in the world.

Unfortunately this meant Agnes had to pay for everything out of her one wage, and a lot of scrimping and saving went on in their house as a result, hence the tiny scrape of butter Grace allowed herself for her toast. At times she felt guilty for even existing.

Agnes had moved on to another topic now. 'And as for that Tilly O'Hare girl, walking off the bus from Tralee into the square wearing a shirt and tie over her skirt, and her hair short like a man's. Bad enough she wears her dead father's overalls around the farm, but a *shirt and tie*! I don't think she's right in the head. Every seed, breed and generation of the O'Hares were...peculiar. So you'd better stay away from her, Grace.'

Grace took a bite of her toast as a way to hide her grin. She rather wished she'd been there to see it when Tilly got off the bus and caused such a scandal in the town. Agnes was a firm believer in always looking respectable. Today she was wearing a long black skirt, though almost everyone wore knee-length now, and a buttoned-up black cardigan with a white blouse underneath. With her fair hair set in waves, light-blue eyes and heavy tortoiseshell glasses, she looked forbidding, but Grace assumed that was her intention.

'I mean,' her sister continued, with a deep sigh, 'that brother of hers, Alfie, going off to Russia. In all honesty, what would take a Christian God-fearing man to that cradle of sin? And her older sister Marion, shacked up with a married man above in Dublin? Did you ever hear the likes? No shame.'

Agnes pursed her lips in such a way when she said that last bit that Grace nearly laughed, because it put her in mind of Flossie the tabby cat's bum; she had to bite her lip to keep a serious face. It was a shame, because it wasn't as if Agnes was ugly. She would be pretty if she only smiled a bit more.

'So I have your word? You'll have no more to do with her?' Agnes's china-blue eyes were fixed on hers.

Grace hesitated. She usually went along with whatever Agnes said she should or shouldn't do, or who she should or shouldn't talk to. But Grace was very fond of Tilly, who had written to her a lot while she was in hospital. Those letters had been a lifeline for her. Agnes had been far too busy with her work to write; by the time she'd marked the books of the whole school, because she had no assistant, the most she had time for was a card at birthdays and at Christmas.

'Tilly was my best friend from school, Agnes,' she reminded her sister carefully.

'Maybe she was,' said Agnes, looking very put out. 'But that was when you were twelve years old. You didn't see her at all while you were in hospital, and you've barely seen her in the year since you've been back. It won't be any trial to you not to see her at all.'

Grace remained silent. She hadn't told Agnes about Tilly's letters so as not to sound like she was criticising her sister for not having written more herself. And she tended not to mention the times she and Tilly got together for a walk on the beach, because she knew Agnes might not approve.

'I don't ask for much, Grace,' said Agnes, with another deep sigh. 'God knows you are a worry to me with your flighty ways, but I care for you and ask for nothing in return. I don't mind one bit having to pay for everything in this house out of my own wages while yours go into a savings account. And all I want in return for all my sacrifices is a commitment to stay away from the likes of Tilly O'Hare, and if you can't grant me that one small request, well, 'tis a sorry state of affairs, I must say…'

Grace shrunk inside. She knew she was a burden to Agnes. Being so young when their parents died; then catching polio and driving Cyril Clifford away; coming home from the hospital with her right leg all twisted and shorter than the other, thus ensuring no man would ever look at her, let alone marry her; failing all her exams; being too soft on the bold children in her care because she didn't understand how to teach properly. How could she go against her sister, who was only trying her best to keep her respectable, in the way a schoolteacher had to be?

'Grace? Are you paying attention?'

'I am, Agnes.'

'Then promise me you'll –'

At that moment their late father's brass carriage clock on the kitchen mantel struck the half hour. It had been given by the Irish National Teachers' Organisation for services to the profession, and it kept excellent time. Grace stood up as quickly as she could, a clumsy, noisy, clattering effort because she couldn't bend her bad right leg in the calliper.

'It's half past eight, Agnes. I'd better be going over.' She hoped her sister wouldn't notice that she'd managed not to give a commitment to cut Tilly off.

Agnes nodded, satisfied, as she helped herself to another cup of tea and a second slice of thickly buttered toast with more marmalade. Because Grace was only the assistant, she was the one who made sure all the children were in and accounted for, the fires lit and the two classrooms ready for the day. 'Make sure the blackboard in my room is fully clean, Grace – you left chalk on it yesterday. And tell young Mikey O'Shea I want to see him before school is over – he was trick-acting in the back of Mass on Sunday with his wastrel of a father.'

Grace's soft heart sank. Poor Mikey was only six, but she knew if she sent him to see Agnes, he'd get the leather, the poor misfortune.

Agnes took being headmistress very seriously. She felt responsible for all the souls in her care, and that meant beating any child who showed a tendency towards sin.

In fact her readiness with the leather strap was the first reason she'd fallen out with the O'Hares, because Mary O'Hare was the only one who had ever dared challenge her.

Grace would never forget it. Agnes had slapped Tilly so hard one day, she made her hand bleed. It was in the year Grace's parents had died, and she and Tilly were still only eleven. Agnes had taken over the school and was finding it difficult because she was having to fill in for both her parents and teach forty children instead of twenty, so it was hard for her to keep order, particularly with children like Tilly, who was always encouraging the others to laugh.

The next day Mary O'Hare appeared in the classroom, walking stick in hand, the *tap, tap* of the metal tip on the floorboards heralding her arrival before they saw her. Mrs O'Hare was a small, stocky woman, with a slow gait and a dark moustache of hair on her upper lip. She was a martyr to the rheumatism, but she marched right into the classroom, no knock or a bit, and raised her walking stick at Agnes.

'You're only a long string of misery, Agnes Fitzgerald, and no wonder your man Clifford has been trying to escape you for years.'

'Get out of my classroom!' gasped poor Agnes, white with shock.

'I will when I'm finished, but listen carefully to me now.' Mrs O'Hare punctuated each word with a point of the stick in Agnes's bony chest. 'You lay a scrawny finger of yours on my Tilly ever again, and I swear 'tis the last thing you'll ever do.'

'You can't threaten me with violence,' Agnes had protested, her brow furrowed and her shoulders back. 'You'll be sent to prison.'

'I will not, because I won't lay a hand on you. But I've fairies on my land, remember that, and I've been good to them and they've been good to me.'

Agnes's face went red. She opened her mouth, probably to say only ignorant people believed in the fairies, but then clearly thought better of it and closed it again.

'And don't ye take a tack of notice of this auld *cailleach*,' Mary told the class, looking around at them all.

Little Grace knew that everyone called Agnes a *cailleach* behind her back, the Irish word for a witch, but this was the first time someone had said it to her face; this would surely go down in the history books as a day no child present would ever forget. She remembered thinking she should speak up in defence of her older sister, but she'd just sat there in silence, feeling a guilty mixture of delight and terror.

Remembering about Mary O'Hare gave Grace an idea that might save Mikey. 'If only John O'Shea wasn't so fierce bad-tempered,' she said softly as she left the room. 'I've been told he's a history of cursing anyone who crosses him.' She hoped against hope that Agnes would believe her, even though John O'Shea was the nicest little man you could ever meet.

His father, Seánie O'Shea, had been a *seanchaí*, a storyteller of renown all over the peninsula for his wonderful stories of *púcas* and the *bean sidhe* and the fairies. He told tales of curses that spanned generations, of thwarted love and wicked people, as well as of great passions and things that happened long ago that were so funny, you'd cry laughing at him.

The *seanchaí* were an ancient role in Irish life, the descendants of the bards of old, and very well respected. A family would never refuse hospitality to a *seanchaí* for fear of being cursed, so she hoped Agnes might have the same concerns about John O'Shea. Agnes said she had no time for the old ways, the mythology and the old *piseógs* – silly superstitions of ignorant people, she called them – but she was wary of Mary O'Hare for that reason, and she would never go outside the door on the feast of Samhain for fear of the dead.

Six-year-old Mikey O'Shea had the same sweet nature as his father, but he was a lively boy with a cheeky grin, and last Sunday he'd been hopping around a bit. The canon had been giving a particularly long sermon, but he expected full and complete attention from everyone.

He had scowled down from the altar at John and Catherine O'Shea, who were standing at the back with their tribe of small children, and made some pointed remarks about people lacking true devotion.

Grace didn't think that was true. The O'Sheas would give a beggar their last bite, even though like many in Knocknashee, they had real problems raising a large family while working a small farm. Catherine was expecting another baby any day now, and Grace couldn't help feeling that if the O'Sheas didn't look entirely engaged with keeping

Mikey in order, maybe they were trying to figure more important things out.

She left the kitchen and limped to the hallstand. The leather and metal splint that went from the top of her thigh to her foot, where it slotted into a built-up shoe, was uncomfortable. She managed, but there were times when she longed to walk upright and straight.

Then she would remind herself of all the other children she'd known in the Victoria Hospital in Cork, struck down by the horrible infection. The little ones who had to go into the terrifying iron lung because their chests were affected, or those who died. And some children had both arms and legs paralysed. She was very lucky; she was spared the worst. All she had was one discoloured and twisted leg that was permanently cold and a calliper to strengthen the muscles weakened from the disease. Dr Ryan, the local GP, had checked her over when she came home and told her she had Dr Warrington to thank for being as mobile as she was. The Cork consultant was a great man and someone Dr Ryan much admired.

Standing at the mirror in the small hallway, she brushed her thick auburn hair, frustratingly curly, and pinned her hat on. She had Daddy's hair and also his eyes – large and green and flecked with amber. She didn't have his height; he had been over six feet, but Grace had never been tall, and the polio had shortened her even more, so she was only four foot eleven. Sometimes she thought she looked like one of those collectable china dolls with her pert little nose and curved, slightly pouting lips.

'I'm right quare looking and no mistake.' She sighed as she fixed a stray curl under her hat, but then she mentally shook herself and told herself to count her blessings, as she did every night when she said her prayers before bed. She might never marry or have her own children, but she had the children of the town to look after, and it was a wonderful job and she loved it. She had a roof over her head and a way of earning her living. She had her books to comfort her; she was currently reading *The Count of Monte Cristo*. And at least she wasn't a prisoner in a dungeon like Edmond Dantès. She was alive and free.

Come on, Grace, she ordered. *You've so much to be grateful for. So put your best foot forward – isn't that what Dr Warrington used to say?* A littl in-joke since she only had one good foot. She often wished she coul see the good doctor and his wife again, but they had other little girl and boys to care for, and they could hardly be expected to keep i touch with every child who had passed through their hands.

Chapter 2

GRACE WALKED AWKWARDLY down the front path and turned next doo to the two-room Knocknashee National School. The school and he parents' house shared a wall, so she didn't even have to go out on th street, just through a little gate, to enter the schoolyard.

There were sixty-five children enrolled and taught in two rooms The building was bright and sunny, as their parents had built it to b thirty-five years ago, and the two long classrooms were of equal size but there the similarity ended.

Grace tried to have the juniors' room looking the way she remem bered her mother keeping it before Agnes took over: lots of picture of the baby Jesus, showing donkeys and cows and shepherds an kings, all worshipping the tiny, smiling child, and some of her moth er's paintings of flowers and meadows and the ocean. It would hav been nice to get the children painting a few pictures to peg up on line across the room, the way her mother had done, but Agnes said th school funds wouldn't run to paint, and besides, paint made a terribl mess, so Grace had to give up on that idea.

The only thing Agnes allowed as decoration in the seniors' roon where she taught the older children was an enormous brown an beige replica of the Shroud of Turin, the length of linen in which Jesu was wrapped for burial and which bore the miraculous imprint of hi face, complete with crown of thorns. It was a very holy reminder o the suffering of Jesus, but Grace thought it was a scary image to shov children; it used to make her sad and frightened when she was a child in that classroom.

Crossing the yard, she saw a few of the older children were ready for the day and were kicking a real leather football.

'Did you get that for your birthday, Patrick?' she asked a red-haired lad with freckles and ears that stuck out like a toby jug.

'I did, miss.' He was clearly delighted with his gift.

Paddy and Eileen O'Flynn wouldn't have much going spare with eleven children, so she was glad they'd been able to get him something so nice. 'Ten is a big age – it should have a fine present.' She smiled at him. 'But maybe you should let me put that in my bag for now?'

He nodded that he understood and ran in alarm to get the ball and bring it back to her. 'Yes, could you mind it, Miss Fitz? I'd be afraid…'

'Of course I will.' She took it from him. 'Come to my room after school and I'll have it for you.'

It would be nice if Patrick and his friends could play with the ball at breaktime, but it was too risky. Two months ago Agnes confiscated a football from the Murphy boys for fear of them breaking a window, she said, and it was never seen again. It was as well not to run the risk of another such incident.

With the ball safely hidden in her big cloth bag, she went in to light the fires, then she rang the bell and the day began, all the children running in to take their seats before Agnes arrived through the gate into the yard.

Once everyone was settled, Grace closed the door that separated her room from the corridor and told the little children to get out their books.

Mrs Warrington might have been wrong about Grace being bright, but she tried her best to be a good teacher. The children came to her without the ability to read or write or do any arithmetic, and they left her for her sister's room with a neat cursive, all the classics in their little heads and able to add, subtract, divide, multiply and make a percentage. They wrote stories as well as essays, and she'd found a set of tin whistles in the spare room among her parents' things and taught them a few simple tunes. Every evening before they went home, she played the school piano for them, their joyful young voices ringing out; it would do your heart good to hear them. But most importantly she wanted them to leave with a love of learning. She suspected that love would dwindle under Agnes's sterner methods, which were more focussed on saving children's souls than teaching them about the wider world beyond Knocknashee, but she hoped some of the joy would remain and come back to them later.

Today she did their letters and numbers with them, but then she moved on to history and geography, telling them about the world in simple ways.

At the moment they were learning all about the explorers, so the children of Knocknashee who went to sleep to the sound of the Atlantic in their ears dreamt they were on that very ocean on board the *Santa María*, or with Cortés as he burnt his ships in the New World to further encourage his men to seek their fortune. She showed them pictures of Montezuma, the Aztec emperor, and told them where the gold and silver taken from Mexico was used. They gazed in amazement at the picture she showed them in a book of the ceiling of Santa Maria Maggiore church in Rome, where the gold leaf came from gold that the conquistadores sent back to King Ferdinand of Spain, who in turn gifted it to the pope.

People from this little town didn't go far, many being born, marrying and dying in the parish. For some of them, Dingle, the town six miles east of them, was an every-five-years excursion and Killarney might as well be Kathmandu. So many of Grace's pupils might never see Rome – most were unlikely to go beyond the county bounds their whole lives – but Grace had learnt through her illness that the only boundaries to the exploration any person could do was imagined. There were books, there were paintings, and now there were film reels – the world was there for all to see without ever setting foot outside the parish.

The morning flew by. She supervised the children playing in the yard at lunchtime, after they'd all eaten a small snack and had a glass of milk. She paid attention to those who had no lunch – times were hard – and she discreetly gave them some bread and jam. Mrs

O'Donoghue from the grocer's supplied her with a loaf and a pot of jam for free as she needed it, and she stored them in a cupboard where Agnes wouldn't find them. For a reason Grace couldn't specify, she just knew Agnes wouldn't approve of handouts.

Lunch duty was always left to Grace, because Agnes didn't want to be exposed to the sun and the wind. It was Agnes who had inherited their mother's delicate complexion, along with Kathleen's long narrow nose and fine fair hair. Daddy's and Grace's skin tone was different; he said there must have been a bit of a Spanish sailor in him since he went so brown in the summer.

In the afternoon, Grace read her children the next bit of the tale 'Tóraíocht Dhiarmada agus Gráinne', a mythological story of a beautiful girl and the man she bewitched to fall in love with her as they were chased all over Ireland by the old warrior Fionn mac Cumhaill – Fionn wanted the young girl, Gráinne, for himself. Grace read it in English, as all the children spoke Irish at home and their English needed work. They hung on her every word as she sat on the desk, her right leg stretched out in its calliper and the children gathered around her. She did the voices of the different characters, and if she got confused and mixed up one character's voice with another, the children were quick to point it out.

Then they translated the list of local townlands from Irish to English, and they used the map to go all over the peninsula, learning why places were called the names they were.

Knocknashee, where they were from, meant 'the hill of the fairies'. The high mound that gave the village its name was gentle and green, with some scree at the top. The legend said that the fairies danced up there, and that it was a portal to the underworld. On certain nights of the year, one had to be careful; people around here still believed in fairies – the *bean sidhe,* or banshee in English – and would never interfere with their ways. Oíche Shamhna, the pagan festival of the dead, what people called Halloween now in English, was the most dangerous. It was widely believed that on that night, the worlds of the living and the dead were closest. There was a risk a fairy would steal a baby and leave a changeling, a fairy child, in its place.

Before she knew it, it was less than an hour to home time, and she was beginning to feel confident that Agnes had heeded her words about the fierce curses of John O'Shea. But then came a knock on the door. One of the older girls stuck her head into the room and, looking a bit nervous and sheepish, said the mistress had asked to see Mikey O'Shea at once.

The little boy looked terrified, his eyes filling with tears. As he got up from his seat, his legs trembling, Grace felt a burst of rebellion. She gestured to him to sit down again and followed the senior girl back into her sister's classroom. Agnes, who had the strap already waiting on her desk, looked confused and annoyed when Grace appeared instead.

'Can I have a quick word with you, Mistress Fitzgerald, in the corridor?' asked Grace. In front of the children, she was not allowed to call her sister Agnes.

Agnes didn't look at all happy, but she followed Grace out into the passageway. 'What's the matter, Grace?' she snapped as soon as the door was closed behind them. 'Didn't Sinead tell you to send Mikey in to me?'

Grace stood facing her, determined not to back down but shaking inside. 'She did, Agnes. But I don't think you should slap him. He hasn't done anything, and he's very upset and terrified.'

Agnes looked as if she couldn't believe her ears. 'The boy was trick-acting in the back of the church during Mass.'

'He wasn't really, Agnes. He was only doing what his parents were letting him do.'

'Exactly.' Agnes's mouth was pinched, her sharp nose quivered, and her delicate skin became patched with red. 'And that's why he must be punished. He needs to know his parents are wrong in the way they behave, unless you mean to let him follow them down the path to damnation?'

'Ah, Agnes, surely you don't think...' Grace could hear her voice failing. It always made her doubt herself when Agnes accused her of not caring for her pupils' souls. She tried to inject more strength into her voice. 'He's only a small lad, and he meant no harm –'

Without waiting for her to finish, Agnes stepped past her and whipped open the door to the juniors' room, barking, 'Mikey O'Shea! Come here at once.'

As the poor boy slowly emerged from the room, Grace longed to snatch him in her arms and run away with him. But she couldn't run, not with her leg – it would look ridiculous. Hating herself, she walked stiffly back into the juniors' room as poor Mikey was marched by Agnes, his head drooping, into the seniors'.

She shut the door and picked up 'Tóraíocht Dhiarmada agus Gráinne' again, hoping if she read aloud in a strong enough voice, she would spare her pupils the horrible sound of Mikey's punishment. But it was no good; there was only a thin partition wall between the two rooms. The slap of the leather was loud and clear, and Mikey's wails made the children go pale and quiet.

Grace found herself unable to speak as the leather sounded again like a crack of lightning in the still air.

No. Just no.

Without saying a word to the children in front of her, she walked out of her classroom and into Agnes's room without knocking. The scene that greeted her steeled her resolve. The older children were watching, sitting bolt upright, terrified to move in case they were next. Agnes stood at the top of the room with her arm raised high, the leather gripped in her fist, gathering all her strength to slap poor, tear-stained Mikey for the third time.

The arrival of Grace made her stop, mid-wallop. 'What are you doing here?' she demanded, lowering the leather.

Grace swallowed the terror she felt and clenched her fists to stop them trembling. 'I've come to take Mikey back to my room,' she managed to say, quietly but firmly, as she crossed to where the boy and her sister stood.

A series of emotions in quick succession appeared on her sister's thin, pale face. Confusion, indecision, followed by cold fury as she raised the strap high again…

Before she could bring it down, Grace pulled Mikey away. 'Come with me, Mikey. It's time to go.'

The little boy turned to her as his saviour and grabbed he outstretched hand like a drowning man on a rope. Together the walked out of Agnes's classroom.

Once back in her own room, she tried to hush her excited chat tering class, but they were too thrilled by what had just happened t quieten, so she dismissed them with twenty minutes left on the clock News of what she'd done with Mikey would be the topic at ever dinner table for miles around this evening.

A few minutes later, after tidying up her own room, she also left Normally she stayed behind to clean the senior room as well, bu Agnes would have to do that today. Another mad act of defiance. Sh crossed the schoolyard with her head held high, not looking bac towards the windows to see if her sister was watching, her hear beating furiously.

She felt strangely exhilarated. Whatever the consequences of he public defiance of her sister were to be, and she dreaded to think, sh would face them. Because Agnes was wrong.

CHAPTER 3

By the time she let herself back into the house, she wasn't feelin quite so brave because she'd begun to panic about the children. Ther was a real chance Agnes would dismiss her from her post, and th prospect of leaving the little ones to be taught by her sister filled he with anxiety and guilt, even if by saving Mikey she'd done the onl thing she could do in that moment.

As for herself, she'd survive, even if Agnes turfed her out on th street without a penny. She hated the idea, though, because this wa the only home she'd ever known; it was full of her precious childhoo memories, even if it was a very different place from when her parent were alive.

Eddie and Kathleen Fitzgerald had been very busy people, and th household they'd kept was warm and bright but also slightly chaotic Since they drowned, Agnes had kept it much tidier, but also dark an cold. She never lit the fire before November because 'turf makes mess and coal is too dear', and she liked to keep the cotton curtains drawn 'to stop the sunlight fading the upholstery'.

The many trinkets – Mammy loved finding odd-shaped stones that she gathered on the windowsills – had been thrown out, and everything else – the books, their mother's artworks, their father's fishing rods and knitted jumpers – had all been consigned to the storage room upstairs.

At least the piano was still in the sitting room, though hidden by a dust cover, and the gramophone, pushed into the corner and also covered with a cloth. Mammy had bought the gramophone the summer before she died. Her favourite recording had been *London Calling!*, a musical revue written by Noël Coward of sketches and skits and funny songs, and it made her laugh every time. Mammy had been such a light-hearted person; in Grace's memory, she seemed to always be laughing. And Daddy would be smiling too, delighted by her.

Hesitating in the hallway, torn between staying downstairs to face her sister or hiding away in her bedroom, Grace's heart missed a beat as she heard the creak of the gate at the end of the path. But instead of the front door flying open with a furious crash, there was a soft, nervous knock. It was just Patrick coming to get his precious football back. Of course. She'd left the school with it still in her bag.

'Miss Fitz, you were wonderful,' he whispered as she gave him his ball. 'But the mistress is awful mad. She didn't say nothing, but her face is red as Janie O'Shea's hair and her eyes have gone all strange looking.' And having imparted this breathless information, he scuttled away with the ball clutched to his chest, glancing nervously around him in case the dreaded mistress suddenly appeared.

Grace glanced towards the gate in the wall before closing the door, her stomach churning with anxiety. It wouldn't take Agnes long to lock up the school. Maybe giving her some time to calm down would be a good idea.

She headed for the stairs and climbed them as quickly as she could. She had to lead with her left and pull the right leg up after her.

She stood on the landing to get her breath, her hand on the banister. There were four bedrooms off the landing. The first was the largest, her parents' room, which Agnes now used as her own; like the sitting room, it was now a lot tidier but less welcoming somehow.

Grace tried to keep her own room, which she'd had since she was a baby, more in her mother's style. The rag doll Mammy had made for her when she was five, which she'd brought with her to hospital, was called Nellie after Dame Nellie Melba, Kathleen Fitzgerald's favourite singer. It rested against the pillow of her single childhood bed, which was still big enough for her because she was so small. The red wool rug on the dark wood floorboards had come from her *mamó's* house, Daddy's mother. Some of her mother's paintings were on the walls, and Grace had crocheted a bedspread in all different colours, mostly taken from woollen jumpers she'd outgrown. She knew Agnes thought she lived in a pigsty, but Grace found it a bright, cheery oasis in their cold, too-tidy house.

Now, instead of going into her own room, she went into Maurice's, which was opposite hers and was kept the way Agnes liked it, empty except for the bed, which was always made up and turned down, even though the absent priest had not been home to sleep in it since before their parents died. The window of this room looked down at the schoolhouse next door, and she could see Agnes still in her classroom, going through the filing cabinet that stood by her desk. She hadn't cleaned the blackboard yet, so whatever her sister was doing, it looked like Grace still had a few minutes to spare.

The last bedroom off the landing had belonged to Agnes but was now the spare room, and it was full of things Grace remembered from her childhood.

Boxes of old schoolbooks, Mammy and Daddy's clothes and personal effects – the room was full to the ceiling. Nobody but Grace ever went in there. It was where she retreated when she wanted to feel close to her parents.

She went in there now and did what she often did for comfort – she held Daddy's old *báinín* sweater to her cheek. It had been knitted by Mammy with wool that had the lanolin still in it, to keep out the rain and the spray, and the scent of it brought back the image of him, tall and strong, striding through the schoolyard on a soft misty day, his pipe held in his teeth, a permanent smile on his face. He was the master, but the children knew they had no more to fear from Master Fitz than they did from Santa Claus. He never slapped a child, ever. He handled poor behaviour by giving the child a few extra jobs, or if it was a repeat offence, telling the errant young criminal how disappointed he was, how he was sure they were better than that, how he hated to see them let themselves and their family down in such a way. And sure enough, it worked; they couldn't bear to disappoint Master Fitz.

Mammy was loved by the children too, and she also would never hit a child. She believed that teaching them art and music was just as important, maybe even more important, than arithmetic and writing. Mammy's easel was here in the spare room too, leaning against an old dresser, and her paintbrushes were on the shelf. Grace wished again that Agnes would let her teach the children to paint, the way Mammy had done.

Also on the dresser was an old Boland's biscuit tin, with a picture of a little girl with a parasol on the front. It held a bundle of letters that had been written by her parents to each other when her father was in teacher training college in Dublin and her mother was at home in Knocknashee. This was what Grace had come for.

She picked it up and carried it into her own room, shutting her door behind her. On impulse she pushed a chair under the handle to block the door from being opened too suddenly, then sat at her dressing table and brought out her parents' letters from the box. They were worn on the creases from her reading them, but even though she knew them by heart, it always made her happy to read them again as they were so full of humour and love.

There were her daddy's funny observations of life in Dublin. It was before the Great War, and he described the dresses of the ladies he saw as he walked to and from the college. Her mother replied that while she had asked him about the fashions, he was not to be looking at the ladies too closely. She spoke of how lonely her life here was without him.

Daddy wrote of how hard he found the mathematics part of the course and how he feared for any child learning mathematics from him because he had no numeric skills at all.

In another letter, Charlie McKenna was mentioned with warmth; he and his late wife had been great friends of her parents. Agnes didn't allow Grace to talk to Charlie, even when he brought the post. It was a pity – he might have good stories of their parents in the old days. But Agnes disapproved of him because he took to the drink after his wife died and his children were taken into care. It wasn't until Nancy O'Flaherty from the post office rescued him with the offer of a job that he'd begun to piece his life back together.

It sounded like Charlie had been a different person when her parents were friends with him, a warm, funny, loyal, trustworthy man. He had no land or boat, so he had worked as a farm labourer for some of the more wealthy families who could afford to pay a man.

She opened another letter. Her Mamó Nóinín, her mother's mother, died the year Daddy was in Dublin. *Nóinín* was the Irish word for a daisy, and every time Grace saw one, she thought of her *mamó*, wishing she'd met her. In this one and a few that followed, Mammy poured out all her loneliness and loss. She wrote of seeing a robin on her windowsill every morning in the months after, and how it gave her comfort in her grief. Mammy was a big believer in signs and always told Grace that a robin was the soul of a loved one passed on, of that she was certain. And then she spoke again of how much she missed Daddy and longed to have his arms around her.

Resting her chin on her hand, Grace wondered if she would ever have someone to write to in such a passionate, loving way. Sometimes she wished she was the kind of girl men looked at, the ones with the trim figures and pretty faces, the ones with hair curled with rags at night and washed in rainwater for shine, the ones with two good legs. Like Tilly, who was so beautiful and drew men's eyes, even when she was dressed in a shirt and tie. But she wasn't beautiful like Tilly. And no man would ever want her. Who'd want a person like her staggering up the aisle to meet him? Nobody, that's who.

She had no one to write to, no one to whom she could pour out the pain and worry in her heart. She wished her mother were still alive, as she was the kind of person one could confide in, however hopeless one felt…

St Jude. The patron saint of hopeless cases. That was who she'd write to. If any saint was the one for her, it would be St Jude, because Grace was nothing if not a hopeless case.

She took out her notepad, a fancy one she'd bought when she was fifteen on a rare trip to Cork City arranged by the nurses to give the children a break from the hospital. Sister Ailbhe, a very kind nurse, had asked Dr Warrington, and he'd not only allowed it, he'd accompanied them, much to the children's delight, and gave them each a shilling to spend. The ten children well enough for the outing were taken down the main street, St Patrick's Street, on the electric tram, and allowed to visit the Munster Arcade. Dr Warrington told them how, as the biggest department store in Cork, it had been destroyed by the British the night they burnt the city to the ground in 1920 as a punishment for the rebellious actions of the IRA; but the Corkonians were not called the Rebel County for nothing and had built it back up again. Dr Warrington was an Englishman, so it was funny to hear him speak in this way, but he had come to love his adopted home and everything about it, and he was as proud of that city as any Corkman you'd meet.

Grace had spent her shilling on some fancy notepaper and a pen that could be filled with any colour ink you wanted. She'd selected a bottle of purple ink, called Lilac Dream, and had imagined using it for writing love letters when she was older, but that was never going to happen now. She'd written to Tilly from the hospital, but that was all.

Maybe she should write to Tilly now…

But Agnes had forbidden her to talk to her old friend ever again, and although Grace hadn't expressly agreed not to do so, she'd been defiant enough for one day.

No, she would stick to her plan of writing to St Jude.

She filled the barrel of her fountain pen with the lilac ink and began, in her small, neat, cursive hand.

Dear St Jude,

I am writing this to you because I have not a single soul in my life in whom I can confide. I feel a bit silly, but I have to get this out of me someho and given your portfolio, I thought we might be a good match.

My name is Grace Fitzgerald, and I live in Knocknashee, Co Kerry Ireland. I am seventeen years old and an assistant teacher in a school run b my sister, who, God forgive me, I am very angry with right now for beating little boy for messing at Mass, and I made matters so much worse for mysel by walking in and taking him out, mid-punishment.

I wish my parents were alive. They were the teachers before Agnes and and they never slapped anyone. I suppose I should be happy for them being i heaven with you and all the other saints, but I miss them.

By the way, I do realise I'm very lucky that, thanks to my sister, I have roof over my head and food, when so many go poor and hungry. It's not tha I'm ungrateful, and she has some wonderful qualities, and she only is hard o the children because she thinks it's for their good in the end, but still. It was very hard day today. She thinks I'm too soft. Maybe I am.

I had polio and was in hospital for four years, and though I have a lim and my back often hurts, I know I was spared far worse.

Dr Warrington says it's important to rise above the polio. He says som people let their illness define who they are, that they allow the world to se them through the lens of a disease, that they even like the attention it bring but mixed in with the attention is pity, and that's not something that doe any good. Dr Warrington encourages all his young patients to stand up an be counted. We had polio, that's a fact and can't be changed, but he drilled into us, 'You have polio, you are not *Polio with a capital P. You're a Perso with a capital P, with something to contribute to the world. Don't let th world see you as a Polio Victim and not a Person. Don't let it win.'*

He's very funny, Dr Warrington. He says each child in the polio ward allowed two minutes of an organ recital every morning. That's what he calle our complaining about all our aches and pains. He used to encourage us to b cross, or sad, or frustrated, or downright grumpy – he said it was good to le it all out. He even let us say one bad word about the polio once a month – that was a very funny day – and then no more. He said complaining was bad habit we shouldn't cultivate.

He's right, and I will try harder to do as he says. I know I'm letting him down whenever I feel sorry for myself about the fact no one will ever marr me and I'll never have children. It must be ten times worse for Agnes than it is for me, because she knew what love was and she was expecting to get married until Cyril's mother persuaded him to leave her because I had polio and she was afraid of the disease. And so my sister's heart is permanently broken, which I think is what makes her so sad and unhappy.

I know I complain too much, and I know I am so blessed by the beautiful mountains and sea around me that God made for our enjoyment, and being able to read books and escape that way from what sometimes feels like the smallness of my world. If I'd worked harder at my exams, maybe I could have gone away to teacher training college...

As she wrote this line, a tear dropped onto the page, smudging the ink not yet dry. It didn't matter, though; nobody but St Jude would ever read this, so she might as well get it all out.

But Knocknashee is my world now, and I'm sure it's for the best. I just wish I knew better how to get along with my sister. Why can't I love her like I know I should? Or love her at all?

She's going to be absolutely livid with me for what I did today, and I'm scared stiff of her, that's the truth.

Here she stopped and read back over the lines, and a pang of guilt and shame washed over her. What sort of a person could not love their sister?

Please help me, St Jude. Please intervene so Agnes doesn't sack me, leaving the little ones at her mercy, and could you also make sure she doesn't throw me out on the side of the road, because I have absolutely nowhere else to go.

The front door slammed. Sharp footsteps crossed the hall and mounted the stairs. Her heart beating rapidly, Grace tore the sheet from the pad, quickly folded it and put it in the pocket of her skirt.

The doorknob rattled, but the door wouldn't open because of the chair wedged under the handle. Grace stayed frozen at the desk. What should she do? How stupid to push the chair under the knob; of course it was just going to make things worse...

'Grace, open this door immediately,' snapped Agnes. The knob rattled again. Her sister tried to force the door, but the legs of the ring-backed chair were wedged against a floorboard that stood slightly proud of the others, so it didn't budge. 'Grace, I will count to five, and if you do not open up, then I will... I will...'

You will what, Grace wondered. And then, as if writing the letter to St Jude had already taken a weight off her shoulders, she stifled a daft giggle at the prospect of Agnes shouldering the door and eventually bursting in covered in dust and splinters of wood like you saw cowboys doing at the cinema. A big, very bad part of her wanted to wait, to see if it might happen.

But the kinder and more sensible part of her knew that to upset her sister even further would be wrong and would also make Grace's situation worse. She stood and crossed the sunny bedroom. Quietly she removed the chair.

Before she could open the door, Agnes made another attempt to force it and burst into the room with an almost comical expression of surprise, stumbling forwards and tripping over the rug with a squawk of fury, landing on her hands and knees.

Grace would have saved her if she could, but she couldn't move that fast. And then an even worse thing happened. The giggle she had suppressed at the idea of Agnes bursting through the door like a cowboy rose up in her again, and the next minute she couldn't help herself – she laughed and laughed, her hands pressed to her mouth. It was the funniest thing...

'How dare you mock me, Grace Fitzgerald!' gasped Agnes as she clambered to her feet. 'How dare you! How dare you... Stop laughing at once!'

But Grace couldn't. 'I'm sorry, I'm so sorry,' she spluttered. 'So...' It was no good. She had to get out of there. Every time she even looked at Agnes's outraged pink face, it set her off again. With as much dignity as she could muster, she headed for the stairs. She wished she could make a speedy exit, but she had to ease down them one step at a time, clinging to the banister, which made the whole thing even more comical, and in the end, she was laughing as much at herself as at Agnes.

'Where are you going?' screeched Agnes from the top of the stairs, enraged. 'What are you doing? For goodness' sake, you're not a child – stop behaving like one! Don't you dare go out in the street like that...'

Still breathless with merriment, Grace took her coat from the hall-stand, placed her felt hat on her head and let herself out the front door. She had no idea what she was going to do next, but she felt it was better she stay away from Agnes for a while.

IF YOU WOULD LIKE to read on - please visit here:

https://geni.us/Lilac-Ink

ABOUT THE AUTHOR

ean Grainger is a USA Today bestselling Irish author. She writes istorical and contemporary Irish fiction and her work has very flat-eringly been compared to the late great Maeve Binchy.

She lives in a stone cottage in Cork with her lovely husband Diar-nuid and the youngest two of her four children. The older two come ome for a break when adulting gets too exhausting. There are a ariety of animals there too, all led by two cute but clueless micro-ogs called Scrappy and Scoobi.

ALSO BY JEAN GRAINGER

The Tour Series

The Tour

Safe at the Edge of the World

The Story of Grenville King

The Homecoming of Bubbles O'Leary

Finding Billie Romano

Kayla's Trick

The Carmel Sheehan Story

Letters of Freedom

The Future's Not Ours To See

What Will Be

The Robinswood Story

What Once Was True

Return To Robinswood

Trials and Tribulations

The Star and the Shamrock Series

The Star and the Shamrock

The Emerald Horizon

The Hard Way Home

The World Starts Anew

The Queenstown Series

Last Port of Call

The West's Awake

The Harp and the Rose

Roaring Liberty

Standalone Books

So Much Owed

Shadow of a Century

Under Heaven's Shining Stars

Catriona's War

Sisters of the Southern Cross

The Kilteegan Bridge Series

The Trouble with Secrets

What Divides Us

More Harm Than Good

When Irish Eyes Are Lying

A Silent Understanding

The Mags Munroe Story

The Existential Worries of Mags Munroe

Growing Wild in the Shade

Each to their Own

Closer Than You Think

The Aisling Series

For All The World

A Beautiful Ferocity

Rivers of Wrath

The Gem of Ireland's Crown

The Knocknashee Story

Lilac Ink

Yesterday's Paper